tell me something TRUE

by

Katherine Owen

TRUTH IN LIES *book 3*

The Writing Works Group

Seattle

tell me something TRUE

by

Katherine Owen

TRUTH IN LIES *book 3*

COPYRIGHT

Without limiting the rights under copyright reserved above, no part of this publication may be reproduced, stored in or introduced into a retrieval system, or transmitted, in any form, or by any means (electronic, mechanical, photocopying, recording or otherwise) without prior permission of both the copyright owner and the above publisher of this book.

This is a work of fiction. Names, characters, businesses, organizations, places, brands, media, and incidents are either the product of the author's imagination or are used fictitiously. The author acknowledges the trademarked status and trademark owners of various products, bands, and/or restaurants or people, places, or things referenced in this work of fiction, which have been used without permission. The publication/use of these trademarks is not authorized, associated with, or sponsored by the trademark owners.

BURNS poem used with permission by author Erin Hanson.
All poems by author r.m. drake used with permission.

Copyright © 2015 by Katherine Owen

All rights reserved.
Published by: The Writing Works Group
Visit our website: http://www.thewritingworksgroup.com

ISBN: 978-1-943337-04-0
eISBN: 978-1-943337-00-2

The Writing Works Group

Book Design - Cover & Interior by The Writing Works Group

Printed in the United States of America

First Edition

BURNS

She threw herself at heartbreak,

Like a moth drawn to a flame,

Patching up her broken wings,

Just to try it once again,

And the world all thought her foolish,

For she never seemed to learn,

But how do you save somebody,

Who's convinced that they should burn?

~ Erin Hanson

PART 1 - OMISSION

"The truth may be stretched thin,

but it never breaks,

and it always surfaces above lies,

as oil floats on water."

- Miguel de Cervantes Saavedra, *Don Quixote*

"loving me will not be easy.

it will be war.

you will hold the gun

and i will hand you the bullets.

so breathe, and embrace

the beauty of the massacre that lies ahead."

~ r.m. drake

PROLOGUE

young and beautiful

TALLY

"Tell me something true.
You know you want to. But can you?
Will you? Will I?
Because sometimes telling the truth—revealing the truth—will
hurt the ones you love the most.
And it turns out, being set free by the truth is sometimes the last
thing you want.
Sometimes, you have to ask yourself: How much is true and how
much can you handle?
How much are you personally willing to gamble?
And truly? How far will the lies take you?
Just how far from the truth are you willing to go?
~ Talia Landon Presley

FAME. EVERYBODY SEEMS TO WANT IT, probably by the time they reach the age of twelve.

I'm sure Lincoln Presley said it or wished for it. "I'm going to grow up and be a famous baseball player." Certainly, his father must have said it because he made damn sure it happened for his son no matter what the cost.

And me?

I said it to my twin sister Holly. We were ten. "I'm going to grow up and be a famous ballerina like Madame Tremblay."

Holly didn't seem to get it. She frowned and asked me, "Why? She'll make you dance every single day, Tally. Where's the fun in that? I'm going to be fall in love and get married and have lots of babies like Momma. You should do that, too."

"I don't like guys all that much. And who has time for love?" I airily waved a dismissive hand at her. "And I don't like babies at all." I rolled my eyes and Holly had just laughed.

"Oh, but you will." My twin smiled wide as if she knew a secret. "Someday, Tally. Someday, you'll fall in love and marry a prince and love him more than life itself even when you are a big star, and then you'll have lots of babies, and nothing else will matter."

"Why would I do any of that?"

"Because love is everything. Love is all there is."

"Sometimes, you are just so naive it is impossible to even talk to you. What do love and princes and babies have to do with being a famous ballerina? Nothing. Absolutely nothing."

I laughed at her and told her that all I needed to be ready for was being rich and famous. "A prince? Marriage? Love? Babies? Really, Holly? That's what fairytales are for; go read one. I don't believe in love and neither should you."

Holly was right, of course. About meeting the prince, love, and babies, and even predicting I'd become a star. Some five years later after that strange conversation with my twin—two little girls fantasizing about their future—I remembered it like it was yesterday.

I got the guy part right. Perhaps, not the prince part. Five years later, I was all about guys. I liked guys. A lot. With studied intent, I found guys were a nice diversion from the fast track of fame that I was on. Guys eased the pressure building deep inside about being perfect. At ballet. Perfect at everything really. Of course, I performed ballet perfectly, but I was pretty adept at hooking up with guys, too.Guys served as nice distractions, however temporary. I realized fairly early on that random sex with them mysteriously diffused the ticking bomb inside of me.

The pressure in my life was intense. Half the time I felt like I was ready to implode from it all.

The expectations for me to do well with ballet were high; they were insane, actually. Constant pressure from my parents to be perfect as well as added pressure from my dance teacher and mentor took its toll. Being perfect became the quest for all to see, but the deviant side of me broke all the rules.

By the time I was sixteen, I realized that hookups with guys not only alleviated the pressure that came with my life, but helped bury the pain with an increasingly troubled home life that I secretly carried. My mother's drinking raged out of control. Holly and I were the ones left to take care of my little brother Tommy as well as my drunk mother, while my father was absent from home more nights than would be considered normal.

Random hookups became a salvation for me—a way to cope. Random hookups ruled and like a secret game I was playing, lying became part of the repertoire as well. Guys were easy enough to lie to and they believed whatever I told them. As long as they didn't want anything from me other than sex, we were good. I didn't have time for a relationship. I didn't want a commitment. Most guys appreciated these particular nuances about me. It was a mutual thing. Guys became easy enough to use and be used by. It was a win-win for everyone.

By the time I turned seventeen, my ability to finesse a lie was standard operating procedure and random sex served as an even better distraction from the never-ending chaos in my life. I welcomed the distraction random hookups provided and since love and emotion of any kind didn't play into it at all for me, I missed all the signs—*the triggers*.

Those would come later.

I was playing with fire. I would get burned. I just didn't see it at the time.

I didn't believe in falling in love and happily ever-afters the way my twin sister did. In fact, I didn't fall in love until this guy in a Stanford Cardinal baseball cap with grey-blue eyes looked straight into mine and ultimately saved my life the same day I lost Holly and a part of myself forever.

After Holly's death, my mother was never sober for long, and my father still remained absent. And yet? The baseball player became everything good still left in the world.

He brought out what was left of the good in me. In many ways, Lincoln Presley saved us all.

Even so, like our tragic beginning, things were never simple for us. There were lies.

My past.

His.

The triple threat fears—of failure and falling and losing—those still dominated along with our shared quest for perfection both in our personal lives as well as our professional ones.

The way we both coped with chaos and tragedy, although different in some ways, was similar in others.

And so it goes, it always seemed to come back to those demons—those fears—for both of us and the different ways we chose to cope because of them.

Ah, love.

The truth about us—about his being my air and me being his water—was clear enough when we both finally admitted to each other that love—*our love*—was the only thing that mattered.

But that was the first day. The day we said, "I do." The day the demons seemed to leave us alone, at least, for a little while. Nevertheless, there were other days, when all the lies of the past and our ways of coping with our fears caught up to us.

And, this is *that* story.

If you believe in fairy tales and happy endings,
and you want to stop right here and bask in the wonderment and joy
of it all, please do.
If you want to know the rest of our story,
you need to take a deep breath

and tell yourself that everything will be okay,
that everything works out,
and life happens,
and in the end
love is all you need.
Someone has to tell you these things,
just like someone had to tell me.
All I know is that the truth never dies,
and it does set you free, whether you want it to or not.
And in the end? All you have is love.
Love is all there is.

   ~ Talia Landon Presley

CHAPTER ONE

the state of dreaming

TALLY

Miracles happen every day just not to me.
But today? I believe in miracles.
I just married one.
  ~ Talia Landon Presley

July 17th

YOU CAN TELL A LOT ABOUT a man's views on marriage by the way he handles feeding wedding cake to his bride. There are the cake smashers that are more intent on making a mess of their beloved one's face all but ensuring a good laugh from the crowd. To me, it's the subtle side of cruelty hidden beneath a veneer and continual quest for a cheap laugh no matter who it hurts in the process. It never ends. Personally, I don't think those guys ever grow up. They're more intent on pleasing the crowd, not the bride. I think that follows them throughout their lives and doesn't bode well for love or marriage.

Then, there are the precise ones. They always cut a small piece from the bottom of the cake as instructed by the bride or her maid of honor and delicately place the cake on the bride's tongue. They are, for one, too afraid to mess up, but also too afraid to be funny. Never capable of making up their own mind without getting direction or opinions from others; it's a little pathetic and most definitely boring.

Finally, there are the winners. They don't care what anyone else thinks because all they care about is the person standing in front of them—the one they've just declared themselves to, the one they love the most—their bride, their soul mate, and their future which they are absolutely certain flows into forever. They consider feeding their bride cake to be the first of many amazing experiences and do this with the utmost care and compassion. It bodes well for the marriage, for themselves. Those are the winners. For life. In love. More often than not.

Lincoln Presley is a winner – through and through.

Transfixed by his intense gaze solely for me, I can't stop smiling. He carefully peels back the silver cupcake liner and divides the cake in half and then quarters. I'm reminded of my uncanny ability to mutilate a burger in much the same way and tell him this. He laughs and holds the cake out like some kind of peace offering and blithely instructs me to open my mouth. Of course, for cake, I'm more than willing to do anything and tell him so.

I swallow the cake down while he's busy kissing the side of my mouth and licking off the remaining crumbs and frosting from my lips. It's a subtle enough move, yet still sexy with enough promise about what we're doing later, that I have to hope my mother isn't watching too closely. I laugh when he whispers what he plans to do with me later and tells me it involves both cake and frosting. He laughs with me as I judiciously feed him his cake and promise a similar seduction for him later, too.

Cameras flash all around us, and I kiss him back.

It's the perfect moment.

This is bliss.

"I love you." Linc has this dazzling smile just for me.

"I love you, too."

Joy for all of this lights me up and the heat for him rises, even as we stand here looking calm, cool, and collected for all of our friends and family and declare ourselves, yet again, with wedding cake.

The crowd buzz falls away, and it really becomes just the two of us standing here. We revel in the wonder of it all. This is love. This is what it's all about. Together, we can do anything, survive anything. It's such an overwhelming feeling of pure happiness—and a new one for me—that, on this day, I believe in. In joy. In happiness. In love. In this man.

Linc's arms come around me. He lifts me up high in the air and the crowd whistles and starts to clap. Another photograph is taken.

Eventually, I slide downward and meet up with his lips and taste the sweetness of this man whom I have just pledged my life to.

"He's sweeter than butter cream frosting," I call out to the small crowd gathered all around us. There is more clapping and more laughter. I gaze only at Lincoln Presley savoring this moment in time with him.

This is it.

This is what Holly meant.

I have it all—the prince, love, and babies.

Holly's right; love is everything.

Love is all there is.

"All right, break it up, you two. Bride and groom dance coming up, and then you two can get a room," Marla says from our left.

The crowd responds with more laughter, and so do we.

And all is right in our world on this day. Everything is perfect. My demons are at rest and allow me to believe that anything is possible, and my life is perfect and is going to be from this day forward.

Miracles happen every day just not to me.

But today? I believe in miracles.

I just married one.

Cara is not pleased with the sleeping arrangements. She's about to throw a temper tantrum over the elaborate plans we've made seemingly without her.

"Mommy and Daddy want to spend some alone time together. You're going to stay with Marla and Charlie. You *love* staying with them. You'll get to play all week with Elliott."

"I want to go with you and Daddy."

"I know, but not this time, sweetie. Next time. I think Marla said she was going to take you two to the zoo."

"I don't want to go to the zoo without you."

"You *love* the zoo. You're going to have a great time."

"Will I get ice cream?" Cara gets this impish look as if she doesn't already know how to run the show at Marla's at this point.

"I'm sure Marla will get you and Elliott some ice cream. Just be a good girl for Mommy and Daddy while we're gone." I lean in and kiss the tip of her nose reflecting how I sound just like my mom and wonder what kind of expectations I am already setting. Then, the worry about leaving her in first place and being so far away seeps in. Yet, I try to control the trembling in my voice and overcompensate. "Just be good; okay? You're going to have so much fun! You won't even miss us."

She grips my face with her little hands. "Mommy, I miss you already."

"I know. Me, too."

"But you'll come back, won't you?" She looks uncertain.

"I'll always come back."

"And Daddy, too?" she asks with sweet wistfulness.

"Daddy, too. Promise." I try to smile while the thought of leaving her weighs me down even more. Three days is the longest I've ever left Cara with anyone, including my mom and dad, since she was brought back to me. Three days is a long time. But now, we're talking about more than a week away from Cara, and she won't be with my mom; she'll be with Marla.

My mom's been sober for almost ten months, but still I worry about things as it relates to her drinking, which is why we decided Cara should stay with Charlie and Marla. It's for the best. Marla knows what to do for Cara. My mom? I'm not so sure and I don't want her to stress out, to mess up, or falter from the rehabilitative path she's been walking and somehow end up going on another binge and falling apart in front of my kid. No child should have to witness that. No child should have to live with that. My own childhood memories back up on me; I push them down.

Still, I worry now.

About Everything.

"I'll be good." Cara gets this sweet smile as she looks up at me. "I promise. And then, you and Daddy will come back like you promised."

My little girl senses my uncertainty in leaving her at all. And I don't have to wonder how she does. "Promise. We'll be back before you know it."

Yet, her smile wobbles. "You won't die, will you, Mommy? You or Daddy won't die," she whispers. "Like Anna and Elsa's mommy and daddy?"

Her little face scrunches up. I hug her close. *Frozen* is still Cara's favorite movie, but she always gets anxious about Linc and me when the parents die in the beginning of the film. She's watched it a thousand times, but she'll still bring this up every single time needing reassurance. "You won't die, will you?"

"Noooooooo."

How do you explain death to a child?

I can't even explain it to myself.

I pull back from her and gaze at her sweet face and smile wide. "Nothing is going to happen to us, Cara. We're all going to be fine. We're all going to live happily ever-after."

I've gone into Disney mode.

Now, I can't find my way out.

"Promise?" She holds the sides of my face with her chubby little hands.

"Promise."

The word holds such optimism.

And yet?

The fears I still carry attempt to rise up once more as soon as I say this.

CHAPTER TWO

valley of the dolls

TALLY

Happiness is so fleeting—a butterfly, really.
It's here one minute and gone the next.
And, I know this already.
~ Talia Landon Presley

July 17th

THE RECEPTION STARTS TO WIND DOWN. All the bride and groom festivities and traditions have been accomplished. Marla looks pleased with herself. Now, we're just hanging out at the bridal table together, decompressing and lamenting the fact that we can't indulge in the fine champagne being served at my wedding. We make a solid plan for six months from now to drink profusely and properly celebrate one night.

"Hopefully by Valentine's Day or soon after," Marla says to me.

I roll my eyes and attempt to conquer the sudden panic that comes with realizing I'm pregnant if only by a few months. Valentine's Day seems a long way off which I remind my best friend of. "Please don't freak me out anymore than I already am about *that* news."

"No worries. You've got this. You look amazing. I know you feel amazing. Your life, girlfriend, is all kinds of amazing."

Marla gazes at me thoughtfully.

"You just used the word amazing like three times in a sentence. Are you *drunk*?"

"Don't I wish."

We clink our water glasses together sealing the deal to drink heavily and *merrily* as Marla puts it, on or around Valentine's Day.

"Amazing, indeed." I start to laugh but it quickly dies away when I notice Linc is in a deep conversation with his father to my far left. Linc doesn't look any happier than his dad.

Soon, the two Presley men move away from the celebratory guests that remain and eventually disappear down the long hallway that leads to the changing rooms we spent so much time in before the ceremony.

Fifteen minutes later, there is still no sign of Linc. Feeling a little unsettled at his unexpected absence and deluged by more than a few guests already asking me where my groom has disappeared to, I stand up and announce to the lingering crowd my need to change.

Marla absently nods as she's attempts to distract her kid and mine. Cara and Elliott are not as enchanted with being at this reception anymore. Dress-up time has lost its luster. Naps were missed. They've had more than enough cupcakes and all they really want to do now is go outside and play on Pastor's Dan beautifully manicured green lawn. Marla and I have taken turns in telling them *no* quite a few times already. We share a look.

"Good idea. Go change. It's not going to get any easier." Marla pats the top of Cara's head and silently mouths, *when you leave her.* Out loud she says, "So yes, go change, so we can L-E-A-V-E."

Linc and I have plans to stay the night at the Ritz-Carlton here in Half Moon Bay and head to the airport and fly out of San Francisco for Miami tomorrow. Linc has a game in Miami. We will take a semi-honeymoon in Miami alongside baseball.

It works.

Mostly.

Linc really wants me at his first game after his return to the Giants, and I have promised to be at his baseball games more often while he's promised to attend more of my ballet performances. It's part of the new us. The new bond we forged just five days before to now with an exchange of wedding vows and a pledge to a life together, a mere two hours ago. Unfortunately, our declaration of love with these nuptials is under a time crunch. We have tonight. Then, we will leave for our flight to Miami mid-morning.

"I won't be long. Thanks." I shoot her a grateful smile and head down the hallway in the same direction Linc and his dad took fifteen minutes ago.

After I change out of this dress, Linc and I can slip out of the reception and get some much-deserved alone time together. I'm beginning to regret getting married at the tail end of his time off instead of at the beginning, but he's assured me it will be fine. I'm not too excited about the long flight clear across the country either but Linc booked us into first-class seats, so we'll have a little more room to ourselves. He's promised blankets and sparkling water and secret fun stuff to pass the time on the long flight. He's told me it will be worth it just to spend the time alone with me.

What can I say? We're in love.

Holly would be so happy to hear me say this. She probably *does* hear me say this.

Meanwhile, most everyone else is heading back to San Francisco tonight. This is what happens when you do an impromptu wedding ceremony on a Thursday afternoon during the week off in preparation for the Major League Baseball's All-Star Game.

Davis is returning to San Fran to fly out on a red-eye on a different airline in order to cover Linc's return to the line-up this weekend for ESPN. My dad has to go back for an early shift tomorrow morning at the hospital as does Charlie. My brother Tommy has his own baseball game, he can't afford to miss. The list of obligations elsewhere consumes just about everyone now that the ceremony is over.

Linc and I are the only ones still free for the next couple of hours. *Free*, in the sense that we just said, "I do" and life is epically joyous at the moment and all kinds of amazing according to my best friend Marla. We'll have a few precious hours together on our own on the drive down to the airport and on the flight and while in Miami. It's the best plan we could come up with. It's almost perfect. It *is* perfect. We're together. That's all that matters. I want to believe it can always be this way. Linc has assured me several times today already that it will always be this way, and I try not to doubt him.

Today, I have a firm grip on euphoria. I plan to hold onto it as tight as I can.

I'm still smiling for a very good reason—*Lincoln Presley*—as I make my way down the hallway when I pass a set of double doors that are slightly ajar on my left and catch the sounds of Linc and his father arguing.

Linc sighs. "I'm still trying to get my head wrapped around it. It's only been a few hours. We're married. We're happy. Don't ruin it."

What is he talking about? My heart starts to beat rapidly. The happiness I've carried with me all day starts to fall away. Somehow, I know Linc and his dad are talking about me. *Us.* Something doesn't feel right. I lean in closer.

"You'll be fine in Miami. Just take it one pitch at a time. You've been doing great with the Grizzlies. This should be no different. Better hitters, but you've got this. Just don't get distracted." Davis sighs. "I'm not sure taking Tally on the road right now is the best idea."

"Tally goes. I need her there with me. She's the reason I came back from the head injury at all. Tally is my singular focus. She's the only reason why I'm pitching so well. *Trust me* on that. She's been my singular focus all summer. She's the reason my stats are so good and why I made it back to the Giants' roster at all, so *my wife* goes where I go."

"Okay. Don't get all bent out of shape. If you think she's your talisman, fair enough, but that doesn't change the issue at hand. You still need to have her sign it."

I glimpse Linc's dad through the slit of the door frame.

He sighs again with impatience. "We do what we have to do to play this game to *stay* in this game. Trust me. That's baseball. I'm glad your new wife serves as your inspiration, son, but you need to focus on your performance as well as the contract with the Giants because that second-year bonus is guaranteed, and a run at the playoffs may mean even more money being flung your way. And, if those two things don't convince you to have her sign this prenup, nothing will. Not even me."

"Dad, I love Tally. Like I already told you. We don't need a prenup." Linc practically growls at his father at this point.

I've never heard Linc this angry before. I step back from the crack in the doorway. My mind races. He wants a prenup? At least, his father does. And why didn't he tell me this before the ceremony? Maybe *that* is what he was really trying to tell me just before we said our vows.

"You're being foolish. You have *millions* at stake," Davis says in frustration. "Even your mother and I had one."

"You did?"

I wince at hearing the sudden wavering in Linc's voice.

"Your mother was already pretty famous," Davis says. "I was just starting out in the league. It was a good idea for us. It made things clearer. It takes money off the table as an issue. *Trust me.* Money can be an issue. A prenup neutralizes what can be a volatile situation if things don't work out. If she loves you enough, she won't think twice about signing it. This is major league. It doesn't get any bigger than this unless you get traded or take advantage of free agency down the road. You need to think about it; protect yourself in case things don't work out with her."

"Things are going to work out with Tally and me. They already are. You make it sound like a test or something of her feelings for me. I'm *sure* of Tally. She's sure of me."

"It's not a test. More like a *testimony.* If she doesn't care about the money, she'll sign it. The only way to find out is to ask her. That way you'll know for sure."

"Why can't you accept Tally? I don't get it. Why are you being so hateful towards her?"

"I like Tally, but I still don't trust her. I thought I made that clear by taking care of this detail with the prenup for you. I mean, what do you know about this guy, Sam Wilde; she was seeing before you?"

"They're friends. She says they're just friends."

"What if they were more than friends? I can't believe you rushed into this thing with Tally. I thought we talked about this? Taking your time. Getting to know her again."

"I *do* know her. I remember her, Dad. *Mostly.* I remember her more and more. I love her. We have Cara. We're a family. Why can't you see that and just be happy for us?"

"That's the thing. I care about you and your happiness, believe it or not. But this whole thing just seems rushed. You're just returning to the Giants. Your life is going to be all about baseball from here on out. You worked so hard to get back here. I just don't want to see you distracted and throw it all away over some girl. The whole thing just seems rushed and I don't—"

"Tally is *not some* girl. She's my *wife.* She's pregnant. We just found out."

Davis sucks in air. I look through the opening in the doorway and see the dismay all over his face. Linc's dad looks like he's about to have a heart attack. His face goes red. "How do you even know it's even *yours*?"

"It's mine."

"How do you know for sure? You told me this Sam guy has been hanging around her for months. *Months.* You've been in Fresno traveling up and down the West Coast playing baseball. Exactly, what has Tally been doing? Look. I'm trying here, son. I came to the wedding. I gave her that dress. But your lawyer and I are recommending you have Tally sign this prenup. If money isn't a major concern, she'll sign it. It's the only way you'll know for sure. And if there's another kid involved now, well, I know I'm right about all of this."

"I can't believe you're saying all of this! I'm sure of Tally. What I'm not sure of anymore is *you*!"

Glass splinters against the far wall causing me to step back from the partially opened door. There is a part of me that wants to go to Linc and stand with him against his father, but there is another part that is unsure he would appreciate my interference on any level. Doubt seeps back into me as if it had never left.

How well do I know Linc? This *version* of Linc.

Again, there are versions of Lincoln Presley.

I love him. I do.

We just declared ourselves to each other for the umpteenth time just five days ago. But how well do I really know him now? I don't know him anymore. He's different, not the same.

The doubts I had about him—about us—while I was in Fresno, months before, rush back. Doubt in all its blazing glory seeps back into me like a virus surely does into its most unsuspecting victim.

We rushed into this. We did.

We felt so sure of each other and our future together mere days ago. But now? The doubt takes hold again. I absently brush a stray hair feeling the sweat form on my face and upper lip.

The demons return. Not long gone after all.

There are still lies between us.

And what if it doesn't work out?

"I'm just trying to do what's right here. This is bigger than the two of you. You have Cara. Another child on the way. But are you sure it's even yours? How can you be sure? She's lied to you before. So many times. There are millions at stake here, Linc. *Millions.* I just want you to be certain and to take the proper precautions. You two have had a rough road. I'm glad you're happy. *Together.* But a prenup is for your own protection. Yours and hers. If things go south it makes the breakup that much easier. Just think about it."

"Dad…" There's a long silence in which I hold my breath and await Linc's answer surely as much as his father. "Okay. I will," he says quietly.

The air leaves my lungs in one long whoosh, but the doubt remains ever steady and starts to grow exponentially. Disappointment, too, in Linc, and his inability to stand up to his father comes rushing back.

We've been here before.

I've been on the receiving end of Davis Presley's wrath. We are never going to be close. Davis and I. The man tore Linc and me apart months ago. Obviously, he'll do it again if he feels it's warranted. Like now.

But what of a prenup?

Does it really matter to me?

Should I sign it?

Wouldn't that make things easier for Linc with his dad?

I hold my breath in search of calm, but it only lasts for a few seconds before I'm gasping for air. The warning signs of a panic attack emerge.

We just pledged to forge a life together a few hours ago and already Davis Presley is interfering in our marriage. *Do we stand together or do we stand apart? Aren't we together no matter what?*

Worried at being discovered by Linc and his father and still not sure how I feel about any of this, I pick up the hem of my dress and race down the hallway before anyone discovers me standing here. I frantically try a few doors and finally find one unlocked on my right.

Two minutes later, I'm sliding down the interior of a closed and locked door seeking comfort and familiarity in the dark confined space of a janitorial closet. I rest my weary head in my hands and sit amid the white creamy folds of my beautiful wedding gown and feel the last vestiges of happiness seep away from me this day.

Anger takes its place and surges outward. *Davis Presley. That bastard.* I guess the dress was some kind of pay-off or appeasement or a very good bribe. Or none of these things. Maybe it's just been another way to manipulate the situation and his son and me, well, most definitely the two of us. And why did I finally think that things with Davis had changed for the better? I can only hope that Linc will someday stand up to his father and recognize the man's treacherous ways, but I'm not entirely convinced that he ever will.

And where does that leave us? The two of us? Nowhere.

I lament that we wasted all this time in declaring ourselves and finally getting married only to have it start to unravel a few hours later at someone else's hand. Davis might be right; it does feel like we just rushed into everything all over again without thinking things through.

I hold my breath as I hear Linc and his dad still talking rather loudly to one another as they must walk away down toward the other end of the hallway. When the tapping of their dress shoes against the hall floor gets more distant, I take in air and let it out.

Breathe.

Breathe, Tally.

You know happiness never lasts. At least, not for you.

"Ready?" Marla asks from the open doorway. My best friend looks so beautiful in the blue maternity sun dress she's changed into for the road trip back home. "You make being pregnant look fashionable."

"So will you."

I say a little prayer that I can pull off the same look in three months time. But right now, I'm caught in the thrilled-but-fearful-I'm-pregnant-stage-and-how-is-that-all-going-to-work-out? stage. I still haven't told Mikhail. I'm intent on avoiding *that* conversation for several more weeks. Maybe a few months if I can manage it like I did with Cara.

I grin at my best friend. "Ready."

"You didn't change?" Marla gives me this quizzical look.

"I changed my mind. I love the dress too much," I mumble.

I don't want to get into the details of what I heard Linc and his dad arguing about. Marla doesn't need to worry about anything else right now. She's a little over five months pregnant. She's taking care of my kid for me. She's got enough on her plate, and I don't want to add to it.

Instead, I lean down and kiss Cara one last time and then helplessly watch as Marla takes my child's left hand and escorts her out the front door of the church. From the open doorway, I watch as Linc swings Cara up into his arms and kisses her good-bye.

Then, he walks over to me and slings his arm across my shoulders. I attempt to shut down the uneasy feeling of letting Cara go as well as all the doubts about us by pasting on a wide smile as Charlie and Marla and the two children wave to us as they are about to drive off.

"She's going to have a great time."

"I know." I don't believe what I say, and my weary tone must confirm this for him.

Linc kisses the side of my face. "She's going to have a great time and so is her mom. I'm going to make sure of it." He leans in and kisses my forehead this time.

Are you?

I avoid looking directly at him and instead fully concentrate on our little girl who frantically waves at the two of us from the back passenger window.

Uncertainty has returned for a second time on this once spectacular day. I wonder what I've just done in marrying Lincoln Presley so quickly.

What were we thinking?

Can we really have it all?

I reach out and air blow Cara a kiss in a futile attempt at capturing happiness once again hoping to bring it back to me.

Happiness is so fleeting—a butterfly, really.

It's here one minute and gone the next.

And, I know this already.

CHAPTER THREE

your body is a wonderland

LINC

"I breathe in air and the delicious scent of her
and lean in close and promptly lose my soul to her."
~ Lincoln Presley

July 17th - 18th

SHE'S QUIET. TOO QUIET. WE HAVE the biggest suite at the Ritz Carlton at Half Moon Bay and the rest of the evening to ourselves before driving to the airport to get on the flight that leaves for Miami around ten tomorrow. It's not ideal. It's not Paris or Maui, but we agreed to make the best of it. I've already promised Tally after the season's over we will make better plans and take a proper honeymoon.

Tally finally admits she didn't really eat at the reception, so I order up enough food for four. A half-hour later, we're grazing the room-service table with an array of breakfast, lunch, and dinner entrees plus an array of desserts that the bellman just brought up to us. I know my bride; she won't actually eat much of anything. She nibbles the edges of a piece of buttered toast and delicately push her fork at a steak and the sauteed vegetables while I wolf down just about everything that's in front of me.

I'm tired. I'm stressed. I'm married. I'm only happy about one of these things.

My head aches. I pop a few Oxycontin to stave off the pain, not pausing long enough to even acknowledge it's a narcotic, and I should be more careful about taking them. I've heard that often enough over the past several months; I don't want to hear it now. My wife of a few precious hours starts to form a question upon her alluring parted lips.

"Don't," is all I say.

Things are not going exactly as I envisioned. At first, I thought she wasn't really talking to me because she was worried about leaving Cara. Let's face it; after tomorrow, we'll be pretty far away from home for the next week or so, and I know leaving our four-year-old for any length of time still makes Tally uneasy, even if it is with Charlie and Marla.

It will be just the two of for the next week or so as we travel to Miami and then onto Philadelphia for baseball. We'll be together, just the two of us, which should be perfect, but it's not.

The news of today, which should be all about marrying Tally, has been usurped by the unforeseen argument with my father over a prenuptial agreement. Hard to forget that. Not that my dad will ever let me forget it regardless of what my decision might be. He's already sent me three texts demanding to know the signature status since he left us two hours ago.

I know my dad loves me, but he has a weird way of showing it at times. My dad has this way of making me doubt what I truly believe and the whole side conversation about Sam Wilde has put me on edge. *Is the baby even mine? Does it matter? It matters to me. I know I'm being a jerk on some levels even questioning it, but it matters to me. It would make a difference to me.*

I covertly study my lovely bride as she moves about the hotel suite and absently touches the mahogany furniture and the artwork adorning the walls and traces an invisible pattern wherever she goes.

Yes, she moves, but remains just out of arms reach. My reach.

She's preoccupied. Uncertain. Her anxiety matches mine, but for very different reasons.

We are…Mr. and Mrs. Lincoln Presley. We should be so happy right now. And yet, the troubles of our shared past and even baseball have followed us here on this day.

Tally stands over at the bar and proceeds to fill a glass with ice and pours sparkling water over the top. Minutes later, she struts over to the vast window that takes up one entire wall of the suite and stares seemingly unseeing out at the turquoise blue of the Pacific. We have an unobstructed view of Half Moon Bay from this suite for just the two of us to admire.

"It's colder here by the Pacific."

She's said this a few times already. "Sure," I answer for the third time, getting more concerned by her distant demeanor.

In an effort to play it cool, I loosen my tie and pour myself a brandy at the bar, mimicking her same movements from moments before, and continue to watch her via the bar's mirror. Her face reflects this unmistakable anguish, when only a few hours before, she radiated with happiness. Somehow, I know I've done this. I've made her unhappy. I sip the brandy in search of liquid courage and try to organize my thoughts. I have to tell her about the prenup and the fight with my dad. I have to make this right with her because without Tally none of this will work. From my vantage point with the mirror, I watch as she moves to the desk and opens a drawer.

"I'll sign it." She turns toward me holding out a pen.

I swing around so fast, I spill my drink down the front of my dress shirt and splash the bar counter. "What?"

"I said, I'll sign it. It's like a test, right? I sign it and then you're convinced I love you enough. Something like that."

I frown while all the air in my lungs escapes. "How much did you hear?"

"Enough," she answers. "So? Where is it? The prenup that will protect your *assets* from mine." She manages a tight smile for my benefit while her emphasis on the word *assets* would have me laughing in any other situation but this one.

I sigh big again. "Tally. I. Love. You. No prenup. *Really*, it's okay." I take in air in a valiant attempt to come clean with all of it. She deserves that from me. "I told Dad about the baby. He…"

She nods with understanding. "My due date is around Valentine's Day—the 16th of February, actually, according to Dr. Eldon with the ultrasound."

Yes, she heard most of it if not all of it.

"The math says it's yours." She looks uncertain. It doesn't make me feel any better.

"I already knew that. I don't know why I let him get to me like that. I never should have even questioned it—the baby, I mean—being mine. I'm sorry I told him. He just doesn't understand. I *never* should have told him."

"He would have eventually figured out that I'm pregnant, but we do need to keep it quiet. I'm trying to keep my job here, and I'll tell Mikhail when the time is right. He can't fire me outright over it, but if he finds out before I tell him; well, I wouldn't put anything past Mikhail. That's just the way he is. My being pregnant is going to seriously mess with his fall schedule."

"I know. I shouldn't have said anything. I just thought…I thought my dad would understand and be excited for us. Obviously that didn't happen." I sigh big. "I just wanted a couple of hours where everything was perfect and I went and fucked it all up by listening to anything my dad had to say at all." I hang my head and then finally manage to gather enough courage to look at her again. "I'm sorry. It's a raw deal. You finally say yes to me and marry me and a few hours later I'm questioning the paternity of our child and bringing up a prenup. I'm an asshole." I shake my head side-to-side. "I'm sorry. My dad…I just let him into my head sometimes."

She lifts her chin looking all defiant. "Maybe, one day, he'll see I'm the best thing that ever happened to you." She gets this wry smile and then it fades. "But if you keep letting him come between us, then he'll come between us."

"I should have just talked to you first."

"That's right because you're *married* to me, not *him*." She's said this so softly, it's difficult for me to tell whether she's angry or just upset.

I walk over to her and have my answer when I see a lone tear trail down her beautiful face. I touch her lips and trace the contours of her collar bone, finally resting my palm against her heart feeling for its fast beat. *How I love this girl.*

"I love you. I didn't mean to hurt you with any of this. I don't want to ever lose you, Tally. I'm sorry. Please forgive me for not saying something to you right away about the prenup. I should have talked to you first. I can't lose you over this. I can't lose you. Not ever."

She just looks at me. Her vulnerability is as palpable as mine. Her heart beats faster and so does mine. I breathe in air and the delicious scent of her and lean in close and promptly lose my soul to her.

"You won't." She holds each side of my face and frowns ever so slightly. "But we're in this *together*, Linc. It's you and me. That has to come first. *Always*. Like Pastor Dan said again today when he married us." Her lips part. She hesitates.

Finally, she takes a deep breath. "We can't let the challenges we face with other people and even in our careers to come between us. Enough people have tried to break us up already, but we have to believe in us. So? Next time, you need to talk to me first. Put us first. Okay?" She sighs. "So, I'll sign it because that will make things easier with your father and frankly, your money doesn't really mean anything to me."

I slowly nod. I'm a little dazed by her conviction. She's not normally this sure of us. Right now, she's sure enough for both of us.

She signs it with a flourish. "It's better this way."

"Is it? It doesn't feel better." Although secretly, I feel this profound relief as I take the agreement from her outstretched hand but then, the guilt takes over because I've been doubting her for the past few hours since the heated conversation with my dad. I hang my head because I've given into my dad's wishes and hurt Tally in the process. *Again.*

"I'm sorry."

"Sorry for what?"

"Making you feel this way. Making you sign it because it makes things easier with my dad."

"It's a piece of paper," she says slowly while her long, dark hair sways back and forth captivating me. "Don't let it change anything between us. Your dad doesn't get to come between us. Like I just said, it's you and me. *Together.* The prenup's easy enough to sign because it doesn't really mean anything to you or to me. It will make your dad happy. And? Years from now, he'll finally have to admit that I'm the best thing that's ever happened to you." Her smile is benevolent and beautiful.

She is extraordinary, and I don't deserve her.

"Like you just said, it's you and me. No one else. We're in this together. Forever." I kiss her forehead and then pull back and grin at her. "You have my heart and my soul. No amount of money or even baseball will ever matter to me as much as you do. You know that, right?"

"I do."

"You're it for me."

"You're it for me, too, Elvis."

Her face exhibits such honesty. Normally she's so guarded it's incredible to see her this way. Pure joy cascades through me because now this girl is mine. She's my wife. The day has finally come to pass where Tally Landon said *yes* and married me. My life is made. "I love you, Tally. So much. Nothing is ever going to come between us. Nothing."

I slide the signed documents into the envelope my dad provided and seal it. Then in the next two minutes, I toss the entire package into the fireplace where it flames up and starts to burn away.

Tally gasps from behind me. "What are you doing?"

"Something I should have done when my dad first brought this whole thing up. We're in this together. Me and you." I grab her hands and bring them to my lips. "Until death do us part and maybe not even then." I smile at her. "No prenup. Nothing comes between us. It's just us. Okay?"

"Okay, then," she whispers softly.

"Okay then." The elation that crosses her features is all I need. That's the exact moment I know burning up the prenup was the absolute right thing to do.

"So." She shyly traces a pattern on the carpet with the point toe of her white satin shoe. "Can we consummate this thing or what? I think we've waited long enough; don't you?"

"Yes, Mrs. Presley, we've waited long enough." I pull her into my arms and kiss her hard and long.

Soon, I'm busy trying to undo all the pearl buttons on the back of her beautiful wedding dress; she insisted on wearing until we checked in, swearing as I go, while she laughs softly at my feeble attempts at getting the dress off of her voicing my complaints aloud at this impossible task. She tells me it's not exactly seductive. I get a paper cut from one of the loose threads. I'm sucking the razor-thin cut and cursing the bridal shop and the dress while Tally just laughs.

"Fuck it." I rip down the back of her dress, and some thirty buttons scatter across the floor sounding just like marbles when they hit the travertine tile. Tally laughs harder. Indelible sounds that I am intent on making her do every single day from this one forward. I kiss the back of her neck and push the dress down off of her beautiful body and toss it aside.

She's wearing this sexy, bridal lingerie underneath, and I start to tear that too, but then she quickly moves out of my reach. Now, she stands away from me in nothing but her high heels and this white lace bridal lingerie with the palm of her hands out warding me off.

"Hey! This stuff was expensive." She gets this lascivious grin. "You might want me to wear it again, someday, Elvis. Slow down." She does a sexy strip tease with the lingerie first unhooking her bra and then stepping out of her white lace panties and tossing them my way.

I finger the lace but keep my eyes solely on her. "Nothing does justice to that gorgeous body of yours, and you've been hiding it from me all day."

"Nothing you haven't seen before."

"It's been a while and not nearly enough over the past five days. And now, it's different. You're really mine. For keeps. Forever." I rise from the bed where I've been watching her undress and dispense with my tuxedo, dress shirt, and briefs in under ninety seconds. "I'm sure I've just set some kind of record for grooms in shucking the gear."

"I'm sure you have. Do you have to win at everything?" she asks with a playfulness I've been missing in her for the past few hours.

"Tally Landon Presley." I come towards her unable to stay away from her any longer. "Thanks for marrying me." I smile wide. "Now, do you promise to be my wife forever?"

"I already said those vows and made that promise earlier. Do you need to hear it again?"

"Yes, yes, I do."

"Okay then. Yes, I promise to be your wife forever."

She dons the sexiest smile I've ever seen from her and just boldly stands there until I meet up with her. Our outstretched palms fit together, and we slowly move into each other. Everything between us seems to slow down, but the connection between us becomes electrified.

"This is the good part," she murmurs when her lips finally meet up with mine.

"It is."

I lightly kiss her and then start a gentle exploration of her eyelids planting kisses on each one and then my lips down travel down the right side of her neck. I pause for a few seconds and feel her pulse beat wildly beneath my lips. Her breath hitches at my tender touch. I really want to savor the moment and make it last just like her finest perfume permeates the air, even after she leaves a room. She rocks my world and now that she's promised me forever I want to enjoy every minute of it with her.

"What do you want *Miss Cloves and Vanilla?*"

"You," she whispers.

We try to match one another with this slower pace, but I can feel her impatience growing as the heated passion between us starts to dictate where we will go next. She becomes the aggressor as she pushes me backwards, my knees hit the bed and then I'm falling and she's falling with me.

She gets this lascivious grin as she starts her own exploration of me while my heart wildly beats. Soon, she presses her face against my chest to listen. "That is the greatest sound, Elvis. You have no idea how happy it makes me to hear it in a moment like this. Your love—this heart—is all I need." She pushes herself back and straddles my lower legs and leans down and slowly takes me into her mouth. Then, she looks up and winks knowing I'm loving what she's doing to me.

"God, Tally."

"Not me," she says pausing for a moment in her seductive exploration. "You're the god around here."

Then she laughs and I'm soon lost as she brings me all these new sensations I've never felt with her quite like this before. She is an artist, and I'm not talking about her dancing.

Within minutes, what she's doing has me just about losing control. "I'm not going to last, babe."

She lifts her head and smiles.

"That's okay. We've got all night. It's just you and me. We have time. No baseball tonight. That's tomorrow. Tonight? You are most definitely all mine. Lay back and enjoy the ride, Elvis. I've got this. You're mine tonight, and I'll have my way with you and take my sweet ass time doing it." She laughs and then I lose my mind all over again because of Tally.

CHAPTER FOUR

somewhere only we know

LINC

"From this day forward, it's you and me.
And you and me? We're all that matters."
~ Lincoln Presley

July 17th - 18th

THE MOON RISES UP IN THE dark sky and lights the ocean water at Half Moon Bay. We lay side by side on the bed holding hands and silently marveling at the fact that we're newlyweds and life is perfect. She's said this a couple of times already. I lean over and trace her lips and then bend to kiss her. "I could do this with you forever."

"What is this? You finally found something you like to do better than baseball?" She grins at me and slides out of my grasp. She crawls over to the nightstand and takes a sip of the one and only glass of champagne she's alloted herself. She's pregnant, but we're being careful. We agreed on this one thing because it makes her happy, and I'm all about making this woman happy. We've done enough research and decided it was okay.

She smiles wide as she makes a point of swirling the champagne around in her mouth and then she's hovering over me proving carbonation can be its own erotic sensation. I think she knew this already. I'm hard again within seconds and more than ready for what comes next between us.

"My turn." I move to kiss her collar bone and then linger at each of her breasts. I span her tiny waist with hands on each side amazed my fingertips actually meet. "Are you sure you're old enough?"

"Are you sure you're young enough? Closer to thirty than twenty there, Elvis."

"I'll do anything to keep up with you."

"Anything?" she asks pulling on my hair.

"Anything." I caress her smooth skin first with my tongue and then with my lips while she cradles the my head with her sweet, loving hands. I catch her left hand in mine and stop to finger the wedding band and diamond for a second or two admiring the significance and then begin sucking each of her fingers one by one. After a while she makes these little moaning sounds that seem to turn us both on.

"You're mine forever." I gaze into her eyes. "Say it."

"I'm yours forever."

My fingers travel up the inside of her thighs discovering her delicious wet center. I focus on going slow knowing she's being pulled over the edge one smooth fingered caress at a time. Blissed-out passion dominates her features; she starts to fall apart with just the insistent movements of my hands, but I encourage her to keep going, to hold onto it. My tongue finds her. Her ecstasy spills over. She grips the sheets as if it's a way to maintain control and then seems to give into the need all at once. I watch her face as the waves of her orgasm roll through her.

"Oh, God, Linc," she says as she goes over.

Tonight, she replaces the setting sun's rays. Outright joy radiates off of her. This dreamy look of pure contentment comes across her face that she doesn't attempt to hide from me. She's blissed out.

I cup the back of her neck and bring her to me as I lay on my back and she swivels her hips around and climbs on top of me.

"Not yet," I say before she can sink further. She arches an eyebrow looking mildly curious while I make a valiant attempt control the pace with her. She sighs and then settles down on my chest. I kiss her forehead and gaze in fresh wonder at the beauty of this woman who is all mine. Intent on showing her how much I want her and what she does to me, I raise her hips up slightly and roll her onto her back. Keeping the pace slow and methodical proves to be a physical as well as a mental challenge for both of us, but I want to take my time and explore all of her.

Her needs become more urgent while my touch becomes more insistent as it seeks her to satisfy her. "What. Do. You. Want?" I enunciate each word slowly as my fingers magically perform pushing inside of her bringing her to a new high.

"I want you." She practically pants each word struggling to both breathe and control herself. "Please, Linc. *Now.* I need you now. Inside me."

"There's my girl. You want it bad, don't you?"

"Don't make me beg." She tries to laugh but the intensity is making it harder for her to even talk. Watching Tally lose control brings all kinds of erotic satisfaction to me.

"Say it, Mrs. Presley. What do you want?" I like seeing Tally this way—all pent-up and needy and ready to seek relief from me in any way I can give it to her. She seeks me. She wants me. She needs me. I like being needed by her.

Her fingers dig into the bed as she starts to lose control all over again. She moans. "Linc." She raises her head off the bed and looks straight at me. "Linc, please. Please now."

I can't wait for her much longer so I slip inside of her. She arches her hips up and our connection deepens. The slow pace with doing number nine on her Fresno list is eschewed in deference to the urgent need to feel this exhilarating wave and go over the edge together.

She moans and playfully bites my shoulder as we reach the crescendo of our connection almost simultaneously. I push into her deeper while her body writhes beneath mine seeking her own kind of relief. I meet up with her and leave a part of myself inside of her.

It is the most amazing feeling being with her, sharing this intimacy and knowing we're together for all time.

Anything seems possible. In this singular moment of time, I believe that.

Much later, she makes this weird face as she hovers above mine. She looks hopeful for the first time I've seen in a long while, maybe ever. "What happens to us now that we have everything? Like this? Like now?" she asks.

"That's easy." I tuck a strand of her hair behind her left ear and smile. "We win."

"What happens if we lose?"

"Tally, don't you see? We've already won. We have everything. We have each other. Love is all we need."

"Did you…did you just turn what we have into a Beatles song lyric?"

I laugh. "I guess I did. I don't know how else to convince you. This is it. We made it. We won. This is you and me winning. Love *is* all we need. We have each other into forever from here on out."

The introspective look still dominates her features. "Don't overthink it, babe. Enjoy the ride. We deserve it. This bliss. This happiness—this here and now—after all we've been through to get to this moment. All you have to do from here on out is believe in it, believe in us. Tally, it's real. We're real. We're something together and nothing apart. That's the lesson we've learned. A few times as I recall. So all you have to remember is we've got this. From this day forward, it's you and me. And you and me? We're all that matters."

"It seems like…it seems like somebody wins but somebody else always loses," she says with hesitation. "That's how it usually works. We can't win forever."

"I think we can. I've always been a winner even in the worst of times and especially this past year, because, deep down, I still believed I'd make it. And once I learned about you and all of what we had, and when the memories of us started coming back to me, I knew you were all I needed."

"Love was all you needed? Me?" I nod. She tilts her head to one side, lost in thought for a few seconds. "So we've already won is what you're saying."

"I believe I came up with that brilliant concept five minutes ago, but I've always known even when I didn't remember you at first that you were it for me."

"You're it for me, too. I thought I already told you that."

She traces my lips. "We've won."

She still sounds uncertain.

"Tally, we've won and we can't lose. We'll never lose. Trust me. In fact, let me show you more about what I mean about winning. Let me teach you as to what all is involved when it comes to winning."

"Yeah, show me again." She laughs as I move in on her. It truly is the best sound in the world.

It's a long while, before the atmosphere of the room returns to normal. It's as if the air molecules have somehow come together and changed, and we've just begun to notice. It's past midnight.

We hold hands and share in the sweet essence of sweat, profound exhaustion, and this unbelievable euphoria as we openly gaze at each other. She sits in my lap and we look out at the moon which seems to signify our coming together as if we choreographed the entire thing.

"I knew it could be this way with you. You know, now that I've made an honest woman out of you." I laugh softly.

She turns her head and looks at me with fresh curiosity as my meaning sinks in. "I *like* being an honest woman with you. Thanks for helping me out, Elvis." She radiates this beautiful smile as if she holds the world's best secret.

She is happy. Satisfied. Blissed out.

And all *mine.*

I grab my cell from the nightstand nearby and snap a photograph capturing her beautiful essence. "Your smile says it all. Just remember who put it there. Your *husband.*"

I show her the photograph. It's up close. You can't necessarily tell she's been having sex all night long, but you could take a wild guess and be right. She stares at me. She's got that look going like she knows the biggest secret of them all. She probably does.

"I'm going to remember this moment forever. Just like this," I say. "I think I'll make a point of looking at this photograph at least once a day for the rest of my life just to remind myself how lucky I am to be with you. I'll call it your pure bliss smile—your best one—and remember this day as the one on which my perfect married life began."

"You are seriously whipped, Elvis. You better slow down." Her smile falters. "I'm less than perfect, far from perfect."

"You're perfect to me, and I'm the only one that counts."

"That's some ego of yours. You just have it all figured out; don't you?"

"I do. Just remember that and you'll be fine. You're doing a bang-up job as Mrs. Lincoln Presley." She giggles at my phrasing. "I'm duly impressed and we're just getting started."

"Technically, it's the day after the perfect day you married me," she says with a sly smile. "Your perfect married life began *yesterday* when we said, *I do*. We're on day two of this ride together, Mr. Presley."

"Okay. Get technical." I grin. "Just think, Tal, we've already beat Pastor Dan's record for blissful happiness. We made it to Day Two."

"So we did." She laughs. "Yay for Mr. and Mrs. Presley and to think people had the gall to predict it wouldn't last."

Tally this happy is an amazing sight to behold. I aim to keep it that way from this day forward. That's my promise to her. I sweep my bride up into my arms and kiss her fine lips. "It should always be this way with us, and it will be. I promise."

"I promise, too." She gazes at me with ardent longing as if she's just won the best prize. She takes my hand and pulls to her to me and brush her lips with mine. "Promise," she says again.

Promise.

Tally's promise is all I need.

CHAPTER FIVE

wake me up when September ends

LINC

"Love is composed of a single soul
inhabiting two bodies."
~ Aristotle

August 31st

On the outside, life appears to be going according to plan. Not ours, but the Giants. The team is playing good baseball in late August. Rumors continue to swirl about my being possibly traded in early December and even my agent has begun to think so. There are usually only five starting pitchers on the roster. My return made for six, and I'm still coming back from a head injury so that leaves me out of the starting lineup more than I would like as the Giants make good on their season with the possibility of post-season play looking more than likely with each game we play and win.

It's not that my pitching hasn't been great; it's just that Mad's pitching has been so much better than mine, or anybody else's in baseball, for that matter. Somebody gets to be the MVP, and it isn't going to me this year. Granted, I feel lucky just to be here again, but it hasn't been long enough to make a standout contribution to the Giants' front office or most of the coaching staff.

Nika has already warned me about this just days ago after one of our home games against the Brewers. "He is having an exceptional year."

She'd pointed to the talented pitcher as he was making his way across the parking lot to his car. She had leaned in close to me as if to only tell me this one undeniable fact just days ago.

"That loss against the Royals didn't help you, and your contract is going to be a problem, Linc. That guy. He is going to be far too valuable to lose, and they're already looking for the additional money to pay him." She paused for a few seconds and touched my forearm. "You know; I could be fired for even saying this to you, but I was around when the talk started in mid-July. A trade deal fell through right around the week of the All-Star Game when they called you up from Fresno. Your name came up, but your pitching coach fought hard and argued you deserved a chance in the Giants' line-up before they made a move like that. Anyway, his contract renegotiation and others will change things up, and you need to plan for that. If I hear more, I'll let you know when I can."

"Wow, they were going to trade me right after the All-Stars? Thanks for the heads-up."

"Money rules the world, Linc. You *know* this."

"Well, my world anyway. What's it like not to need the money when you have someone like Thorn around?" I asked her with as much nonchalance as I could conjure up. I knew things weren't looking good for me but I didn't know that it had been so seriously talked about already. She smiled at the Rob reference and the undertone of jealousy I couldn't quite hide.

We had history together.

Nika and I.

But I love Tally.

Still.

Rob Thorn? I didn't get it. I didn't like it. Right or wrong. My problem or not, Rob and Nika being together didn't sit well with me. Regardless that I had no right to feel this way.

"I'm sorry. I'm sure your *wife* wants to remain in San Fran." Nika frowned revealing her own jealousy in spewing the word *wife*.

This little crevice formed at her nose bridge when she frowned, something that always happened when she was contemplating serious thought. I wasn't exactly sure if it was at the utterance of the word *wife* or my contract problems that posed the biggest problem for her. All I remember thinking was that Nika was still beautiful. She's manipulative in every other way, but Nika Vostrikova was still easier to manage on many levels than Tally would ever be.

"She does. We're expecting a baby around Valentine's Day."

Nika took this bit of news rather well, although she was working up her jawline pretty hard. She always clenched her teeth when she was angry. I didn't recall my entire life; there were still large gaps. And yet? There were these weird little facts about Nika I remembered.

I looked away from her searching gaze as she said, "Congratulations."

Meanwhile, Madison drove away with a wave in our direction as he passed us. "He's got it going on all cylinders." I inclined my head in the direction of Madison's retreating car. "I know that. And thanks for letting me know. You didn't have to do that, but you did. I appreciate it." I smiled at her. The wind blew her long blond hair forward. I tucked it back behind her left ear without even thinking about it. She looked momentarily surprised.

"I thought you hated me," she said softly.

"I could never hate you, Nik. We've been through a lot together. You were there for me. Plenty of times."

"Not always. I never said how sorry I was about Moscow. I'm sorry."

She looked so troubled and vulnerable, I took a hold of her hand. "I can't really remember much about Moscow, so there's nothing to forgive. And, if there is?" I grinned at her. "You're forgiven."

She looked relieved and something else. *Driven. Purposeful?*

I dropped her hand and ducked into my car, suddenly intent on finishing up this conversation and getting home to my wife. I didn't like to overshare my memory problems, and I certainly didn't want Nika to get the wrong idea about us. Out of the corner of my eye, I saw the photographer taking photographs of the two of us, but I was too preoccupied by Nika's revelation about my contract, a possible trade, and discussing our past relationship to even think about stopping him from taking them.

"That's good to know. Thank you. I just thought, given our history, I should try to help you out. You know, so you're prepared for what's up ahead," Nika said as she leaned into the open window of my car.

"Right." I nodded slowly as she looked at me seemingly to gauge my reaction. "Like I said earlier, Tally's pregnant. We have a lot going on. We're trying to keep her pregnancy quiet. Please don't say anything to anyone." I instantly regretted bringing it up again, but Nika seemed to take my unexpected request for discretion in stride.

She subtly smiled as if she'd just learned an important secret. "Rob and I…are getting married soon. You two should come. It'd serve as some kind of closure among all four of us, right?"

"Sure. Yes, send us an invitation. I'm sure you and Rob will be very happy together."

"What's that supposed to mean?" She shielded her face from the fading sun as it set behind me. I couldn't see her as clearly, but I heard the wistfulness in her tone.

"Nothing. Congratulations, Nika. You and Rob. Marriage is great. You'll be great at it."

"Well, you're already married and having a baby with her," she said softly. "A lady's got to move on. I did." She shrugged and her smile faded.

Then, she looked at me for a long time through the open car window. I'd finally reached out for her left hand and fingered the big diamond resting there. "It looks like you have. Thanks for letting me know about the other thing, too. I just want you to be happy, Nik."

"That's what we all want. Right? To be happy." She didn't ruin it with a smile.

"Right."

"Take care of yourself, Linc. I'll see what I can do about keeping you in San Fran, especially with a new baby on the way. Rob might have some influence where I don't."

I didn't know what to say to that, so I just thanked her for trying. I wasn't aware of how big or how far Thorn's money or power went, but it wouldn't surprise me if he or his dad had some kind of influence with the Giants' owners. Thorn Enterprises was everywhere. They were big in this town. Even with the Giants.

Then, Nika had jolted me from my reverie about the Thorns when she openly traced my jawline and then leaned in and kissed my mouth in the next. I was stunned but not stunned enough that I didn't kiss her back. All these memories of the two of us together came rushing back. "Nik," I groaned. "We can't. Yes, we have history, but things are different."

"I know," she said stepping back from the window with the trace of a smile. "Be happy, Linc."

"You too."

The whole encounter had been surreal. I'm sure the photographers got a shot of that kiss, too. Yet, I'd watched her as she sauntered off toward her own car—a white Mercedes, sleek and beautiful, just like she was—without looking back at me. I felt the disappointment of that for a few seconds before I shook my head at the surreality of our encounter. However brief. We had history, Nik and I. But it was over. *Clearly.*

She slid into her car, and I continued to watch her for some undefinable reason trying to remember any of the reasons why we broke up. Kimberley had told me enough times to stay away from Nika at all costs, but the details of why we split up remained unclear to me.

Nik and I. Together.

Why?

Because it was easy.

Because *she* was easier.

Because, as much I remembered it, my life with Nika had been a whole lot easier.

And things were far from easy and far more complicated with Tally.

Easy sounded good for a few precious seconds.

Kissing her had been easy too. Maybe I was reeling from news of the trade. Maybe I was just an asshole for even playing with temptation with someone like Nika Vostrikova. And I kissed her back but I didn't mean to, although I imagine Tally would have a tough time believing that if she'd seen it. Nika waved at me as she drove past, and like a besotted fool, I'd waved back. And yes, I imagined the photographer got that money shot, too.

But I didn't think anything of it at the time.

Instead, I'd turned the key in the ignition and kept going over in my mind Nika's exact words regarding my baseball career with the Giants and our shared past more than a few times on the drive home and really ever since then.

I knew Tally hadn't quite figured all of the contract implications and how baseball trades worked and what that meant for us ultimately.

Clearly, Nika had; and she took a big risk in telling me.

I owed her that much. Didn't I?

CHAPTER SIX

landslide

TALLY

You start to make all these plans.
You begin to believe that things will work out, and often they do,
but then there are those other things that wreak havoc
on your very soul and threaten to tear you apart from the inside.
Those things rule your head and attempt to destroy your heart.
I've seen it.
I've felt that kind of loss. More than once.
Those things will wreck you. Those things.
Those things that attempt to drown you every fucking day.
Those are the things you have to watch out for.
And there are the lies that go untold. There are those, too.
Just waiting to reveal themselves one day when you least expect it.
~ Talia Landon Presley

September 8th

YELLOW. BABY'S BREATH YELLOW. NOT PINK or blue. We wanted to be surprised. Well, Linc wanted to be surprised, and I wanted that for him, too. Boy or girl. It didn't matter. We didn't care. Well, we did, but we told each other we didn't. Secretly, I wanted to give Linc a son and even without asking him directly I knew that's what he wanted, too. Even so, we didn't say it out loud.

Not to each other. Although my thoughts were so loud, it's as if I'd spoken them.

So. The baby's room was to be painted yellow. It had been decided.

Baby's Breath Yellow. It was a pale yellow, almost white. I was not sure how it's going to look on all four walls, but Linc assured me it would be fine when I talked to him about the color three days ago before he left for the weekend series with Detroit.

And yet?

In the back of my mind, I was already thinking this was a bad idea that we're testing fate this way, which hasn't always been good to me, by painting the walls yellow. Something didn't feel right about planning ahead in painting these walls at all. It was a commitment to something that has yet to arrive. I didn't like looking too far out into the future. I spent too much time running from my past.

The truth was we were both secretly counting on this baby to be born on time, right before Linc's spring training for baseball, and my return for SFB's spring season because life should be perfect and fall into place like that. And yet, the thing was I already knew you could never count on things to go the way they were supposed to go.

Let's face it; I was having trouble reconciling hidden thoughts that invaded my psyche that questioned the likelihood of this baby being born at all. Bad thoughts these. I knew it. I tried to outrun them, too, just like in the past, but they were still there. And whenever Linc and I were apart for more than a few days, those were the thoughts that took over.

How I wished I didn't think this way. How I wished mistrust and distrust, and thoughts of impending disaster didn't always rule my head and heart. But they did. Because that's been my life, right?

You start to make all these plans.

You begin to believe that things will work out, and often they do,

but then there are those other things

that wreak havoc on your very soul

and threaten to tear you apart from the inside.

Those things rule your head and attempt to destroy your heart.

I've seen it.

I've felt that kind of loss. More than once.

Those things will wreck you. Those things.

Those things that attempt to drown you every fucking day.
Those are the things you have to watch out for.
And there are the lies that go untold. There are those, too.
Just waiting to reveal themselves one day when you least expect it.

Baby's Breath Yellow. That's what we said we wanted. "Baby's Breath Yellow," I said to the painter Linc hired.

This tall giant of a man nodded in utter silence and continued to stir the creamy yellow color with a flat stick that resembled a ruler but without the markings.

Silence still bothered me, so I filled it in. "Okay then." I forced a smile and started to back out of the room attempting to damp down the eerie feeling this hired hand gave me. Luther. Luther W. Swanson was what his card said. It's a peculiar name for a strange man. I turned back to him. "So, I'll leave you to it. Just lock up when you leave. I have to take my daughter to preschool, and I'm off to a doctor's appointment and then a business meeting and then possibly the studio …" He nodded as if he knew all of what I was talking about but kept on stirring the paint. "Is everything all right? Are you going to be all right here by yourself?"

He looked up at me then with these deep brown eyes that openly revealed such profound sadness. "Are you?"

"Am I what?"

"Are you going to be all right here by yourself?"

I shivered at the starkness of his words and his seeming clairvoyance. The house was big. *Too big.* Linc…was always gone. I hated it. And how did Luther W. Swanson sense all of this in the mere thirty-five minutes we'd spent together since I first met him at the front door?

After the painter's arrival, we'd looked at the paint samples. Again. Linc and I had already finalized the color. Nervous and unsure, I spent an inordinate amount of time pointing out the location of the upstairs guest bathroom where he could wash his paintbrushes and clean his hands. Why was I going on about this? Because the house was so big, and I felt this vague sense of fear in being all alone in it and in this life.

Linc was hardly ever here. And I was alone in this house with Cara all the time. And now, with a painter, who I did not know that Linc assured me was bonded. *Bonded. Whatever that means.* Linc said he used his services before—for the house—before we got back together. His dad recommended him. Davis recommended him. *I didn't find much solace in that.*

I contrived another smile—a winning one this time. Luther stared at me with his mouth partway open. The paint dripped onto the floor from his suspended paintbrush, and he seemed not to notice. "I'm fine here. Everything is great. Thank you." I played with my hair, and he watched me do it. I filled in the growing awkwardness with more words. "I don't know when I'll be back, so have a good day. You said it would take four days. A day for each wall?"

"Four days."

"Okay then. Thank you. I'll see you late this afternoon or tomorrow morning again."

"Thanks for the key."

"Sure." I slowly met his sympathetic gaze. "Linc didn't give you one before?"

"He did. But you changed the locks again."

"We did?"

Luther nodded slowly. His lips parted halfway, with not quite a smile, which, on his face with his melancholy demeanor, would have seemed incongruent.

He permeated with such profound sadness, which was probably why I was still here talking to him. Kindred spirits of sorts.

Finally, he said gently, "It's your house, Mrs. Presley. You *do* live here, right?"

"I do?" It came out more of a question than an answer.

I again started to back out of the room because I thought Luther W. Swanson had guessed way too much about me in the past thirty-five minutes. "I think I do." I kind of laughed. "Okay then. See you tomorrow."

"Yes. See you then, Mrs. Presley. Have a nice day." His solemn tone somehow soothed me.

Thirty minutes later, I placate the Cara's pre-school teacher by promising to be on time to pick her up with a solicitous wave for both teacher and pre-schooler and make the short drive to Dr. Eldon's office. And that is the moment where my perfect life begins to unravel.

CHAPTER SEVEN

chasing cars

TALLY

"You can't get real happy or real depressed when you play baseball. Baseball is a great sport in that it offers a player a lot of opportunities for atonement."
~ Mike Piazza

September 8th

TALLY STILL DOESN'T FOLLOW BASEBALL THAT closely even when she's sitting in the stands at my games, but the reality is I'll be playing baseball somewhere else by next season just like Nika warned me not so long ago. My contract is far too big to ignore, and those dollars are going to be sorely needed for their star pitcher's own contract renegotiation with the Giants soon enough. Nika's right. They'll have to trade me. Yet, I keep that reality to myself. There's no sense in getting Tally all worked up about a possible move clear across the country or even to Toronto, Canada before the trade takes place. And yet, keeping this from her these past few weeks has been harder than I thought it would be.

All I wanted most was for us to be settled into married life here in San Francisco; and yet, it's not going to be long before we are literally pulling up stakes from this place and having to start all over again some place else. I just can't bring myself to tell Tally that.

Not yet.

"Yo, Linc. You ready to throw? They need to see you throwing," Mad says to me now. He gets this lopsided grin as he hands me the ball. It's hard not to like him. He's easygoing but his intensity in the middle of a game cannot be denied. It's why his record is practically unbeatable at this point.

Focus. I toss the ball up in the air and easily catch it one-handed and signal to Wyman with the other that I'm ready to warm up. "Sure. I'll go." We shift positions. I take his place on the mound while he turns to head toward the dugout.

"Everything okay with you?" he asks turning back toward me. "You look a little too serious for this game." He's a man of few words, but when he does get to talking, his North Carolina's accent dominates.

"They're going to trade me." My voice is low, so I won't be overheard. "That's what my agent is telling me and others."

"Probably." He holds little consolation, but then he looks at me straight on and grins wide. "You'll be a Yankee despite your best efforts to stay out of their lineup. They've wanted you to play for them for a couple of years now. No denying that. And I'll be schlepping it here for some time the way things are going."

"Hardly schlepping." I subtly nod at him indicating he's probably right as well as so damn good and with that one exchange, we openly acknowledge the Giants cannot afford both of us in the lineup. The rumor mill about me and my contract is already rife with speculation. He's right; the Yankees are chomping at the bit to get me in their lineup. I've let my agent float a few numbers—astronomical ones—their way, hoping to stall them because I'm still unwilling to face the inevitable, but even the high floats going around haven't put them off of me. New York is willing to pay. They've said as much to anybody willing to listen to them, including my agent.

"The life of a baseball player." He sighs and shakes his head back and forth, but then looks all serious. "You're going to have to be honest with your ballerina, sooner rather than later, Prez, and ensure she understands all of this. You do what you have to do to play. We all do."

A little taken aback by his honesty and spot-on assessment of my situation, including Tally's highly predictable reaction, I can only watch with grudging admiration as the best pitcher in baseball walks away from me toward the dugout. No truer words have been spoken to me all day. All year in fact.

I grip the ball tighter preparing to throw my best fast ball because he's right of course; Tally is going to have to accept our reality with my baseball career. It's what I love. It's all I know. It's everything. Even so, there's a big part of me that already knows that Tally doesn't actually accept that fact. The reality is our careers clash more than they harmonize. Baseball and ballet don't go together. We've been ignoring that undeniable fact for the past several weeks.

Instead, we naively attempted to settle into married life as if settling in actually describes what we have going on. Chaotic is probably a better description. Constant chaos and turmoil. We've been to Miami, Philadelphia, New York, Milwaukee, and Kansas City since we got married, but after four weeks on the road with her and Cara traveling with me for most of the games, we came to the inevitable conclusion that it was better for all of us, for the most part, when she and Cara remained behind. Being pregnant and a little on the cranky side, Tally has little patience for baseball's grueling schedule. As a fan in contrast to being a player, the travel proved to be too much for her and Cara.

So, yeah, we're married but the road is as lonely as ever because I'm hardly ever home. Every other week I'm out of town, and I'm not sure Tally has come to terms with all of that.

My response that "this is baseball" is met with resentment as opposed to understanding more and more often. My memory is still less than a hundred percent, but Tally's dislike for baseball when it comes to my schedule seems vaguely familiar.

We've been here before.

We've fought about this in the past.

Even our little girl seems to sense the rising tension between us. "Is Daddy *ever* going to come home?" is the most frequent question put to us from Cara, these days.

Meanwhile, Tally's been preoccupied with keeping her career on track, while her boss, Mikhail Rostov, subtly gives her a hard enough time still not knowing she's pregnant yet. Tally is still trying to hide that fact from just about everybody right now.

I didn't want to add to the tension between us by freaking her out with the possibility I may be traded because of the lack of playing time and impatience of the Giants' coaching staff with my slow return to the mound, but time is running out. The Giants are winning even if I'm not a major part of that yet and going into the postseason is becoming more and more likely. My trade seems inevitable. It's only fair to tell Tally about the possibility while there's still time to determine where a trade will end up taking us.

Still, I hesitate to say anything—fearing things between us as it related to our clashing careers of baseball and ballet—will just make things worse.

CHAPTER EIGHT

catalyst

TALLY

"Dates matter.
Math is an intrinsic part of life.
And lies never become true."
~ Talia Landon Presley

September 8th

AFTER A THIRTY-MINUTE WAIT FOR MY gynecologist for my monthly prenatal check-up, Dr. Eldon sweeps into the exam room with a cheery greeting. "Tally! How are you? You look great."

My gynecologist smiles and proceeds to ask me all the usual questions as it relates to how I'm doing, eating and feeling. Then, she hands me a readout that she's just printed off.

"What's this?"

"Well, I made a note last time to check the baby's measurements again. The last time you were here, it was a bit rushed, remember? I re-checked them after you and Linc left because your baby's measurements actually put you at eighteen weeks, not nineteen. Everything else looks great."

I hear her but I'm busy staring at the dates for conception. "Huh. This can't be right though, can it? It says I conceived on May 20th. How long do sperm live?"

Dr. Eldon's smile seems to slip a little perhaps subconsciously knowing she may have just rocked my world. "Five days at the most. Just remember, predicting dates with conception isn't exact, but we have a pretty good idea. Your baby's measurements put you at eighteen weeks with a revised due date of February 9th plus or minus a few days either way. Your cycle is more like thirty-five days from what we've been able to track."

"February 9th, plus or minus a few days," I echo her words while my heart races, and my brain attempts to do the math all over again. I swallow hard and quietly ask, "Five days?"

She looks up from reading my chart. "Yes, sperm can live up to five days after intercourse depending on a number of factors."

"Only five days." I close my eyes. Blacking out feels like a real possibility.

"Tally, are you okay?" Dr. Eldon leans into my face and quickly moves to take my pulse. "Lie down. Do you feel faint?" I just nod. "Tally, is there a problem with the due date?"

"There may have been a problem all along." I try to smile, but I'm far beyond coming up with one at the moment.

"Did you have sexual intercourse with someone else during the same time frame?"

"Yes."

I close my eyes again and allow the reality to swoop in on me for a few seconds. When I open them, Dr. Eldon is staring at me with notable sympathy. I struggle to find the words.

"There was someone…else I was seeing. Linc and I broke up in mid-May—on the sixteenth of May to be exact. We were together that night and then we had a huge fight and I broke up with him and left." I take a sorry breath. "And then, I was with someone else just one time."

I'd been a little pent-up and crazy after the Fresno thing with Linc. I showed up at Sam's place and barely stopped to look around the apartment he'd never even let me see before because I was so determined to erase Lincoln Presley from any waking thought I had.

I basically seduced Sam. He didn't have a choice.

Were there condoms? Yes. Maybe, the first couple of times but probably not the last time.

I was crazed and out of control and like the great guy Sam is, he just let me work through it. Afterward, in doing the deed several times, he was the first to say it was great to be with me, but he hoped next time I wouldn't be so all up in his grill for being a guy and taking it out on him and that maybe we just needed to slow things down a bit. We had laughed and it was fine, and then we agreed to take things at a slower pace in our relationship and lovemaking.

For a few months with him, I tried my best to hide my conflicted feelings for Linc but Sam saw through me. I know he did.

Dr. Eldon hands me a calendar and has me fill in the dates for when I was with Linc and when I was with Sam. The dates don't look like I would want them to.

"Like I said I was last physically with Linc on the sixteenth of May and with Sam from the seventeenth of May until the first part of July."

"We could still be off by a few days. The baby is small, but I can't be sure until we do some blood work to determine paternity if that's what you want. It's a non-invasive test. I just need a blood sample from one of the potential fathers and then we can determine a match or eliminate one of them. That's the surest way." She runs the calculations again and prints off another sheet of paper for me to look at. "Based on my calculations even if we change the due date by a few days you still conceived this baby around the 20th of May. And yes, based on those and the dates you've identified, there could be some overlap in terms of who is the father."

I'm shaking my head and attempting to get a grip on this new reality.

"Is there anything I can do?"

"No. Not right now. I just need to get my head around all of this and figure out what I should do. Linc really wanted this baby." I frown. "But he doesn't exactly *know* how serious things got with Sam because I never actually told him. No one knows. I barely told myself. I was very confused at the time and very pissed off at Linc and acted out with someone else. It's…" I start to lose my composure.

"Complicated," Dr. Eldon says with sympathy.

"It always is, right? I mean we're talking about me and my life here. Of course, it's complicated."

"Do you want me to put in a request for the lab work? It's a matter of one of them showing up at our lab and providing a blood sample. Then, we just need a small sample from you. Like I said, it's a non-invasive procedure and fairly accurate. Otherwise, we wait and do an amniocentesis which I'm not inclined to do given your history and the probability of miscarriage with anything invasive like that. With the non-invasive blood test, we just compare the DNA results to that of you and the baby and the potential father. Would you like to do that—the blood test? Just to eliminate or confirm the possibility?"

"Yes. We need to do that. I…let me think about all of this. I need to think it through. It could really mess things up with Linc. I mean, maybe it's some kind of miracle and I have my cycle dates all wrong and the math is wrong."

"Maybe." She nods slowly. "Your cycles are erratic. The best way to determine this would really be with a paternity test sometime before twenty weeks or after the baby is born." She touches my hand and looks at me intently. "You have a little time if you want to consider other options with this pregnancy. I would insist on counseling you about those in any case."

"I'm not sure I could do that. I mean I know we have the male ego involved here, and it will wreak all kinds of havoc on my marriage because of my omission in not telling him how serious things got with someone else, but still… I don't know. I have to think this all through."

"Like I said, you have a few weeks. I'll order the lab work and you can send one or both of them in for the blood draw and we'll go from there?"

"Okay."

"And Tally? Try not to worry about it. Let's just get the results back and then review next steps. You're pregnant, and you need to take extra care with yourself. I don't want you overly stressing about this until we actually have some results. Conception is not an exact science. If it was we'd have far more women who want to get pregnant getting pregnant. We know how it works to a certain degree but there's a miracle factor in all of this as well. In your case, getting pregnant— with your history and what your body has been through—is an achievement. So, don't stress. We'll figure this out. Right now, I put you at eighteen weeks and everything looks good. Why don't we make another appointment for a week from now and see where things are? That will give you some time to think about what you want to do and how you want to proceed."

"Okay."

No. No. Not really but what can I say?

I screwed up.

Look at me pretending to be this good wife.

This good mother.

Yet, I never told Linc I slept with Sam after we broke up. Marla doesn't even know how far things went with Sam. And now, the baby I carry could possibly be his.

Ironic.

Cosmic.

One of those.

"I'm okay," I say when Dr. Eldon must see the tear rolling down my face and asks me if I'm doing okay. "I'm *fine*."

She sets up the mini ultrasound telling me it's good to have more data when I walk out of here. She tells me we might be able to find out the gender if I want to know. And I do. I want to know. I want to know how badly I may have screwed this whole thing up.

"I'm so sorry, Tally. I know this is upsetting. We can make estimates but the size of the fetus tells us whole lot more. See this measurement here?" She points at the monitor's screen and I stare at it hoping the 3D image of this beautiful baby will reveal a different result. Be Linc's baby. No question. No doubt.

I don't really hear what my doctor is saying. She's said enough. Far too much already.

"I marked it here and here from last time. The baby's grown since then, but I would definitely put you at eighteen weeks based on these markers from last time to now. Oh lucky. I can tell the gender. Do you want to know what it is?"

I nod already knowing what she's going to say.

"It's a boy."

Of course.

"A paternity test is the only way at this point to tell us more," she says. "Let's meet again next week and see where we are. Okay?"

I nod slowly, unable to form words because I am still repeatedly doing the math in my head and silently berate myself for lying to Linc about my involvement with Sam. Sleeping with Sam was something I never planned on having to admit to. Not even to myself.

I attempt to look like I have it all together for Dr. Eldon. Even so, on the inside, I can feel myself falling and can only wonder if I've hit bottom yet.

Dates matter.

Math is an intrinsic part of life.

And lies never become true.

CHAPTER NINE

fear and loathing

TALLY

You can never go back in the past; can you?
And if you could, would you change some things?
Or change everything?
Regret. We live with regret.
And mistakes.
And lies.
  ~Talia Landon Presley

September 11th

PARTIALLY BLOOMED WHITE ROSES IN TALL crystal vases are virtually everywhere. The funeral and the graveside service are touching eulogizing the good parts of her life and all of her good deeds. She would've been touched by it and all the people who came to pay their last respects to her. Even so, burying my mother on a Thursday when she only died on Monday was quite a feat, and I pulled it off. She would've been proud of me. That much is true. There's that.

Linc clasps my hands so tightly, I practically gasp with the pain. I steal a glance at him. His head is down, but I catch sight of the tears traveling down his face behind the Ray-Ban mask. I knew today was going to be hard, but seeing Linc cry just about pushes me over the edge.

I lean into him a little more. He adjusts his body and moves into mine.

Soon, he lets go of my hand and slings his arm across my shoulders. His body weight bears down on me, but at least I know he's there.

For now.

He presses in on me further. "We will get through this, Tally; I promise."

Oh, the irony of a promise.

We've all made those.

"Promise." My response is rote, and I know he notices. He leans back and studies the side of my face but I continue to look out at the black-clad, designer-dressed crowd standing graveside that have come to witness the burial of my mother. I can't respond to the uneasy, questioning look I see in Linc's eyes these days. Not today.

"Promise," he says again squeezing my hand.

His utterance assures me of his rescue.

Once again.

Yes, but for how long will he want to stay and rescue me?

I shiver despite the warmth still present in mid-September. My lips part in a concentrated effort to smile when I glance up at him for a few seconds. "Okay then."

"Okay then." He attempts to smile back, too, but it doesn't quite work for him today.

My mother is dead, and Lincoln Presley can't change this horrible outcome.

He can't fix it.

Any of it.

Not today or any other day.

And, there's the lie—the one lie.

The final one?

The lie hangs over my head like a guillotine's blade ready to mete out a punishment and decapitate this sinner, once and for all.

Because I lied.

And the lie will change everything between us.

Disconnected thoughts race through my mind. What will my dad do now? What about Tommy? Tommy attends Lowell High School, but he may want to go to Paly like Holly and I did. Get out-of-district permission and go to Paly like Holly and I did. They could move back and reestablish a home here again. Maybe, they can wrangle a deal and get the old house back. *What will they do?*

My mother is dead but I know she tried to be here for me as best she could. God knows she tried to be here for all of us. *She tried.*

That's what we should inscribe on her headstone.

She tried.

What will I do?

My mother has always served as the proverbial albatross around my neck—the mental worry of her always weighed me down. She anchored me to this earth, in some ways. She was never someone I could count on, but the weightlessness I experience with her loss makes me feel completely untethered now.

I'm unanchored.

How will I stay?

Who will anchor me when Linc stops altogether?

Because the math is wrong. The math is still wrong.

I feel myself get ever smaller under the pressure of Linc's arm.

Will he still tether me to this world when he learns the math is all wrong?

Yes.

Maybe.

No.

Not forever.

There is no forever anymore.

You can never go back in the past; can you?

And if you could, would you change some things?

Or change everything?

Regret. We live with regret. And mistakes. And lies.

Which day it will be that I actually disappear altogether?

Not a Monday.

Not a Thursday.
Another day. Soon.

"You guys want to stay over with us?" Marla and Charlie still call the guest house at Charlie's parents *home*. I doubt she has enough room for Linc and me. I don't even know how she's going to fit another baby into that house. She's already confided in me, more than once, she wonders the exact same thing.

I shake my head. "We have a room here so does Dad and Tommy."

I wave my arm around the elegant surroundings of the Four Seasons. It was nice of the hotel staff to accommodate us on such short notice but then again, copious amounts of money really do make a difference. I opened our checkbook, and things got done.

Still, it's a *hotel*. Granted, it's the Four Seasons, but it's not exactly what one would expect to be utilized as a venue to accommodate guests after a funeral. We needed something near Atherton and Holy Cross Cemetery for after the service because we're a homeless gathering. Last year, my dad sold the family home in Atherton we had here and moved the family forty miles north to be closer to me and Linc at my mother's insistence. We didn't have a home left in Atherton. We didn't have a home left.

Holy Cross Cemetery was the natural resting place for my mother. It's where we buried Holly. In fact, we buried my mother right next to Holly.

At Holy Cross.
Near home.
Home that isn't home anymore.
For any of us.
You have to have some consistency–some sort of plan—as to where you bury your dead regardless of the nomadic existence you now lead.

Where's home?
I do wonder because the math is still wrong,
and my life is about to disintegrate even more.
Beyond my mother's death.
I can feel it.

The truth is my dad hates the house in Saint Francis Wood. *Hates it.* My mother loved it. I wonder what he'll do now? I glance over at him. My dad stands by himself looking lost and a little out of it. He absently greets the latest arrivals from the service with a stoic face—his best doctoral bedside manner—the one he uses for delivering bad news he normally reserves solely for his patients. The persona seems to be working for him today.

What will he do now?

What will I do?

"Okay. Well, if you change your mind, let me know." Marla looks a little unhappy with the plan for sleeping arrangements. We don't see each other often enough anymore. Palo Alto is a long way from Sea Cliff.

"It was just easier," I say in an attempt to make her feel better. "We can pick up Cara from your mom's on our way back to Sea Cliff and get ready for his game."

A half-hour later, with the event running smoothly in the capable hands of the caterer and the wait staff, I glance around the hotel bar in search of Linc. I eventually find him conversing with my dad in a far corner of the bar. They both hold onto crystal highball glasses filled with generous amounts of scotch with obvious intentions of drinking their way through the next couple of hours in order to survive. I study them intently noting how Linc's dark hair contrasts directly to my father's golden looks.

They must be talking baseball because Linc is demonstrating how he holds onto a slider. My dad is actually smiling as he mimics the hold Linc has just shown him. I smile, too, because in this moment, I'm grateful that Linc is here for him. For me. For all of us.

Linc looks up and over at me. This inexplicable bond that feels like an electric wave passes between us.

It's been a while since we've had a connection.

Since the math became wrong. Before that?

And yet, with one look, we are reestablished for a while.

We are tethered.

Today, we are tethered.

Today I can stay, and he can anchor me to this earth.
Today, he can do that for me.

I table all the other thoughts trying to invade my psyche. I cannot go there today. I will splinter into a million shards of glass all over again if I do.

"I love you," he says to me from across the room.

Why?

Why do you love me?

"I love you, too," I say back to him.

Linc turns his attention back to my dad while I search around for my brother Tommy. At sixteen, my brother has had to face a harsh reality; he's lost his mother. It has to be worse for him than when we lost our sister Holly. He understands it now. Surprisingly, my younger brother's grief appears to be masked behind promiscuity. I find him in the opposite corner further hidden from view of the majority of the guests with his arm firmly strapped around the waist of some blonde I haven't seen before. They're not talking from what I can tell. They're doing other things. He's been with his girlfriend Felicity for more than a year so this is a surprise. Felicity didn't come today and now I know why.

Tommy raises his head and looks straight at me outright daring me to question his motives. He shakes his head. The look of defiance he sends my way is a familiar one. It speaks volumes. It appears we share the inclination to use sex as a way of coping in order to alleviate pain and heartbreak.

I've been there; I've done that.

I fight the incredible urge right now, right this very second. I've fought this powerful need to bury myself into somebody since the frantic phone call from my dad on Monday night telling me she was gone. The desire to feel numb and be nothing but numb has dominated me for some time now. The compulsion for illicit sex gets stronger with each passing hour, since that fateful call on Monday. *Before then?*

"Tommy can take care of himself," Marla says as she comes up to check on me again.

I look at her quizzically and then turn back and watch my brother wander off with the girl in the direction of his room. He doesn't look back. I wouldn't either. "Do you think they have sex?" I smirk and incline my head in the direction that Tommy just took off with the girl.

"*Tons* of it." Marla laughs. "The Landon libido cannot be denied."

"True that," I murmur still watching the young couple retreat to the furthest dark recesses of the hallway.

Marla grabs my hand and leads me over to a couple of lounge chairs situated at the edge of the hotel bar. "How are you holding up?"

I reward her with my best and brightest answer. "I'm *fine*."

"Sure you are." Marla rolls her eyes. "And how's your husband?"

"A more complex question." I wince. "He's fine. I think he's fine. I don't know." I shake my head. "It brings back a lot of memories for him with losing his own mom. He was close to mine. They kept in touch all the time we were apart even when we broke up before. They went to lunch in the City whenever he was here. She told me that not so long ago. She loved him so much and he loved her. He's going to miss her just as much as me."

"Yeah, but he has you."

"He has me. And I have him." *For now.* I'm sure my face looks bleak for a few seconds for a myriad of reasons that Marla will never begin to understand or guess at.

"You okay?"

"I'm fine." I practically choke on the words this time when I say them.

She studies me intently. I quickly turn away in a concerted effort to avoid her laser-like gaze. A mind meld with Marla is something I do not need today.

"Not today." I shake my head while the hollowed-out parts of me threaten to implode and make a point of sipping my club soda in a vain search for some kind of courage or hope or validation or a way out.

I haven't cried for my mother. I haven't cried in four days since Dr. Eldon's doctor visit changed my life and course and then my dad called to tell me that my mom had been in a serious car accident and she died at the scene probably at the exact same moment the pieces of my life seemed to have fallen apart just like a crystal vase shatters when it falls to a marble floor. That's the moment you realize nothing in the world is going to be able to fix all those broken shards of glass. *Nothing.*

Or me.

Or us.

We are.

We will be.

Unfixable.

"What's going on with you? I mean, I know we just buried your mother, but there's more; isn't there? When are you going to tell me what else is going on with you?"

Marla's clairvoyance is stunning. It always has been.

"Not today."

"Tally." Marla seems to experience a little of the pain for me and casually wipes at her eyes with the back of her hand and tries to smile. "Look at me. I'm a mess. I cry at anything these days." Then, anguish comes across her face. "I'm here. Tell me when you're ready."

"I will. But please don't feel sorry for me, today," I say in warning. "I couldn't take it."

Her sympathy is palpable. I can hardly stand it. I resist the urge to reach over and slap it right off her face. Just barely.

This incredible rage is real and continues to build inside of me. I finally understand Linc's rage, although his is the aftereffects of brain trauma and subsequent memory loss that still plague him almost a year later after being hit by that line drive. Add to that, the sporadic use of painkillers—those blasted mood-altering drugs—that he takes when his headaches get too hard to handle has changed him. He's different. Still. We're different together this time around.

On the day we got married, he told me he remembered me. Or rather, I filled in those words for him the day we said our vows. "You remember me? Don't you, Elvis?" I think we both wanted it to be true that day. But the thing is he doesn't remember everything about me; he doesn't necessarily remember me at all sometimes, and he's different, not the same. He lied to me. He wanted to remember everything. He wanted to remember me. He doesn't. Not always.

So each day we forge together seems to present new ways to navigate our marriage. Every day, we seem to face a new challenge in order to find our way back to each other. Some days, we all but admit we need to choose a new and different path altogether.

Some days, he's fine.

Some days, he's pissed.

Most days, he's not here so it really doesn't matter.

"I've got this," I say to Marla's questioning look.

"I know. I know you do." She doesn't sound convinced. But then again, I have trouble convincing myself these days.

I take a risk. I decide to tell it to her in various phases. "Hey, guess what? Dr. Eldon changed the date. It's not an exact science I guess." I shrug for good measure. "It happens. Anyway, the new due date is the 9th of February. Seven days earlier." I struggle with maintaining a light tone, but it seems to work.

Marla nods with a modicum of understanding, but then again, she's not really understanding it at all, and that's what I'm counting on. I breathe a sigh of relief when I see this. Maybe, it is just that easy. Maybe, I can try to say the exact same thing on Linc. One day soon. After the season ends. After the playoffs. After the World Series. After that.

"Oh, but it would have been so epic to have the baby on Valentine's Day. I mean, to bring a new memory for that day," she adds quickly.

I shrug with indifference. "Anyway, I don't have an appointment for another couple of weeks with Eldon. Everything is fine. I'm fine. Dancing up a storm. Keeping Mikhail at bay. Wearing Spanx faithfully although I'm still not showing quite yet. Eating a lot." I frown because nobody is going to believe that, least of all, Marla.

Right on cue, she says, "Yeah, right."

"Of course, I'll have to tell Mikhail soon. I've got another week now. I bought an extra seven days or so. I'm eighteen weeks and right now, Mikhail is fairly happy with me. *Swan Lake* starts early next month. I'll finish that show and then I'll tell him about not being able to do *The Nutcracker* at Christmastime. But we've got some reciprocity program going with ABT and he told me he put my name in for it. So, you might be looking at the next star for *Giselle* with the American Ballet Theatre in New York come next May."

The setup proves exhausting. I've run out of good things to say. I've pulled things out of the air—fabrications, little white lies—just to say them and throw her off. Marla looks momentarily confused by it all. "It's all good; right?" I tact on while she looks at me in newfound wonder. The facade is getting hard to keep up.

"I don't know, is it?" Marla laughs a little. We both glance over at Linc and my father. I involuntarily shiver. They're still talking baseball. Linc now demonstrates a recognizable windup with his pitching arm. The way he holds an invisible baseball in his right hand is a dead giveaway of his best pitch, the fastball. *My husband, the baseball star, seems destined to go all the way.*

"It doesn't get much better than this. We're in a good position right now." Linc told me this very thing last week before our world cratered in.

He's right; it doesn't get much better than this, but not for the reason he thinks.

Marla turns her attention back to me. "February 9th. What does Linc say?"

She doesn't know how close to the edge she treads.

"I haven't told him yet."

"You haven't *told* him yet? Why not? And isn't that like right before he leaves for spring training? So, that's better, right?"

"It's better, I guess. We'll work it out. *Please* let's get this season over before we think about the next one. Things got away from us this week. My mother fucking died on Monday. Let it go," I say with a hint of irritation. "I can't worry about baseball, right now. Well, I can, but I choose not to. He's focused on getting to the playoffs, possibly going all the way." I shrug with nonchalance trying to throw her off, regretting I've said anything at all, regretting this trial balloon I've offered up.

What do they call it? A false flag?

"You're acting kind of strange, Tally, weirder than usual." My best friend looks a little worried.

"I know." I force myself to smile while guilt and grief take turns punching me from the inside.

With an exasperated sigh, Marla pulls herself up out of the chair rather masterfully for being with child and makes her way over to the bar to chat up the bartender who instantly reminds me of Sam. Again.

I look away and concentrate on the ice melting in my glass and only look up when Marla returns a few minutes later. She hands me a fresh glass filled with ice and what I take to be cranberry juice topped with a thin slice of lime.

Ninety calories in an eight-ounce glass.

Some things never change.

My obsession with food intake for one.

Math.

The math isn't hard.

Unless you get the math wrong, and then it ruins absolutely everything.

Your calculations are wrong, and your life is about to blow up.

That happens. It will happen.

And, your mother is dead.

I gulp the drink down and then gasp. "There's vodka in this."

"I think you need it. Liquid courage. Honor your mother properly. Partake in her favorite beverage."

"You're such a bitch," I say airily as I take another generous sip.

"Yeah, but a good one. A good bitch," she says with a sad smile, "I'm here to support my best friend."

"You're doing it. Good job." I salute her with the glass. I haven't eaten in a few days. It doesn't take long before the alcohol hits my system and courses through my veins spreading warm, fiery wonder everywhere. I nod slowly and finish the drink down in one long swallow. *Stalling.* Buying time for myself. Whatever. A few minutes pass. I order another drink from a passing waiter to fill the uncomfortable silence that follows because Marla suddenly looks as grim and unhappy as I feel. We both know it has nothing to do with my mother's death.

"I wondered how long it would last." Marla looks at me quizzically. "Happiness," I supply. "It only lasts eight weeks. That's the maximum. That's all you get. Then, it all goes to hell." The waiter returns with a fresh cranberry and lime drink just like the last one.

"You and Linc will get through this."

"Will we?" I slur.

"You need to slow down…" Her voice trails off, and she's looking rather intently right behind me. "Oh God. Rob and Nika are here."

"Now, *those two* I know I don't need," I say even as I come to stand and prepare to greet these late arrivals.

"Tally." Rob takes my right hand and squeezes it in his. "I'm so sorry."

"Thank you for coming. Thank you *both* for coming."

Nika stares daggers at me and doesn't say anything, while Rob and I commit to small talk. He asks about Cara. And tells me about his latest travels. Paris. New York. They settled in San Francisco instead of New York because of his dad's business and Nika's publicist job with the San Francisco Giants and his startup company. Better funding prospects here. They're here to stay.

It's such a small fucking world.

Linc and I can't seem to shake our exes from our lives.

Here stand Rob and Nika.

Just what we need.

It's a been a long while since I've seen Rob. He looks good. Happy. I go on to tell him about Linc's house—our house—in Sea Cliff. Rob looks surprised when I mention this.

"You guys live in Sea Cliff? By me? By *us*, I mean." He quickly corrects himself as Nika jabs him in the side with her elbow.

Never forgotten our girl, Nika.

Not by me anyway.

Bring your enemies closer and all that jazz.

I lock my gaze with hers.

She hates me. I'm not too fond of her either.

"Yes. We moved in a little over a month ago? Boxes are still everywhere. There's still time to give us a housewarming gift though." I actually laugh. Half the room seems to hear me and turns to the four of us standing here probably wondering what could possibly be so funny on this day.

Marla's grabs my elbow vying for my attention all at once.

"Thanks for coming," Marla says to Rob and Nika. She's clearly taking over. "Tally, your dad needs you."

I turn and start in the direction of my father, but neither Linc nor my dad is there. I raise an eyebrow at Marla, but she quickly steers me toward the bar and away from Nika and Rob.

CHAPTER TEN

habits

TALLY

*"I'm drowning, and he doesn't even see it. He can't.
He's drowning somewhere else."*
~ Talia Landon Presley

September 11th

AFTER A BRIEF CHAT WITH THE wait staff about closing out the open bar tab, Marla deftly steers me toward the women's restroom.

"What's wrong with you?" I attempt to shake off her tight grip on my arm as we push through the restroom door at the same time. "What is going on?"

"I'm saving you from yourself. From Rob."

"Are you *serious*? You're cock blocking me now?"

"Always have. Look, the eye fucking you had going on with Rob gave off all kinds of signals. *Bad* ones. *And,* Nika saw you doing it, and she was furious."

"She was? I did that with Rob?" I feign innocence, although the deviant part of me knew exactly what I was doing.

Marla rolls her eyes. "I guess the past never stays buried. *Sorry.* Bad choice of words given today."

She starts again. "Look, I don't want to get in the middle of your marriage, but you have a tendency to fuck with your happiness or other people on your way down the dark abyss. I know you're suffering right now, and I know better than anybody else what you tend to do in situations like this."

"What do you know?" I'm seething now and a little disturbed that she is already onto me, although I've never been able to hide anything from Marla. And I *know* this.

"You act out, Tally. You always have. Sex is your coping mechanism and, in all the ways it counts, it's your Kryptonite. Someone unattainable is even better. They're getting *married* in a few months. Rob and Nika. It's the perfect scenario for you. Been there. Done that. Watched it many times before with you. Don't do it."

"Do what?"

"Mess with her. Mess with him," she says softly but with warning. "Let's just stay focused on the present and not dive headfirst into the past and repeat the same mistakes all over again. Instead, let's explore all the whys and wherefores and therefores of how perfect you and Linc are for each other."

"Not perfect," I mutter.

"Perfect!" She stands up straighter and looks me in the eye and jabs her index finger into my shoulder.

"Ow!" I rub my shoulder and step back from her. "Take it easy, Marla. I've got this. Back off."

"No, I won't back off. You need to listen to me. She will take you down. You do not want to mess with her. She'll destroy you, Tally, and she'll do it in any way she can if she feels threatened by you. She hates you if for no other reason than you exist and when you're around Rob, she doesn't. And *that* she does not like. Plus, the fact that you're married to Linc—her ex-fiancé—which probably continues to fuel her hatred and fervent need to destroy you in any way that she can. Just remember she had Linc first and the way she views it; you took him away from her. She is *not* going to allow that to happen again with Rob."

"Rob and I were already over long before Nika came along. It's ancient history. I'm sure she doesn't even think about it that way."

"Of course she does. She plays to win. Always." I start to laugh which just makes Marla madder and even more intent on proving her point. "You *know* it's true. That's how she views it. Stay clear of her. I saw the way she was looking at you when you were talking to Rob. She is *not* your friend. She never will be. She is enemy number one. She always has been."

I roll my eyes. "You're overreacting. Rob and I have history. So what? It's over and done."

"She doesn't see it that way, and you're in a bad place right now. I know it. Don't look at me like that. I'm on to you. I know what you feel like doing right now, but fucking your way out of this isn't going to bring your mom back."

I cringe at what she's said and so does she." Sorry, I don't mean to make you feel bad; I just want you to listen to me and think long and hard before you make a mistake with Rob or some other random guy you cannot undo."

"Rob is *not* random. He's a good friend."

"Yeah, I *get* that part. He fulfills some twisted need of yours to try and be Holly. It's not good for either one of you. You can't be Holly. You never were. That's why it ended. And now? That's Nika's problem, not *yours*. Don't underestimate my clairvoyance in knowing that you see fucking him as a way out of your grief in some convoluted way that only a psychiatrist could figure out. You always have. Look, I know things are tense with you and Linc right now. I—"

"Things? *Things?* You don't even know the half of it. You live forty miles away. I'm alone all the time. My mom just died. He's at a funeral on his one and only day off for the next week or so and then he's gone again. It's all tidied up, and life goes on and my mom is still dead, and I'll still be here all alone trying to make it all fucking work. This is it. This is all there is. *Things?* Things are *tense* between us. Just like they always are. I mean really when have they not been tense with Linc and me? A few days here and there together are all we've had in the past month. It's not enough. It's not enough to save us." Marla takes my hand.

"I'm drowning, and he doesn't even see it. He *can't*. He's drowning somewhere else. Don't you see?" My face twists up with grief.

"Why did we naively think that getting married would solve everything? Tell me why we thought that?"

Marla leans in and hugs me tight then steps back. "I don't have those answers, babe. No one does. We seek normal. We foolishly believe and seek happily-ever-after. It deludes us into thinking that life doesn't need to be complicated and that happiness is just around the corner because love of any kind makes us feel good but it doesn't work that way. All we can do is try our best and try not to repeat the same mistakes, survive the tragedies and carry on and hope that love is enough to get us through the hard times as much it is when we're happy. That's all any of us can do. I'm just asking you as your friend—your very best—to just stop and think first before you do something you'll regret, do something you cannot undo."

My throat tightens, my eyes sting, and I attempt to swallow in order to maintain some kind of grip on reality without blurting out the truth to Marla. Defeated, I lean against the sink and tip my head back looking for answers on the ceiling that I already know aren't there.

Finally, I look over at her. "What if it's too late? What if there's something I did that I can't undo?" I hold my breath for a few seconds then blow it out. "If he ever finds out, it will ruin everything." I run my hand through my hair and sigh. "I don't know what to do. Everything is so fucked up and there's no way out."

"Just tell me so I can better understand what's going on and help you. It can't be that bad."

"I can't tell you, Marla. The only person I need to tell is the one person who can never know."

Her eyes lock with mine. She nods with true understanding. "He loves you, Tally. It can't be that bad."

I incline my head. "Oh but it is and…" A sudden noise from the farthest stall captures my attention.

We were careless. We didn't check to make sure we were alone in the restroom. I signal for silence while Marla glances past me when we here a toilet flush.

"Holy shit." She gives me our secret stand down signal because from her vantage point she sees the person emerge from the stall before I do. Her eyes widen and panic seems to surge through her.

I suck in air when I finally see Nika Vostrikova walk out of the bathroom stall and strut towards us. The woman virtually sucks up all the remaining oxygen in the room.

Yet, she doesn't even glance at our way. No. She takes her time soaping up her hands and running them under the streaming water as if she's a brilliant surgeon waiting to cut somebody's heart out. *Mine.*

Strangely transfixed, I watch as she proceeds to dry her hands off with a fresh hand towel the hotel provides like she has all the time in the world before commencing with this timely execution of hers.

She owns time.

This moment.

Me.

The look on her face tells me this. She gazes at me in the mirror while she styles her long blond locks already without a single strand out of place. Like the final act in a scene, she withdraws a red lipstick from her bag and patiently lines her lips. I note the designer look she's sporting from the sleek black dress which is so low-cut it almost reaches her navel, and the black Louboutins that adorn her feet. She looks like she's attending a black-tie affair for some fundraiser instead of my mother's funeral.

Disingenuous.

Dishonest.

Destructive.

The words march through my head like little alarm bells. Each one tolls louder than the last.

"I'm so sorry about your mother." She feigns an unhappy sigh as she turns to face me. I practically fall into a trance under her laser-like gaze. "Rob and I are getting married in late November just like your friend here said." She seemingly smiles and inclines her head toward Marla, who stands frozen between us now. "And she's right about me in a lot of ways. I do take what I want. I do get what I want."

The smile slips from her face as Marla moves to be right next to me.

We are a united front—Marla and me.

Nika glares at us. She doesn't have any friends.

"Stay out of my life and I'll stay out of yours, but if you fuck with me or Rob in any way, I will take you down. Don't fuck with my plans, or I will most definitely fuck with all of yours. You got that, Mrs. Presley?"

"I believe we're clear," I say coolly. "You stay away from my husband, and I'll stay away from yours."

"That's right. And this is your one and only warning when it comes to that."

I shake my head unable to quell a need to taunt her. It's a valiant effort to gain the upper hand if only for a moment. "So. I stay away from Rob, and you stay away from Linc? But how does that work exactly when you're at all the Giants' baseball games and see my husband pretty much every day? I can't even pretend to understand your need to work for a living, especially with the San Francisco Giants, when Rob has more money than God these days. But just how am I supposed to trust you to keep your word?"

Nika shrugs. At a gut level, I experience envy at her obvious self-confidence and the easy way in which she displays it. I shrink a little more because the woman is made of steel, and I am not in a good place right now to do battle with her. She makes me feel powerless and I begin to wonder, too late, of course, what all she put together in overhearing our conversation.

"I like keeping my options open. I like baseball players." She smiles wide. "What can I say?" She shrugs. "Besides, in a few months, when the baseball season is over, I won't be working for the Giants any longer. I'll be married and living my perfect life and running Rob's start-up company as his chief financial officer because I'm good at math."

She laughs while I take a step back and experience a fresh round of pure panic at her mention of math knowing it's only a matter of time before she puts it all together about me. She'll tell Linc first if I don't. The look on her face tells me this already. Nika Vostrikova would take great pleasure in bringing me down and literally burning me to the ground in the process.

"And Tally? Just so you know, the math is never wrong. Now, we humans? We make mistakes all the time, your friend here seems to already know that about you, but the math is never wrong."

She purses her lips together and intently studies me while I seem to wilt further under her judgmental gaze. "All is not well in paradise. Do tell, Tally. What can be so bad that you would *lie* to your husband about it?"

"You're the last person on earth I would tell."

"Uh-huh. Well, good luck with that then." She moves past us and grabs onto the door handle and then turns. "Piece of advice, Mrs. Presley?" Her eyes glint with contempt. "I've always found that it's better to stay two steps ahead of everyone else so there are no surprises. Perhaps, you should try it sometime. And just remember, we do what we have to do. We all do, *eventually*."

It is beyond tempting to smash her beautiful face in with my closed fist. Marla seems to sense this. She steps into my path. "Let it go. She's not worth it."

I nod and don't say anything. I don't have to.

"What the hell was she going on about math for anyway?" Marla asks after Nika's slinks out the restroom door.

"I have no idea."

The lies still come so easily.

They fall from my lips like dead petals from a dying flower.

CHAPTER ELEVEN

lies

TALLY

*"We know how to hurt each other.
We know how to inflict deep wounds
with words or a single look.
We are each other's catalyst to the chemical reaction,
whether the combination goes right or wrong
or annihilates us both in the process."*
~ Talia Landon Presley

September 11th

Iᴛ's ᴀɴᴏᴛʜᴇʀ ʜᴏᴜʀ ʙᴇғᴏʀᴇ ᴛʜᴇ ғᴜɴᴇʀᴀʟ crowd disperses. After one last familial group hug in which we mourn the loss of my mother without really saying anything and briefly exchange a knowing look that conveys there are no words to describe our loss, my dad and Tommy move off to their respective rooms. My dad leads the way with Tommy trailing behind him toward the other end of the hall away from the suite Linc and I are staying in. My brother turns and proudly holds up a card key for his own room and puts his index fingers to his lips with a little smirk. I'm pretty sure he's going to hook up with the blonde I saw him with earlier. The girl is nowhere to be seen. I suspect she's already waiting for him inside his room.

That's what I would do. I've done it, in fact. Sex consoles.

Oblivious to his son's deviant behavior forthcoming, my dad calls out goodnight to me before disappearing into his own room. Tommy performs a cool guy wave at me, and then he's gone too.

Now, I am even more weighed down by the despair that's so palpably felt from my dad and brother, the unexpected confrontation with Nika, and the truth I still withhold from Linc. With some foreboding, I slide the card key through the lock base, watch the lock light flash from red to green, turn the suite door's handle and enter the hotel room.

My husband of two months pours himself yet another drink at the hotel suite's bar. "Haven't you had enough of those for one night?" the fish wife that I am asks.

Never mind the two I threw back breaking all the steadfast rules of pregnancy. Apparently, I'm living by the mores of the 1950s before fetal alcohol syndrome was named a thing—a consequence for stupidity—and judgment for imbibing hadn't been invented yet.

"Apparently not."

"What's going on with you?" I unzip my black dress, slip it off, and toss it over a chair. Linc's arms go around me. His drink sloshes on me as he does this and I gasp at the sudden fiery feel of ice and heat.

"Sorry." He sets the drink down on the desk with one and keeps hold of me with the other. "What's going on with you? I heard you got into something with Nika." I stop undressing and turn around in his arms and look at him, incredulous. "She told me you were upset about something, and that I should talk to you." He clenches his jaw. "Apparently, she did not like the way Rob was looking at you anymore than I did."

"You two are seeing things. That woman is crazy. She wears some slut designer black number to my mother's funeral slit to her navel and slinks around like she's attending some party. She is beyond inappropriate and will be forever insincere. She's the devil barely disguised. She hates me and the feeling is mutual."

"She is all of that, but we agree on a few things. I didn't like the way you were looking at Thorn either and touching his hand in that familiar way of yours wasn't exactly a consolation prize for me."

"I *barely* talked to him."

"Oh Yeah? Well, the eye-fucking you two had going was more than enough for me and apparently for Nika, too. Christ, Tally, they're getting married in a few months."

"I wasn't eye-fucking him, but we have history. You *know* this."

"Yeah, but do I *remember* all of it, Tally?"

Linc's tone is dangerous. He's pissed and unhappy and most likely drunk. I should let it go, but I don't. "I don't know, do you?"

We know how to hurt each other. We know how to inflict deep wounds with words or a single look. We are each other's catalyst to the chemical reaction, whether the combination goes right or wrong or annihilates us both in the process.

"I'm sorry," I say as he stumbles away from me toward the center of the room looking mighty fine in his dark Armani suit and turns to stare at me. His face reflects such deep anguish and sorrow, remorse rushes in at me. "Let's not do this to each other tonight. I'm sorry."

The disenchantment I see on his face tells me it's too late for apologies tonight.

In looking back on my behavior over the past few hours, I silently admit to myself that I was eye-fucking Rob, and I knew I was doing it. Marla might have been guessing, and I might have pretended to be surprised by it, but I knew what I was doing, and I knew why. But is it fair to go there the night of my mother's funeral? Probably not.

"I'm sorry."

"Are you?" Linc finally asks. "What do you want from me, Tally? Right now? Right this second? What do you want?"

He comes over to me and fingers the lace of my black bra. He pushes the cup down on one and then the other. He lowers his head and nips at my nipple eliciting exquisite pain encircling it with his tongue and then blowing on it. The sudden chill coming from his lips ignites the passion surfacing within me. I grab his hair and pull him in closer. His lips find mine. I moan louder.

"What do you want from me, tonight, Tally?"

I raise his head and grasp each side of his face and look into his eyes. "I want you to fuck me. Make me numb. Take away this pain. Burn it away. Make me feel alive again."

He undoes his belt and tosses it towards the bed. He swipes

everything off of the desk and turns me around and bends me over the chair. We both look up in the mirror as he drives his way inside. I'm already wet for him having desperately sought relief in any way I could find it for quite a while now. Marla was right. I was ready to take Rob into one of the hotel's rooms and let him fuck me senseless. Rob knew it, too. That knowable hunger in his eyes was there when he looked at me the first time. Linc has it now—the I-want-to-possess-all-of-you-let-me-fuck-you-senseless look.

"Come back to me."

His desperate words and actions bring me back to the here and now. "I want to."

I bend further at the waist to receive more of him and he drives into me deeper. I need this man to fill up this emptiness trying to take me over. I need him to draw me back to shore and keep me from drowning and make me whole again. I need him to anchor me down before I completely disappear, and I think he finally realizes this. I shudder with the ecstasy and the restorative feelings in being this intimate with him brings as he finishes quickly. I merely nod my acquiescence to him in the mirror. He looks frustrated. I start to laugh, which doesn't make any sense to either one of us. Then he's pulling me by the hair and half-dragging me over to the bed.

"Let me in, Tally," he commands. Fresh passion flashes in his eyes turning them from grey-blue to granite. He pushes me down and then he's on top of me holding my face between his major-league hands. "Let me in, Tally. You have to promise me that you'll stay with me."

"Where would I go?" I whisper up to him.

"I don't know, but I can *feel* it; I can feel you leaving me." He touches my chest sensing the rhythm of my beating heart. He lowers his head to listen and then brushes his lips against my breasts. Then, he kisses me harder bruising my lips with his. In the next, he lifts his head in confusion and studies me, but then his face clears with fresh understanding. "You've been drinking."

"A little. Marla got them for me."

"How many drinks did you have?"

"Two. Only two. Let's face it, Linc. It's been a shitty day. A shitty week since Monday."

He frowns. "You won't eat, but you'll drink, and you're pregnant." Judgment colors his features as well as his tone.

I lift my head in defiance and brazenly look at him. "Not tonight. Tonight? I'm not pregnant. Tonight, I'm not anything."

The first tear for my mother falls. He watches it roll down my face for a few seconds and then catches it with his index finger just before it lands on my shoulder.

"Let me in," he says again. He renews his advance holding my neck with one hand and exploring me between my legs with the other. I tense as two of his fingers slip inside but soon relax as the pleasure he elicits begins to take me over. "Say it," he says against my lips. "Tell me what you want. What you need."

"I need you, Elvis. Tonight, I need you so much."

He pulls aside my panties and pushes his way inside and begins to slip in and out in a regular rhythm. I acquiesce all the raging thoughts and embrace the reprieve from sadness and start to move with him. Even so, the current of despair becomes stronger. Linc begins to feel very far away. As if sensing my retreat from him as the grief overpowers me, he stops what he's doing and looks at me intently. "Stay with me, Tal."

"I don't know that I can."

There's profound solace in being honest.

I'm not sure he knows what I'm referring to, but I'm no longer convinced it even matters.

In the next few moments, he moves ever slower, his hands working magic along with the rest of him. "Stay with me, Tally," he says again while I moan at the mix of pain and pleasure his advance causes. "There you go, baby. See how good it feels? Don't let the grief rule you. Let me."

He withdraws his hand while his fingers push me further. I arch upward in search of release as the pleasure he invokes takes me still higher and works itself through me better than any narcotic ever could. He pulls back teasing me, and then he stretches and fills me up. I tense up for a few seconds with the intensity but then relax as his tender movements break me free from the grief.

He slows down and I prepare for him to fill me up and alleviate this painful sadness. I scream out his name as the euphoria begins to course through me. My nails dig into the silk sheets and then the mattress as I search in vain for some kind of release as the pressure from him and what he's doing continues to build within me. His ability to focus and keep going surprises me. In awe of him all at one, I can only gaze at his handsome face and body as he clearly exhibits this god-like mastery over me. We go over the edge together and sign with contentment as the same time. It feels like hearing the finest piece of music ever played for the first time—that same feeling of joy and wonder seems to encircle us both.

He is a god. I don't deserve him.

Together we lay entangled in each other's arms and revel in this secret intimacy, too exhausted to actually move. His body covers mine for a long while but then he moves to one side and begins tracing my spine in a familiar pattern.

I turn into him and smile knowing he wants to do it again soon. "Thank you."

He is the light and I am the dark, but somehow we make it work.

Somehow, we found each other.

I can't lose him.

I won't lose him.

"Tally," he whispers. "Why won't you tell me what's really going on with you? Earlier tonight, Nika said you had something you wanted to tell me but were afraid to."

I look up at him, uncertain all at once again. "I want to keep this—what we have. Don't you?"

"I do."

"Then, trust me? I have this. It'll all work out. We're together. Us being together is all that matters. Nothing else can come between us. Not Rob. Not Nika. No one."

His face becomes shadowed. He looks uncertain. "Someday, soon. You're going to have to tell me whatever it is. What I can tell you right this second is that we can handle it—whatever it is, but only if we stay together. We can get through it *together*, Tally. That's the only way."

I lay on my back with my arms above my head while he strokes my stomach in the same kind of mesmerizing rhythm he used before. Grief over my mother is replaced by guilt about this baby's paternity.

"Stay together. I want that, too," I finally say as I look at him.

"Come on the road with me next week. To Chicago and Washington D.C."

"What about Cara?" I ask.

"We'll bring her with us."

"Because we could do what we just did with a four-year-old in our hotel room? She won't get up in the middle of the night and ask for a drink of water and wonder why Daddy is doing that to Mommy?" I look at him quizzically and then reward him with a secret smile. He returns it.

"Don't bring Cara," he says. "Andy can watch her for the next week or Marla can help out, too."

"I don't know." I hesitate at the idea of leaving Cara but being with Linc—all alone with him on the road—is really what we need.

"*Please,* Tally. I need you. We're winning. You and me. We need to be together. Cara isn't going to require therapy if you miss a couple of weeks with her and come out on the road with me." His wistfulness moves me.

"Okay," I finally say. "We'll pay Andy triple and she can watch Cara for a week or so. Happy?"

"Almost. I think we need to do number nine, and then take a shower, and then sleep together." He grins wide and then it starts to slip. "It doesn't seem like we do any of those things together anymore, does it? And soon you'll be busier with the fall show unless you've told Mikhail you're pregnant." He gives me a quizzical look.

"I haven't told Mikhail. I don't need to tell him until the time is right." I trace his jawline. "But you're right, we don't spend enough time together and we need to. I need you, Lincoln Presley, so much. I need us together right now more than anything."

"I know. Me, too," he says on a sigh.

We've done number nine nice and slow. We've showered. We've just remade the bed and pulled the covers back. We share in this weird ritual of never getting into an unmade bed to sleep. We slide in together. He moves into me from behind and flings his arm over me and pulls me close.

His scent is amazing—a combination of fine soap and his signature cologne. He soothes me in so many ways.

It's after three in the morning. Our liaison tonight robbed us of about three hours of precious sleep, but I don't think either of us would have wanted to be anywhere else.

We needed this. We need to be together.

Weathering this grief together is the most important thing. It's the only way we'll survive this.

The loss of my mother has unanchored me, worse than Holly's death, which astounds me on many levels. In the last year, I began to depend on my mother, and now she's gone. The sharp edges of grief begin to roll in on me once again.

Linc pulls me into him further. "I miss her, too."

I give voice to my pain and turn toward him. "It's weird, you know? She was never a normal mom. I could never count on her, but she really tried hard this past year or so to be there for me, for Cara, for you, for all of us."

Linc plays with a strand of my hair. "I know."

I lay my head near his heart and listen to its steady beat. "It's just so ironic that it would end this way. I feel abandoned by her. I feel lost and unanchored all over again like I did when Holly died. Another part of me feels like it's just gone. I don't know what to do with all of this sadness or how to process it."

I look up at him. "It's suffocating me. Yet, I can't even cry for her yet. What is *wrong* with me? Why did this have to happen to us? And how do I explain it all to Cara?"

Linc traces my lips. "Sometimes, I think kids have an uncanny understanding that allows them to accept the outcome of death far better than we ever do as adults. Right now, you don't need to worry about Cara. Let me do that. Let Andy do that. Right now, you just need to let me take care of you, and maybe I'll let you take care of me."

I try to smile with reassurance. "I'll take care of you, Elvis. I promise."

"I like that promise." His smile fades, and he looks haunted for a few seconds. "Don't ever break it."

"I won't." I move in closer to him encouraged by his words and intent on giving him reassurance for once.

He clasp his left hand with mine and fingers the wedding band there. "We'll get through this, Tally. We will. Together, we'll get through this."

"We will."

I listen to the steady beat of his heart for a long time. His breath sounds become more even. I take solace in him just being here for me.

I need him.

He's all I need.

Going out on the road with him might be the best thing for us right now.

It might be the only thing I can do or should do.

Us together.

That's all that matters.

Perhaps, it's the only answer I should be seeking. Maybe it doesn't matter that the math is wrong because together we'll make it right somehow.

Us together is all that matters.

That's the answer.

It's the only one that should count.

CHAPTER TWELVE

wicked game

LINC

Winning.
The euphoria wears off much like a party balloon leaking helium.
Winning doesn't last forever
and it's not nearly long enough.
Eventually, it's all about the next one.
~ Lincoln Presley

September 14th

I**T'S TWO O'CLOCK IN THE MORNING** when I finally return home after pitching a crucial win that has us continuing our march toward the playoffs. It's mid-September and every baseball player in the league wants to be playing baseball in October and it looks like the Giants will be. Yet, with every game the stakes get higher. We play to win, to be a part of the winning team.

The coaching staff has been cautious in working me back into the regular starting pitcher rotation so the guys wanted to celebrate a little in the locker room with my win. We stayed in our uniforms long enough that the champagne that first soaked them dried completely. Photographs were taken. Statistics were shouted. Congratulations were thrown my way like free candy at a parade.

What a ride.

It felt good to pitch a winning game. I'd forgotten how much I enjoy winning in the major leagues. It's been a while. It's different than the minors where baseball is still a sport rather than a business and a brand. Players still want to win at the highest level, in fact, I would hazard a guess as to more so, but there's a lot more money involved and there are the owners and the fans and the media, and everyone wants to be a part of it when you're winning, but when you lose, nobody wants to be reminded.

Winning.

The euphoria wears off much like a party balloon leaking helium.

Winning doesn't last forever

and it's not nearly long enough.

Eventually, it's all about the next one.

Winning.

I'm lucky to even be here, but the whole celebratory thing leaves me feeling hollow inside. After interminable amount of celebratory time, I shove my favorite glove into my bag along with one of the game balls that Mad Bum snagged for me and prepared to leave the premises. Most of the guys were going crazy over the latest win and not worrying about who did what during the game or whose pitching was almost perfect or who helped the most to get us here or worry about the mistakes that were made. By me.

That was my problem. Solely, my problem.

One of the world's best pitchers in baseball glances over at me more than once, while he reigns supreme over the media surrounding him in the locker room. "It's a team sport, a team effort," I hear him say a few times to the press.

Some time later, the guy rewards me with a smirk as he tells the reporters to go and talk to Presley about the art of fastballs. He saunters off from the fanfare with a wave of his amazing arm.

I can't help but think that one of the best pitchers in baseball seems to have it all figured out. Envy starts in my gut and makes its way outward.

What is wrong with me? I should be happy.

I have everything. Don't I?

Tally left the stadium a few hours ago. And now, I sit in my car outside of our house for another half hour trying to get my head around as to why I feel so amazingly empty. Slowly, I make my way across the foyer and head for the kitchen and pour myself a generous shot of whiskey and down it quickly. I pour another. After two more, I lean against the kitchen counter for support admitting to myself that the last shot of tequila with the guys probably wasn't such a good idea after all now that I've switched to whiskey. Still not a good idea. I breathe in deep in an attempt to clear my head.

Figuring that Tally has probably been asleep for a couple of hours, I quietly slip into our bedroom hoping not to wake her. Nevertheless, she sits straight up in bed as soon as I stumble on something in the middle of our bedroom. It's one of Cara's dolls. I place it on the chair so I won't repeat that performance in the early morning hours when I'll probably still be awake and pacing.

"I was beginning to wonder where you were," she says from across the room. "You okay? You happy?"

"Looks like we'll make the playoffs the way things are going. It's all good."

Only one of these things is true, and the lie comes easy enough. I won't tell her about the bad encounter with one reporter, who didn't waste much time in congratulating me on the win and then quickly moved on to ask all kinds of tough questions about all those trade rumors.

He told me the inevitable trade of Lincoln Presley was already slated to be the next month's headline for his sports column. A few too many shots in, as well as a raging headache, almost had me swinging at him, but Mad came to the rescue. The reporter couldn't believe his luck in getting to ask a few questions of one of the Giants' most winning pitcher, and quickly turned his attention away from me. I was saved.

"Everything is fine." This time I manage a smile to go along with the lie.

It wasn't.

It wouldn't be.

"You don't seem exactly fine."

"I am."

Tally sighs and then gracefully slides out of bed and walks up to me. She puts her arms around my neck and pulls me in order to kiss me. "And you won the game for them. Nice job."

"Six and a half innings, Tally."

Six and a half innings wouldn't be enough.

"They believe in you. I think they just want to give you time to settle back in."

"I'm too expensive to be awarded much time."

"But you have a contract."

Here's my chance to tell her about the trade, prepare her for the next move. Still, I hesitate. Things are going all right between us. I want to keep it that way. I don't want to upset the balance.

I've missed what all she's said and force myself to bring my mind back to the present and to her because she's made a ton of effort. She came to every game this week and even flew back and forth for the games against the Tigers last week. She sat in the stands with all the other wives for every game, which she hates doing, but she gutted it out with me for the past ten days. Tally remains silent and supportive, apparently knowing I need that more than anything else from her right now even though I think she might be starting to put things together when it comes to me and my playing time, or lack thereof.

She's wearing one of my Fresno Grizzlies baseball shirts. She's five months pregnant and still barely shows but she looks so damn cute. I shelve the idea of telling her about my trade talk worries and just hold onto my wife.

"We're in the good part," she whispers into my chest. "You won the game for them." She looks up at me and gets this little smile. "Everything is going to be okay." She's told me this a few times before, parroting Dr. Eldon's words from the last week's check-up. It appears that even Tally has begun to be happy about this baby.

"It's just one game in a long season, but we'll be playing in October if we keep playing like this. It's what every guy plays for."

I should tell her about the trade rumors, but instead, I kiss my wife intent on focusing solely on her and silencing her questions about baseball and my playing time. I don't want to talk about baseball anymore tonight. I don't want to deal with rumors of being traded right now. I want my wife. I *need* my wife.

"We're in the good part." I force a smile even as my head pounds with fresh pain. "Did you eat today? I mean, earlier?"

She gives me a withering look. Her eating has been a constant battle between us, but we've called a truce around this one thing in the past couple of weeks and I'm not supposed to be bringing it up. There's no need for Tally to know that I still keep a tab on the food inventory at home and even when I'm away and have told our nanny to do the same. I pay Andy good money to ensure the house is stocked full of good healthy food and that Tally's stress level is kept to a minimum. Our live-in nanny is well compensated for all the extra duties I've delegated to her without my pregnant wife knowing anything about them.

"I ate earlier. Let's not talk about my eating habits, okay? We agreed."

Now, I concentrate more fully on Tally because she has this vexed look. *Is it guilt? Anticipation. Both?*

"Mikhail's hired Ian Sands for some of the fall performances," she says softly. "He wants to meet with me tomorrow over lunch to go over things."

I tiredly run my hands through my hair and try to remember what she just said. "So much for going with me to Arizona."

"Yes, I realize that. I'm sorry. But it must be important to Mikhail to meet before rehearsals start up again."

"So *who* did Mikhail hire?" I ask.

"Ian. Ian Sands." She gets this solemn face.

"Ian Sands? I take it you *know* him?"

Tally looks a little uneasy and steps away from me. "He's from The London Ballet Company. He's good. It's quite a coup that he would guest star at SFB. He told Mikhail he wanted to come to San Fran so he could dance with me which could get a little tricky in the next couple of months." She points to her slightly protruding stomach and makes a face. "I performed with him in London and Milan about three years ago. Maybe four. A while ago." She smiles a little too brightly for me now. "Anyway, Mikhail asked me to meet him for lunch tomorrow. It's probably to talk about the fall line-up and Ian's guest starring role."

"You still haven't told Mikhail you're pregnant. And, I take it this Ian doesn't know you're pregnant, married, or *both*?" I try to keep my tone even but the jealousy creeps through anyway.

"No, I haven't told Mikhail yet but I'll do that tomorrow. I mean, I'll *have* to tell him now. He's starting to plan out the late fall schedule especially with Ian coming here. Wait. You're not seriously jealous; are you? Ian's part of the past. I mean, *really…*way way back in the past." She laughs nervously and plays with her shirt again, tugging it this way and that and walks further away. She picks up a brush and starts running it through her long dark hair.

"How far in the past? And how well did you know him?"

She turns to me with the brush mid-air as if she's been caught in a lie. "We spent some time together. I was nineteen. Rob and I were on the outs. He showed me around London…Europe. We went to Milan together. It was a long time ago."

"But you slept with him."

No trade talk tonight.

Now I have a new problem to contend with—Ian Sands—as if Sam Wilde or Rob Thorn weren't enough.

Now there is this Ian Sands.

Jealousy takes over; it's instant and destructive.

"I did in fact sleep with him for the better part of that spring. But it's old news. I'm sure he's changed a ton. I'm sure he's married, too."

"Don't sound so resigned or disappointed by the fact that you're married." I try to make a joke of it but it doesn't quite work with jealousy racing through me now like a lit fuse. I'm sure she hears it in my voice.

She comes toward me with that dancer's walk—a strut more than a walk. I'm instantly captivated as she moves in that regal way of hers. *Ethereal.* When she reaches me, she slides her hands along my chest and then nuzzles her face into my neck by standing on her tiptoes to reach me.

"Don't be jealous, Elvis. You've ruined me for anyone else. You *know* this." She laughs a little.

"Don't make me jealous then." I kiss her roughly and then proceed to maneuver her towards our bed. It seems we're both a little turned on at the rough play. I'm determined to show her she's mine in every way. She echoes the sentiment back in her sexiest voice laced with the same intent for me.

"Why do you have to fuck with me like this?" I ask in exasperation after a few minutes of kissing her everywhere as jealous thoughts of Ian Sands begin to rule. I study her beautiful face for one long moment.

"I don't know." She frowns slightly and then her face transforms and portrays this wry, little smile. "Sometimes, I can't help myself. I have a tendency to sabotage the very best things in my life that are actually good for me. You know that's true."

The sweetness in which she's said this is a complete turn-on, and I completely ignore the truth of what she's just admitted to me about herself.

"Do you think maybe just once you can try *not* to sabotage the best thing in your life? *Me*, for instance?"

Her green eyes flash but then this steely excitement takes over as she brazenly gazes at me. "You *know* this about me," she whispers. "You know it better than anybody else. I'm scared of being this happy, Linc. There's always a dark side. Things don't stay happy forever."

"Maybe they will this time." I can't quite hide the wistfulness in my tone. I feel it, too. The feeling that everything is temporary and about to break apart. Maybe even us. Tally's right; things don't stay happy forever.

She takes my hand and glides it across her almost flat stomach. "I'm scared to hope too much, to love too much. I wake up every day and thank God for what my life with you has become. It's perfect because of you and Cara and even this baby." She frowns. "But I don't want to hope for too much. It can all fall apart so easily. You *know* this. *I* know this."

I rub her stomach, hoping to feel this fluttering that she should be feeling at this stage. She tells me it hasn't happened yet, but Dr. Eldon and this new specialist whose name escapes me isn't worried either. "He has a name." I grin at her.

She doesn't want to talk about gender or baby names or her due date or anything to do with this pregnancy. She's too busy hiding it all from her boss right now.

She nervously licks her lips and then looks away and says, "*He* could be a *she*. We don't know yet. But if you want to name him go right ahead, but you know what I think about that. It's too soon."

"Theo," I say softly. "If it's a boy his name will be Theo. Theo Elliott Presley. And if it's a girl we'll call her Holly Tessa Presley."

Tally face contorts. "I told you it was not a good idea to name this baby yet. We don't know yet what it will be, and it's too soon." She looks decidedly unhappy. "I can't hope for too much. I'm just taking it one day at a time right now."

"Everything is going to work out." Although even as I say this I know just telling her about the possibility of me being traded will send her into a fresh panic. I hold my breath and don't say anything more. Instead, I slip my roving fingers inside of her and elicit her mighty fine response in a completely different way. We move in on each other exploring each other in ways that have become both familiar and necessary.

"Let's not talk about this Ian Sands or Sam Wilde any more tonight. You're mine." I lift my head after kissing her thoroughly.

"Who's talking about Ian or Sam? You are. I'm just hoping to get lucky with the best pitcher in baseball." She lifts her chin while her green eyes mildly dance in the semi-dark and then seemingly darken. She looks troubled for a few seconds and then her face goes almost blank.

"I just want to make sure *you know* you're mine." I lean over her and kiss her hard. "Lest you forget your name, Talia Presley, you *belong* to me. Only me. You don't get to fuck anyone else anymore. We're married. Remember?"

"I do remember. And I could never forget you." I wince at her words and so does she in realizing what she's just said.

"Sorry. That was cruel." She tries to smile at me but it doesn't quite work this time. "I'm sorry. I didn't mean it the way it sounded."

"Yes, you did."

She doesn't deny it. Instead, she looks away from me. The atmosphere becomes electric as the unspeakable tension between us runs even higher this time.

It's like we're two adversaries poised to strike out at each other in battle. Or better yet, she's the Black Widow spider and I'm her prey, dizzy under her spell, just before the inevitable demise of my very soul.

Or, I'm the monster.

Or, she is.

Or, we both are.

I hate it when she teases me about my memory—the demons that plague me. Sometimes, I resent that she remembers what I still can't about us. She knows this bothers me to no end, but she brings it up anyway at unexpected times like this one. My memory has mostly returned, but there are bits and pieces still missing—like a jigsaw puzzle that's only half-finished—and sometimes she vividly reminds me of this—my past failings of her, of us.

I know there's a part of her that she holds back from me. She remains unsure of me. Of us.

I'm not the same. My memories of us are not all there. I work within the confines of my life only seeing sporadic scenes of an unfinished film at times.

Sure, I can make out the gist of the movie of our life together and what it is all about, mostly, but there are all these blank scenes that may never get filled in. Memories of her and me—of us—that may be gone forever.

There are times when I look at Tally where I can still see the questioning look in her eyes. The distrust. Of me.

I'm not quite who she remembers me to be. She won't say otherwise, but I sense her doubt. I'm left to silently wonder how that translates to who I am to her now, and how much she really loves me deep down. Not all the parts of me have returned; surely, not all of them are back or may never come back as Brad Stephenson has warned me about more than once.

And other parts are different. I have sides to my personality she's never seen before. She's told me this. The headaches continue to rage. I still battle this anger and these weird-ass mood swings. They surface unexpectedly. Like now.

There is definitely this cruel part of me that takes her like this without her granting me permission first. Admittedly, I get turned on in ruling her this way because I think I can and do. Sometimes, our love for each other feels so strong as if nothing can ever sever the bond between us and at other times—times like these—I feel its fragility.

I sense her uncertainty. And mine as well.

I can't fix it. Not everything.

And she can't fix me. I sense her disappointment in that, too.

I'm not a superhero after all, and Tally knows it.

The silence grows between us even as our breaths quicken and soon synchronize at the close proximity of our bodies that invariably ache for one another. Physical attraction to each other has never been our problem. Sex has never been our problem. Or, Tally's problem. She's been with more guys than I care to think about, and yet I do anyway while the jealous rage for all the others who have been with Tally surges through me from deep inside.

"I don't want to fight with you anymore. No more fighting," I say with a heavy sigh.

"I don't want to fight with you either." She runs her hands through my hair and pulls my head down to hers and kisses me.

The jealousy over the other men she's been with is suddenly set free and swarms to the surface. All at once, I don't wait for her acquiescence. I don't gently slide off her panties or casually remove the baseball shirt she's still wearing. Instead, I tear at the silk lingerie and immediately thrust my way inside of her before she's even ready. I feel the resistance of her flesh and yet still push my way into her. Her body tenses beneath mine.

"Linc? What is going on with you?"

"I don't like Ian Sands. I don't like that he fucked you in London or Milan or anywhere else, for that matter. I don't want to think about Sam Wilde or Rob Thorn or all the others you've been with. I want you to be mine for all of time." I unleash this almost uncontrollable rage at our circumstances, and allow the jealousy over this Ian Sands and all her previous lovers to take over. Plus the precariousness of my professional baseball career also coalesces and rules my ardent behavior for the next several minutes.

Tally responds to the rough play of my lovemaking, if you can even call it that, by arching her back and opening herself to me even more. Rage takes all control. I finish quickly leaving her incomplete. I pull out and move to my side of the bed away from her while the twin feelings of being out of control, and guilt attack me from all sides.

For a few minutes, Tally lays perfectly still next to me and catches her breath.

I close my eyes. I can only imagine what she's trying to discern from what just happened between us. Remorse comes for me.

Then, she leans over me. Her long dark hair brushes my chest as her head sways side to side. "What was that all about, Elvis?" Her voice is gentle and soothing. Two things I don't normally associate with Tally. The guilt worsens.

"I'm sorry. I'm not…myself."

It is times like these, even when she looks at me the way she is now with nothing but love—even as she strokes the side of my face in this loving, tempestuous way and tells me she loves me that I can still sense her disappointment because I am not the same guy who saved her from that fiery car crash on Valentine's Day almost six years before. Because I'm not that Lincoln Presley anymore. I'm this other guy, who is not going to be the MVP of the Giants, and who will soon be traded to New York or Toronto and neither of these places will please my wife.

I'm failing, and Tally knows it.

Nevertheless, I don't tell her any of that now. Instead, we start over again, slower this time as my body responds and hardens at her insistent touch and even more so with her all too willing mouth. Eventually, she slides down on top of me and establishes the rhythm for both of us. I span her tiny waist with my hands and ultimately brand her deep inside with my seed even though I still silently rage at her in the only way I know how where I can retain a semblance of control because it doesn't feel like we have everything, and even if we do, it is tenuous at best.

After we finish again, I promise myself that I will finally tell her about the trade talk rumors and what it means for us as the possibility that we'll be moving somewhere else after all becomes all too real.

I'll tell her.

Tomorrow.

CHAPTER THIRTEEN

starring role

TALLY

The thing is I knew it was something.
Even then.
~ Talia Landon Presley

September 15th

IN A FOG, STILL UNABLE TO fully comprehend that my life is un-raveling, I finally manage to glance down at the address Mikhail sent me via text late last night about meeting up today. I give Suri the command to take me there and don't put it all together until I am driving down the once familiar street. I park the car in front of *The Promissory Note's* front door entrance after verifying the address is correct *twice*.

My former life in Alamo Square and with Sam comes rushing back. It's been months. And how ironic today of all days to wind up here. *This will be awkward.*

"Mrs. Presley? Your table's ready."

The maitre-d gives me this sly smile that tells me he knows who I am and also must like what he sees. He's already dispensed with my black coat, gingerly hanging it up in the closet right behind his podium. Now, he eyes my simple black dress with this somewhat suggestive approval while I raise an eyebrow in his general direction and have to hope the Spanx is still hiding my unexpected burden, I mean, baby. *Not a burden per se. Not really.*

I mean my gut instinct tells me my career may be on the line here. Something Linc fails to grasp.

Shit. I'm a bad person. A bad mom. A bad wife.

My eyes start to sting. The guy clears his throat as he touches my hand and asks if I'm okay. I just nod at him and follow. *Nod and follow.* My mind drifts, vaguely intrigued by his obvious interest and the battle of guilt and fear that continually rages inside of me. *What kind of vibe am I giving off?* Maybe, it's the dark-red shade of lipstick staining my lips that has him nodding at me in this notable seductive way. Or, it's Robert Palmer's *Addicted To Love* lyrics conspicuously playing this sensual beat in the background as if I've planned this whole setup just for the two of us to ponder. This stranger and I.

We can ponder.

Even my hair looks chic today. It's pulled back in a chignon making me look older and wiser, and well, put together for once. It's just one of Marla's many recommendations when I called her, after hanging up with Linc before he left early this morning for Arizona, in seeking my fashion guru's advice on what to wear to this unexpected lunch meeting with Mikhail Rostov.

"Maybe he's going to offer me the *Swan Lake* gig, especially since Ian Sands is going to be here," I'd said with all the confidence that my position in the pecking world of dance afforded.

"I'm sure that's part of it," Marla said soothingly. "But why the special lunch date? Aren't you technically off for a few more weeks before fall rehearsals start up? Maybe there's more. Maybe he wants you to get the starring role *and* the title. That would be epic and so well-deserved. I mean he should be doing that for you just for putting up with his shit. Gah, you so deserve the promotion, Tally."

"Maybe. Let's not get ahead of ourselves. I haven't paid that many dues yet. But…Mikhail's been slightly better. *Lately.* Of course, I haven't seen him for the past month. He was pleased with my performance of *Giselle.* We had a good crowd for the entire run earlier this summer."

"Yes, he's been better. What a few months, at the most? Since you and Linc got married? But before that? Let's face it, Tal. He's a dick, and he knows it. *And,* he doesn't even *care.*"

Marla was right of course. "Yes, he is a dick, and he knows it, and he doesn't care," I say with a little laugh, "which is why I have to be two steps ahead of him at all times."

But was I two steps ahead of him now?

Or, had Mikhail outplayed me and finally found a way to oust me out of San Francisco Ballet's prestigious line-up.

After all, Mikhail Rostov had been an Allaire Tremblay fan through and through. He didn't know all my history with my former mentor, but he knew some of it. The fear of failing stayed with me. You would have thought that I would be over it by now, but that particular fear was so deeply ingrained within me that it took over my ability to breathe more than half the time. Literally, I walked around in life holding my breath half the time in a futile effort to combat failure. Even now.

The waning silence between Marla and me developed into something more. Neither one of us dared to fill it. Until I heard her say, "yo, Tal! You listening? I asked you if you've told Mikhail yet. About being pregnant. You're going to have to *soon.* I mean he's bound to notice soon enough, and his whole fall schedule is going to be seriously fucked up without you in it."

"Yeah, I know." The words come out defensive. I sighed. "Spanx helped me keep the curious at bay up until now. I haven't gained that much weight, but I know I need to tell him now, and I will tell him. Tomorrow."

"What if he already knows?" Marla asked sounding anxious all at once.

"No way. I've been careful. Nobody knows. There's no way he could ever find out."

"Are you sure about that? Linc told his father. Davis could make trouble for you."

"He promised he wouldn't say anything. Linc talked to him about that specifically. And, Mikhail doesn't pay attention to little details like that. How could he even tell? I've worn Spanx like a religion and worked twice as hard as everybody else. The early summer production of *Giselle* went off without a hitch. Mikhail's happy with me right now. I'm sure he just wants to talk about the fall line-up. They want to do a *Swan Lake* production as well as *The Nutcracker*. He's probably just worried about the logistics with all of that. I can go another month or so and at least do the *Swan Lake* performances. I'll be fine. I'm sure this lunch meeting is just to get a jump on all of that."

"Probably." Marla didn't sound convinced. "Just dress to the nines and be ready for anything. That's the only way to handle someone like him. You've got this."

"You know? You're the only one who believes in me all the time. You're always there for me, Marla. *Always.* Thank you. I know I don't say that often enough."

"Ditto. Stop it. You're getting all sentimental on me. What? Are you becoming Holly these days?" she teased.

"Hardly."

We've made progress we can bring up Holly and sometimes laugh.

"Maybe, it's nothing more than a friendly, you're-doing-great-we-want-you-to-star-in-Swan-Lake-for-us-this-fall speech complete with a meal he's paying for," Marla said with detectable wistfulness.

Fear circled like an invisible noose and seemed to constrict my throat with the ill intentions of cutting off my air supply after she said this. "Well, if he does know, all he's going to want to do is fire my ass in a nice public place away from the studio so the idea of making any sort of scene is virtually impossible," I said feeling uneasy all at one. I tried to laugh but it really wasn't funny.

Would Mikhail do that?

Fire me?

My contract offered me no protection from that particular career demise. See? That's what happens when you sign a contract in haste like I did over a year ago.

SFB was a means to an end. To Linc. San Francisco Ballet just meant going home. To Linc. So no contract clause protected me if Mikhail decided to fire me. Something Sasha would never do, but Mikhail could and he just might.

"Maybe it's nothing. Just a friendly, you're-doing-great-we-want-you-to-star-in-Swan-Lake-for-us-next-year speech complete with meal he's paying for," Marla said with heartfelt consolation even as the waning silence between us grew into something more. Yet, neither one of us dared to fill it.

Yet the growing sense of failure had already set in as if a fuse had been lit. It crawled its way through me in the same way that ink seeps into paper leaving a permanent mark. Falling, failing, and losing—the triple threats—never left me for long. I knew this.

"Maybe," I'd said faintly.

"Let's hope so."

Maybe it didn't matter if I wasn't the lead in Swan Lake.

Lost the part.

Lost the job.

Maybe.

It did, of course.

The job was everything.

My ballet career at SFB meant everything.

Without it? I'd have nothing.

Except Linc, Cara, and this baby.

And the math was still wrong…

"Don't worry so much, Tally. It's probably nothing," Marla had said just before our call ended.

The thing is I knew it was something.

Even then.

The summer break for SFB lasts another two weeks before rehearsals start up in late September. I suppose that thought alone manages to set off a new round of anxiety all over again. I can actually feel myself get even more uptight as to why Mikhail wanted to meet me here of all places for lunch.

My back aches. My head hurts. My stomach tightens. Add to that that the timing is suspect, too. Technically, this is my vacation from SFB. I start to tremble even more after the maitre d' begins to lead me forward into the dining room.

It's feels like I'm being lead to an execution rather than a lunch meeting with my boss.

My only relief ends up being when the head host informs me that today is Sam's day off.

Yes, there is a God.

Temporarily relieved at the news that it's Sam's day off, I smile at the maitre d' in appreciation at his obvious approval of my fashion ensemble one last time while he extends his long arm to secluded table farthest away in the dining room. Sam's done some remodeling since I was here last. The dark-red colors of the chairs blend with the wood quite nicely while the starched, white linen table cloths make for a rich contrast.

Sam's been busy. That's good. Good for Sam.

He deftly pushes in my chair for me and lingers near my face for a moment too long. Then, he is pointing toward the television that's been turned on in the opposite corner, displaying the game between the Giants and the Diamondbacks.

"Nice, that they're winning," the guy murmurs in my right ear which jars me to the present.

I get it. I do. It appears he has a fascination with the ballet world and, most definitely, me, and baseball for the win. I put on a fake smile. "Yes." I reward him with a lascivious look as the fear of failure swarms me. I grab hold of his forearm. "Can you do me a favor?"

"Yes," he says as he displays a nice white smile.

"Can you swing back by here when my lunch date arrives? I may need a witness." I give him a winning smile.

"Of course, give me a few minutes to make sure things are all set upfront."

"Thank you." I openly watch him as he saunters away but then the smile slides from my face while nerves get the best of me. My hands shake, and my heart beats so fast it feels like it is actually going to make its way out of my chest.

Breathe.

Breathe, Tally, breathe.

This is nothing.

This will turn out to be nothing.

Just be ready.

Get it out fast.

I look around at the restaurant decor for something to do as the fears I battled earlier take on new life. I note the new lighting and the dark crimson colors Sam has put here in the dining room. There's a large painting of a ballerina from Swan Lake on the far wall. I scrutinize the artwork more closely thinking it's Tremblay from years before, but my own face stares back at me.

My face feels hot and I fan it hoping to quell both nerves as well as this uncomfortable, overwhelming sensation that Sam has paid homage to me in this secretive way.

Then the fears rush in again, and they make me feel worse the longer I sit here waiting for Mikhail. The biggest one of all circles like swirling dust. What does Mikhail Rostov really want? I'm not sure exactly why Mikhail wanted to meet me here. I've been stalling on telling him about the pregnancy thing. *Stalling for far too long* as Linc would say if he were here. But since Linc is in Arizona, *winning,* I have to handle this whole thing in terms of this pregnancy and my career and Mikhail Rostov all on my own. I told Linc all of this during our brief phone call this morning, right before he hung up and raced off to his away game, while I proceeded to call Marla seeking reassurance.

The reality is Linc is almost eight hundred miles and a time-zone away from me today. I feel his absence deeply. I need him today. I need his special way of reassuring me. I seek out the t.v. screen in the bar but I can barely see it. It's him, of course, on the t.v. doing his favorite windup for a fastball. I watch my husband for a few minutes, like a devoted fan, as he pitches a few more fast balls and strikes the guy out. He looks good. Fast balls. *Those* I recognize. I start to smile because I am married to Lincoln Presley, and he loves me and we have Cara and this baby is coming. And love is enough.

It is.

Love is enough.

Love conquers all.

And then, it comes to me all over again. The plague of grief that never leaves.

My mother is dead.

It's all wrong, isn't it?

And, the math that is never wrong is wrong.

Perhaps, that's only the sign of what is to come next.

Bad news comes in threes. I've already lost my mom. The date with this baby is all wrong. *What else will it be?* I don't get the chance to wonder about that for too long because Mikhail Rostov suddenly stands in front of me. I frantically look around for the maître d' but he hasn't returned yet.

My timing is off.

I'm not two steps ahead.

I am two steps behind.

Like a dark angel's unexpected visit in a horror film I realize I am not about to be knighted or be promoted. No. I am about to be annihilated. *Fired.* I can tell by the look in Mikhail's dark eyes when he slides onto the chair opposite mine like we're just old friends just gathering for an intimate chat.

"Talia, it's so nice to see you," Mikhail says too easily.

Is it?

No words come. No air either.

"You, too," I finally manage to choke out because I already know what's coming. "I'm pregnant. I've been planning to tell you."

He frowns and shakes his head slowly. "Yes, well, I was informed of your condition by one of our patrons—a very reputable source. And yes, we have some concerns about your ability to perform and maintain the terms of four performances per year per the contract you signed with us. Talia, keeping this from us—*from me*—has led us to a degree of liability we weren't prepared for. You should have told us sooner but you didn't. It puts us in a very precarious position. You've brought unnecessary jeopardy to SFB and to yourself. Your omission is inexcusable. I'm afraid we have cause to let you go, Talia."

Five minutes tick by where I just stare at Mikhail too stunned to speak.

"You're firing me?" I finally ask.

The director nods. "We're letting you go." He doesn't look unhappy. He looks rejuvenated as if the wicked witch is finally dead, and he's the one who gladly killed her.

My newfound friend—the maître d'—returns, but he's far too late and my severe look tells him this. Mikhail is enjoying this crucifixion far too much to take much notice of the tuxedo-clad servant who has so audaciously swung by our table to join us. I wave the guy off shaking my head at him.

The meeting with Mikhail goes downhill from there.

There is food. There is severance. There are actual walking papers. Mikhail produces them all with a surgeon's precision exacting cuts are that are deep and permanent.

I manage to maintain a stoic face in spite of the humiliating experience of being fired in such a public place while Mikhail ticks off my long list of sins in terms of insubordination and defiance as if he's reading them off from some ancient scroll.

It takes less than thirty minutes for Mikhail to finish his dirty work with me. It's replete with allegations and legal innuendos while he hints that any sort of retaliation by me will have me blacklisted. *Blacklisted.* As if I haven't been already. He reminds me I'm under a non-disclosure agreement. A non-compete for six months. I'm surprised he didn't produce handcuffs to further drive his point home.

I can't say anything. I can't do anything. I'm finished. He's made sure of it.

My artistic director—now, former employer—slinks out of the restaurant much the way he arrived. I valiantly watch him as he stops to profusely thank the patrons of the arts that recognize the famous director just before he reaches the front doors. Yes. Mikhail Rostov basks in the spotlight while having just extinguished mine as he takes his leave. For all the right reasons, he told me.

Because SFB is going in another direction.

Because he doesn't want to hold me back.

Because you should have told us sooner but you didn't.

Because it puts us in a very precarious position.

Because you've brought unnecessary jeopardy with your omission to SFB and to yourself.

I'm afraid we have cause to let you go.

Because your omission is inexcusable.

Because he knows.

And, my career?

It ends just like that.

CHAPTER FOURTEEN

how to be a heartbreaker

TALLY

Failing, falling, losing. They're all here for me.
~ Talia Landon Presley

September 15th

THE MAITRE D' SWINGS BACK BY.

"Is there anything else I can do for you?" he asks.

"No. No, thank you."

"Will you…be staying much longer? We kind of need the table. If Sam were here, he could arrange …"

"Sam. If Sam were here." I force a smile. "Yes, if Sam were here then everything would be okay." I shake my head back and forth while his dismay at my display of outright craziness erases the enraptured look he had for me thirty minutes earlier. "I'm just leaving. I'm *leaving*. Thank you. You've been…a great help." I cock my head to one side and look up at him. "What's your name by the way?"

"Joshua." He gets the all-is-forgiven smile.

"Well, Joshua, thanks for the…help." I look past him at the t.v. screen displayed in the bar, but the baseball game is over. "Who won?" I ask softly.

"The Giants. Your husband did."

Neither of us miss the double meaning of what he's just said.

"See you again sometime? I'm always here," he says as he saunters off.

I absently nod as I make my way toward the front doors although it seems half the dining room is watching me leave or the paranoia for what just happened to me has finally set in.

Failing, falling, losing. They're all here for me.

I walk out of the restaurant, *The Promissory Note,* which I now realize has never really held much promise for me—shaking my head side-to-side and trying not to cry at least until I reach my car.

I'm unemployed.

I'm motherless.

The math is wrong.

I've failed.

I've fallen.

I've lost.

I need my mom to tell me everything is going to be okay.

Or Linc.

Somebody please tell me it's going to be okay.

"Mrs. Presley."

I whirl around at the guy's words, and for a brief moment wonder who he is talking to. *Who is Mrs. Presley?*

Joshua holds out my black and the walking papers. I start to laugh while a single tear rolls down my face, as if on cue.

I do manage to say, "thank you," before I begin the long walk down the sidewalk toward my car.

I make it to the curb and awkwardly sit down on it and proceed to quietly break down.

This numbing sensation takes over as pure panic engulfs me. The wheezing sound fills my ears. It drowns out everything else.

It feels like forever before my dark world begins to fill in with color again.

I only look up when I hear someone calling out my name.

"Tally? What are you doing here? What's wrong?" Sam Wilde kneels next to me grasping my hand. "Are you all right? What's wrong?"

"Everything. Everything is wrong, Sam. And you can't fix it, so don't even try."

"It's going to be okay," he says.

I catch him looking at the severance papers scattered to the sidewalk next to me. "I don't see how." I crumple inward and inadvertently seek out his reassurance. "My mom died." I look up at him again seeking comfort.

"I know." He squeezes my hand and pulls me up in the next. He sweeps up the papers and steers me towards his restaurant. "Come on. Come back inside. We'll get you something to eat and talk it through."

"Why would you be so nice to me after everything that's happened between us?" I ask faintly.

"Because I care about you."

"I saw the painting. Why, Sam? Why?"

He shakes his head side-to-side and doesn't say anything for a few minutes. "It's my favorite ballet and my favorite ballerina. It goes with the room."

I nod not understanding what he's said on any level but don't say anything more because I don't trust myself to come up with the right words for either one of us right now.

"It's your day off. I'm sorry. I shouldn't be here. I know you have a lot to do. You always do," I say even as I attempt to shoot him a look of gratitude as he pushes me down in the soft black leather confines of his office chair.

"I have too much to do around here. I took the morning off." He gently dabs at my tear-streaked face with a cool wash cloth.

We are too close. My libido decides to come to life.

I breathe in his masculine scent and already know I shouldn't be liking it this much.

"What happened, Tally? Why are you here? What happened out there?" Sam points his thumb toward the front door and the street curb beyond where he found me. He's been waiting to ask me these questions for the past half hour.

I close my eyes and strive to center myself and keep it together long enough to escape his scrutiny and not confess my latest sins. I don't want him to know about the subsequent firing by Mikhail Rostov or my gynecologist's latest math calculations. His sympathy would not be welcome. I haven't had a chance to thoroughly process what just happened to me as it relates to my job and I can't think about the math right now nor redo the calculations or admit aloud that the baby I carry might be his.

"Tally." He brushes his lips against mine.

My eyes fly open. I reward him with a beseeching look. "Sam. Don't." My tone doesn't hold much conviction for either one of us. I try again. "*Please.* I can't do this."

He leans back away from me and searches my face. "Why? I miss you. It could be like before."

I hang my head refusing to look at him. "It was always going to be Linc."

"How do you know that for sure?" He lifts my chin with one hand and while with the other he encircles my face and effectively imprisons me.

But instead of pushing him away, I move in closer. "I can't fully explain what I have with Linc. I don't understand it myself but he's my center—my very core. The best part of me," I pant the words because Sam's kiss is having a profound effect on me. "He's the reason…I can even breathe."

He kisses me with more intent. My body responds of its own volition.

He lifts his head from mine and looks at me. "He's the reason right now? Right this second? Because I hear your breath coming faster, and I think it has everything to do with me." He smiles and begins a fresh assault. I do not turn him down.

His tongue probes my mouth. It is hot and erotic and my arms come up around his neck. Sam has always been patient with me but now he seems like he is barely able to hold onto his control. It's strangely erotic and my body automatically responds to his passion. "Even when he's clear across the country pitching a base…ball." Sam lifts me up from the chair without breaking our connection. He kisses my face and my collar bone and he fingers the filmy material of the dress I'm wearing. "Even then. Like today. I love him." Sam's touch becomes more insistent and I feel myself coming apart in his arms. "But I love you, too, Sam."

Now why did I have to go and say that?

"I love you, too," he says sounding utterly amazed as he looks down on me. He gently kisses my mouth and then his tongue explores me deeper. I groan with all the inexplicable desire he's released in me and lean into him further. He takes my ringed left hand and places it on his rapidly beating heart.

"I want you," he whispers. "Just like before. Like always."

The math is wrong.

It's so wrong.

I'm such a liar.

I shouldn't be here because I belong to Linc, and this is so wrong.

Everything is wrong.

But maybe Sam can fix it. Maybe Sam can do the math.

"Is there some place we can go?" I ask in sudden desperation.

He takes me by the hand and leads me out the front door much to the utter surprise of his employee.

"I'll be back later," Sam says to Joshua as we pass. The guy looks upon us with pure dismay and obvious disapproval.

I am playing with fire, and I will burn. And I know this.

Like a white knight solely designated to be my rescuer, I aimlessly follow Sam down the sidewalk away from the restaurant, away from my car, away from my life with Linc.

Surprisingly, within minutes, we arrive at Tremblay's place. In a daze, I climb the stairs holding onto Sam's outstretched hand to me. In shock that he lives here now, I vaguely hear him tell me that Linc approached him weeks ago about leasing it, and the offer was too good of a deal for Sam to pass up.

"So you're friends with my husband now?" I ask.

"We'll never be friends. We love the same woman."

I don't know what to say to that. I don't know why Linc failed to tell me he leased my house to Sam. It didn't make any sense. But then, none of this makes any sense.

Why am I here?

Sam unlocks the front door and allows me to walk in past him. Then, he steps into the room after me and just stands there gazing at me like Thor looks at Natalie Portman in the movie scene where half the town is destroyed around them, and yet it is only the two of them. Everybody wants to be Natalie in that scene. No one could turn Thor down.

"What's going on, Tally?" His voice is husky and softened with desire.

It's like before. I need before.

Some part of me must believe that Sam can help me find the way out. I step toward him.

Surprisingly, he frowns ever so slightly and backs away looking troubled all at once. "I leave in a few days for Afghanistan. We're doing some contract work there; and *no*, I can't tell you about any of it. I'll be gone for at least six months, maybe longer, but I'd come back for you."

His look is all telling. I know he wants me. Now. Six months from now. Even so, he seems to hesitate as he stays about five feet from me clearly assessing, weighing, and perhaps determining the odds for both of us.

He does math.

I smile even as I say, "Mikhail fired me."

"So I gathered. He's a dick, Tally. You never liked dancing at SFB with him there. It was better for you when you were working with Sasha."

"Well, it's the only ballet company in town, so I've kind of had to put up with him. He says I put the company in jeopardy. I'm a liability. He has cause. He probably does."

"That doesn't make any sense. You can fight this. You have a contract; he can't do this to you."

"He just did. He said I breached it. He threatened to have me blacklisted. It's a small world, Sam. He can do that. He can make it nearly impossible for me to get a job anywhere else. He can do that, and he threatened me and told me he would if I say anything about what he's just done. He has the leverage. All of it."

"He's bluffing. He can't do that. Kimberley will have his head. She can make his life a living hell. You *know* this already."

'I haven't told Kimberley yet."

"Well, let's *call* her. We'll get her working on it." He picks up his cell phone and starts to dial."

I run over and press the button ending the call. "Not right now. I can't talk to Kimberley right now. She'll be wondering why I'm here with you. Let's not complicate things anymore than they already are."

"So, you're still protecting him. You're still *with* him."

His question is bizarrely easy for me to answer considering where I'm standing and what we've been doing for the past twenty minutes. "*Yes.* I'm *married* to him. Let's not forget that."

"How could I forget that?" Sam says bitterly.

There is a very long silence while we openly gaze at each other.

My chin lifts in defiance and he smiles ever so slightly at seeing it.

"Tally, you can go anywhere. Be with anyone." He points to his heart and gets this rueful smile while I gaze at his massive chest and the passionate desire for him comes to life. "You're a star, but you were flaming out here, and you know it." He frowns. "And Linc's holding you back. He always has. You sacrificed it all for him. Does even he *see* that?"

"Only sometimes." My lips part and I try to smile, but it doesn't quite work this time because what Sam has said begins to resonate.

"Wait a minute. I don't understand something. What kind of leverage does Mikhail have over you anyway?"

"I'm a liability. I may have infringed on the terms of the contract with them. Or, I'm about to do that." I look over at him and sigh. "I didn't tell them…and he found out from someone else that…I'm pregnant."

"Christ, Tally. That changes things." He runs his hands through his golden hair.

"It does. You have no idea how much."

I pause for a long two minutes and battle with myself about telling him about the baby and the math. I eventually lose. "The math says it might be yours."

  Katherine Owen

I've never seen Sam at loss for words. He looks stunned. Then, his face lights up with such an incredible joy it is impossible to describe.

He becomes the golden god in my eyes again, and the golden god is very pleased at this news.

He lifts me up off the floor and twirls me around in his powerful arms. "Is this true? You think it's *ours?*"

He didn't say you think it's *mine?*

He asked, you think it's *ours?*

Ours.

I *hear* and *feel* the difference.

He twirls me around again, and it feels good to laugh and share in the joy of this baby with someone who doesn't expect me to be perfect. His elation is powerful. He is a god. His embrace makes everything feel okay. He makes me happy, and for a few minutes, I allow the wonder of it all with Sam to claim me.

"Dr. Eldon says I'm due the 9th of February. The most recent due date calculation would make it most likely yours."

He lowers me down and encircles me with his arms. "This changes everything," he says. Then, he's kissing me everywhere. And we're laughing together.

The sands shift.

I'm busy trying to remember when the last time was that Linc, and I laughed like this together. Things between us have been all about power shifts—winning and losing—and mood swings, his as well as mine. Together we've battled far too much sadness and angst to ever be happy for very long together.

And yet?

I can't do this to Linc.

I cradle Sam's face between my hands and look up into his amazing blue eyes, and even though I feel found for the first time in months I break his heart for a second time in the next moment.

"Sam. I can't do this. To him."

"I'm here, Tally. I've got you."

"Sam. I can't do this. To him. I can't be with you." He must finally hear what I've said. *Twice.*

He steps back as if I've run a sword straight through him. "What?"

"I belong to Linc. Good or bad. Right or wrong. I can't be yours. I have to go back. To him."

"Don't do this to us, Tally. If the baby is ours, I have every right to claim you both, and I plan to."

I press my finger to his lips. "No. I can't do this with you. I can't. I have to tell him first about the baby. I have to figure things out with Linc and see where we stand. I can't make any promises to you. I can't lie anymore, but we can't go back to the past either. I belong to him. I belong with him."

The golden aura around Sam effectively disappears while the fire in his beautiful eyes is all but extinguished. His disappointment is profound and I know the hatred for me will soon follow. It seems to reach for me already.

"I'll always be second place with you, won't I?"

I don't say anything.

He sighs big. "He doesn't deserve you."

"I...don't deserve either one of you."

"That's probably true," he says.

His cruelty wounds me as intended. I nod in acceptance and move towards the the front door, but then glance back. "Goodbye, Sam. Thank you."

"Please don't thank me. Not right now." He gets this look of regret. "I'm sorry. I shouldn't have said the thing about you not deserving either one of us. It was cruel. I shouldn't have said it. You don't even know how amazing you are. You really don't. God, Tally, how can you be so sure of him? Even now?"

"Because I love him." Sam gets this wounded look. "I love you, too, Sam, but it's different with you. It's easier."

"Not the same," he says in defeat. His hands clench at his sides. I can't decide if it's because he wants to put his arms around me and is willing himself not to or because he just wants to strangle me with his bare hands and end the misery I've caused him all over again.

Our eyes meet.

"A bit of both," he says sadly.

I nod and feel the loss of him. "I have to go. Please be careful in Afghanistan. Write to me and tell me how you are."

"No." He goes and stands away from me with his arms crossed across his chest as if that might be the only way to hold himself together and withers me with a single glance. "I can't… do this. If the kid's mine, I'll do right by the baby, but I can't do this with… you…anymore." He sighs big. "Like I said, I'll be gone in a few days. And where I'm going, I won't be able to contact you. That's best anyway. And, when I come back?" His blue eyes turn glacial. "I can't see you anymore, Tally. It's just too hard. I'll do right by this baby if it turns out to be mine, but I can't do this with you anymore." He winces and then gets this shameful look. Even so, I strain to hear his next words which I know will prove to be the final blow. "I can't be the one…to rescue you anymore. You need a rescue? Call your *husband.*"

His goodbye is clearly final.

Blinded by new tears, I walk out of his house—Tremblay's house—down the street toward my car where I put it into drive and point it toward home.

Home—this huge empty house—where I seem to live all alone and continually wait for Linc to come home and try to keep the last lie I've told at bay for a while longer.

Because if the lie remains untold,
if the secret keeps,
the truth remains hidden.
It can, can't it?
Sure it can.
But for how long?

CHAPTER FIFTEEN

you don't really know me

TALLY

"There was no fairytale in sight.
I didn't abide false hope for love.
I didn't abide love."
~ Talia Landon Presley

October 24th

THINGS GOT WORSE. LOSING MY JOB with San Francisco Ballet proved to be a catalyst for sinking further into the dark abyss I now find myself drowning in. Deep down, even I knew I couldn't keep it together for much longer. Keeping the truth about the baby from Linc became almost unbearable while the grief over my mother's unexpected death six weeks before and my destroyed career consumed the rest of me.

I was in a living hell, burning up in an inferno mostly of my own making with no way out. I couldn't breathe. The panic attacks grew worse and more frequent and lasted longer when they happened to me. I am losing time now—with each attack—blacking out on some level.

I get more desperate, more despondent and I know it. Linc has begun to question what is really happening to me.

He insists I talk to Brad. He *demands* it.

Meanwhile, the Giants are in the World Series playing against the Kansas City Royals, and Brad and Kimberley are in town for that. I am desperately trying to keep it together, but each day becomes harder to do so. Even Marla sides with Linc, she thinks I should talk to Brad, too. And so I do because I not sure I will be able to hold it together for even another day. It seems Brad Stephenson is my last lifeline.

Let the confession begin.

Confessions. Most of them anyway.

"What I will tell you first is that I stopped believing in fairy tales long before Holly died. No knight in shining armor on a white horse was going to ride in and save me. I'd just turned fifteen when Danny Solon and I did the deed for the first time. It was fast and awkward. The word messy comes to mind. And yet, I convinced myself that first times were like that and next time would be better. I made sure it was by adopting a cardinal set of rules. No backseats. No promises. No talking during. Gum. Breath mints. Condoms. A little music was always a bonus. A nice bed was optional. A secluded place was a requirement. Again, no promises. No looking back. No talk of a relationship. There were no expectations. Ever. And no promises. I already said that, didn't I? Those were my rules. The rules worked for me. Until they didn't."

"After Holly died."

"Yes."

I nod and search for air and manage to contort my face into a practiced smile for my newest audience.

"Up until that moment, I approached sex much like my mother planned Christmas each year, predictably, right down to the flocked tree. Little touches were the best. Necessary. Talk was optional. Like I said, no promises."

I sigh in this quiet agony at revealing my dark view of the world, of illicit sex with guys, even strangers, while playing the perfect protégé for my parents, for Allaire Tremblay, for the world. I clasp my hands together to keep them from shaking from anguish and the inexplicable anger that rises out of me in relation to my past.

Shame finds me, too. I force a fresh smile for my newest audience member. "The Pill became my best friend. Promiscuity with a lot of guys became my vice. I convinced myself it was better than food." Bitterness creeps into my voice. "Illicit sex comforted me in this strange, twisted way. I didn't care what others thought of me. Tally the rebel. To the very fucking end." I hold my breath and can only hope the words will still come. Or stop. One of those.

"You're still here."

"Am I?" I've spoken those two little words aloud. My face flushes at my carelessness.

"Go on."

I nod with contrived acceptance but feel compelled to continue my life story. "Like I said, I stuck to the mantra that sex was my vice and constantly reminded myself that there would never be a knight in shining armor riding in on a white horse to rescue me. No guy was ever going to be around long enough to save me. And that for worked for me. Sex was the goal—and always served as the ultimate endgame—as long as available and willing guys remained the conquest." I sigh big.

"And that was my life for a very long time. You see I was a very good liar. My parents didn't have a clue about me and what was going on. Just my sister Holly did. And I liked my life just the way it was because to the world I was this talented protégé—the next up and coming Polina Semionova—and to myself I was the girl who finessed her way through life surviving with a lot of sex and a lot of strict rules around sex.

"Fooling myself, fooling everyone else that I was perfect, and I didn't need anything or anyone. All I really cared about was ballet. It's in my DNA, I think. Ballet. I won't apologize for that." My listener nods clearly enraptured with my story. "All true. There was no fairy tale in sight. I didn't abide false hope for love. I didn't abide love. Real life ended up being so different from any fairy tale my mother had ever read to us, and I was fine with that. I'd accepted my reality. And then, like I said before, Holly was killed in a car accident, and the best part of me died right along with her." I pause for impact. "Because I was driving."

I look up at the bright baby blues that gaze so intently back at me and falter with my speech for a few seconds. I manage to break eye contact by looking around the room gathering up all the thoughts about all of my sins.

How much should I tell him? It seems to be one of those all defining moments.

"Tally? You were saying?"

I look over and take in air. "The thing is you're surrounded by people that tell you it's not your fault, but you end up spending the rest of your life trying to outrun that one indelible fact that cannot be changed—you were driving—it manages to follow you around everywhere and never truly goes away no matter how far away from home you go. It's still there. It lives inside of you and slowly tears away at the remaining best parts of you. You're permanently scarred by the guilt and the horror of what you've done. I was driving. Nothing changes that. Of course, it was my fault." I take a long, sorry breath, hold it in, and fight the inexplicable urge to tell him everything. The real reason as to why I'm here. I lied. To Linc. Telling my husband the truth will break his heart as well as mine.

"Tell me, Tally." Brad's voice is gentle. Soothing. Mildly seductive. "Tell me all of it."

"Then, I met Lincoln Presley, who not only rescued me the first time we met, but has pretty much been my savior ever since. Then and now." I dip my head unwilling to meet this man's penetrating gaze that seemingly sees all the way into my very dark soul. I sigh deep. "The truth is. The truth is…I'm having a difficult time believing in the fairytale—of Linc and me—let alone living it. I try to hide this from him most of the time, but it doesn't always work, which is why I'm here. He insisted I talk to you."

"And so you came to see me because you think I can help you? Or, because Linc told you to?" It's a mild reprimand laced with a white smile.

"Both." I flash him a winner-take-all, star smile and shake my head at him. "He's worried about me. He doesn't remember everything about me like before, and we've been fighting. Not fighting, really. There have been differences between us. In us. For a lot of reasons you know already." I sigh. "Linc thought if I talked to you about it, maybe you could…" My voice drifts off because the semblance of this meeting being a good idea begins to wane.

"Help you."

"Help me?" I don't hide my contempt for the word help. "No. Of course not. I wouldn't presume to get that far, to think that I could ever be helped, or forgiven for the past, or let alone be allowed to forget what happened to Holly."

My laugh is somewhat harsh and decidedly inappropriate given the dark revelations I've been spewing. Yet, he just watches me in this veiled fascination.

I am the unexpected find on a slide under the lab researcher's microscope which holds such promise in discovery. I can feel the fascination come off of him in waves. Fascinated waves. I am a bona fide living enigma of crazy. I try again.

"It was my fault. I was driving. I've had to accept that. Live with that. I guess all I want…all I really want…I just… I just want to be normal. I want to be a good wife to Linc and a good mom to Cara and —"

"You want to be a good wife. A good mom. Those are roles we play. Let's start with the person beneath that veneer of being good. What do you want? What does Tally want?"

I stare long and hard at the psychiatrist. Dr. Bradley Stevenson is an acquaintance. I'm trading on his relationship as Kimberley Powers' husband and as Linc's former psychiatrist and current friend—for his secrecy, for accommodation in his seeing me so quickly—even though he and Kimberley are only supposed to be in San Fran for a few more days and this is not a formal psychiatric undertaking. I'll have to fly out to New York if I continue along this path in talking to him, eliciting his confidence—and perhaps even taking his advice. I'll have to pay him more than four hundred dollars an hour to do so because Dr. Bradley Stevenson is that good. He helped Linc so I'm hoping he can help me if only a little. That is, if I continue to give in to this irresistible urge to talk about my many demons, as if I really want to be saved.

Be a good wife.
Be a good mom.
Be Tally.

I want those things, don't I?

I do; don't I?

I try again. "Really, I just want to…be able to breathe again."

"Breathe," he echoes the word back to me as if I'm being knighted. "And why wouldn't you be able to breathe, Tally?"

It's an innocent enough question. My heart stutters at his sudden intensity.

He sits directly across from me in the opposite chair and openly studies me now.

Now what? This visit was supposed to be cursory—a one-time thing, a simple way to placate Linc—and yet, it has just gotten very real. Brad watches me even closer now as I begin to unravel by essentially giving a voice, breath, and life to my darkest fears. I'm emotionally exposed. I go for defense.

"Don't." I shake my finger at him in a now frantic attempt to appear outwardly in control and all powerful while my long-held fears attempt to work their way out of me for him to plainly see. Then, I smile wide for added effect. "Don't."

"Why are you *really* here, Tally?"

Not fooled.

Five minutes tick. Dr. Bradley Stevenson watches me closely the entire time. Finally, I take a deep breath while my body involuntarily shudders. I clasp my hands together in an effort to try and make it stop. "It was an extraordinary day. It was one of those middling days of late summer where the temperature rose high enough for early September and made good on its promise to all of San Francisco that warm weather was here to stay for a little while linger. A promise to remain.

"My 23rd birthday was in early August, over a month before, but we'd been out of town traveling on the road with Linc for most of August. She'd forgotten one of my birthday presents and brought it over that weekend. We talked of ordinary things. Mostly. She and I. She'd marked almost a year of sobriety, and we drank Pelligrino Sparkling Water with slices of lemon to celebrate the significance. We kept vigilance over Cara as she played in the shallow end of the pool while we waited for Linc's return from an early-morning practice.

"We solidified ours plans for a late celebration with the family later in the week. I told her the actual day didn't matter, celebrating with her and the family was all I cared about. So, we made plans to get together later in the week when Linc didn't have a late game, on his only day off, that Thursday, when all of us could be there. After all, life was good. Everything was perfect. Even I could say that. We laughed when I said that. Still, she wanted to acknowledge my birthday, we'd been in New York the actual weekend of August 2nd. Yet, my mother insisted on making a big deal out of it even though it was more than a month past. She gave me my present saying she wouldn't delay any longer."

I swallow hard. "There was a part in the conversation when she sweetly touched my hand and told me how proud she was of me. How happy she was for me. With Linc and Cara and the baby coming. That life was just as it was meant to be even if Mikhail was giving me a hard time. I still hid my pregnancy from him. But overall, our life was good. My mother deemed it so. And I agreed. On that day."

It gets harder to breathe. I'm too hot, fanning my face in the next. My eyes sting. "There's that," I say softly in an attempt to find the words to stave off drowning in the grief. "She gave me a charm for the bracelet Linc had given me so long ago—a ruby heart with a diamond teardrop." I sigh again. "'It's too much,'" I'd said. And she said, "'No. You love with your whole heart, Tally. You deserve so much more. Just know I'm so proud of you.'"

I take another long sorry breath and attempt to swallow, but my throat starts to close up and at the exact same time my eyes fill with unshed tears. Brimming over, threatening to spill down my face.

There is too much sadness. Too much grief. These things plague me all the time now.

"Go on," Brad says gently.

I try to take in air, searching for air, always searching for air these days. And the will to continue.

"My dad called around six. Linc and I were just heading out for dinner with just the two of us because he was home, and Andy agreed to watch Cara for us, and it was just so rare to have a normal date, and I wanted that and so did he." I hold my breath for a few seconds.

"Dad said the guy veered into her lane and hit her head-on. Apparently, he started drinking early and didn't stop. The paramedics on the scene said she died instantly. They said it was a blessing that she died. *A blessing.* It doesn't feel like a blessing."

I look up at the ceiling and study a cobweb that's been missed by the cleaning service. "They found a half empty bottle of Jack Daniel's behind the driver's seat of his truck. Almost a year of sobriety so she could be killed instantly, head-on, by another drunk. It doesn't get more ironic than that, now, does it?"

"No. It's tragic."

"Tragic." I smile inappropriately at Dr. Brad Stevenson. "Explain that to me."

"It can't be explained."

"That's right; it can't. Do you know you're the only one with that honest answer? Most of her *friends.*" I quote the air with my fingers at the word. "Most of her friends stay with the mantra that it was God's will and say little prayers as if that helps. They take solace from their beliefs and, in the next, deliver overcooked casseroles vying for my suddenly eligible father's attention."

"It might help them whatever their motives might be." Brad gets this wry little smile. "What do you think is going to help you?"

"Nobody can help me."

"Linc thought I might be able to help you."

"I know what Linc thought. Thinks. Feels. I don't…need anyone's help," I say with a defiant lift of my chin. "I'm fine." I look at him intently and go for the light-bulb smile. The one that conveys I'm fine; I'll survive this. Brad looks startled by its brightness.

Then, my own words betray me. "Linc has a game tomorrow night. He's pitching. In the World Series. This is his moment. He wants me to be fine. He needs me to be fine. He wants me to be there in the stands with my brother and my father and pretend everything is fine. He wants all of us to be fine. He wants me to be fine. Believe me, he's just as disappointed as I am that he can't fix any of this. That he can't fix *me.*"

I sweep my arm through the air while the psychiatrist scrutinizes me even more.

"What else?" he asks quietly. "Tell me. There's more. Tell me all of it."

I look him straight in the eye. "I have some doubts. A few." I incline my head.

"About?" he prompts with such ease.

"About Linc and me. He's different, not the same. Before…" I take a shaky breath. "Before my mother died, I felt…I *believed* that everything was finally going to be okay. Now? I don't believe in anything. Not this." I stroke my barely bulging stomach. "Not anything, really. Haven't you heard? Bad things happen in threes, so I'm just waiting so I can prepare myself. I don't know what it is, but it's coming for me. I can feel it. From a long way off. And I can't talk to my husband about it because he has his own stuff to deal with. The Giants are in the World Series. I don't want to worry him about me or get him off of his game anymore than he already is. He's already struggling. We all are. We're searching for normalcy where none can be found. Linc has enough to bear, and I can't burden him right now with all these fears that refuse to let me go. Not right now. He can't handle my brand of crazy."

"You're not crazy, Tally. You're grieving, having experienced a tremendous loss. I'm so sorry about your mom. You need to tell Linc what all you're afraid of. To be fair. It will help him understand why you've been so—"

"Difficult?"

"I was going to say distant and—"

"An outright bitch to him? Maybe." My throat constricts on this harsh laugh. "Everything has fallen apart and he can't fix it. Neither of us is coping too well with that fact. He loved my mom. I think losing her brings it all back for him, about losing his own mom. Right now, I can't even look at him because the transference of his pain to me is more than I can handle. We're not good for each other, not right now."

"Is that what you believe? Really? So even if I tell you the one and only thing you can count on is each other, you wouldn't believe me, would you?"

"No," I say gently, attempting to let the psychiatrist down easy. "I want to. I really want to believe that love is all I need, Linc too, but I don't. Not right now."

"I'm so sorry for your loss, Tally."

"I know. Everybody is. Everyone is so sorry." I go with another winning smile. He looks disconcerted by it. "And that helps," I add softly just to placate him so I can escape this room and his intense scrutiny. Talking to Dr. Bradley Stevenson has become a very bad idea and I have no intention of telling him anymore. "Thank you. It's just these bad things come in threes for me. So, what's next, Brad? Tell me what's next so I can prepare myself and possibly survive."

"That's just a superstition. You don't really believe that, do you?

"I wish I didn't."

"Tally." The famed psychiatrist takes my hands in his and squeezes them, reminding me of my mother and my birthday and what feels like a whole other lifetime now and so very far away from today. "You *will* survive this. You and Linc. You need to tell him more about how you feel, so he better understands where you're coming from right now. He shares your grief over the loss of your mother. You need Linc, and he needs you. That's how love works in good times and bad."

"Is it?"

CHAPTER SIXTEEN

I'm a ruin

TALLY

He wants answers.
I'm not wired to give them.
~ Talia Landon Presley

October 24th

BRADLEY STEVENSON STEEPLES HIS HANDS TOGETHER across the bridge of his nose as if in deep thought. We've slipped past the first hour of talking into the second. I text Marla and tell her I'm running late and she texts back telling me she's fine to wait. I steel myself to keep the secret but it haunts me and I know the intrinsic fear in accidentally revealing it shows on my face whenever Bradley Stevenson looks at me for too long. My world is about to be obliterated by my own hand. I have no choice. No choice at all.

"There's more. What else?" Brad lifts his head and watches me closely.

I nod slowly acknowledging already what he may have just guessed and decide I may as well come clean with some of it. "I keep having these nightmares. About Cara. About losing her again. I gave her up when she was first born. For a variety of reasons. One of which was I was eighteen. I had a demanding dance career. Linc and I weren't together. I didn't think I'd be a good mother. Then some three years later, Allaire Tremblay—the woman who adopted her, my former mentor—dies. Cara's brought back to me. And sometimes…I just wonder because I still don't know what I'm doing—"

"But, you're a great mother."

"Sometimes." I nod every so slightly and then look down at the plush beige carpet and trace the pattern with my shoe.

"Everyone has doubts."

There's that gentle seduction again. He's good. He's really really good.

"But *why* are you really here?" He seems to hold his breath as he stares at me. *Hard.*

He wants answers.

I'm not wired to give them.

I shake my head again and return his intense stare. "I promised Linc I'd see someone. I don't know if it's with being pregnant again." I shrug for effect. "I suspect so. I just…I have this recurring nightmare about losing Cara. All the time." I take in air and start over, but the words still escape in a rush. "A few days ago, we were at the park by the new house in Sea Cliff. Linc's house. I had a panic attack. I don't know for how long I was out of it. When I came to, I couldn't find Cara on the playground for a few minutes. *I lost her.* I freaked out. I've had panic attacks before when I first met Linc, and before that even when Holly died, but never like that one in the park a few days ago. It took a while to come back from it. Like more than twenty minutes and that whole time, I didn't know where Cara was. *I lost her.* I'm her *mother.* I'm not supposed to do that. *Lose her.* Let her go. Like *ever.*"

"A panic attack is a symptom for something else. What's really bothering you?"

The math is all wrong.

Say it. Say it out loud.

Tell someone.

Instead, I convince myself that silence is fine.

I convince myself for five minutes that silence is fine.

"What does Linc say?" Brad finally asks.

"He doesn't know…about me losing Cara, about that particular attack and the ramifications of it…he doesn't know about all of them."

"What's really going on, Tally? Tell me." Brad reaches for my trembling hands. Like his tone, his grip is warm, comforting.

Don't slip up. Don't tell him.

"I don't know." I give the easy answer everyone uses. I let him hold my hand. I give in to his unspoken empathy and ignore the fear of being seen as weak for a few precious seconds.

"Sometimes, our fears manifest in this way. But these panic attacks. Have you been treated at all for these?"

I smile, despite myself, in recognizing he's taken a different approach. "No." My throats constricts and that single word comes out a raspy whisper. I feign another weird smile and let go of his hand. "I usually have them under better control. Linc helps. Usually. Sam before that." I wince at mentioning Sam to him.

Brad looks at me quizzically while I shake my head. "Sam?"

"Sam Wilde. He's my…" I stumble over the word. How do I explain Sam? How do I explain Sam when I haven't told anyone just all what we did or meant to each other? I wince at Brad's confused face. "Sam used to help me with the panic attacks. Talk me down. Get me to breathe. We're not…together anymore." I frown at stumbling over the word *together*. "Since I married Linc."

Brad tries to smile with a hint of understanding, but it doesn't quite work. I can sense his doubt about what I am telling him about Sam—his growing doubts about me and what all I am telling him as much as what I am not saying.

What's true?

What's not true?

Doubts. I have them. I must be transferring some of my own to him now.

Because the math is all wrong.

And the lies will catch up to me. They already have.

"Okay. Go on. We'll get to Sam."

Brad smiles with reassurance. I don't return it.

I am not reassured.

"These attacks are different," I say slowly, trying to regain the upper hand. "Like I said, I've had more trouble getting them under control and there has been more and more of them. Almost daily. And I made a promise to Linc to get checked out because I've been feeling sad about my mom, and I thought I could tell you about the panic attacks to see if you could help me stop them. Maybe. Somehow."

"I leave in a few days, Tally." Brad sighs and then runs his hand through his blond hair in notable frustration. "This isn't an easy fix."

"I know. I just thought maybe you could give me some pointers. Maybe, you could tell me the reasons why I am having this kind of reaction."

"You're scared. You have issues with your past. For starters, decisions you made then that you are not proud of now." He's quiet. *Introspective. Conciliatory.* "And you obviously have triggers."

I wince at his use of the word *triggers*. "You sound just like Sam." I don't intend to sound wistful, but I do.

Now, Brad looks at me even more intently. "*Now*, do you want to talk about Sam?"

"No. That's over. I married Linc. We both understand that."

"So it's complicated." I nod and so does Brad. "This isn't something that just handing you a prescription can can solve, Tally, and being pregnant makes that even more complicated. You really need to talk to someone about this."

"Yes. And, I am." I gaze at him boldly, daring him to deny my request for help. Just a little help. A little understanding. Just *something*.

"Tally, I live in Manhattan—three thousand miles away and—"

"You worked with Linc. You overcame the distance with Linc."

"I did, but I shouldn't even be talking to you. I'm doing this as a friend, as a favor to my incredible wife and to Linc because he asked me to, those two think I can help everyone. It's—"

"Complicated," I say while he nods. "I'm asking too much of you. I get it. Okay." I get up to leave. "I'm sorry. I didn't mean to impose on our social, somewhat familial connections. You helped Linc. You can't in good conscience help me. I get it."

"That's not what I meant. Stay, Tally. Sit down."

I let go of the hotel door knob and turn back to him even as my lungs begin to wheeze. *Not here. Not now. Not in front of the great Dr. Bradley Stevenson.*

"Just breathe, Tally. Just talk to me. Let me see where this goes. Let's start with giving up Cara. Let's start there. You were eighteen years old. You gave up your baby to a loving and reliable person with—"

"Allaire Tremblay was a good mom as far as I could tell. I just saw her with Cara the one time after, but I don't know if I would go so far as to call her *loving*." Just the thought of Allaire with Cara has me shaking. I fold my hands together in an attempt to hide their trembling and gain some semblance of control while Brad continues to watch me. "Cara will say something every once in a while that catches me off guard, even now, almost a year and a half later—"

"Like what? What does Cara say?"

"I was giving her a bath one night and she said, 'I really want you to stay, Mommy. You won't leave me, will you?'" I shake my head in an attempt to dispel the memory of how my breath had caught and my hands stilled in the bath water at those all telling words.

"I remember trying to think of the right thing to say. I so wanted to tell her something true. I didn't want to lie to her, but I didn't want to scare her either. Finally, I told her I'd never leave her, and that I would always stay. I don't know what all she remembers about being with Allaire, but I try to assure her that everything is okay. Imagine me, assuring someone everything is going to be okay. Talk about ironic. And how does that work when I tell her I'll always be here when we just buried my mom six weeks ago? How does that work? It doesn't. It's not true. I don't know anymore. Life is not a guarantee. *Nothing* is a guarantee."

I shake my head side-to-side and then look over at him. "The truth is I don't know what to say to her when she talks about Allaire like that. I haven't told her anything about what I did. I haven't told her the truth about any of it. She's four years old. I just want her to be happy and feel loved and I have to hope that she is and does, but I don't know what the truth about giving her up will do to her if she ever finds out. And I don't understand all that happened to her with Allaire, how they lived, what all Cara saw in that car accident. It took hours for them to find her. That's what they said. Cara didn't talk for months after. Until Linc came back into our lives. And then he was gone again because of the line drive accident. He didn't remember us. Things were a mess for all of us for a long while. But then, she started talking again when he came back to us and she loves him so much."

Brad grabs my hands again to still the trembling that's started up all over again. His hands warm mine.

"She loves you too, Tally. I've seen it. The thing is you might have to tell Cara one day—when she's older—about what happened to her when she was a baby. You might have to tell her how people make choices. Decisions. But I don't think you need to do that right now. Like you said, Cara just needs your love and support. Show her that you and Linc are permanent fixtures in her life and that the two of you are not going anywhere. She needs the stability, the nurturing, and the love given to her by her two devoted parents. From what I've seen in the past week, she has all of that with both of you and so much more."

"Right." I get up and start moving about the room intently touching the fine fixtures and the swanky prints that adorn the W Hotel walls busying myself with the artwork in order to stave off the panic that has already ignited deep inside.

"Linc and I want the same things for her." Brad leans in further just to be able hear me. "A stable home life. A *home*. I know she's feeling a little out of sorts since we moved to the big house. That's what we call it—the big house." I force a smile Brad's way but he doesn't look convinced by it. "She and I lived at Tremblay's place in Alamo Square. It's all she's known. That's where she and Tremblay lived before." The brittle smile slides from my face. "I just want her to be okay, you know?"

"I think Cara is going to be fine. I think she *is* fine. It's you I'm worried about. You need to understand that you can't change the past. You can't fix it. It's over and done. All you can do is move forward—the three of you, soon the four of you—together. That's all you can do. It's all you have control over."

I take a deep breath finally deciding to wade into at least one of the reasons as to why I'm actually here.

"Do you think it's possible to be so afraid of being happy that you actually sabotage your own happiness? You go out of your way to fuck everything up because you cannot deal with the idea of being so happy knowing what it feels like on the other side?"

"The other side?"

"The loss of everything…on the other side. I've seen that side. I've *lived* it."

"Sometimes," he says after a long silence.

"What do you tell crazy people like that to do?"

"You're not crazy, Tally. A lot of people have anxiety and sometimes it can be over getting everything they want. I think people like that—especially those who have experienced profound loss in their lives—are extremely vulnerable to feeling this way. They really just can't afford to lose it all again."

"Can't afford to lose. That's it; isn't it? I can't afford to lose it all again. That's my problem. Probably my biggest fear."

He looks at me intently while I attempt to get the haunted feeling that must be all over my face under better control. He is entirely too close to witnessing the complete unveiling of the worst part of me.

"Look, I think you're under a great deal of pressure. You don't have an easy career to navigate either. How's that going by the way?"

"Not a good topic or a very subtle change-up there, Brad." I try to laugh but then I wince as a fresh round of panic roars up from deep inside. I have trouble getting air. "Didn't Kimberley tell you?" He shakes his head no. "Mikhail fired me. A little over five weeks ago. Right after my mom died. He let me go. We haven't made a public statement yet. We're working with Linc's contract attorney to see if there's any recourse. My director was…less than enthusiastic about all of this. Somehow, he found out before I officially told him I was pregnant. It happens. Just not to me." I gesture towards my protruding stomach. I finally look pregnant but the math is still all wrong and it's getting harder to keep the truth from Linc.

Now, Brad studies me intently. Somehow, I can tell he's begun to make the connection to this baby.

This baby and me.

And the math.

And as to why I am really here because you have to tell someone.

Someone has to know the lies and understand the truth.
This baby will destroy everything. That I now know.

Instead, I manage to say on topic. "I was going to let him down about the fall line-up. He was not happy with me. *At all.* It's San Francisco Ballet Company's busiest time of year. Most lucrative. I was to be the big draw. So he fired me and hired someone else to take my place." I cross my arms in an attempt to keep it all together before I lose it completely and tell him everything. "And, I'm in a precarious position and like I said we've been in contact with a lawyer to see how steadfast the terms of my contract are, but apparently, I didn't negotiate that great of a deal. I was solely focused on getting to San Franc and leaving all of New York behind me. My previous boss, Sasha Bennett would have been completely understanding. But now she's in Moscow heading up the Bolshoi Ballet Company. So it's ends up; it's a pretty standard contract. There were a number of loopholes that Mikhail exploited. He found them all. So I don't have a job to go back to next spring."

A single tear trails down my cheek before I can stop it.

"What will you do?"

I contrive a smile. "There's always Moscow, I suppose. Sasha's there. My former director?" He nods and I'm grateful I don't have to go into great detail about Sasha or Moscow. "She'd hire me in a nanosecond. I burned quite a few bridges in New York to come here."

Brad doesn't quite know what to do with that answer. "I see."
He doesn't see. At all.

And suddenly, I'm agitated that he doesn't see. That Linc doesn't see either.

"I'm out of a job. Unless I dance in the corps. A little hard to do after you've been the star on your way to being named a principal ballerina. Thirteen years to get to this point in my career—swiftly lost—because I messed up with birth control *again.*"

"I'm sorry. That must be hard on you."

"You have no idea." I look straight at him. "Linc doesn't either." I lift my head in defiance. My eyes must glitter with unshed tears and this unforeseen anger takes over. "Sam knows. There's the difference. Right there. In pretty much everything about the two of them."

There is a long protracted silence.

Brad has that look of dismay as if he's gotten a lot more than he bargained for in this conversation and is now unhappy with his prized find.

The experiment under the microscope has taken an ugly turn.

We do not like what we see.

That's right.

We don't.

"Do you want to talk about Sam?"

"No."

The good doctor goes for diplomacy. "You have a lot of stress factors going on in your life, both personally and professionally. My advice for you right now would be to give yourself a bit of a break. Take the fall and winter off. Enjoy this time with Cara and Linc. Put all of your efforts into forming a strong family unit. Get used to all of you being together under one roof. Then, when the baby comes, you'll be ready for all the new stuff and then you can decide what's next with your career. You don't have to have all the answers right now, Tally. And you can change your mind down the road. Everyone does. Right now, it seems Linc and Cara need you more than ever—"

"I'm not sure about that."

"Yes, you are. The thing is you've experienced a great deal of loss for someone so young, including the latest blow with your dance career, but you've survived all the heartbreak and adversity. You'll survive this. You're actually in a good place. You have Linc. You have Cara. You have this baby. Those are the things that count the most. Embrace it. Trust it. I think if you do that, the anxiety over losing again, other than the job, will go away. Trust your life, Tally. Trust your path. Trust being happy."

"Trust being happy with my life?" I shake my head. "Those things have never been said together in the same sentence when it's related to me." I force myself to smile at him.

He's not going to be able to help me.

He doesn't see it—the terror threatening to obliterate me.

"Maybe not. But that's my advice. Here's my card. I want you to call me in the next few days or, at the very least, the first part of next week. We'll work something out, whether that's meeting in person again in New York before you can't travel, or we'll just talk by phone. You're really okay, Tally. You just need to start believing that."

The terror takes control. My frozen smile is in place, and it's big enough and real enough that he really believes that I'm okay. Some salvageable part of me goes in for a hug, providing him with the full-force stage performance of a ballet star.

I am still thanking him profusely just as Kimberley walks in and pronounces, "All is right with the world because the Giants are in the World Series, and Brad can fix anything and all of us."

They both laugh.

My lips part enough with some kind of capricious smile; and yet, I can't even really breathe.

I hide it well and long enough that I manage to transport myself all the way out of their hotel suite and into the hotel's swanky elevator before I collapse against the mirrored walls and slowly slide down to the carpeted floor.

Luckily, I'm alone.

I stare intently at the girl in the mirror who looks back at me.

"The math is all wrong; isn't it?"

The girl in the mirror nods. "Why can't you tell them something true?" She shakes her head side-to-side and presses her lips together because there's nothing more to say because none of it is true, and she already knows this.

"Life isn't perfect." The words echo around the mirrored prison and reverberate back to me.

"No kidding," I whisper to the hallowed-out girl in the mirror.

The girl in the mirror begins to cry, feeling so far from normal, it hurts to even breathe.

CHAPTER SEVENTEEN

hurricane

TALLY

The need for absolution on some level must be met.
~ Talia Landon Presley

October 24th

I FINALLY ESCAPED BRAD'S HEIGHTENED SCRUTINY OF my state of mind but only after I promised to meet with him again just before they fly out for the Giants' series of games in Kansas if those become necessary. Linc's pitching in the World Series tomorrow, Brad reminded me with a little smile.

But tomorrow is too long to wait.

Things will be settled long before then.

Obliterated. My life.

Long before then.

Marla waits in her white Escalade for me. She drums her long, beautiful fingers against the steering wheel. You wouldn't think you can describe a best friend's fingers as beautiful, but it is like everything else about Marla; she is all of that. And, I am her bizarre and tragic best friend, who secretly hates her, but loves her just as much for being all of that.

It's been a little over two hours that she's been waiting for me. Of course, it's her own fault for being so damn sweet and benevolent, not trusting me enough to go on my own, not trusting me enough to go at all.

Marla knows me well. She always has. For a very long time.

"How did it go?" Marla asks launching right into the inquisition.

"*Fine.*"

I have look away from her because Marla is capable of guessing far too much about me with just the one laser-like gaze she's flashed my way. Instead, I intently study the landscape by squinting at the car window's glass and pretending to care about green foliage and rhododendrons that grace the curbside walk. The truth is I'm weak and barely functioning. After the better part of two hours with Brad, much of my defenses have been broken down. I shared far too much with the psychiatrist, and I'm about to do more of the same with my best friend. I can feel that coming on.

The need for absolution on some level must be met.

"I'm all cured. I will never cry again. Among other things…" My voice drifts off when I glance over and spy her wizened look.

"I doubt even the famous Dr. Bradley Stephenson could promise that." Marla shakes her head side-to-side with mild disapproval and proceeds to start the car and contemplate our next move. "So, how did it *really* go? Truth time."

She frowns ever so slightly as she seemingly studies the oncoming traffic and begins to nose the car into it while I grip the passenger door handle and attempt to look at ease, although I am far from it. *Me. Cars. SUVs. Car accidents. We go way back.* I thought I conquered most of these fears last spring, but lately they have managed to rear their ugly heads and worm their way directly back into the very front of my psyche. Marla guns the engine and whips the car onto the road when she spies an opening. I catch and hold my breath and with morbid desperation prepare for the sounds of screeching brakes and shattered glass.

Nothing happens. I take in a little air in and let it out and try to settle back further into the passenger seat. Eventually, I'm able to casually look around and verify we are safe and manage to avoid Marla's quizzical stare altogether.

"Truth time."

She's not going to give up today. I think she's even pretending not to notice I just had a silent freakout about the traffic because there are worse things, and we both know it. I am regressing, and my best friend knows that, too. That's why she insisted on driving me here today to meet with Brad. She's getting worried about me, maybe, even desperate. She and Linc have been talking. That much is true. *Talk to Brad.* They both said *talk to Brad.*

And so I have.

The thing is I know that Marla is a little bit afraid for me now. I can sense it.

I'm a little afraid for me, too. The end is near. So near.

Kimberley and Brad are in San Fran for the next week as part of the presser events that come along with Kimberley's job of having a famous baseball player for a client whose team has made it to the World Series. I know Kimberley's worried in the sense that I've become a distraction for Linc and the team, or am about to be. Somehow, her sixth sense is telling her this.

I take solace in knowing that only Sam knows about my little math problem and Sam's in Afghanistan now. We said good-bye. Our final good-bye. And nothing and no one can change that now. I mourn the loss of him like all the others.

I covertly study Marla in an attempt to determine her trustworthiness. These days, everything I tell Marla goes straight to Charlie, which leads directly back to Linc. It's a problem of epic proportions because there are times when all you want to do is share your darkest thoughts or confess your darkest deeds.

And yet? You can't tell anyone. Like now.

So no one is more surprised than me at her next question.

"When did you *know*, exactly?"

"Know what?" I force myself to laugh but it comes out sounding like a clown being strangled.

Marla snarls in my general direction and looks completely put out. "Don't *lie* to me, Tally. Save it for everyone else, but don't you *fucking dare* lie to me."

Her sudden intensity lights me up. The rage I've held in check for weeks spills over. Granted, I should be most angry with the man who killed my mother and seemingly proved to be the catalyst that darkened my life once again just when I was beginning to believe it could possibly be light again maybe be light into forever. Yes, my anger is most definitely directed at the wrong person. Still, I form the words and say them before I have a chance to think them through. "What's it like watching from the cheap seats, Marla, continuously watching my life get blown up? Am I as entertaining as I appear to be from the outside with you looking in?"

"You are *not* the only one with problems, Tally. Even so, I'm going to let that somewhat awful remark pass because I know you're distraught and what I just asked you about hits entirely too close to home, as it were. The truth. Your version of it anyway. So when did you figure it out and did you tell him? Are you going back to him?"

The color drains from my face. Passing out appears imminent. I feel the train whooshing through me and the descending blackout that invariably follows. *How does she know?*

"No." I shakily breathe the words out.

"No," she parrots back to me, incredulous now. "He's so loyal; he's practically blinded by you. He'd do any for you. They both would."

She pauses for a few seconds and tilts her head to one side. We're stopped in traffic but I stare straight ahead, hoping for a reprieve that I already know isn't coming. Still, I hold my breath and begin to pray she hasn't guessed correctly.

"Sam," she says with such deadly accuracy that I feel annihilated all at once. "You think it's Sam's baby; don't you?"

I don't say anything. The silence becomes deafening while the truth hangs between us like a medieval guillotine blade swinging back and forth intent on severing both our heads and ties forever.

"You need to end it," she says.

"There's *nothing* to end." I clasp my hands together in my lap to keep them from visibly shaking because Marla has intentionally strayed entirely too close to the truth. "We. We said goodbye. He's… gone. He left for Afghanistan. Linc doesn't know about the baby possibly being Sam's."

"So how long have you known?" she asks. I start to answer but she cuts me off. "Don't *lie* to me. And quit lying to yourself."

"How do *you* know?" I stall because I'm not ready to answer her.

"The due date. It took a while but then it dawned on me to look it up. Based on the date, even the revised one, you could have gotten pregnant *after* Fresno and Linc wasn't here to do that deed," she says quietly. "I guess things got pretty hot and heavy with Thor."

"Something like that."

"You told him?"

"Yes, I told Sam it might be his baby based on the math."

She nods. "What did Sam say when you saw him and told him?"

"He wanted me back. I told him I loved him, but it was different than the way I loved Linc and that wasn't going to change. He didn't take it very well. We said our final good-byes, and now he's in Afghanistan for six months so it doesn't really matter. He said he'd do right by the baby if it was his, but he didn't want to see me anymore. Dr. Eldon had me see a specialist, but that didn't really change the outcome. I'm pregnant, and it might not be Linc's baby as much as I want it to be. Sam and I were together, obviously. It was good for a while. I was so pissed off at Linc after Fresno, and Sam was there. Sam was easy. He just wasn't…"

"What? He just wasn't what?" Marla asks in exasperation. Her reaction is a little surprising.

"He isn't Linc. He could never be Linc. I tried not to compare them, but I still did."

"So you broke Sam's heart all over again."

"Yes. I said goodbye to Sam. A final goodbye. I can't mess up anyone else's life anymore than I've messed up my own."

"When was this?" Marla asks glancing at me sideways.

"The day Mikhail fired me. The lunch meeting was at *The Promissory Note*. Sam was there after Mikhail fired me."

"Did you sleep with him? Because that's what you would do. You'd be desperate. You'd be lost. You'd need sex to cope with all that was going on. So *did* you?"

"What is with you?"

"*Did* you?"

"No! Some sane part of me wanted to try to salvage things with Linc. I told Sam I was pregnant, and it might be his child, but then I ripped his heart out again when I told him I was choosing Linc no matter what. *Happy* now?"

"You really don't get it, do you? You destroy everything and everyone you care about. You always do. You sabotage your own happiness. Why? Why? Tell me why. Tell somebody why. You just spent two hours with one of the best shrinks in the country, and I bet you didn't even get to this part. The *omission*. The genetic makeup of this baby that is tearing you and Linc apart. For what? So you can be lonely—spend your life alone—because it's easier than allowing either of these two men to love you. God, you are so fucked up! I'm amazed you managed to hide it all from Brad Stephenson."

"The light's green."

"*Screw* the green light! We'll wait for the next one."

And she does. She just sits there in her humongous SUV while car horns go off all around us. We sit through the next red light, too, and she finally guns the engine when it turns green for a third time. All the while, she stares at me. Her eyes glint with anger. She's furious more than I've ever seen her.

"What is wrong with you? Why are you looking at me like that?"

"Nothing," she says irritably. "I know you think if you don't tell Linc that the curious math with this baby's due date may just miraculously go away. Or, you'll miscarry." Her eyes narrow. "You're planning for it, right? So you can stage a funeral and greet grief and loss like an old friend. But what happens if things actually work out? What then? Oh, I know! You'll fuck some guy or maybe plan for an abortion or—"

"It's too late for that."

"You thought about it?" she asks incredulous.

"I'm going to lose everything. Yes, I thought about it, more than once, but I couldn't do it."

"Well, there's that. Give the girl her gold star. So, what are you going to do? Annihilate the whole thing with Linc, right?"

I don't say anything. I can't even look at her now.

"Aw yes. The nuclear option. The old Tally Landon standby," she says. "Well, wake the fuck up, Tally. You *did* this. Now, *own* it. Because it doesn't matter how hard you try to end the world; it doesn't *end*. There are worse things that can happen beyond your heart getting broken. Much worse. People die, but we love them until they do. We love them even when they die. We visit their graves. We try to find peace. We make our way in the world, and we survive. That's what we do. So stop trying to fuck up on purpose. Go get some help for that devious mind of yours. Stop fucking other men or even thinking about it. Why don't you try staying with and loving the one guy who still loves you back regardless of how fucked up you really are? Just stop it, Tally. You've got to stop this. Get off the merry-go-round and quit telling lies. You have to."

"I hate you so much right now." I'm wringing my hands I'm so upset by what she's said.

Her eyes narrow in on me. "Yeah, well, the feeling is mutual, my friend. I have grown tired of holding your hand and helping you clean up all of these messes because I've finally come to realize that so many of them are of your own making."

"I'm not asking you to clean up my messes anymore."

"Yeah, well, I'm a sucker for tragic heroines, and I'm still your best friend, and you tend to make sure that I'm all you've got whether we like it or not. Come on. It looks like we have a lot of stuff to talk through."

With a heavy sigh, Marla pulls off at the next exit. She cruises right on in to the parking lot of some dive of a diner and hastily puts the SUV into park.

Then she turns toward me. "I'm not taking you back home until you come clean with me about all of it. *All of it.* You don't get to hold anything back. Not one thing. You're going to talk it through with me, and we're going to figure this all out. You'll talk to me, and you'll tell me everything because there is no going back." She sweeps her hand through the air for emphasis.

"You already know everything I know," I say quietly. She glares at me. "You *do.*"

"Well you're going to tell me the entire story all over again just to make sure you haven't left anything out. Just in case, there's some bizarre little lie you've forgotten that can still come back to haunt you and fuck everything up all over again even if we fix this one. And then, we'll go from there."

She glares at me. She's still furious. It doesn't take any special powers to figure that out.

"Where exactly are we going to go?"

"Doesn't matter. Somewhere. This diner here." She waves a hand toward the dive in front of us. "We'll figure it out. And, you're going to tell me everything or you won't get to tell Linc any of it because *I* will tell Linc all of it. And let's face it; your life story is far from a fairytale as we both know."

With a dismissive wave of her hand, she slides down out of her side of the SUV with the grace of a dancer. I marvel at her a little because even at eight months pregnant, she's still agile as ever. With this inexplicable sense of relief, I follow her into the diner. There is something freeing about finally telling her all of what's going on, well, most of it. Plus, it will give us a chance to say a final goodbye.

It appears that telling her the truth has set me free in some way. I can feel it.

CHAPTER EIGHTEEN

time to pretend

LINC

*"Everything is done, but it's far from perfect.
It hasn't been perfect for some time."*
~ Lincoln Presley

October 24th

Tally is home. The dinner I cooked for her hours ago—still lingers all around as I stand here waiting for her. I angrily watch her sneak through the side door from the garage and make her way into our house. It's after eleven. Cara is still up. I've listened to her periodic giggles while she plays with her dolls in the downstairs playroom just off the kitchen and waits for her mom to come home just like I have been.

Everything is done, but it's far from perfect. It hasn't been perfect for some time. I'm pissed on a variety of levels. Tally's been checked out of our life for weeks. And tonight this sets me off.

When she innocently looks up at me, I can no longer contain the anger; I let if fly. "Where have you been, Tally? I called Brad and Kimberley. They said you left their hotel room *hours* ago. Where have you been?" She sighs in exasperation and already looks pissed off at the obvious interrogation that's spewing forth from my lips, but I'm unable to stop myself. "Where have you been?"

"I'm not sure. I took the bus home. I got on the wrong one. It took a while to find the right one." She pulls the gold headband from her hair and plaits it out and essentially ignores everything I've just said.

"Charlie called. He said you were with Marla. I know she drove you to the appointment with Brad. That's what Charlie said. Yet, you both have been missing for hours. *Hours,* Tally. Why?"

She doesn't answer. She just drifts away and takes her sweet-ass time shedding her winter coat and putting it away in the hall closet. I'm aware she's avoiding me. All in an attempt to forestall what is coming. I hate it when she gets like this. All distant from me. She shuts me out more than she lets me in. More and more these days. The honeymoon appears to be over. It's long gone.

"I didn't think to call you."

She steps back into the room and smiles ever so slightly but her lips tremble. She's nervous for some reason. She is pale and looks decidedly wrung out. Sympathy for her automatically starts to kick in. I push it down.

"I thought you knew I'd be late with Brad and Kimberley," she says. "Marla and I stopped at this diner for an early dinner. I made a mistake. I should have let you know we were running late."

She shrugs and seemingly makes an attempt to make light of the situation but I'm not buying it. "A lot of mistakes. You've made a lot of mistakes. Jesus, Tally, I called the police!"

Now she watches me in some kind of twisted fascination as I pick up the land-line phone and dial the San Francisco Police Department lead detective's cell number. "Detective Tolt? I found her. She…" I throw an angry glare my wife's way for good measure. "She just walked in the door. Apparently, the Metro was giving her a hard time. Yeah. Not sure why using a cell phone was so impossible all day. Anyway, thank you. She's been found." I end the call and whirl back to face her with my arms crossed and bestow her with this stony glare. For a second, my heart lurches at the sexy sight of her but my fury obliterates any of those salacious thoughts in the next. "You drive me crazy, you know that? *Crazy.* I'm out of my mind worrying about you, and yet you waltz in here like nothing is wrong. Where the hell have you been all day, Tally?"

She hastily pulls out a kitchen chair, slides down onto it, and attempts to hide her face in order to somehow avoid the direct onslaught of my anger.

"I don't know." She sounds like a child, all muffled, speaking from behind her hands. Eventually, she lifts her head up and glares at me. "I lost track of time. Marla dropped me off at the Metro downtown because Charlie insisted that she head home to Palo Alto. We were trying to save her some time, but I had to find the right bus. My cell phone went dead."

"Your cell phone went dead. This is what you say every fucking time. Every fucking time. Jesus, Tally. Do you care about us at all? You left home at ten o'clock this morning more than thirteen hours ago. I told you to take the car. You said you would. Yet, I find it still sitting in the driveway when I leave for practice."

"Marla drove me to the appointment with Brad. She waited for me." Tally's shaking now and she looks even more worn out since she first arrived, but I can't let it go.

"Andy had to stay late to cover for you tonight until I could get back from practice. It's the *World Series*, Tally. I can't exactly skip practice because my wife decides to go AWOL!" She looks away. "I started worrying around five. It's been hours. It was so late. And you're pregnant, and out only God knows where. So tell me what happened because you're not getting out of this. You'll tell me what happened to you, and why you're so late, when I know for a fact, you left Brad and Kimberley more than six hours ago. Tell me!"

"God, am I on a leash or something?" She pushes out of her chair and faces me with her hands firmly clenched at her sides. "I *told* you my cell went dead. That's why I didn't call you. And I took the wrong bus after Marla dropped me off at the station. I got lost. We went to Alamo Square and we had a drink and dinner at some diner. There's a lot going on that you don't know about and—"

"You had a drink when you can't drink. At *The Promissory Note*?"

She looks down at the floor and traces some invisible pattern with her shoe. "No. It was some diner. I didn't see Sam tonight."

"But you saw Sam at some point." My voice breaks. "When?"

I rented Tremblay's place out a several weeks ago to Sam. It was after we moved her and Cara into this house. I didn't tell Tally I'd leased the place to Sam. A one-year lease. To Sam. Why I was trying to make friends with him made no sense at all. Keep your enemies closer? I guess so.

"I saw Sam at *The Promissory Note* the day Mikhail fired me over a month ago." Her chin lifts in defiance. Her green eyes sparkle with fresh anger. "I was with Marla tonight. I drank club soda. So did she. It was a *drink*—a carbonated soda. I never see her anymore. We needed to talk. Me and Marla. That's all. I wasn't ready to come home yet."

Her mention of Sam cuts me to the core and the rest of her little speech barely registers. I step back from her as if she's somehow burned me from across the room with this admission alone.

"What else?" My face contorts at her mention of him.

Tally and Sam. I still hate the idea of them, however far in the past he might be to her. Months? Days? Weeks? Do I even fucking know?

"Nothing else. There's nothing more to say." It looks like there's a lot more to say. Her hands shake. She moves to hide them when she sees me watching her. "It's just like when *you* saw Nika, which that damn tabloid so sweetly captured. The two of you. Together. Like old times. But you kissed her. I saw the photo, Linc. It's in your office. She sent it to you. I saw it. Now, the world sees it, too. So who is the biggest liar in this room tonight, Linc? You? Or me?" She starts to wheeze and holds up her hand at me as I start to come towards her. "Don't answer that."

She sweeps out of the kitchen like she's performing her most famous role from *Romeo and Juliet*. My reaction time is slower so I don't follow her right away but I manage to meet up with her in the hallway just outside of my office. She pushes the clipped newspaper article into my chest.

I take it from her and dully scan the headline even though I already know what it says. Now, I can't even look at her. The guilt over the photograph with Nika comes full circle to haunt me. "I'm sorry. I should have told you."

"Doubts. Secrets. Lies. We all have them."

Her accusation cuts through both of us like a serrated knife. "Even the most famous one among us in this very hallway has them," she says softly.

The tabloids had a field day with the photograph that shows Nika leaning through my car window and kissing me. The angle seems to show me kissing her back.

Trouble In Paradise Already?

In the photo: Socialite Nika Vostrikova is seen in deep conversation with one of the Giants' starting pitchers, Lincoln Presley. It's not a complete surprise that these two would be together, since the couple was engaged to be married two years ago. However, this past May, Vostrikova became engaged to Rob Thorn, heir apparent to Thorn Enterprises, one of San Francisco's elite real estate investment firms. Lincoln Presley married Talia Landon, San Francisco Ballet Company's star ballerina in July during Major League Baseball's All-Star break, which Presley was clearly absent from, having recently been brought up from the Fresno Grizzlies after having recovered from a head injury due to a line drive the season before. Presley has been playing well and seems well on the mend, but who is he on the mend with? Landon just relinquished her starring role in SFB's Fall production of *Swan Lake* because the prima ballerina is expecting her and Presley's second child early next year. Yet, it would appear that Presley has someone else on his mind other than his wife.

Nika's handwritten note on the bottom of the article sinks me now.

Don't get me into trouble, Linc. –Nik

Damn. It looks bad.

"I'm sorry."

"How did they know I was *pregnant*, Linc? Nobody knew save my family and Marla. Well, Mom's dead so she couldn't possibly have said anything. Your dad? Who told the press I was pregnant?"

"Oh…geez. I told Nika a few months ago."

"You. Told. *Nika?*"

Tally is shaking she's so upset.

"It just…slipped out. I'm sorry."

"You're sorry. Do you know what this means? Nika is the one who told Mikhail. That's the only way that could have happened. He *fired* me. Does that even register with you? By telling your Russian whore I was pregnant; the two of you effectively killed my career. Do you realize this? Do you *get* it?"

"She's not my whore. She means nothing to me. I said I was sorry. Tally, I told you from the very beginning you needed to tell Mikhail. You needed to come clean with all of this."

"Come clean with all of this. Do you *hear* yourself? Do you *know* how it works in the dance world? I already risked my career *twice* for you. Once with our first encounter by quitting the New York City Ballet and now this baby—ill-timed as ever. There are no third chances for me, Linc. This is *it*. Where would I go, huh? In this town? San Francisco Ballet was *it* for me. The last stop. I guess there's Moscow. The Bolshoi Ballet Company with Sasha. I'm blacklisted here in the States. Mikhail has all but made sure of that."

"Kimberley can help you out. She has before."

"Don't bring up Kimberley as some kind of solution here, Linc. She's *not*. She can't solve my problems. She could have leveraged the shit out of things and made Mikhail believe I'm in demand, but my reputation precedes me these days. *I'm pregnant.* Nobody hires pregnant dancers."

"You don't even want this baby."

"You have *no idea* what you're talking about."

"Don't I? I don't see you rushing out to buy baby things or even bothering to tell anyone you're even pregnant. You don't eat. You were still dancing and would be if Mikhail hadn't found out when Eldon told you to stop at twelve weeks. Twelve weeks, Tally! Do you see your pattern? You don't want this baby. For all I know you were still doing the jumps when I *told* you stop doing them weeks ago." Her face gets flushed. "You were; weren't you? You did the jumps and jeopardized the life inside of you every time you did one. Why Tally? Why couldn't you just sit this season out and tell Mikhail you were pregnant months ago? Why did you insist on lying or at least omitting the truth? Why? What's so important that you're hiding?"

"Nothing!"

She shakes so badly that she begins to pace the floor back and forth just like the caged Bengal tiger at the zoo we saw last summer. It would be comical if the heat of our argument wasn't running so high threatening to spin out of control.

"I can't fix everything, Tally. Your mom died. Your career has been put in jeopardy."

She whirls around with her fists clenched. "My *career* is *over*. You and Nika made sure of that. And I don't expect you fix everything. Just one thing would be nice."

"Which thing would you like me to fix?" I ask in exasperation. "Pick one. I'll see what I can do."

"Forget it." She resumes her pacing.

"I'm sorry about telling Nika. I was excited about sharing our baby news. I momentarily forgot that we are supposed to lie and hold our best secrets to ourselves. I'm *sorry*. I just wanted to be normal for once. I didn't think that announcing the amazing news that you are pregnant would lead to ruining your fucking career. Maybe you should put this family first for once and not worry so much about your career. Have you ever thought of that? Maybe that's what fate is trying to tell you. Maybe you should learn from your mom's sudden death. Life is precious. It's short. You have to make the most of it. Take your one chance to believe in miracles."

She whirls around again. "Don't you *dare* bring my mother into this. And screw your philosophy, Romeo. Don't you dare turn this around on me. I need you, but you are *never* here. Never here. I'm lonely and still I wait for you, and hope things will get better. And yet, they keep getting worse. I'm weighed down with grief every fucking day. My mother died. And Mikhail fired me. And now, there are pictures of you everywhere kissing your ex-girlfriend. Why? Because Nika makes you feel good? Well, great. Well, okay then. You're sorry. Thanks a lot. Thank you so very much. At least, *your career* is still intact, Linc. Mine has been annihilated because you had to feel normal and tell someone—the woman who hates my guts the most, my mortal enemy—Nika Vostrikova. Well, thanks a lot. I hope it was good for you." Her eyes flash with anger. "I guess it's all good for you—the great and very famous Lincoln Presley of the San Francisco Giants—has it all while his wife holds onto absolutely *nothing*!"

"I'm sorry." She turns away from me ignoring my apology.

Instead, she calls out for Cara. At about the same moment, we both spy our kid standing in the doorway. Cara looks anxiously from one of us to the other. Tally gasps probably knowing our little girl has just heard every word we just said to each other, but she seems to quickly recovers. "Mommy's home," she says too brightly. "Time for bed, sweetie. Did you have a good day?"

She sweeps Cara up into her arms and starts up the stairs leaving me to stare after the two of them from the landing below.

"Tally, I'm sorry. I should have told you about Nika. It's not what it looks like. She kissed me. I...I didn't kiss her back." My words come out in a rush. I sound like a compulsive liar.

Tally whirls around with Cara in her arms from the top of the stairs. "Save it. You're *lying*. It takes one to know one," she says with a lift of her chin. "She kissed you and you kissed her back. Pictures tell a thousand words, and photographs don't lie the way people do. At the very least, it doesn't look like you tried very hard at all to resist her, Linc, and you didn't tell me about it. So, all I can do is guess that you didn't tell me because it meant something to you. Because if it didn't you would have told me. But you didn't. So it must have meant something. And then, you told her I was pregnant, and she called it into the press and probably told Mikhail as well. She's the only one who could have done that. She's the only one vicious enough to want to destroy my career with a few easy phone calls." She waves her arm dismissively at me. "Whatever. I don't want to talk about this anymore. Not tonight. Not with you."

"So when would you like to talk about all of this? I pitch tomorrow in the World Series, remember?"

She doesn't remember. The guilt at not remembering the most important game of my career shows up on her face. Then she just glares at me. In the next moment, Cara vies for her undivided attention by holding Tally's face between her little hands. "Mommy, will you read me a story?"

"Sure, baby. Mommy will read you a story."

All the doubts about us rush at me. I look up into my wife's accusing face and feel her indifference for me all the way from the top of the stairs. "Tally." My words are smothered in desolation as I look up at her. "We need to talk this through. Don't walk away from me."

She doesn't say anything. She just walks away from me.

CHAPTER NINETEEN

I'm not the only one

LINC

She is so far away from me.
She's slipping away from me now.
She's already gone.
  ~ Lincoln Presley

October 25th

IT'S TWO IN THE MORNING BEFORE I come to bed. Game four of the World Series is later today and I'm pitching.

Her breaths are shallow as I lean over and just stare at her amazing face. In sleep, her beauty is absolute. It takes my breath away. After a prolonged study of her features, she still doesn't open her eyes. She must really be asleep. Part of me is still angry at the way things are and the way she treated me earlier today by not calling. Her thoughtless behavior doesn't sit well with me. It seems to be happening more and more.

We're drifting away from each other existing in a parallel universe. It started with her mom's death and spun outward.

Then, there were the mind games that Mikhail Rostov played on her. The loss of her job with the San Francisco Ballet has put her further into a tailspin. She's been depressed for weeks about her mom and her career, which is why I finally insisted she talk to Brad.

Even so, I should have told her about the tabloid photos with Nika. *Why didn't I?*

I pull away from my uninhibited study of my sleeping wife and sigh deep. I need to concentrate on getting some sleep. Tomorrow I'm pitching the biggest game of my career. Everybody who cares about baseball will be watching. It's important. It's full count. I settle in on my side of the bed and solely focus on breathing steady in and out, nice and even.

I long for sleep. It doesn't come.

The truth is I long for forgiveness. For peace. For salvation. I need them all right now. I will be playing in the biggest game of my life tomorrow. I'm pitching and here I am worrying about my marriage and trying to undo the damage that one innocent kiss, her obnoxious boss, and her mother's untimely death—all three so causally related—have most assuredly ignited the palpable strife that grows exponentially between us.

Maybe, it's the pregnancy that has her edge. Maybe, it's marriage itself. This house. Cars. Accidents. Death. Trust. Love. Maybe it's Sam Wilde for all I know. The truth is I don't know. Tally's been out of sorts for weeks. Months, really. Since her mom died. *Before that?*

All I really know for certain is that I don't have all the answers, and Tally isn't trying hard enough to find them for either one of us. For me. For us.

The mattress dips when I shift and settle in closer to her. Yet, Tally remains ever still next to me.

The minutes continue to tick by, but I'm still awake and even more restless. I turn again and lie on my right side this time and take in the essence of her and just end up listening to her breathe.

My anger fades.

Remorse takes its place.

I stare out into the darkness and wonder how we have already gotten to this point. We fight more than ever. Things should be great, but they're not. Everything is fucked up, and I cannot figure out which event to blame the most for all of this. Tessa Landon's death? Tally getting fired? My lack of playing time? My never-ending travel schedule? The long baseball season? Which thing was it that caused us to lose the firm grip we had on happiness when we first said *I do* in the middle of July? How did we end up here contending this never-ending malaise that has taken such a complete hold of both of us?

Which thing was it?

What can I blame?

Who can I blame?

How do I undo all of this turmoil between us?

How do I fix us?

The illuminated red numbers project on our bedroom ceiling displaying the time as half past three in the morning. And I still can't sleep.

How did we get here?

How do I fix this?

Time stalls out. Remorse settles in on me further. I have to stop getting mad at her so often. Yes, she should have called, but did I have to take it out on her like that? Because what I'm secretly worried about, besides our marriage, is this trade. It's going to happen. Mad has just about got the MVP title all locked up. I need to pitch the game of my life tomorrow just to remain in contention of the starting lineup for next season or wherever I end up. I need to pitch. For somebody. Anybody. I can't keep hoping and waiting for things to change; I have to bring it to the mound. Like my teammate said once, *we do what we have to do to play this game. Wherever it takes us. We all do. We just do. We have to.*

Tally stirs next me. She slowly opens her eyes. "What happens if we were to get everything?" she whispers. "To us? To Cara. To this baby. What happens after we get the starring roles? If we do. Or, appear in the starting line-up? If we do. Or get the MVP title? If we do. What then? What happens now that you're pitching in the World Series? Win or lose. Or, if I were to get the lead in Swan Lake someday?" Her voice catches on the word, *someday*. She hangs her head and sighs deep and then looks over at me intently in the dark.

Her face reflects such profound anguish that I reach for her in the darkness suddenly needing her more in that moment than any other. "Then, we win."

I try to sound certain. I'm not sure that I do. I'm not sure that I am anymore.

"No. The bigger question is what if we lose in the end? What then?" She turns her body more fully into mine and briefly nuzzles her face into my chest. I think I feel the wetness of tears but Tally rarely cries. *Is she crying?* Then she is holding onto me so tight it's as if her life depended on it.

I slides my legs in between hers and drape my left arm over her body and pull her in closer. "We won't lose. We'll never lose. We *can't* lose."

"That's where you're wrong. Somebody always wins, while somebody else always loses." She gets this solemn face, and then she winces as if she's in serious pain. Tears cling to her lashes. She *is* about to cry—the woman who never cries. "That's the way it works. Somebody wins. Somebody loses."

I trace her jaw line. Then, kiss her gently as if with this one simple act can silence and perhaps even annihilate all of her doubts and biggest fears.

"It's going to be okay," I say against her lips.

She sighs deep as if it's her very last breath as if there will be no others. Meanwhile, the physical parts of me come to life against her finely-shaped thighs revealing my next greatest desire for what we should do next in the middle of this night. I grip her arms and stare at her longingly. Even in the dim light, I can still make out her face, but I get a little lost in her deep emerald gaze, and I'm struck by her beauty just as much as I was the first time I laid eyes upon her.

Then, instinct kicks in because I suddenly know we're not talking about baseball or ballet when it comes to winning or losing. We're talking about *us*.

"Stay with me, Tal."

She flinches at my choice of words and starts to pull away. "I can't."

The words are barely audible.

The next are stronger and more final as if she's giving a sermon and finally found her theme. "That's how it works, Linc. Give and take. Somebody gives. Somebody takes. Somebody wins while, invariably, somebody else loses."

I half-smile still naive about what is about to transpire besides making love to her and ending this night better than it began. I casually tuck a strand of her hair behind one ear.

"I don't know about all of that. That's almost at a mathematical level or physics or something. I just know this universe." I reach beneath her t-shirt and stroke her stomach and reach further down. She grabs my hand and effectively stops me from exploring her further. "All I know about my universe is that you're in it, and you're it for me, and I love you. And I will always love you no matter what. I just wish for one day you would believe me. Just one day, Tally, that's all I'm asking for. Come with me…to the game tomorrow. I'm *starting*. It's the World Series, Tal. Be there in the stands. Watch me play. That's all I ask. All I really want is for you to be there when we win."

I allow hope to overtake me while she gently strokes my face as if seeking all the answers there. My wistfulness is hard to ignore. I know she wants to believe me; I can sense it. But there's something else, too. It's there in her eyes, and in the way she's looking away whenever my gaze meets up with hers. All at once, I realize that she's avoiding telling me something.

Dread comes to life deep inside.

The instinct to survive whatever this is starts to kick in. "Stay with me, Tal."

This time there is no denying the tremors my request causes her. She's shaking. Her whole body trembles. She covers it up by hugging me a little tighter, but it's still there overtaking her.

"Why didn't you tell me about Nika?" Tally looks up at me for the answer as if this is some kind of test and already knows I'll fail miserably.

"It didn't mean anything. There's a lot going on. It meant nothing. She…means *nothing*."

Tell her about the trade rumors. I stay silent.

"She's a part of your past. I imagine life with Nika was a whole lot easier than life with me, wasn't it?" she asks quietly. "I know I've been down with what Mikhail did in firing me. My mom. The move. I've been out of it lately. That's why I went to see Brad. For you. For me." She sits up in bed.

I hear her take a jagged breath. "The thing is…I'm barely hanging on. Cara. This baby. You. Marriage. This house. Baseball. You're never here. It's all a bit much to take in. I just kept waiting…"

"Waiting for what?"

"Waiting for something else to go wrong."

"What if it doesn't? What if everything goes like it supposed to? What if we win?"

"What if we've already lost? What then?" Her words are offered up like prayer. She looks so lost and so sad that I pull her into my arms, cradle her neck, and kiss her desperately as if I can somehow reach her all the way to her soul by doing so.

"What if we've already won?" I capture her chin in one hand and force her to look at me. "You and me. We've won. We're together. You and me. That's enough. Isn't it?" I tack on the last two words because of the sudden look of resignation that crosses her features.

She holds my face between her hands and gazes at me long and hard before she actually shudders and attempts to take a breath. "We've already lost."

Clairvoyance kicks in. "Don't tell me," I beg. "I don't want to know."

"I slept with Sam."

She's told me.

I knew it.

"Don't tell me anymore." I pull away from her grasp and hold my head between my hands to hide my face and stem the onslaught of pure terror. *Fuck!*

I switch on the bedside lamp with a shaking hand. I have to see her face now. *Clearly.* She flinches with the bright light but she doesn't stand down she just keeps talking.

"In late May," she says with indifference. "After Fresno. I lied to you about it. *Him.* I didn't think it would matter. But then, Dr. Eldon recalculated the due date and I saw that it mattered. It had always mattered. I talked to Marla about it. She's right. The truth sets you free while the lie imprisons you. And, I can't live like this anymore. She told me that everything would work out. That I would figure it all out. But, it's not working out. Nothing is working out. I don't know what to do but I can't live like this anymore.

"The due date is February 9th. You can do a paternity test, but it doesn't change the date they've estimated. It's unlikely that the baby is yours. And I needed to tell you. To come clean with this. It isn't fair to you. It isn't fair to Sam."

"It isn't fair to *Sam*? It isn't fair to *me*? How are you going to make it *fair* to either one of us, Tally? Exactly, how are you going to do that?"

"I don't know."

"How did this happen? When did this happen?"

"After Fresno. I was so angry with you, and Sam was there for me. We were together. We didn't tell anyone. We kept it to ourselves. I don't think I told myself. Marla didn't even know. And yet, the entire time I was with him all I did was compare him to you. I was fucked up. I am still fucked up. My mother's dead. My career with SFB is finished. The paternity of this baby is questionable, and I went there. I thought about never telling you and just solving the problem, and I thought about an—"

"Don't even *say* it."

She hangs her head and stops talking for a few minutes and then looks over at me with new determination. "I couldn't do it because you can't just take care of it because it's inconvenient or somebody's feelings are going to get hurt or your marriage is ruined. I couldn't do it, but I can't do this either." She slices the air with her hand. I can't decide if she's angry with me or more angry with herself. "After the thing in Fresno with you, I went to Sam. I slept with Sam. We didn't tell anyone. We kept it to ourselves. It was just him and me. And I lied to you about it. I was wrong and—"

"The *thing* in Fresno? Us together in Fresno is now a *thing*?"

But she just keeps on talking as if she's reading off of a note card. "You came back to me, and I wanted to believe in forever with you. I wanted to move forward and stop looking back. I thought I was done making mistakes. And yet, the biggest one of all was yet to come. I lied to you when you asked me about Sam. I did that and I got caught in the lie in the most unexpected way because I am looking at you now and telling you that this baby I carry is most likely Sam's. I've been to two different doctors and had two different ultrasounds trying to confirm the exact date.

"I kept hoping that the math was wrong. That the dates would work out. Hope didn't change anything. Denial didn't either." She shakes her head slowly side-to-side. "The math isn't wrong, Linc. *I am.*"

Now, she gasps for air, while in the next, she effectively takes my breath away.

"You saw Sam. Did you tell him the baby might be *his?*" My voice breaks just upon uttering the last word.

"Yes. I'm sorry," she says as she hangs her head and avoids looking at me altogether, "I knew I needed to tell you, but yes I told him first."

This is a lethal blow; I feel mortally wounded.

"Tally?" My voice breaks. "You always put him first."

She shakes her head again and gets this sad, resigned smile. "He accused me of the same thing with you."

Still, the truth starts lining up and begins to resonate with me. "You slept with Sam after we were together in Fresno? Did you sleep with him a few weeks ago when you saw him?" I can't bear to look at her knowing her next words will slay me either way.

"No," she says gently. Then, she looks all kinds of guilty. "But, I wanted to."

"*What?*" I let go of her then and she slides from the bed in one lithe move like always and moves farther away from me.

She is so far away from me.

She's slipping away from me now.

She's already gone.

My head pounds but my heart demands to be heard. "We can work this out," I say giving life to my sudden desolation.

"No. We can't. It doesn't ever work out. Marla's right about me and what I do and how it works. It doesn't work out. It never does. But I have to own this, and that's what I'm doing. I'm owning it now. I won't lie to you anymore. I can't. I hate myself for what I've done. I wanted so much for everything to be good between us. I wished for it. I prayed for it. But the outcome is still the same. I can't live with the lie anymore. I can't live here in this house with you and live a lie. I didn't know what to do for the longest time, but then I finally came clean with Marla, and I told her all of it, and now I know what

I have to do. I have to try to make something good happen despite all the things I've done wrong and the people I've done wrong to as well. Like you. Right or wrong, I have to own it, beginning now. And I can't be with you or Cara. I'm no good for either one of you right now. I'm not."

"Tally, take a breath. It's all too much. Just *stop talking*. Just stop. You're spinning out of control," I manage to say in the breach when she stops to take a breath.

But it's as if I haven't spoken. She doesn't hear me.

"I can't live like this. I can't live like this anymore, Linc. I've known all this time since the day my mom died that the math was wrong. But, I can't do this anymore. I can't do this with you anymore."

I lift my head from my hands and watch her slowly as she slowly nods while her darkest confession descends upon me like heavy black smoke rises from a fire and obliterates the blue sky. In the next shitty moment, I reach out and grab her by the forearms in some desperate attempt to relieve this sharp physical pain I feel. I reach for her desperate for some kind of sanity harboring the sudden wish to inflict the same kind of pain upon her with my vice-like grip. She winces but doesn't try to escape.

Instead, she stares past me, unseeing, out the black windows that grace one whole side of our bedroom and overlooks the fantastic view of the Pacific.

The view we never stop to admire or even look at.

The view we never really see from this huge house.

This huge house she hates.

And I know this.

She's lonely.

She's been tortured by grief and plagued by the constant fears of falling and failing and loss.

And she's felt all three all over again recently.

I know this, too.

So, why did I think she'd stay?

That she'd be happy.

That she'd try?

Fuck!

Tears slide down my face unchecked. It appears, I am unable to recover. I will never recover, and I cannot fucking breathe now.

"Why are you doing this to us, Tally? Why?"

"It has to be done. The math is all wrong. It's all fucked-up." She slowly shakes her head side-to-side. "Fucked-up, I can deal with. Happily ever after? Obviously, not so much."

"You love me." My words are bitter and flow upward and out like the worst kind of bile, and she stares at me for a long while apparently unable or unwilling to fill the void they make in the room and within the two of us.

"I don't know what love is anymore."

She effectively skewers my heart with her sobering words and slices the air with her hand in frustration in the next. And yet, somehow, I'm captivated by the sparkle coming from her left ring finger but within ten seconds she's twisted off the diamond as well as the platinum band that's been there for the better side of three months. Then, she moves across the room away from me and tosses it onto the dresser where it lands right in front of the silver-framed wedding photograph of the two of us that she put there right after she and Cara moved in.

She turns and, with her hands on her hips, lets the accusations fly. "You're never here. Sam's always been there. He doesn't need anything from me. He doesn't expect anything from me. It's never about winning or losing or anything in between. It just is. It's just *us.*" Her voice breaks on the last word as if she's forgotten where she is at in this particular scene as well as her very next line. She seems to have trouble speaking as she makes these sobbing sounds and starts to break down.

"Why won't you let me do any of that? We'll work through this. We can. We'll have this baby, and we'll be together because we still love each other. We can get past this."

"Don't you see? It's *ruined*. We were doomed from the start. I *lied* to you. I told you nothing went on with Sam, but it did. It happened and I'm pregnant, and the math is wrong. It might not be yours. It's more likely his. We won't know more until we do a paternity test. And what's the point? Do we judge this baby or ourselves? *Me?* And, I lied to you about it. I did that. And now? Knowing the truth destroys everything between us."

"No, it *doesn't*," I say simply.

She winces as if she's in physical pain. "Maybe not today. Maybe not tomorrow or the next day or a year from now, but someday after you've processed it all it will change everything for you, for us because it just *does*. It changes us, and you know it. I cannot undo this, Linc, and neither can you."

Her sadness and the resignation clearly etched upon her face guts me. Now that her confession is over, she's having trouble getting air into her lungs. Still, I try again to win her back, to reach her in some way. "Please, Tally, we'll get through this."

"We won't."

She's adamant all at once, and it pisses me off.

"I get it. You want me to hate you; don't you? That's it; isn't it? Well, no fucking way. I want to be here for you, take care of you, *love* you, Tally."

"I. Don't. Want. You. To." The words come out of her mouth as complete sentences, and it is like driving nails into my heart, hitting their intended target one by one. "I don't want you to love me anymore."

While I gasp for air, she drags her suitcase out from our master closet.

She's already packed.

How many times has she left me?

How did I not see this coming?

How did I think this would last?

Some part of my brain hears her little speech about this being for the best and being fair and being over.

And then, she's gone.

Just like that.

I swear it's four in the morning before I actually feel my sorry ass self take another breath.

I've been annihilated.

She's left me again.

I briefly give into the pain that now plagues every part of me.

But then, there's a noise near the open doorway.
Tally's back.
She's changed her mind.
She's come back to me.

I look over instantly realizing it's a pathetic wish lasting all of two seconds. Cara stands in the open door. The moonlight lights up my little girl's face and her long, dark hair. She is the exact replica of Tally except for her big grey-blue eyes, which stare back at me reflecting my DNA and a child's simple wish for the truth.

"Daddy?" she whispers rubbing her eyes with her sweet little hand. "Where did Mommy go? Why was she crying?"

Daddy doesn't have those answers.
On the other hand, he has far too many.

All I really want to do is set a world record for spewing the most clever uses of the f-word right now which might inadvertently relieve this incredible heartbreak that has managed to already burrow its way into my soul since Tally left me less than an hour ago.

Even so, sanity prevails in the next precious moments where I manage to hold onto silence, but it's close. Without a word, I open the covers and my four-year-old crawls into the bed with me.

It's a long time before I can speak. "Mommy's just sad. She's going to go away for a little while to figure some things out. That's all. It's you and me, kid, for a little while."

I tell lies almost as well as this little girl's mother, but I have to hope on some minuscule level that Cara actually believes mine. I attempt to smile at her in the dark, and my little girl snuggles into me and closes her eyes with an innocent sigh.

"She'll be back. She's coming back…for you soon." I remember Tally saying something about coming back for Cara, but she didn't exactly say when.

We share a few minutes of daddy-daughter silence. But then, my little girl interrupts my racing thoughts. "She said she'd never lose me again. She promised."

"*Lose* you? When did she lose you?"

"In the park." Cara plays with my fingers and then innocently smiles up at me.

"She lost you in the park? When?"

"I don't know." She pats the back of my hand.

"It's okay, Daddy. She found me."

"Were you scared?" I hold my little girl close.

"I was scared for Mommy. She couldn't breathe for a really long time."

It takes a few seconds to process Cara's revelation.

Tally lost Cara. Tally had another bad panic attack and didn't tell me. That's why she left Cara with me.

"She'll never lose you, Cara."

But, will she?

She lost sight of Cara in a park because she suffered a panic attack.

That's a scary proposition for both of them, for all of us.

I tuck the covers in around my child's little body. "Your mommy loves you very much. She always will. She'll come back for you." I'm not sure why I feel the need to defend Tally right this very second considering she just ripped my heart out, but I have. "She'll come back to us."

Perhaps, if I say it often enough it will become true, and it won't be a lie after all.

PART II - CONTRITION

"Stars, hide your fires;

let not light see my black and deep desires."

-William Shakespeare

CHAPTER TWENTY

better than that

TALLY

Death takes us all prisoner; nobody wins.
~ Talia Landon Presley

November 18th

The Giants win the World Series and dominate the sports pages for an entire week and then word begins to circulate about Linc and me splitting up. The tabloids take pictures of the moving van which was only parked for less than four hours in front of Linc's humongous house, and have begun to spin out numerous headlines about the break-up of the famous baseball player and me—the used-to-be-famous ballerina.

Not satisfied with the *no comment* angle both parties involved have adopted, the press begins putting together their own stories as to the reason for our break-up and dig up photographs of Linc and Nika, and Linc and Trinna Danner, and then the speculation really begins to fly.

We are off to the races.

I have been designated the role of the victim, and Linc is anointed the part of the villain. They have it so so wrong, but nobody corrects them, not even Kimberley.

Then, they find some obscure photograph of Sam and me from months before. And when that doesn't work, they trot out photographs of Rob and me. And then, there's the final two blows—me pregnant with Cara and the questions surrounding the paternity of our first-born begins to make the rounds while speculation about the one I carry runs rampant as well.

The please-respect-the-couple's-request-for-privacy press releases that Kimberley issues go largely ignored while the news stories themselves get more salacious with each passing day.

I'm waiting for the antics in Fresno to make the rounds because I know they will. It's only a matter of time. I'm surprised they haven't shown up already.

It all hurts wounding me deeply. The lies are just as twisted as the truth they unintentionally annihilate.

Even so, I deserve this pain.

And yet, I remain secretly fascinated—addicted, really—to the speculation about our complicated relationship that takes place throughout the land of social media and tabloid gossip. I wade through the newspaper and sports pages like an obsessed fan trolling for any bit of news, intent on feeling all of this visceral pain even as the tabloids dissect and virtually destroy our private life.

Meanwhile, the truth dies a little more each day. As do I.

I spend a fair amount of my time just avoiding my life including the paparazzi because I'm so intent on hiding out, mostly from myself.

Hiding out from the press proves much easier than I thought it would be because I've become quite adept at avoiding anyone who has anything to do with my former life, including my four-year-old daughter. I am a *bad mother*; she may as well learn that now. I fucking own that title and all the others as well, including *bad wife*.

Kimberley calls. Brad calls.

My voice mail overflows and cannot even record their messages. I like it that way because then no one can leave me one.

I spend all my time at my Dad's playing video games with Tommy. I have managed to avoid the endless phone calls from Lincoln Presley and Marla Stone for the past three and a half weeks as well.

I am unfair and unrepentant. I will do this thing on my own whatever this thing is. Well, let's be clear; I am fucking up my life. I am good at that and even my little brother seems to think so now.

He glances at me sideways now. "He just wants to talk to you."

"Stay out of it, Tommy." My body goes rigid at my brother's mention of Linc. It's as if I've been stabbed. I attempt to get it under control and hold my breath until the pain subsides and then proceed to jab the gaming controller buttons, feigning utter concentration and a vested interest in mastering *Halo* and winning this round because I am all about blowing guys up and away, at this point, in real life as well as video games. I think my brother regrets teaching me to play his favorite war game.

"Dad thinks you should talk to him. I can't believe you're doing this to Linc, right now. It's harsh, Tally. Pretty fucking harsh."

I take my eyes off the screen and turn and scrutinize my brother. These days, he is sixteen going on twenty-six. Mom's death has hit him hard. With our Holly's death, he was too young to understand, but with Mom, he effectively gets it.

Death takes us all prisoner; nobody wins.

"Don't swear like that. Girls don't like it." My brother looks confused and probably wonders at that truth when he knows I swear all the time now, especially when I'm gaming or whenever I'm awake. "Besides when would you have talked to Dad about me and…the baseball player? Dad's at the hospital all the time now. You don't see Dad around here anymore than we used to; right?" He shrugs. "So how would Dad *know* what I should do? He's already checked out as much as I have."

Tommy can't really argue with that assessment. My dad is never here. He is always at the hospital, and since I've spent the past three weeks at his house in lieu of my own that has been confirmed.

After I left Linc, I thought about moving into Tremblay's place again, since Sam is still out of the country, but that would just constantly remind me of my failures with Sam, too, so somehow I ended up here.

I cook breakfast, lunch and dinner for the Landon men and turn into my mom a little bit more with each passing day. Although, I merely *study* the vodka bottles instead of partake in what is inside of them. On some subconscious level, I must know that adding drinking to my never-ending list of personal problems would be catastrophic.

For now. There's that. I can't make any promises down the road on that front, but apparently I can keep them for now.

Contrition. I think I've found it on some level. All that time, *years*, where I was never around or *present* for my family. I make up for it with them now, for the two remaining.

Yet, I can't even think about Cara and what I've done by leaving her and how I've made her feel. I lost her. I can't be trusted with my own kid to watch her and take care of her. Hopefully, she understands that on some level. I love Cara; I just can't take care of her. Not right now.

Yet, I am quietly desperate because what is left of my sanity little by little ebbs away from me into this ever eternal oblivion.

I am slowly dying from this heartbreak. I can feel it. But I did this. I deserve this.

"What are you going to do?" Tommy asks some five minutes later.

"About what?" I raise a quizzical eyebrow at the youngest Landon, mostly, because I don't know what I'm going to do, and I'm not sure what all he's talking about. I have no intention of telling my brother anything like ever because he is entirely too close to Linc.

"About the baby? About Cara? About Linc? About *you?*" he whispers.

My eyes start to sting. "I don't know." The words leave my lips nice and slow, but I gasp at the air anyway in just thinking of Cara and this baby and Linc. And, in the next thirty seconds, I manage to lose the game.

I lose. Just like everything and everyone else.

My cell rings.

It's Marla.

After almost a month of no contact with my bestie, I finally pick up my phone and answer her call.

"Hey," she says without preamble. "I need a favor. I'm tied up at Dr. Eldon's in Alamo Square. Not literally." She laughs.

"It's just taking longer than I thought it would. Can you pick up Cara from preschool? Elliott's with my mom and Charlie's got a late shift at the hospital, but I'm going to be at least another half-hour and you know how those people are about parents being late for pick-up."

"Hi to you, too," I say into the breach when she finishes her mini rant.

Neither of us are particularly fond of the teachers at the preschool. They're not too fond of us either since we're always running late to pick up our kids, yet they have no problem tacking on the $25 late fee to ensure we curb this nasty habit. We're on *their list* for sure.

"Where's the baseball player? Why can't he do it? You know I'm kind of out of the picture right now."

"Pull your head out, Tally. It's your *daughter*. She needs you. So, you lost her at the park one day while you were fighting off a panic attack, get *over* it."

"You *know* about that? Who *told* you?"

"Cara told Linc. *He* told me. Geez, I lost Elliott at Target for four minutes the other day. We all do it. We recover. We move on and try not to do it again."

"Marla, it's not that *simple* for me, and you know it." I sigh with impatience and mortification because now Linc knows how fucked up I am as a mother, too.

It just keeps getting worse.

"I think it is. Now look, don't get all bent out of shape. Your daughter *needs* you. You can *do* this. Go get her from the preschool. You can spend like an hour with her, and she'll be thrilled. Swing by Dr. Eldon's office and I'll take her home with us."

"*Why* is she staying with you anyway? She should be with Linc."

"You *filed*, Tally. He's a little upset right now about that. In fact, we all are. Right now, he's too despondent to handle the loving care involved in taking care of his four-year-old. What is going on with you? He *loves* you. *You love* him. And yet, you're destroying your life on purpose. We already talked about this. So what if it turns out the baby isn't his? He wants it to be. He'll take care of you." She breathes in deep and sighs. "He thinks you're with Sam, but we both *know* you're not. We both know that ship sailed some time ago."

"It's okay if he thinks I'm with Sam. That makes things easier."

"Sure, sure, but does it make it honest? When are you going to start dealing with the truth? The truth about the two of you and how great you are together. Quit destroying everything, Tally, just because you're afraid of losing it doesn't make it all right to destroy it on purpose. He's hurting. Quit doing that to him and just grow the fuck up." She sighs big again. "Sorry. Look you have me swearing and I'm supposed to be stopping."

"Yeah, well, I swear more than ever since we made that pact. Another bad plan gone awry."

"Now," she says gently, "go get your kid because I can't make it there on time. Oh and Dr. Eldon says *hi*, by the way, and she wants to know when you're coming in again. You need to reschedule your appointment with her, apparently, you missed the last one."

"Let's just take this one thing at a time. I haven't even agreed to pick up Cara yet."

"I can't find Linc. He isn't answering his cell phone. Get it together, Tally. Go pick up your little girl and call me when you get there so we can arrange to meet up at Dr. Eldon's office or somewhere else. You've put me off long enough."

She's hung up on me. She doesn't do that very often.

I'm momentarily stunned by it and then thoroughly pissed because Linc is leaning on my best friend instead of doing his job as the designated parent in charge. Nothing has changed. Somehow, Marla has reeled me back in because she can't find him. Gah! I'm so pissed right now.

I yell at Tommy telling him I need to go pick up Cara because Marla can't do it.

My brother sticks his head around the corner of the kitchen and grins. "*You're* picking up Cara?"

"Marla's at the Dr. Eldon's. She can't find Linc. I guess it's down to me to get her from preschool."

"Great! Bring her back here. Tell her there will be ice cream. I'll order us a pizza. She's loves pizza."

I'm frantically searching for my keys. I'm tugging at my hair and plaiting it out with my fingers. I'm changing out of my sweats and into a sweater and maternity skirt that I finally broke down and bought since my normal clothes are no longer fitting me these days. I stomp into my favorite black pair ankle boots cursing Linc the entire time.

Tommy just watches me in stupefied wonder and eventually starts to laugh. "*Why* are you getting all dressed up for this?" he asks.

I swing into my leather jacket and glare his way. "I haven't seen her in almost a month. I don't want to scare her with my latest gamer look." I reward him with a withering glance.

"Good idea." He grins shaking his head. "Tally, it's going to be fine. She's going to be thrilled to see you."

"How do I look?" I ask as I finish putting the finishing touches of a little mascara and lipstick on.

"You look beautiful. Perfect. Go get her. See you in a half-hour or so."

See you soon." I grin back at him. "It'll be at least forty-five minutes before we make it back." I slide into the driver's seat of my car and wave at him where he stands in the doorway sending me off.

"Tally," he calls out to me, "it'll be okay. She's going to be thrilled to see you. See you soon." My brother waves and has this big grin on his face. He loves Cara; he misses her, too.

I focus on the car—starting it and warming it up. Linc had it delivered a few weeks ago along with Cara's car seat. His thoughtfulness makes me crazy. *Crazier.* I don't need him being thoughtful. I need him signing those divorce papers I had couriered over a few days ago. I want this thing with him finished so I can move on. So I can do *something.* Whatever that is.

I slowly back out of the driveway, wave at Tommy one last time, and head out.

Marla's right; the teachers at the preschool, the director, especially, do not like it when parents are late. I wonder where Linc is and why he has shirked his parental duties and handed them over to Marla so much these days. The whole point of leaving her with Linc was so she'd be taken care of by the best parent among us. It's supposed to be him. *Why isn't he doing it?*

He's hurting. I'm hurting.

I gave him Cara. I don't deserve Cara.

I lost her that time in the park. Until the panic attacks subside,

I'm no good for her. And they haven't stopped altogether although they've been less frequent for some unidentifiable reason.

Maybe because I've stopped trying to be so perfect?

Let's not go there.

I'm far from perfect at this point.

And here I am going to pick up my little girl by myself so what does it matter? I'm it.

Grow up, Tally.

You're the parent here. Act like one.

Okay. Okay. Okay.

I stand in front of Cara's pre-school for a few minutes. The dread washes over me much like a rogue wave at a beach. I summon up a modicum of courage, push open the front doors, and step inside assailed by the ever present laughter of children and the distinct odor of drying fingerpaints. The smell of sugar cookies also fills the air. It must be Tuesday. They do an art project with sugar cookies and frosting on Tuesdays.

"Talia, it's great to see you," says Katie Strongman, the school's director, as soon as she sees me. "It's been a while."

Let the judgment begin.

"Yes. Yes, it has. How's she doing?"

"She doing okay. She's been a little off lately what with everything going on at home. Children adapt, of course, but they're sensitive to change."

"It's been a little rough. I haven't been at my best." My voice breaks on the word best. Tears threaten. *I cannot cry in front of Katie Strongman.* The woman is perfection, and she doesn't tolerate weakness of any kind in her parents or the children. Every parent who brings their kid here knows that. *No whining allowed.*

"She'll be so happy to see you." The director touches my hand and actually smiles. I know my assessment of this woman is dead-on, and I can barely handle her being this nice to me. I'm not a charity case, and I'm no fucking saint as has been well established by every newspaper in the country at this point. They're probably tittering to themselves whenever Linc shows up hoping to catch his attention and wondering how this all might work out for them personally now that he's eligible again. "Sorry to hear about San Francisco Ballet. They're going to miss you."

"Uh-huh. We'll see. There's an opportunity for me with The Bolshoi Ballet in Moscow. I'm just weighing out my options."

"Will you take Cara with you to Moscow? Wow, what a cultural experience that will be if you do. Children can learn a second language so quickly. You'd be amazed."

"Yes, I'll take her with me. She'll be going." I smile brightly suddenly as intrigued by the idea as a plan for Moscow begins to automatically formulate in my mind.

Cara and I will go to Moscow.

We'll go now before I can't fly, before I'm considered a risk for international flight.

Of course, I already know Linc won't go along with this plan on any level whatsoever, but suddenly I feel strong enough to take on this battle..

"Momma!" Cara runs to me from the other side of the room as the classroom door swings open. "I missed you so much!"

My child heads straight for me. "I missed you too, baby." I sweep Cara up into my arms. "Come on. Uncle Tommy is ordering pizza, and he said there's going to be ice cream."

We wave at the director as well as Cara's teacher and head out.

I realize just having my little girl back in my arms has made everything all right for me again.

I can do this.
Me, Cara, and this baby will be enough.

"Oh, I missed you so much, Cara. Mommy will never leave you like that again. Okay?"

"Okay, Momma. Daddy said you'd come for me. And now, you have." She rewards me with this angelic smile.

My life is made again.

"I love you so much, Cara." I kiss her forehead and hug her close just before I load her up into her car seat.

Katherine Owen

"Love you more, Momma."

"We're going to be okay, baby. You and me. We're going to be fine."

She grabs my hand and kisses it. I laugh and so does she.

My world comes together again just like that. My future is clear. I can breathe again.

CHAPTER TWENTY-ONE

your eyes open

LINC

"If you prick us do we not bleed?
If you tickle us do we not laugh?
If you poison us do we not die?
And if you wrong us shall we not revenge?"
  ~ William Shakespeare

I don't intend revenge, but it's there tearing away
at what's left of my soul leaving the rage
and hatred of her behind and in command.
  ~ Lincoln Presley

November 18th

IT'S BEEN THREE AND A HALF weeks since she left me. The press has had a field day but the anxiety over all of that never reaches me because the pain in Tally's leaving me hurts far more.

My cell rings. *It's Kimberley. For the hundredth time.*

"Do you want me to have them print a retraction?"

"No.

"Are you sure? They're taking swipes at Cara's paternity now. We can clear that right up and probably file a lawsuit for defamation of character and scare the shit out of them."

"That's not a court battle, I'm willing to fight."

Kimberley fidgets on the other end of the line then asks, "she's filed?"

"Yes." I swallow hard at this admission.

Yes, the tabloids have made a valiant attempt to tear my life apart, but Tally has done a stellar job of that all on her own. Not a crier normally. I didn't cry when my brother died nor when I looked at my mom in her casket for the last time in my life. *But Tally leaving me? I swear I cry every fucking day.*

"What are you going to do?" Kimberley asks gently.

She has been a rock. Her and Brad. They have both been there for me while the Giants took the World Series title while Tally virtually destroyed my life in the same span of time. And yet, the sympathy I detect in Kimberley's voice makes me feel like I'm suffering from a fresh stab wound, but then again, it's no worse than the pain I felt at receiving the manila envelope containing divorce papers via courier just two days ago.

Irreconcilable differences.

Well, I suppose that's true.

She's given me full custody of Cara. I don't know why. My lawyer doesn't know why either.

She lost Cara. That's why.

My subconscious knows. Something like that would tear Tally up. I know my wife. I *know* her.

"What are you going to do?" Kimberley asks again.

I tell my publicist what I've told my lawyer. "I'm not signing them. I'm staying married to Tally, whether she likes it or not."

Kimberley laughs. "Well, that is certainly a unique approach."

Two hours later, the doorbell rings. I descend the stairs grabbing a t-shirt draped on the stair railing and manage to slip it over my head, so I look halfway decent as I answer the door. I've been wandering the house in the same pair of sweats for past two days and can only contemplate the idea of taking a shower. Tally actually filing set me back. I can't get my head around it. It makes the past month look like a cakewalk compared to the way I feel now.

She filed.

She wants to divorce me.

And yet, I still don't hate her enough to let her go.

Cara is staying with Charlie and Marla for a few more days. I needed a break, and I'm supposed to be looking for a new nanny since Andy didn't feel it was appropriate she stay on since Tally was no longer here. *Fuck, I don't know. Whatever.* I need a live-in nanny slash full-time housekeeper.

Do those interviews start today?

Can't Kimberley fucking handle this for me?

I open the door feeling nothing but rage for whoever is on the other side. *God, help them.*

I'm staring at Nika Vostrikova.

"You shouldn't be here," I grind out and then promptly turn away and head into the living room knowing she'll follow me regardless of whether I invite her in or not.

Her heels meet up with the marble floor in the foyer; the tap tap of her stilettos is a dead giveaway. The front door clicks then latches while I vaguely note it could serve as an early warning.

Wary now, I turn and stare at my ex. *Ex-Fiancée? Ex-girlfriend. Why did we break up?* Kimberley was never very clear on that. She didn't like Nika Vostrikova and she didn't like spending time filling me in on her after I lost my memory. I remember Nika from Stanford. The rest of my time with her is still unclear.

"Your wife is making a mess of *my* life," she says without preamble.

"Join the fucking club, babe. You think mine is going swimmingly at the moment? Our *nanny* just quit. Tally left us. She's *filed*. Please do tell me what the fuck she's done to you."

"I'm marrying Rob in five days and there are photographs of the two of us—me and you—all over the damn place! He is not happy about it, and you need to stop this."

"I can't help you."

"Yes, you *can*! Lincoln, *please*. It's wreaking havoc on my life as you Americans say."

"Jesus, Nik, stop feigning with your Russian misunderstanding of everything American. You've been in this country for *years*. You know how things work. It's not working on me anymore."

I go over to the bar and pour myself a good measure of Jack Daniel's in a tall water glass and dully note that mixing those two Oxy pills I took less than an hour ago with this whiskey is probably not the best plan. *Who cares?* "You want one?"

No. I have a fitting." She gets this recognizable pout.

"A fitting?"

"A *bridal* gown fitting. I haven't eaten in two days. You can't, you know. Didn't Tally have a fitting for her dress? It wasn't *that* long ago."

I slam back the whiskey and then snarl at her ridiculous statement. "It wasn't like that. My dad bought her the dress. *Off the rack.* We practically eloped. It wasn't very planned out."

"Prenup?" Nika eyes my empty glass with fresh curiosity.

I pour another. "No to a prenup." She gets this incredulous look. "Of course, my father wanted one and Tally signed it, but then I promptly burned it because we were going to last *for-fucking-ever.*"

She laughs.

It should piss me off but instead I find it fascinating.

I haven't heard a woman's laugh in weeks, months really. The pain at Tally's leaving resurges all over again. I wince when I feel it come back up on me.

"Rob doesn't want one either. It's dangerous; right? Getting half of everything."

"She doesn't *want anything*, least of all, *me.*" The anger comes naturally. I think I even sneer. "She gave me full custody of Cara. "

"She gave up her parental rights to *Cara*? Her child? She really *is* crazy."

"That's not how Tally sees it. She didn't leave Cara; she left me. She's in a bad place. She's *been* in a bad place. She lost her mother; she lost her job. And Nika? Please tell me you didn't have anything to do with the press printing that story about Tally being pregnant. Somebody tipped off the press and Mikhail Rostov."

She won't look at me now. My Russian ex remains steadfast and silent.

"I'm sorry, Lincoln," she says sounding all contrite. "I shouldn't have done that. I didn't know she'd get fired. They asked me to comment about the photograph of us, and I denied anything was happening between us. You told me Tally was pregnant, and you were a good guy, and I knew you would never cheat on her because you wouldn't and I didn't know it was a big secret so I mentioned it. I'm sorry, Lincoln." Her simple shrug seems insincere and it sets me off.

"Nika! God damn it! That put Tally over the edge. *One* of the things that did. And I wasn't here when her director fired her. I fucked up. I fucked everything up as much as she did."

"I'm sorry."

"Well, there's that." I let out a sorry breath. "*Forget* it. Tally being pregnant and people finding out became the least of our problems. The baby might not even be mine. It turns out she was with somebody else for a time."

"What? When?" The normally cool Nika Vostrikova looks momentarily confused but she recovers fast. "Who, then?" she asks quietly.

"It was after our big fight in Fresno. We were together on the middle of May and then we broke up. She left me and went back to San Francisco. To *him*."

"Not one of your finest moments with TMZ. Who did she go back to?"

I ignore the TMZ reference. We're way beyond the big fight in Fresno now. "She went back to Sam. Sam Wilde. He owns *The Promissory Note*. The restaurant? Do you know it?"

She gets this intrigued look as if she's figured out Einstein's Theory of Relativity all on her own. "The one in Alamo Square? Yes. Oh now, I see. *That's* Sam Wilde. I saw him with her a few months ago in September. At first, I saw her meeting with her director, Mikhail Rostov, and then she left soon after and then she came back with Sam. The Giants were playing San Diego that day. I was in the bar watching the game and waiting for Rob. She seemed upset and they left together."

"She left with Sam? Jesus. That's the day Mikhail fired her and she was with Sam?" I sit down heavily in one of the living room chairs.

"I don't know. I saw them leave together. They walked down the sidewalk together. I'm not sure where they were going."

"His house. The house in Alamo Square. The one I leased to him. Geez, I'm a fool. Do you think she's been involved with him the entire time we were married?"

"I don't know.

I start talking in circles as the Oxy I took earlier and the whiskey kicks in and begins to dull my pain. "Yeah, well she went back to him after Fresno. I guess I denied it even to myself about how serious things got between them. It turns out Tally did, too. I was just concentrating on baseball and winning her back. She said she wasn't with Sam and I…I just wanted her back so we could be together for—"

"For-fucking-ever," Nika says enjoying her ability to openly toy with me a little too much. She goes over to the bar and pours me a fresh drink.

"Yeah."

She hands it to me and stands in front of me. *Déjà vu plays its part. We've been here before.*

"But she lied to you about her involvement with Sam—how serious it was. And the baby."

"Not intentionally." I still hold onto the last threads of hope and defend Tally without a valid reason as to why.

"Is there an *unintentional* kind?" Nika starts to laugh but I glare at her, and she stops. "I'm sorry, Lincoln. I'm not following this story completely."

She shakes her beautiful head, and I get a little lost in looking at her. Nika is gorgeous and blond, and I'm having trouble remembering exactly why we never fit together. She seems to notice me noticing her. Her stance changes from casual to deliberate.

"Did she tell you about being involved with Sam or not?"

"Not exactly. I guess I should have assumed it because it's *Tally*. She's never had a problem with sex or with the guys trailing after her wanting to be with her. I just…"

"And the baby…she told you it was yours? But then it wasn't? I don't get it. You Americans are always so hung up on sex and who's doing who when it just *is* what it is. Move on, already."

"She thought she was due on Valentine's Day around that time—the sixteenth, actually—when she first learned she was pregnant. But then, the doctor changed the due date based on the baby's measurements. She didn't tell me she slept with Sam. That little omission was intentional. Does an omission become a lie or is it always one from the beginning?" I feel all kinds of wounded in having to acknowledge that Sam and Tally were together.

"I don't know. Does it matter?" The blonde plays with her hair and looks over at me with renewed interest." I'm sorry. I know how much a child means to you, especially a son."

"Not as much as Tally. Never as much as Tally." I shake my head, but it makes me dizzy. It's getting harder to focus on what Nika is saying. "But she doesn't believe that. She never did. I fucked this up as much as she did. I was never here enough. I didn't see how her mother's death and losing her job were tearing her up inside and Sam has always been there for her, whereas I...I wasn't always there."

Nika takes out her phone and hits a few buttons. "Her due date is February 9th?"

"What?"

"Her due date."

"February 9th," I say feeling apprehensive all at once.

Nika looks over at me shaking her head. "Aw. That's why she was so upset at her mother's funeral. I *spoke* to her. We had a less than happy exchange. She was upset about something. Something she didn't want you to know. Now, it all makes sense; she was lying to you then. About the baby." Nika looks at her phones, sighs and then holds it up for me to see. "The baby never would have been yours. See? You broke up with her on the 16th of May. She left you. That's what you said. She went back to Sam. There's no way the baby could have been yours. You weren't here. She lied to you the entire time. If the original due date was February 16th, there's no way the baby would have been yours. She probably already knew that even before you two got married."

"You think Tally *knew* the entire time?"

"Apps calculating due dates are pretty easy to find. I imagine even Tally would have figured that out. It's right here." She shows me the app again. The due date of February 9th puts conception around the 20th or 21st of May.

"How do you know this for sure?"

"Sperm live five days at the most," she says like an informed health studies teacher. "That puts it around the 21st of May for it to possibly be yours. If her dates are correct, it could still be yours, but it's unlikely. The math is never wrong."

"The math is never wrong. Spoken like a true stats major from Stanford." I cringe knowing Nika's right and not wanting to hear it. "Tally lied to me the entire time."

"It appears that way. I'm sorry. I know you loved her. She never deserved you. I *barely* deserved you, but then again we have a lot of history you and I…" Her voice trails off. She gets this familiar gleam in her eyes. I remember this one. I remember more of Nika than I do of Tally sometimes. In moments like this where she's standing entirely too close to me, her signature lavender scent does things to my libido. Her lips curve upward as if she knows that, too.

I breathe out slowly as the whiskey hits me full force. My stomach growls reminding me I haven't eaten today. Probably ten minutes too late, it occurs to me that downing all that alcohol probably wasn't the best idea, especially with Nika around. My head swims with all these outrageous thoughts of Tally and Sam.

I close my eyes to make it stop but that just makes it worse. I open them and sway a bit as the booze does a stellar job of annihilating the pain over Tally. Good moral judgment effectively disappears at about the same Nika kneels down in front of me and slides between my legs and studies me even more intently.

I know this look from her.

And, Nika Vostrikova is dangerous.

And I know this.

"We all fuck up." Her sympathy is notable. "That's what we do."

Nika leans in, grabs my face, and pulls me in. Our kiss is hot as her tongue explores my mouth and I do the same to hers. Stopping is impossible. I pull her up onto my lap and note how she fits quite nicely to my body. All these alarm bells go off in my head at the exact same time. Now, she settles her hips down on me, lift her head from mine, and gives me that fuck-me-so-I-can-feel-it-with-you-baby look.

"We all fuck up," I echo back to her. My words are jumbled. I think I actually slur them. I attempt to lean back from the intoxication that is Nika Vostrikova in an attempt to ward her off and not let this go any further while some remote part of me acknowledges it's far too late for that.

"You look like hell, Lincoln Presley." Her willing hands slowly stroke the sides of my face in her familiar signature move. "Why don't you go take a shower? I'll make you something to eat, and then we'll talk about how you're going to fix this thing with Tally."

I nod, a little taken aback that Nika Vostrikova has apparently decided to back off. Given an unexpected reprieve, I slide out away from her and take the stairs two at a time stripping off most of my clothes as I go. When I reach the master bedroom, I hear Nika gasp from behind me. She's far too close in proximity to be actually be backing off. With sudden trepidation, I glance back. She's followed me and performed the same stripping routine.

She is every man's fantasy. She is tall with these slender legs that seem to go on for-fucking-ever. She has these willowy limbs that bend every which way when you want them to and her long blond hair falls down past her waist. She stands there with the sun's rays and the Pacific at her back in our master bedroom obstructing an already perfect view but she manages to become an even better one.

One moment she's a few feet away from me, but then she purposefully closes the gap between us.

"Go away, Nik," I say with a heavy sigh. I turn away from her, step into the master bathroom, and firmly close the door behind me, and turn the water on full-blast.

Five minutes later, I soap up and breathe a sigh of relief that she's left me alone, but then I'm sucking in the air when her very capable hands reach around for my already hardening cock.

Why does Nika still affect me this way?

Because I'm a guy and she's beautiful, and she used to be mine, and I can't seem to readily recall any of the reasons we broke up.

"Old times sake," she murmurs as she puts her arms firmly around my waist and then reaches down and blatantly strokes me further. It's been a long while since we've been together but my body clearly remembers.

Key to a lock.

We fit together.

Sex with Nika was never a problem and she is proud to demonstrate this for me now.

"We can't do this," I say for both of us but my resistance to her fails me.

She ignores my protests. Instead, she slides down my front and closes her mouth around me before I can stop her. Nika has a long neck and a wide mouth that it is good for a lot of things. She molds her mouth around me and I am unable to form the words that would tell her to stop. A part of me doesn't want to.

I need this. I deserve this. We have a past. Maybe we can have a future.

Tally is with Sam. She's probably fucking Sam right now.

I can't bring myself to turn this woman down.

Within minutes I finish inside her willing mouth and she swallows down. She always did. I remember this about her. Sex in all of its forms with Nika had always been good. That hasn't changed.

My fingers find her. She's wet for me. I slip them in and out in rhythmic pattern and she writhes seeking release as I lift her up and start to kiss her dirty mouth. The combination of Oxy and whiskey make me bold as well as careless. We shouldn't be doing this, but that doesn't mean I don't like it. We're still wet from the shower as I drag her to the bed—the bed I share with Tally. The bed I *shared* with Tally. *Past tense.* The sheets still smell of *Miss Cloves and Vanilla.* Suddenly, I'm ready to annihilate Tally's intoxicating scent from my life like everything else about her once and for all.

She filed.

I grab a condom packet from the bedside drawer, and a few minutes later I drive myself inside the woman who has been there for me before and who is always willing and never tells me no. *Nika.*

I whisper her name over and over. She helps me bury the pain ever deeper over Tally's leaving me, even though I already know by being with Nika I'll lose everything I ever had with Tally if she ever finds out.

She will find out.

The thought assails me as I finish.

CHAPTER TWENTY-TWO

of moons, birds & monsters

LINC

"Tis one thing to be tempted, another thing to fall."
~ William Shakespeare

November 18th

NIKA LOOKS SATIATED AND EXTREMELY SATISFIED. She wears a lazy smile and nothing else. She crosses her long legs and seductively swings her left foot back and forth.

Easy to please. There's a part of me that loves that about her.

"This is one-time thing." She grins and moves in on me again and playfully bites down on my shoulder blade. I realize I enjoy the pain she elicits a little too much as it alleviates the heartbreak by degrees.

"It's a one-time thing. Agreed."

"I can't afford to fuck up things with Rob. Rob and his millions." She smiles but then it disappears when she sees my face. "Don't feel guilty, Lincoln. She's been fucking around on you, remember? I saw her with Sam not that long ago again."

"*You* saw Tally with Sam? *When*?"

She shrugs. "A few weeks ago. They were together at a hotel downtown. I don't think they thought anyone else was around, but I saw them. Hot and heavy those two, since she left you. She stays at his place sometimes where she lived before? In Alamo Square."

"How do you *know*? How do you know she stays with him?"

"Give me a little credit. It doesn't take much to find out what people are up to. You just follow the trails they lead you on, and you make the connections. They have a history. She's been fucking him for months. She probably never stopped. I'm not sure Tally holds much faith in the vow of marriage, do you?"

"No more than you," I say cruelly.

"I'm not married yet. I'll be faithful." She laughs. "Rob loves me. He makes me happy in all the right ways, lots of ways." She gets this uncertain look. "Like we agreed, this is one-time thing. This is goodbye, Linc. It has to be. I can't afford to mess up my life with Rob. I've worked too hard to get this far and I love Rob. He's good for me. He makes me want to try harder. To be good. To be faithful."

"And yet you're here with me." My mouth latches onto one of her breasts and she laughs again.

"You're the best player I know in baseball. You made college fun. We have a past. We share that. But nothing can come between us—Rob and me," she says with confidence, "not even you, Lincoln Presley."

"Nothing?" My hand finds its way to her center again and she closes her eyes as we move in on each other again.

"I'll miss you, Linc. But you'll never be free of Tally. I knew that a long time ago when you screwed around on me with her at her best friend's wedding. That's when I first met Rob." She grins. "*See?* It all worked out."

"I don't want to talk about Tally anymore."

Nika reaches for me. "Then, let's not talk about your *wife—your soon to be ex-wife*—anymore."

And we don't.

We take another shower together. I wash her long blond hair and kiss her fine neck and stroke her up and down in all the right places. It's easy being with Nika again. It feels like before when we were at Stanford. Her needs are so much simpler than Tally's although Nika is complex, Tally takes complexity to a completely different level.

Stay focused. Here and now. This.

I kiss Nika hard and she kisses me back. I crush all thoughts of Tally. I can't afford to think about her anymore.

"What is going on with you?" Nika asks playfully as she picks up her red dress and panties and bra off the floor and slips them back on.

"I'm glad you came. Can you stay?"

She sighs. "I can't. I have a fitting in less than an hour now. I'm going to be late as it is. You're different," she says with fresh curiosity. "Angry. Very angry. Then sweet. It's kind of turn-on. It's going to be hard to give you up, Lincoln Presley."

I wince when she tells me I'm different. "It's the line drive. Remnants of the line drive. Narcotics. Painkillers. I gave them up but lately I've needed them again. Sometimes, I can't even see straight I'm so pissed off."

I know." She fingers my damp hair. "You need to be careful, Lincoln. You need to stay focused."

"You always helped me do that before."

"You remember?"

"I remember."

She signs again and shakes her head. "They're trading you, Linc. That's what I really came to tell you." She gets this wan smile. "One of the reasons I came."

I suck in air. "When? Where?"

"I heard them talking. They didn't know I was there. I was cleaning out my office. I'm not coming back after the wedding. There's enough for me to do with Rob's charities and it appears to be a full-time job to be married to the man and his start-up business is going well. I'll be the chief financial officer for that venture. There will be an IPO next year. You should invest in it. Voluntarily, this time."

"Voluntarily?"

"You don't remember the mix-up with the six million?"

I shake my head. "No. Did I invest six million in Rob's company before?"

"You really don't remember everything from before, do you?" Nika asks looking incredulous.

"I told you I didn't. It comes back in waves. Different things will trigger memories but some are lost forever. Do you need six million, Nik?"

"You could make some heavy-duty cash with an investment like that. A hundred times or more in return," she says.

I pull on boxers and new sweats and a t-shirt. Nika follows me downstairs to the office where I pull out a checkbook and write her out a check for six million. "Don't wash that check; you'll clean me out, but I'm good for this much," I tease.

Nika looks surprised. The girl who is rarely surprised. *This* I do remember. "Why are you doing this, Linc?"

"You never know how far along in this game you'll get to go. If you think, Rob's start-up has the potential to do well in an IPO, I want a part of that action. I can't play baseball forever, and I could use some other financial options. Tally could very well clean me out if she changes her mind, and she could at any moment, and I'd rather invest some of the money before she does."

"And you trust me with your money to invest?"

"I do."

She gets this wide smile. "It's going to be huge, Linc. I mean it. Rob's onto something. This could be worth a lot like I said." Nika looks perplexed even as she slips the check into her purse. "You're different," she says again now. "More of a risk-taker than I've ever seen from you before. Does Tally see this in you, too?"

"Tally doesn't see me at all anymore. Tally appears to be disappointed with this version of me. In case, you haven't noticed she doesn't live here anymore. She's with some other guy and she could very well be having his kid, and she doesn't love me anymore."

"I'm sorry, Linc. She's acting foolish throwing all of this away." Nika grabs the front of my t-shirt and pulls me in and kisses me again. "She really is."

"I don't know. Maybe." I hang my head intent on bringing up again what I really need to know from Nika. "So where is it? The trade. And when exactly?"

"They're getting ready for the trade talks in New York."

"Where, Nika?" I chide softly.

"New York but Toronto wants you bad, too. Seattle, too. But I imagine the Yankees will come up with the most money. I heard figures upwards of ninety plus million. Five years. They were talking a package deal to make it even more enticing. They're looking at a few guys from Fresno, too. Hillman for one."

My head shoots up. "They're serious then."

"Yes, they're serious about a package deal. They need top dollar in order to cover Mad's contract. You knew that was coming."

"I did." I sit down heavily on the sofa in the living room where we've made our way. The trade news hits me hard for some reason. Nika sits down beside me and puts her arm around my shoulders. Nika's tall. Taller than Tally by a good four inches. Probably a better match than Tally in terms of height and proportion to me. Nika is different from Tally in every way, which I take solace in right now.

I'm being traded and Tally is with Sam, and I was just with Nika. The world is all messed up.

"You knew this would happen, Lincoln. It's only a matter of time. Take the money. You can buy your freedom from Tally. And you can start over. Any girl would be lucky to have you."

"Even a stats girl from Stanford?"

"Especially a stats girl from Stanford," she says and then looks at her watch. "I have to go."

"Right. The fitting."

"The fitting." She stands and turns to look at me before she reaches the foyer. "I love you, Lincoln Presley. I always will. We would have been good together."

"You're better off with Rob, Nik. I'm fucked up. Too fucked up. Even for you."

"You're not. You'll figure this whole thing out." She leans in and kisses me. I kiss her back.

"Cancel the fitting." My arms go around her and lift her up off the ground. She laughs and slides down my chest. She's different than Tally. My hands don't go all the way around her waist like Tally's. She slips from my embrace.

This fleeting look of guilt and sympathy crosses her beautiful face. "I have to go. It's a twenty-thousand dollar wedding dress. I'm getting *married*. To *Rob*. This *Saturday*."

"Right. It's always about the money, isn't it, Nika?"

"It's always about the money. That's what makes me such a good statistician and such an excellent choice for chief financial officer for a company that is going to make us all millions. I never lose my focus, not even for you, Lincoln Presley. There's a lesson in there somewhere for you, too."

"Ha! I think I'm learning that lesson. Thanks for the information. For the trade tip. For the trip down memory lane. Thanks for stopping by," I say softly.

"Thanks for letting me in." Her lips catch mine for an instant. She bites my lower lip. I taste my own blood. She is wild and dangerous and, on some level, exactly what I needed today. "Can I see you again before the wedding?"

"I don't think so. It would be too hard to turn you down the next time. I might do something foolish and call the whole thing off." She laughs.

"Am I still invited?" I ask.

"Yes, if you want to be." She smiles as she digs into her bag and pulls out an invitation addressed to Tally and me in the finest calligraphy. "Bring a guest or come stag. We'll make sure you're entertained. It will be quite the party. The Thorns are sparing no expense for their only son."

I kiss her one last time as she stands in the open doorway. Paparazzi be damned. Nika pulls away from me first quietly admonishes me for the slip up of PDA out in the open, but her hand lingers in mine.

"Goodbye Lincoln Presley. You're the best. Don't forget that. Don't let Talia get inside your head. You're worth it. I just wish things could have been different between us sooner, but that bridge has been crossed."

"You're mixing up metaphors, Nik."

"I told you my English wasn't perfect." She smiles wide.

"You're amazing."

"I am *focused*. Stay focused, Lincoln Presley and you will always win." She blows me a kiss as she slides into her car. I watch her pull away in her white Mercedes. She waves at me one last time as she guns the engine and speeds down our street and disappears from view.

CHAPTER TWENTY-THREE

immortal

TALLY

"They're not lost anymore. God found them,
and they went to Heaven.
We can't see them anymore, but they're always with us.
They stay in our hearts forever."
~ Talia Landon Presley

November 18th

I RACE THROUGH THE STREETS GOING A little faster than I should be for a thirty-mile-per-hour zone while Cara chatters on about pre-school and her playmates from the backseat of the car. She keeps going on about the elephants she's been learning about and tells me elephants are her favorite animal this week. She clutches her favorite picture of an elephant in her sweet little hands that she's already held up for me to see at least three times.

I've automatically take the turn toward Linc's house before I realize my mistake.

Linc's house.

Our house? I don't live there anymore.

Linc's house.

"Oops, Mommy made the wrong turn. I forgot where we were going, silly mommy." I briefly turn to look at Cara and smile. "Hang tight, baby girl. I just have to turn around because we're supposed to be headed to Grandpa's and Uncle Tommy's."

"Will Grandma be there?" Cara asks with such wistfulness that my heart starts to ache.

"No, sweetie. Grandma went to Heaven just like Aunt Holly. Remember that picture you drew for Daddy? It was so beautiful with all the clouds and blue sky with Grandma Tessa in Heaven with Aunt Holly. It was so beautiful, baby. We won't see them anymore. Not for a long time."

"They're not coming back?"

"No. They're not coming back."

"They got lost? So they went to Heaven," she pronounces.

I catch her gaze in the car mirror. "Yes. They're not lost anymore. God found them, and they went to Heaven. We can't see them anymore, but they're always with us. They stay in our hearts forever. Right here."

As we come to a stop at the intersection, I swivel around and point to my heart showing her.

She mimics me and points to her heart. "Right here," she says in her sweet voice.

"Right there. Forever. We'll always love them. That's how love works." I smile at Cara in the mirror and then quickly glance away looking toward the intersection as the car shifts into first and we accelerate across.

That's when I see this white Mercedes sedan come flying out of nowhere from the right.

She should have stopped.

She didn't stop.

There's no way we can both be in this same space at the same time and not intersect.

There's a strange hissing sound. Flames spiral upward from a white car. Glass shatters from the intense heat and the sound seems to go on forever. It reminds me of the record player needle that used to get stuck on the 45rpm records that my mom used to play for Holly and me when we were little.

A noxious smell of gasoline and burning rubber starts to gag me. I need air. I can't find any.

Cataclysmic.

This is.

Cataclysmic.

My car has bizarrely spun around. Within seconds, the air bag deploys making it impossible for me to move or see very much around me. It attempts to smother me. I can't move. I'm imprisoned by the white nylon fabric. The world goes dark soon enough.

Holly's here.

"Hey. What are you doing here? You look *amazing*," I say to her in stupefied wonder. "I've missed you. I'm so glad you're here. How long can you stay?"

She reaches out and smooths back sticky long strands of my hair from my face. Holly looks worried about something. She's frowning and shaking her head back and forth. "It's not your time, Tally, you can't stay."

Her words wound me deeply. "I just want the pain to stop. I *miss* you. I want to be with you. *Please.* Let me *stay.*"

"No. You can't stay. Don't cry."

A mysterious silence blankets my eardrums. The voices all around sound faraway except for Holly's. Hers sounds like she's right here.

But how can that be?

"Tell me something true," I say gasping for my next breath suddenly. I'm warm and cold at the same time.

"It's going to be okay."

"Liar."

She grins mischievously as if she's secretly glad to see me but equally surprised by it at the same time. As am I. The way she smiles reminds me of our sixteenth birthday party. Somehow, my parents pulled off the ultimate surprise party. Balloons everywhere. Cake, too. If felt just like this. Holly smiled just like this when we walked in side-by-side together with our arms linked into that amazing party.

Not the same.

Her smile disappears. "You can't stay. It's not your time," she whispers looking more anxious than before.

She stands back from me now. A ghostly shadow. She hovers, but she's further away.

"Don't leave me, Hol. Take me with you. We *have* to be together."

"I *can't*. It's *not* your time. We can't be together, Tal."

This fireman in all his yellow and black gear with the most reassuring blue eyes I've ever seen blocks my view of Holly. He leans down through the broken windshield and looks down at me. He's punctured the air bag and pushed it out of the way.

Such gratitude. Thank you.

In a matter of seconds, he's taken my pulse, but he still holds my wrist between his large hands, and murmurs to himself. It's obvious he's counting beats and for some reason I find it fascinating. His lips move as he enunciates each number. Next, he dons big gloves and gently sweeps the shattered glass away from me.

Then, he's wielding this huge wrench and begins to cut away at the crushed metal of the driver's door to free me. He reminds me of Linc.

"You need to find my…husband." Blood clogs my mouth making it difficult to talk, but I force the words out anyway. I think I even manage a weak smile. My teeth feel slick and unnatural. I cough a little and smile a lot less realizing I still can't move my hand up to reach my face and wipe the blood away for some reason. The fireman does this for me. Like Holly did, he brushes tendrils of my hair away from my face and uses his sleeves to wipe some of the blood away. His sleeve is now a bright red mixed with rubber yellow.

I stare at him, unable to form words, unable to breathe it seems.

I need Linc.

He should be here.

He's the one who rescues me.

He always does.

"Lincoln…Presley. The baseball player?" I take a jagged breath and force air into my ragged lungs. "He'll want to know what's happened. We have to tell him. I should have told him. And where's Cara? She'll be scared. You have to tell her everything is going to be okay."

He looks at me in alarm now. "There's someone else with you?"

"Yes. Cara. My daughter. She's four. Cara. She's in the backseat." I force my head to turn and helplessly stare at the empty backseat. "Caraaaaaaaa." My voice strains as more blood enters my throat.

Blood comes from everywhere now. I can barely see or breathe.

Panic roars through me. "Caraaaaaaaa?" I scream again. I force my arm backwards and desperately reach for her. *She's got to be back there.* A little hand steals into mine. "Cara."

I breathe easier for a few seconds.

"Momma." I can barely hear her but I do.

"She's here," I whisper to the fireman.

He quickly turns away and starts yelling to the others. "There's a kid. Cut from the other side. I think she's on the floor behind the driver's seat. The pole's in the way. I'll stay with Mom. Hurry! We have to move fast here before the other car blows!" He rummages through my purse and holds up my license. "Talia Landon Presley," he calls out. "Age 23. Her breathing's labored. Pulse is thready at 108 over 55 and falling. Come on! Move!"

I look past the fireman's shoulder at Holly who is getting more diffi-cult to see. "Tell me something true," I say again to my twin. Holly is holding Cara's other hand.

How can that be?

I squeeze the one I hold. "Hang on baby. Hang onto Mommy."

I can't hear what Holly's saying to her, but a filmy version of Cara just stands there looking bewildered. Cara mouths the words, "Momma" to Holly. Seeing two of us will be hard to explain. I try to lift my free hand to beckon Cara over to me to try and explain why there are two of us.

"Cara. Stay with me. Stay with Mommy. Stay with me!"

"Got the kid," someone says. "She was thrown onto the floor. We've got her. Labored breathing like Mom. Head injury. The one in the other car is DOA."

The fireman grabs my chin and forces me to look at him. He grips my left hand tightly between his. "You're going to be okay, Talia. I'm not going anywhere. Pete's working from the other side, and we're going to get you out. Stay with me. Focus on me, Talia."

"Just save my daughter. I'm fine. I'm tired that's all. So tired. So very tired."

"I know you're tired, but you have to stay with me." He turns back to the other firemen hovering nearby. "Just cut through. Do it now! She's crashing. We've got to get her out of here."

Cara's hand slips from mine.

Now, my rescuer holds onto my hand so tight it hurts. The pain seems to come from all directions now. There's this loud screech as a saw cuts through metal and then I'm lifted upward. I can see the blue sky and a few wispy clouds from this strange horizontal vista. My rescuer's eyes become a lighter blue in the sunlight but he looks surprisingly scared.

"Talia," he says gently. "Hang in there. Come on. Let's get you out of here."

My twin reaches for me too, and I grab her hand with my free one— the one that the fireman isn't holding. Holly's hand feels light and airy and warm, which is good because all of me is suddenly so cold. Yet, Holly's heat encircles me but I cannot stem the intense shaking, and I still have to get to Cara and tell her everything is going to be okay.

"Come with me, Cara. It'll be okay," Holly says.

It becomes clear who Holly has come for.

"No, Holly, please no. You can't take her. Cara belongs to me. You can't have her. Give her back to me. She's mine." I reach for my child. "Stay with me, Cara. Come to Mommy. Let her go, Holly. She's mine."

"It doesn't work like that."

"I don't care how it works. Give her back. It's not her time either. Go make a deal with God. He's taken enough from me already."

"You've got to let her go, Tally."

"No, I'm not letting go! Cara, come to Mommy. Say goodbye to Aunt Holly. Come on, baby. Come with me." Cara grabs my hand. I can feel her little hand in mine. "I will not let you go, baby. I will never leave you. Mommy won't ever leave you again. I promise."

Suddenly, it's dead calm. I'm weightless as if gravity has deserted me altogether. The light is bright, and the silence is so peaceful. And then, the light disappears altogether and there is nothing but the tomb of darkness, accompanied by these screams that seem to be coming from me as I desperately call out for Cara.

CHAPTER TWENTY-FOUR

hold back the river

LINC

*It is not in the stars to hold our destiny
but in ourseves.*
 ~ William Shakespeare

*We'll get through this.
These are the things we tell ourselves.
These are the things we wish to be true.*
 ~ Lincoln Presley

November 18th

AFTER NIKA LEFT, I PARKED IN front of the t.v. and watched ESPN and vigilantly listened for any baseball trade news knowing the owners are slated to meet next week and start talking and dealing for next year's MLB teams.

I call my agent relaying what Nika told me about New York, Toronto, or Seattle. Scott adds Seattle to the growing list of owners interested in a package deal.

"What's your preference?" he asks.

"Doesn't matter. Highest bidder."

"You know that's going to be the Yankees."

"Maybe."

"I thought you said you'd never play for them?"

"Doesn't matter. Just take the highest number. If I'm being traded I want the biggest contract. It doesn't matter where anymore."

"Things still bad with Tally?"

"I'm pretty sure that they couldn't get much worse. Especially, after today."

Guilt swamps me. I close my eyes as the images of Nika and what we did together assail me from all sides. The memory of her doesn't make me feel better now. I fucked up and most likely lost Tally in the process.

"What happened today?" Scott asks, sounding uneasy.

"I fucked around on my wife."

He sighs deep. "Do you really think that is a good idea, right now? You're kind of playing with fire here, Prez. The paparazzi are already having a field day as it is with you two splitting up. Please tell me you kept it as a low profile."

"Mostly."

"Shit, Prez. You better hope the paparazzi took the day off from camping out at your house."

"I think they did." I swallow hard but my throat starts to close up a minute later when I spy a photographer adjusting his camera lens while sitting in a car parked directly across the street from the house.

Was the car there earlier when Nika was here? I honestly don't know. Does it matter?

"It doesn't matter anymore," I say to Scott.

"Well, it *might*. Lie low, Prez. Things are going to heat up soon enough. Pray a little. Geez, with a huge contract on the line and your soon-to-be-ex-wife; we seriously don't need cause to flip her out even more because you're stepping out on her. They always side with the wife. Got that? This could get messier for you. *Trust me.* I've seen it. You need to lie low because I say so."

"You're starting to sound like Kimberley, but I get it. Just stayed focused on the contract terms when they come through and ensure they're solid. I'll do my part from here on out."

I'm still watching ESPN when my cell phone flashes. I curse myself for having it on silent all this time. I'm a little slow in answering because of the whiskey earlier on an empty stomach and no workout for the past four days and the remorse which has grown exponentially over what transpired with Nika less than two hours ago.

"Linc, it's Adam Landon. Look," he says with notable urgency but then he just stops talking.

I hear him shudder. "Sir?" I'm not sure what to call him now.

"There's been an accident. Tally and Cara. They're here. In the emergency room. Here at San Francisco General. We've been trying. To reach you. Look, it's…it's not good. You need you to come. To General like now. It's important. You need to get here *now*."

He's lost his normal bedside manner. Adam Landon is one of the calmest people I know but right now, he's talking in incomplete sentences and failing miserably at keeping the sharp edges of pure panic at bay. "I know you and Tally have been. Have been going through a rough time. But this. But *this*…it's very serious, son. You need. To get here now."

"Is Tally okay?" I ask fearfully. "And Cara was with her? How can that be? Marla has her. Right?"

"Cara was in the car. With Tally. Tommy said Marla called. She needed Tally to pick up Cara from preschool. Because they couldn't find you." He pauses. It takes another thirty seconds for him to say more. "She's just so small, Linc. But they've got the best working on your little girl. The best working on both of them." He sighs. "Tally's critical. She lost a lot of blood at the scene. The paramedics brought her back in the ambulance when she stopped breathing and they've been working on her since she arrived. They want to get her stabilized before they take her to surgery."

"Tally stopped breathing?" I think I do, too.

"The air bag deployed, and that may have caused some of the trauma and some of her internal injuries. We'll know more after they get her to surgery. She's in trouble, so is the baby. I need you to sign the release forms as soon as you get here since technically, you two are still married; I've broken a few rules already since they weren't able to find you. We can't afford to wait much longer, Linc. You need to get here as soon as you can."

I look down at my phone. It's been on silent for weeks. I have six missed calls on the cell—two from Marla, probably at the same time I was fucking Nika, and four more recent missed calls from the hospital and Adam. "Oh God."

"Just know, we've got the best here working on them. You just need to get here. Get here as soon as you can." My father-in-law starts to cry. With the recent loss of Tessa, I'm not surprised to hear Adam break down. Some part of me refuses to believe he's crying for more than his dead wife.

My wife and kid cannot die; I won't allow it.

"I'm on my way."

I change into some decent clothes and shove on a pair of shoes on and race out the door to get to my family. I leave a message for Marla on the way to the hospital and tell her Tally and Cara have been in a car accident, and they're taking Tally to surgery, and I don't know how Cara is and tell her to call me as soon as she gets this.

Getting traded to another team becomes the least of my worries as Tally, Cara, and my unborn child take their rightful places front and center in my life again, whether Tally wants that or not.

If I lose her, I lose everything.

The guilt over what I did with Nika just a few hours ago swamps me along with Tally's words from the night she left me.

"What if we've already lost everything?"

"What then?"

Tally's going to be fine.

We'll get through this.

These are the things we tell ourselves.
These are the things we wish to be true.

CHAPTER TWENTY-FIVE

solitaire

TALLY

I can't be sure of anything anymore.
Why is that?
  ~ Talia Landon Presley

November 22nd

THE ENDLESS WHIR OF MACHINES PENETRATES my skull which feels like a sledgehammer. There are far too many bright lights compelling me to open my eyes. I don't want to be awake. On some level, I know this to be true. The pain starts to come from everywhere. I valiantly fight the urge to open my eyes despite the persistence of the lights for a few more minutes. And then, I give in, and when I do, the room is blurry and far too bright.

Close.
Open.
Close.
Open.

My throat feels like it's been filled with concrete. I can't move. I start to make these guttural sounds as true terror seizes me. I can't move my head. There's a tube down my throat.

Linc's handsome face swims in front of mine.

He shouldn't be here.
We're separated.
We're done.
We're finished.

"Tally. It's okay. The tube is to help you breathe. It's keeping your lungs clear. You're okay. I'll let them know you're awake. I'm just going to press the call button and get some help. I'm right here, baby."

I squint attempting a variation of a glare because he knows how much I hate that term.

He presses my one untethered hand to his lips. "Sorry. I know you hate to be called baby, *baby.*"

I blink ever so slightly. His eyes go wide. Our attempt at shared communiqué works.

There's a commotion to our right. A nurse comes in and starts turning some machines off and others on. She adjusts the IV drip bag that hangs above my head. She gives me a tight smile.

All at once, I feel tired again. I close my eyes and effectively shut out the brightness.

I hear her say, "She'll sleep for several more hours, Mr. Presley, and then we'll remove the tube; you should go home and get some food and rest."

Typical. I'm the one with a tube down my throat and yet everyone fawns over Lincoln Presley.

Of course I would, too. What does that say about me?
Cara.
Cara.
Where is she?

The room is dark except for the moonlight that shines menacingly bright through the slits of the blinds. Otherwise, it's like a morgue in here. Still and dark.

My throat feels like it has been set on fire. I vaguely recall when the tube was removed, but my sense of time is off.

It takes a few minutes before my eyes get used to the darkness, and when they do, I spy Linc sleeping upright in the chair next to my bed. He looks terrible. He looks worse than when I left him more than a month ago.

I left him and Cara.

I left them.

Cara.

Where is she?

I work my mouth and lips around a bit to form words, but my throat is so dry that I start to cough as soon as I breathe in deep. The coughing attack wakes up Linc. He jumps up from the chair and looks disoriented for a few seconds. In the semi-darkness, I watch this haunted look assail his features as soon as he must remember where he is.

"Sorry. I didn't mean to wake you." I grab at my throat. "Oh God, it hurts too much to talk."

"Then, don't talk."

We warily eye each other for a few minutes. Then, he turns away and avoids looking at me altogether.

Still, I study him. He looks like he hasn't showered in days, and when I do get a glimpse of his face I note his mouth is turned down like the cartoon character Charlie Brown. It looks almost permanent. I want to ask him about it, but it takes entirely too much effort to form more words, and my physical needs become urgent.

"Water," I whisper in sudden desperation.

"Right. Here you go. Not too much. They said it can make you nauseous." He holds up a plastic cup of water in his famous pitcher hands and proceeds to fit a straw between my lips.

I focus on sucking the water up into the straw. It doesn't take long before this simple act proves to be too much. I'm exhausted by the effort.

I shake my head ever so slightly side-to-side not really understanding what is going on here.

"Why am I being treated like an invalid even though I feel like one? What is wrong with you? Why are you looking at me like that? Why am I here?" I spout off the most important questions and instantly regret it. My throat is set afire all over again; it feels worse than before. I moan at the wasted effort because he doesn't answer me anyway.

Instead, he coaxes me to attempt a second sip of water, but it does little to put out the flames that now engulf my throat. Worn out by the exertion, I lie back and settle my head in on the pillow and give up on the hydration effort entirely. Linc sets the water pitcher back down on the side table and settles back into the chair next to the bed.

It completely infuriates me that he hasn't answered me. Instead, he makes a big production out of pressing the call button for the nurse and proceeds to tell the tin-sounding voice that answers back that, "Mrs. Presley is awake."

Just like before, a nurse comes in and adjusts the dosage on the IV bag in quick succession. I begin to feel sleepy in a matter of seconds.

"Stop with the drugs." I choke a little with the effort in getting the edict out. I glare at them both with equal measures of fury.

The nurse murmurs to herself something about, "doctor's orders." Then, she glances at Linc, and he nods at her without either of them exchanging a word and after that she quickly leaves the room.

I helplessly watch him settle back down into the bedside chair but cannot fight the woozy feeling overtaking me to interrogate him further.

"Get some sleep, Tally. You need to rest."

"You sound like the one who needs. The rest. Next time, you need to. Tell me. What's going on. Elvis."

"Next time," he whispers as if the words are being torn from him.

Then, I'm off to wonderland again and vaguely realize I can't be sure of what he's said at all.

I can't be sure of anything anymore.

Why is that?

CHAPTER TWENTY-SIX

teen idle

TALLY

Sometimes, all you can do is breathe.
Or not breathe.
Breathe.
Not breathe.
Why breathe?
There's nothing left.
There's no one left.
Why breathe? God makes the sun come up again just to taunt me.
I hate Him for it.
I already know the sun will never shine as brightly for me again.
On some subconscious level, I know this much is true.
The pain—the incredible pain—consumes me,
and I already know I'll burn with it.
I welcome the darkness that descends upon me.
The darkness can stay.
 ~ Talia Landon Presley

November 23rd

A HUSHED ARGUMENT TAKES PLACE ACROSS THE room from me. I keep my eyes closed in order to concentrate on the words being said as well as who might be saying them. On some level,

I know that they will stop talking altogether if they discover I'm awake.

The sun should not be shining today.

I think I already know the reason why.

I've lost another day and, on some level, I know I've lost so much more.

The bright light already hurts my eyes. I both need and want to keep them closed.

"She needs her rest in order to get stronger. I don't want her upset—" Linc says.

"She *needs* to be told. It's part of the healing process. Believe me, I know this is hard for you, too, but the sooner she knows, the sooner she can start dealing with it." I recognize Dr. Eldon's voice.

"I agree with Linc. We should wait. A few more days. When she's stronger," my dad says.

What do I need to be stronger for?

My heart starts to race, and I try to think about what I remember—what I know to be true.

Tommy's face flashes before me. "I'll order piiiizzzzzzaaaaa."

"You dooooo thaaaaattttt."

And Katie Strongman is telling me that Cara is having a rough time. There are elephant drawings. Cara's. She is clutching them in her sweet little hands.

Her hand.

I held her hand.

I held onto her hand.

I didn't let go.

Did I?

"You don't know Tally the way we do," Linc says. "Trust me. She's not ready. We need to give her a few more days and keep her sedated rather than have her—"

Holly holds her hand.

Holly took Cara's hand.

I let go.

I open my eyes and look at all of them.

The sun is still shining. The God damn sun is still shining.
How is that possible?
Why would He do this to me?
"Noooooooooooooo."

I attempt to sit up by pushing my untethered hand beneath me in order to gain a better hold and weakly push myself up. It works for only a few seconds and then I'm slipping back down into the deep recesses of the bed.

Linc grabs the remote and tilts the bed up negating my failed efforts. I reward him with a small but grateful smile, but he doesn't return it.

His face is swamped with pain. I reach out as if I can somehow wipe it away with my touch, but he turns away from me.

"I can't do this," he says to the room.

I look over at my dad. He doesn't say a word; he just starts to cry.

"Daddy?" Tears sting my eyes but I refuse to let them fall until they tell me.

"Tally." Linc's voice breaks in just saying my name.

"Tally," Dr. Eldon says gently. I turn toward my gynecologist. "You're awake."

I frown because she's stated the obvious. *She's nervous. Why?*

Dr. Eldon starts again. "We've…just been discussing your progress. You're doing so much better, and we want to give you some time to—"

"Let me talk to her," Linc says interrupting my favorite doctor. "Let me talk to her. I'll tell her, but I'll do it in my own way, and I'll do it *alone*."

Dr. Eldon squeezes my hand. "You're going to get through this, Tally. Just know, we're all here for you." She touches my face and tucks a strand of my hair behind one ear. This wisp of a smile tries to cross her features, but then it's gone. I must have imagined it. She leaves without saying another word but I see her as she wipes her face with the back of her hand when she reaches the door and swiftly exits.

My dad leans down and kisses my forehead. "I love you, Tal." Then, he steps back and looks over at Linc and says to him, "I can stay."

The famous baseball player shakes his head and whispers something to my dad I'm unable to make out. Whatever it is Linc has said has my dad has him bolting fro the room.

We're alone.

The room feels like a vacuum, as if all the people just here have suddenly gotten sucked out into space. There is no air any longer.

I can't breathe. My heart pounds so fast it seems to be threatening to leap straight out of my chest.

This is bad.

"Where's Marla?" I ask cautiously.

"You're in the ICU. It's only immediate family."

"Well *lie* to them. I need to see her like right now. You can't keep Marla from me. If it's bad, I need her to be with me. I need her. Can't you see that?"

"She went into labor last night, Tally. She's here in the hospital."

"She had the baby?"

"She had the baby."

"Why are you basically parroting my words. What is *wrong* with you?"

"Tally." The way he's said my name practically crushes me. The weight feels unbearable and I already know the pain is related to what he needs to tell me and that it is far too great to even be said aloud.

His beautiful grey-blue eyes swim with tears. Lincoln Presley, the strongest one among us, the rising star, the greatest man I have ever known starts to break down in front of me.

He cries.

He lays his head down next to my left arm and I catch his tears as they fall onto my outstretched hand and the sheets. I try to stop them, but they just keep coming.

He can't stop crying.

With a trembling hand, I finally reach out and press the call button.

"We need some help here. My…husband…needs some help here," I say in a croaky voice into the intercom when the someone finally answers. Soon, a nurse comes in. Linc lifts his head and makes a valiant attempt to get it together.

"He's in a great deal of pain," I say guardedly. It's as if the words cost me everything. My lungs burn, and my heart seems to be on permanent pause—it seems to have stopped beating altogether. "He won't tell me why."

The nurse leads Linc away from me. He doesn't look back, which feels like an even greater loss.

She returns a few minutes later and proceeds to adjust the dosage on my IV just like before.

"I want to know what's going on. I need to understand why Lincoln Presley is falling apart, but no one will tell me."

"You need your rest, dear." She slowly meets my gaze and the sympathy in her eyes practically annihilates me. She continues to pat my hand while I drift away.

"Noooooooooooooo." The word is painful to say and some part of me already knows why.

And the pain?

This pain feels permanent.

It's dark again when I wake up. It appears I've lost another day. Linc sleeps upright in the chair.

His neck will be in some serious pain sleeping like that.

Lincoln Presley looks terrible even in the limited light from the moon seeping through the closed window blinds. "You look really bad," I finally say.

He lifts his head and looks straight at me. There's a haunted look to his face worse than before. He looks like the sparkly vampire from *Twilight* when Edward believes Bella is dead.

It's bad.

I swear I've never seen Linc look like this before. I shouldn't care. I'm not supposed to care about him anymore, but I reach for him anyway and help him to a stand.

"You're awake," he says.

"And this is the worst news?" He doesn't even crack a smile at my joke. "Tell me what's going on, please." I look at Linc expectantly.

Instead of saying anything more, he reaches for the pitcher near my bedside and pours himself a glass of water with an unsteady hand and attempts to swig it down. He sputters the drink, then coughs and proceeds to spill half of it down the front of his t-shirt.

It's the Fresno Grizzlies one I stole from him some time ago. I'm surprised he's wearing it. A part of me is wondering where he found it. He's been complaining that I must have shrunk it in the laundry by washing it one too many times, and that it doesn't fit him anymore.

And yet, he's wearing it. Why?

"What's going on with you? What do you need to tell me?" My throat doesn't hurt as much with the talking effort today. I glance at him in triumph and momentarily forget my role in this interrogation.

"They gave you some antibiotics. You had a throat infection from the tracheal tube. You should be feeling better."

"Along with the narcotics. Sure. I'm feeling better; I think." I try to smile, but my lips are chapped.

Linc seems to notice this. Within seconds, he's making an effort to line them with fresh Chapstick that appears to have been staged by my bedside for this very purpose.

It takes a few minutes before I realize he's stalling. I can't fire questions at him when he's busy lining my lips with cherry-flavored Chapstick.

Avoidance.

We're both so good at it.

"Cara? Where is she?" I ask simply.

You would think this wouldn't be the hardest question to answer but he actually catches his breath and holds it for at least ten seconds. Then, when he does breathe outward, it comes out as a big sigh and he starts to hyperventilate.

"Are you okay?" I ask in concern.

He nods but moves aways from me and grabs onto the back of the bedside chair and still seems to struggle to get air into his lungs.

"What do you remember?" he finally asks.

"Marla called me. She asked me to pick up Cara because we couldn't find you. Tommy was going to order us a pizza. I went and picked up Cara. I talked to Katie Strongman. She's still not my favorite person sorry to say. She said Cara was having a hard time. Cara drew some elephants. She clutched the drawing on her lap. She seemed fine to me. I took a wrong turn heading toward home instead of Dad's. I was telling Cara about Heaven. She asked where Grandma was and I told her she was in Heaven with Holly. We had ice cream. Pizza. With Tommy. That's all I remember."

He reaches for the water pitcher again. His hands shake even more as he pours himself another glass and slowly drinks it down.

"Enough with the water," I say with growing irritation. "*Where* is Cara?"

He pauses for a long while and then he's shaking his head as if he can't quite believe what he's about to say. He gets this incredulous look laced with pure sorrow. "She's with Holly and your mom."

"*What* did you just say?"

"She's gone, Tally."

"You're *lying* to me. Why would you do this? Why would you say something like that when you *know* it couldn't possibly be true? We had pizza and ice cream. *She's fine.* She is *fine.*"

Linc automatically reaches for the call button and presses it multiple times.

The nurse comes rushing in as well as my dad, who now looks openly devastated. My brother follows closely behind him. Tommy's eyes are bloodshot as if he's been crying.

But sixteen-year-olds don't cry.

Everyone knows that.

"Daddy, is it true?" I finally ask feeling this sudden dread grip me while my mind acknowledges that all the nightmares I've been having have coalesced and become reality.

"It's true, baby girl. Her injuries were just too severe. She never came out of the coma. She died two days ago, Tally. There was… nothing…they could do." The voice of the great cardiologist breaks down. He runs out of words and the ones he's chosen to say out loud are of the worst kind. "She's gone, Tally."

I stare at my brother. Tommy finally meets my gaze. "Is it true?"

Tommy nods.

Tommy cries.

I however stay dry-eyed and refuse to accept this outcome.

"Noooooooooooooo. No! No! No! It can't be true!"

Linc takes my hand and presses it to his lips. "Tally, it's true."

"It can't be. It can't be true. We were driving. I made a wrong turn. I was coming toward the house, but that wasn't right, and so I stopped at the stop sign and then I made the turn to go to Dad's. Tommy had ice cream and ordered a pizza. We went to Dad's and had ice cream and pizza. Cara is *fine*. You're *lying* to me," I say cruelly and look solely at Linc.

"She's not fine, Tally." Linc clasps my hand tighter; the pain of his grip shoots up my arm.

"Let go. You're hurting me, Linc!" Tears cascade down his face. "She has your eyes. She is our one and only truth. She is the greatest gift we ever made. She can't be dead."

His lips part but he doesn't say anything more.

He can't. He's struggling to even breathe.

I've been there. I've done that.

That's what you do when death comes for you or one of your loved ones.

When grief takes over your hollowed-out shell of existence this is what you do.

Sometimes, all you can do is breathe. Or not breathe.

Breathe.

Not breathe.

Why breathe?

There's nothing left.

There's no one left.

Why breathe? God makes the sun come up again just to taunt me. I hate Him for it.

I already know the sun will never shine as brightly for me again.

On some subconscious level, I know this much is true.

The pain—the incredible pain—consumes me, and I already know I'll burn with it.

I welcome the darkness that descends upon me.

The darkness can stay.

"Cara." Just saying her name aloud causes me to shut down. My heart empties while my body convulses.

This does not compute.

This cannot be happening.
The math is wrong again.

The machines go haywire. All the alarms go off at once. The nurse races in. Her eyes go wide as she stares at the machines. "Everyone needs to leave, please. Now!"

She checks my vitals while a few more people in blue surgical scrubs rush in. I gasp for air. The room starts to disappear. Black filmy edges begin to fill my world up. They close in and take over all the color that was there.

"Tally, I'm Dr. Marston," says a blond guy leaning in near my face. "Stay with us, Tally." He turns away. "Pulse rate? Everyone clear the room! Call the code team. She's crashing! Everyone else, leave us!"

With effort, I force my eyes open. My father and brother head for the door. Linc still hovers nearby, refusing to leave, refusing to let go of my hand.

The medical staff starts shouting out numbers at Dr. Marston. The machines go off with even more alarms until Dr. Marston shouts to one of the nurses to completely turn them all off. "Turn them all the *fuck* off!"

It's weird; I almost smile. We are kindred spirits in the use of the word *fuck* in inappropriate settings. *I like him.*

Then, silence entombs me. Their voices get very far away. Like a filmy black curtain on a movie set, my world dims, and it feels as if I'm slipping away. I can't make my lips work. I concentrate on Linc while he exchanges an anxious look with my father and brother as they start to take their leave. Linc has taken up a sentry position near my bedside and holds his right arm across his chest as if it's the only way to hold himself together.

The nurse checks my vitals, shouts the numbers to Dr. Marston and then proceeds to adjust the dosage on the IV bag again per the doctor's instructions. I watch her do it and wonder if I can turn it up all the way when she's not looking.

Cara's dead.
I already knew this.

I open my eyes and seek out my father, who still stands in the doorway trying to make sense of all the chaos. "I saw her, Daddy. With Holly. Holly took her. I asked her not to. I held her hand as long as I could. I didn't want to let go. I tried not to let go." I can't bear to look at the devastation of my dad's face let alone Linc's when I steal a look at his. I close my eyes. "I did this. I let her go," I whisper.

My dad rushes back to my side and squeezes my hand despite the protests of the entire medical team fighting for all the limited space at my bedside. "*No.* You didn't. It was an accident, sweetheart. It wasn't your fault."

I helplessly look at him. "How do you know?"

"I just do." He strokes my hair back away from my face. "It just happened. She was so small. There was nothing they could do."

"Oh, Daddy, I need Marla. Find a way to get her in here," I whisper. "Get me the drugs. I don't want to be awake." My hand slips from my dad's and Linc's at the same time. My body sinks inward and hurtles toward the dark abyss. I silently beg it to take me.

This incredible pain ignites as if I've just been struck by lightning.

The pain—the incredible pain—consumes me, and I already know I'll burn with it.

I'm untethered all at once. That's what this is.

I welcome the darkness as it descends upon me.

Darkness can stay.

CHAPTER TWENTY-SEVEN

weeds

TALLY

You wake up every day and for ten seconds or so your life is normal; you innocently embrace the day's goodness and light and freely smile.

Then. You remember. And then. You hate everything and everyone within the realm of you in this unwelcome silence.

You spend a great deal of your waking hours armoring up for the inevitable sympathy and empty words from people incapable of understanding you or your world anymore.

Your darkest thoughts?

All you really want to do is trade places with the ones you lost.

The worst feeling? One of them? That you're awake. That you live and breathe. And they do not.

You're here, and they're not. And breathing without them seems all but impossible.

The second breath you take in? After you remember? After your reality assaults you? That's the worst one—the worst moment.

Then, there are all the others that follow. Those are hard, too.

And this is your life, now.

Welcome aboard. You liking the ride so far?

~ Talia Landon Presley

November 24th

IT'S SUNNY OUT WHICH I HATE.

I'm alone in the hospital room which I wonder about.

With an intensive dedication for deviant behavior, I take my sweet ass time in unhooking the various connections on my left hand which have me tethered to the IV and the machines. Then, I slowly stagger over to the window—the bright sunny window—that somehow betrays me and allows daylight in.

Bright. Sunny.

What god would allow this? Why does God always gives you sunny days when the darkest days of your life descend upon you?

It must be some kind of cruel joke. His way of showing you, he had the last laugh. The last word.

And he does.

Cruel, indeed.

Perhaps, there is no God because what god would do this? What God would give you sunny days when your twin sister is dead, when your mother is dead, and when your four-year-old daughter—your greatest miracle, your only truth—is dead?

"Cara," I whisper her name in the fervent hope that Holly secured a deal with God and He'll bring her back to me. But God doesn't seem to hear me and I don't know where the hell Holly went to.

I grip the porcelain window ledge so tight my knuckles turn white to avoid falling. Having broken out of my bonds from the IV, the machines' alarms go off.

They sound like train whistles. Obnoxious and unnecessary.

The machines are unhappy. We do not care.

I glance down. Blood slowly trickles down my right inner thigh.

Of course.

Holding onto the walls for support, I finally make it to my destination and vaguely note the trail of blood I've left across the tile floor from the window to the restroom doorway.

I feel faint. The filmy black edges of unconsciousness are back attempting to obscure my vision, but I fight to stay coherent and upright.

I will not pass out.

I. Will. Not. Pass. Out.

I dully watch as the bright red water swirls, goes down, and disappears.

I lost the baby. No one needs to deliver that news.

I feel the emptiness in my womb. No one needs to tell me.

Dr. Eldon peeks in around the corner of the bathroom door.
Forget privacy there isn't any in hospitals.
That much I do remember from the times before.

"There you are. You're awake. We sent Linc home. He should be back in a few hours." My gynecologist takes my arm and helps me climb back into bed.

"Why don't you tell me what's going on." It's not a request of her any longer. It's a command. *Mine.*

Dr. Eldon nods.

She finally gets her wish.

"You had emergency surgery seven days ago. You were in a car accident, Tally. You lost a lot of blood, but the paramedics on scene were really good. It was touch and go for a little while there but they saved you. You had emergency surgery seven days ago for internal injuries and experienced a placental abruption. There were complications. There was just so much trauma and he was in grave trouble by the time you were brought here. He did not survive, Tally." Dr. Eldon stops and takes a breath and then slowly lets it out.

"When can I leave?" I ask slowly drawing in air and trying to keep it together for the good doctor. Delivering this kind of news is not an enviable task. I'm trying to be keep the rage at bay in her presence. I do not understand God at all at this point and what He's taken from me. I time my next words counting out to ten. "I already know this ending. I just want to get the hell out of here."

"It's going to take some time." I roll my eyes. "A few more days," she adds quietly. She tightly grips one of my hands. "You should be well enough to go home in a few more days."

"Well enough." I sigh. "Okay. How many days then? *Exactly*?"

"Three or four. You actually need to take it easy for the next couple of weeks. You've had major surgery. You just lost a baby...and a child." She pauses for about thirty seconds.

"Nothing more to lose, is there?"

"I'm so sorry, Tally. I don't even know what to say."

Her grey eyes fill with tears. "The good news is Dr. Marston repaired your lacerated liver and I was able to save your right ovary. You can have other children, Tally, it's possible that you will. Someday."

"I don't think so."

"Well, you don't have to think about that right now. All you need to do right now is focus on getting well and dealing with your grief over Cara and this baby and all that's happened to you. You need help coming to terms with all of that, and I am here to ensure you get it. I've asked for Jane Nelson to stop by and see you. She specializes in—"

"Crazy, right? I need to see a shrink before I can get out of here."

Of course, I do.

Practically every time I've been in a hospital there's been a Psych consult.

Of course, I'm not going to get out of this one.

"Yes," she says slowly. "I've already asked for a Pysch consult with Dr. Nelson. She can help you. Jane's the best. You'll like her, Tally, and she's going to help you both—you and Linc—get you through this as much as she can. We all are." She shakes her head and frowns. "Losing a child is like no other and it's just going to take some time for you two to process what's happened. You have a support system. Your family. Each other. I know this is hard for you. I know it seems like the world is at an end. You've lost Cara and your unborn baby. I'm not going to pretend this isn't beyond devastating because I know that it is for you and Linc as well as your family. Given your history, I know this feels impossible. But you can do this, Tally. You can survive it, and you will. And someday, when you're ready, you and Linc can try again for another child when the time is right."

"Time," I say and look toward the sunny window and feel the need to curse it for being. "The *time* is never right for us." I look over at her. "Haven't you heard? We're getting a divorce."

"I didn't know that." Dr. Eldon looks a little shocked. She obviously doesn't read the gossip columns or the sports pages. She shakes her head side-to-side. "I don't see that happening right now. He's been here for the past week barely leaving your side. He only left you today because the nursing staff pushed him out the door and threatened to call security if he didn't go home and take a shower."

My lips part. I try to smile. It's funny.

I can imagine the nurses fawning over my husband, practically swooning over him like every woman does. I can't imagine Linc not showering for seven days. But then, my lips form a straight line and guilt lances through me when I remember Cara is dead, and my baby is gone. The world blinks off again, and I stonily stare out the window at the bright sunny day and only wish for darkness. Dr. Eldon seems to notice.

"Tally, you'll get through this," she says with fresh sympathy. She deftly takes my other hand and holds it refusing to let me go.

We sit like this for a long time.

I don't say anything, and neither does she which I so appreciate because there are no words.

There are no words.

There is nothing.

A whole lot of nothing lies ahead of me.

The tilt of the sun's rays actually changes, and Dr. Eldon is still here. She only moves turning toward the sound of the door swinging open.

Linc is here.

"Well, I'll leave you two to it," Dr. Eldon says too brightly. "Remember, no release until you meet with Jane Nelson. My orders. Your surgeon's orders. Everyone's orders, in fact. She's all yours," she says to Linc.

Dr. Eldon leaves.

I glance over at Linc and note his dark hair is still wet. He's wearing a black Polo shirt with faded blue jeans.

"They told me that you'd be asleep for hours. That's why I left."

"Not because they threatened to call security if you didn't shower. Not because of that."

"No."

Silence.

"Do you ever just feel like telling them all to fuck off?" I ask into the void.

"All the time."

"What did she mean by she's all yours?"

"I think it was just wishful thinking." He sighs deep and for the first time since I woke up I think actually catch a glimpse of his former self and the ghost of a promise of his amazing smile.

"They're going to release you this Friday afternoon. You can stay at the house. With me. It's all arranged. I hired a nanny—a full time housekeeper, actually. She's a quasi nurse, too. Her name is Eddie Lightner, Edith actually, but she likes to be called *Eddie*. Kimberley found her for us. She can do everything. She can help us. You can take the downstairs master until you're well enough to climb the stairs again. I've already moved all of your things back in from your dad's place. The doctors think it will be best. To start up your normal life again."

He's babbling. I'm a little fascinated with how much his lips are moving and how fast, and the fact that he's taken care of everything.

I wonder how that is even possible since he's obviously been staying at the hospital with me. "A normal life. What's that?"

"It's *our* life, Tally. The doctors say we need grief counseling and that we should go together."

"That's what they think? That's what they say? Whose *they*?"

"Your surgeon, Dr. Marston. Dr. Eldon. Dr. Nelson; she's the psychiatrist that's been assigned to you. Your dad. Everyone basically. Marla."

That gets my attention.

"Where is she? Why hasn't she been here?"He looks away. Not the reaction I was expecting.

"She's got her own thing going on," he finally says. "Their baby had a heart condition. They weren't sure she was going to make it. Your dad performed the heart surgery a few days ago, and the baby, Alexandra, is doing better now but she's still in the neonatal intensive care unit. Marla's not handling things very well. She's devastated about Cara. She thinks it's somehow her fault. If she hadn't called you. If she'd been there. She's taking Cara's death pretty hard. Charlie's worried about her. He thinks she might have postpartum depression. She's at home. Charlie is taking care of her."

"Charlie is there, taking care of her," I say grimly.

"She's falling apart. Her baby's sick. But at least she has one, right? Whereas I? I have *nothing*!"

"You have me." He reaches for my hand and brings it to his lips. "If you'll have me. I'm here and I'm staying."

"If you''ll have me," I say repeating what he's said. "Why wouldn't I?" He gets this contrite look as if he doesn't deserve a second chance. I lean into his chest and his arms go around me.

I need him.

I need us.

"I lost the baby."

"I know. I'm so sorry, Tally. I know." He pulls back from hugging me. "He was in trouble. Dr. Eldon tried to save him, but you were in trouble and bleeding out. We had to decide. We had to save you. I told her that was what I wanted them to do."

His words land on me like stones. I pull back further. "Him? You chose me over him?"

"I had to. There was only one choice I could live with and that was you. He was twenty-four weeks, Tally, but there was too much trauma from the accident." He takes a deep breath. "He was in trouble and there wasn't much they could do. I had to make a choice, and I chose you."

"He was ours."

"He was ours."

I lay back in the bed and close my eyes. The day is too bright. The sadness tries to suffocate me. Linc lays his head on my chest. Tears slide down my face, unchecked.

"I know, babe. It's hard." He lifts his head and looks up at me. "They want you to talk to Dr. Nelson. I've met her. You'll like her," he says quietly.

"Not today. Today, I don't want to talk to anyone. Just you. Only you." He gets this grim look as if he's unable to fulfill that request or isn't worthy. I sweep my fingers along his face. "Stay with me. Please."

He nods and climbs into bed with me and puts his arms around me. I truly believe it's the only way I'll survive this day.

Knowing.

Knowing Cara is dead.

Our baby is gone.
Linc is all that remains for me.
"Anchor me," I say turning into him.
"I will."

We stay this way for what seems like hours. Occasionally, a nurse pops her head into the room from the doorway but for some inexplicable reason they leave us alone as we weep in relative silence together over the irrevocable loss of our children.

And for some unknowable reason, the loss feels even bigger.

The loss is bigger.
I don't know why.

I wake up in the early dawn only to find Linc is gone.

Linc is gone, and I miss him.
Why isn't he here?
Why did he leave me when I need him the very most?

CHAPTER TWENTY-EIGHT

hypocrates

TALLY

*God provides the world with another day of sun, and
I hate Him for it. Again.*

~ Talia Landon Presley

November 24th

BREAKFAST.
Break fast.
The idea of food seems incongruent for all the right reasons. I poke at the yellow mess that the hospital cafeteria has designated to be scrambled eggs and hate the fact that I'm alive and Cara is not. Next, I make rounded squares out of the green jello blob on my plate with the spoon provided having searched in vain for a butter knife to better complete my artwork, but discovered there wasn't one.

Apparently, I'm considered a suicide risk.

Yet, nobody dares to tell me as the power of suggestion could make it so.

Indeed.

And where is Linc?

It's been hours since I woke up in the early dawn, and discovered he wasn't here.

And he hasn't come back.

And I wonder why.

I have long stretches of time to wonder why. I close my eyes. I still wish for darkness to take me and wish to never come back.

I'm still here having dozed off for the one thousandth time and wishing for more drugs. And yet? That drug-induced haze I've come to expect has not been fulfilled today.

The door swings open. My heart leaps expecting to see Linc.

I need Linc.

I allow myself to *need* him.

Instead, it is a stunning woman in her mid-twenties with dark auburn hair that folds in waves around her shoulders as if she just finished up with her best stylist. She wears a long, white lab coat with a lot-cut black t-shirt that reads, "I'm a psychologist. I will fuck your mind, too," and black jeans with four-inch silver stilettos I know to be Manolo Blahnik's.

My mouth hangs open. She is not what I was expecting. She is a dichotomy of extremes in color and fashion and attitude. Black and white, austere and sensuous, a woman who would tell you to fuck off if she needed to. A Disney version of Ariel if the mermaid was decidedly bad in some way.

Her red-lined lips part confirming everything I've just concluded about her. And, as soon as she smiles, the room seems to change, as if clouds are parting from an unexpected storm and there's a sun and a rainbow and a promise of stars. She's turned the darkness to dazzling light within seconds. And surprisingly? I don't hate her for it. *Yet.*

I wince at the sudden brightness although I still long for darkness for all of eternity. *I'm not sure I can handle this mermaid today.*

"I'm Jane," she says in this low voice.

Forget Ariel. She's got this Emma Stone thing going on with her husky voice and sultry looks.

"I'm Tally." I hold out my hand, and she takes and grips it hard like a man. I'm taken aback. Stunned, really.

"God," she says with a little laugh and a dramatic roll eye roll, "I'm trying to be so *cool* here, but I have to confess I saw your performance in *Swan Lake* last year with my mom, and I just cannot *believe* you're going to be my patient. This is surreal, amazing and it's just going to make Stella fucking flip out when I tell her!" She hangs her head for a brief moment and groans. "Backup, Nelson."

She's talking to herself. I smother a smile because sometimes I do that, too.

"Okay. Sorry. Damn!" She flashes me a fresh smile. "I just used the word *fuck* in my first sentence with you. I'm so *sorry*."

"Not your first sentence. Maybe you're fourth? Your first was, 'I'm Jane.'" I press my lips together to keep from smiling for a second time. Then, I incline my head toward her as if we're kindred spirits. "*Fuck* is my favorite word. In fact, it may be the only thing you get me to say without prompting."

"So if I ask you how you're doing you'll answer…"

"Fucking fabulous. It will not get any better than this. *Obviously*," I deadpan.

"It will," she says softly, "but I try not to argue with my patients on their very first day with me."

I give her the look—the please-fuck-off-and-possibly-die look. It seems only fair that she knows right away that she can't help me.

"What's with the jello?" she asks throwing me off with such a strange question straight out of nowhere.

"They wouldn't give me a knife."

"You're a *flight risk*, Tally. Of course, they wouldn't give you a knife. They run things around here just like the TSA. They'll throw out your favorite shampoo if you let them. Do you *want* a knife?"

I can't tell if she's messing around with me or if this is some hidden mumbo-jumbo way of getting me to talk or winnow her worldly psychic powers way inside my head. "I don't need a knife. I don't need anything from anyone."

"That's what I thought." She goes over to the window and gazes out. "Okay then," she says turning slightly to look back at me over her shoulder with this slightly mischievous look.

"I'm sorry about the fangirl moment, and I'm glad I won't have to apologize for the use of the word *fuck* because, let's face it; that word covers a myriad of emotions, and it is just so *fucking perfect* for expressing just about most everything in life." Her smile fades. "And death," she says sadly.

"Don't start." I hold up my hand. "Save it, Janie. I don't want to hear how I'll *survive* this. That I'll get over this. I just lost my kid and my baby. *And,* my husband—my *almost ex-husband*—has decided to go AWOL for no apparent reason on the sunniest day of the year when I need him the very most, and they're withholding the drugs so that I feel every God damn thing today and no one here will even bother to fucking tell me where he is or why I can't have the drugs.

"So save your little speech for somebody else about how it will all get better. I'm not buying it. So, I *survived.* So-fucking-what? For *this*? So I can feel this incredible pain in my chest where my heart used to be because God decided to pull it out and crush it for all the world to see? *Again?* I don't want to be saved by you or anyone else. You got that? Fucking write that down. Print it up, frame it, and then nail it to your office wall to *remind* yourself that I don't *need* your help nor do I want it.

"Why don't *we* just get straight to the point? I need you around for a couple of hours so you can fill out some damn form and validate for all the wondrous medical team and staff here that I am all fucked-up but salvageable and then all you really have to do is cheerily promise to straighten me all out, and then they'll let me get the hell out of here. Well, why don't we just cut to the chase and save each other loads of time? Why don't you just sign the damn release form, so I can get out of here and go…" My tirade ends without warning for both of us.

The word *home* won't come out of my mouth to even finish the last sentence nor this dramatic scene.

"Anger," Jane says with a nod as if she's beginning a college lecture to one of her favorite students.

"*Anger* is *good*. Now, we're getting somewhere. It's the docile ones I can't stand. I don't tell them that, of course, but if you're not angry, if you're not royally pissed off, then the grief gets the better part of you right from the start. Good job."

She pauses for so long I finally have to give in and look over at her. "Go where, Tally?" she finally asks me with notable curiosity.

"No. Where. *Nowhere.*" I hold my arms around my body to keep myself from falling apart. I've said more in the last five minutes than I have in the past three days since I first awakened from my drug-induced stupor and learned my life was over. I take a decidedly shaky breath. "I just want to go home, but home isn't there anymore."

"Home is where your heart is."

"Hey, Dr. Hallmark, I am *not* buying into that brand of Zen *at all*. I don't have a heart anymore. I most certainly don't have a home or a life to go back to. Skip that part of the lecture, please." I clutch at my chest even more to prove this to her on some level because the pain in my heart is suddenly unbearable. "I have never in my life felt this empty inside."

"It's the worst feeling; isn't it?"

Her eyes are full of sympathy. I get a little lost in her sky blue gaze. I hold my breath hoping the sentimental moment will pass, but it holds onto me.

"It is," I finally say struggling to hide my fascination with this woman who has materialized in my hospital room like a fresh breeze I didn't know I was missing out on until now.

"Hey," she says coming over to me and nudging my tethered-up arm, "are you up for a walk? This place feels like a prison and even though the weather is shitty outside, I think we should take a stroll somewhere together. Get you something *decent* to eat. There's a Starbucks a few blocks from here."

She points at the food tray and my mutilated artwork and makes a weird face.

In another life, I'm sure we could have been friends.

"A walk? A walk isn't going to put my life back together and besides it's *sunny* outside, Dr. Hallmark, I hate to break it to you, but it is." I sweep my hand toward the sunny window. "God has a twisted sense of humor, now doesn't he?"

"If there is a god," she says airily. "Do you think there is?"

"I don't know anymore. If there is a god, why would he create such a nice day when my baby is gone and Cara is dead?" Just saying Cara's name out loud causes me to stop and catch my breath and hold it. I squeeze my eyes shut and hope to recover. When I open them, Jane watches me closely.

Then, she nods as if I've just shared a big secret. "Cara's your four-year-old."

"Yes."

"I'm sorry, Tally. I'm so sorry. I've seen pictures of her already. She's so beautiful. I'm so sorry." She squeezes my hand again.

"Who showed you pictures of her?"

"Your husband. I met up with him yesterday. And we talked about you and Cara and everything." She sports this expressionless look upon her face and continues to study mine.

"What's this? No fangirling over the famous baseball player?" I start to grin and then stop as the world goes a little dim because I'm actually smiling, and that proves impossible. My face twists up. I attempt to recover and retreat back to the familiarity of drownable sorrow. "You're seriously not going to say anything about the guy I'm married to, if only temporarily?" I ask in a hushed tone.

Jane grins for both of us. "I'm trying to keep my fangirl moments to a minimum—only one per day. Lincoln Presley was yesterday's." She actually laughs. "*You* are today's."

I give her a tight smile despite myself.

"It's okay to smile or laugh, Tally. It's part of the process. Grief is a very strange beast," she says gently. "I told your husband that, too."

"And what did you think of my husband?"

Curiosity has me bantering with this woman. She's just so alive. I find it captivating on some weird-ass level.

"I'm not going to lie. I think, if I were you, I'd find a thousand reasons to stay, but that could just be the fangirl in me talking." She leans over to me and whispers, "And I don't even like baseball, but I think I could overlook that." She laughs again.

Her laugh is like the sweetest wind chime. You could surround yourself with her sound and just listen to her all day. She is enchanting, and begrudgingly I admit that I am enchanted with her.

"Neither do I." I shake my head side-to-side. "I don't like baseball either. Not anymore. It's taken too much from me."

She looks momentarily surprised and then introspective as if she's just learned something important that must be filed away for safekeeping. Something she'll tap into later. All I can do is sigh, realizing she's gotten me to say far too much about myself and Lincoln Presley in a matter of fifteen minutes.

"A walk. Let's take a walk."

"A *walk?*"

She helps me get out of bed and come to a stand. Then, she's handing me a white lab coat that is just like hers. "Come on. Put it on. If I have to wear one when I come and do rounds in this place to look *presentable* around here, so do you."

I like Jane. I think I liked her instantaneously.

I'm probably not supposed to like her, but instinctively I know she's going to be the one to help me get out of here, and I am suddenly all about doing that.

She undoes the IV line that has been tethered to the bed and to me. She unhooks the wires connecting me to the numerous machines that monitor me and my bodily functions much like an astronaut and without any hesitation whatsoever she just turns them all off. "Let's break you out of here, Tal." She waves her hand like Vanna White indicating I should slide into the wheelchair she's just retrieved from the closet.

"No way." I stand near the side of the bed in an attempt to keep my balance and fight the sudden vertigo feeling while adamantly shaking my head. "I *can* walk. I'm a *dancer* in case you've forgotten. I don't *do* wheelchairs. As in *never.*"

She just smiles and shakes her finger at me. "Too many liabilities. I'm already in enough trouble as it is. I had to do some heavy-duty convincing of your surgeon to make this even happen. Don't bug out on me now."

Who says bug out?

Where is she from?

Mars? Or Venus?

And then, as if on cue, the nurse who has been fucking with my IV drug dosage for days appears in the doorway. She doesn't look too pleased with Jane, but then again, she doesn't look too surprised either.

"Tally's going for a walk," Jane says as if we're discussing party plans. "She's agreed to go in the wheelchair for safety reasons. I've already cleared it with Dr. Marston. I'll be with her the entire time. Help her into the chair, will you, please, Helena?"

Without uttering a word, Helena puts me into the wheelchair and re-hooks the IV bag onto some pole.

There is obviously some kind of conspiracy going on here.

We're maneuvering out the door before I have another chance to say no fucking way and even when I do no one is listening anyway.

Jane pushes my wheelchair from behind, and we're off.

We garner quite a few strange looks as we make our way down the hall. Jane does most of the work while my arms attempt to keep the wheels straight and on course, every so often.

A wheelchair. Me. In a wheelchair.

There's a first time for everything. Not that I like this one bit, but the call of freedom in escaping through the front doors of this hospital overpowers me.

Jane calls out to the nurses as we glide past that she's taking me for a walk, and she giggles. A grown woman giggling, who has flaming red mermaid hair, as well as high doses of magic is apparently hard to harness or argue with.

The blue-scrub set just stares at us and then all of them slowly nod.

We pass Dr. Marston. He gives her a somewhat stern but still gentle look, and then he promptly breaks out into a bright white smile.

She's charmed him, too.

"See you later, babe."

Oh. She's more than charming him.

This weird, notably intimate look passes between them. I am a third wheel all at once.

"You and Dr. Marston?" I ask softly after we are safely passed him.

"A girl's got to eat…among other things," she says with a laugh.

Oh this girl is all kinds of magic.

It's fascinating just to watch how people respond to her.

"It's not my first rodeo, Tally," she whispers to me.

We meet up with Linc at the elevator. He's wearing his black Armani suit with a fresh pressed white shirt and blue silk tie. I'm wondering what he's so dressed up for. He looks completely taken aback at seeing us.

Jane takes over. "Hey, Prez," she says sweetly, "I'm taking your girl for a stroll roll. We'll see you in about an hour. You want coffee?"

I lean my head up against the steel pole of the IV and attempt to take this all in and remain indifferent since huge parts of me are still pissed off at Linc for leaving me in the room all alone and another big part of me is wondering why in the hell this redheaded siren is calling him *Prez*.

Meanwhile, Jane takes his coffee order like their old friends just running into each other on holiday. Jealousy surges through me at a high rate of speed while the mantra in my head goes off.

Does it matter?

Does it matter?

Does it matter, Tally?

You're divorcing him.

Quit depending on him.

This is what you wanted.

No more than sixty seconds later, Linc's heated gaze reached for me. I finally have to look up at him or stop breathing altogether.

He arches an eyebrow as if to say, *'Are you sure you're okay with this? She's something, right?'* which gins up fresh insecurities about him and Jan all over again. I'm just nodding at him as we exchange places with him on the elevator. He gets off; we get on. Jealousy at the intimate conversation he and Jane were having about his coffee order consumes me and now I refuse to say anything to him at all.

His disappointment over my lack of a response is evident although he manages to semi-wave at us just as the elevator doors close cutting off all contact between us. I swallow down the lump forming in my throat at seeing him and then leaving him again inside of three minutes.

Which is it, Tally?

What do you want?

As if reading my mind, Jane says, "He's something, right?"

"You're fangirling, Janie."

"I know, but *right*?"

I shake my head refusing to answer. She looks at me intently again for some kind of sign. I shut my eyes in an attempt to eliminate the sudden sting of tears. Somehow I already know it is in my best interest to valiantly fight off the feeling that I'm falling apart in slow motion right here in the elevator, but I tell myself that I will not give in to Dr. Jane Nelson's seductive, inquisitive mind as it relates to my relationship with Lincoln Presley.

We're done. We're finished. We're moving on. Everybody knows that. Somebody tell Tally.

Instead, I open my eyes and make a point of studying the elevator panel with all the numbers, some lit up, some dark, and count myself down.

"Here, put these on." Jane hands me a pair of black-framed glasses as we roll off the elevator. She leans down to me. "They're fake. I use them to throw people off in making them think that it's not just about this hot body, but I'm smart besides." Her take-charge-of-all-things face falters a little as I look up at her. "We're breaking a few rules here, Tal. Not everyone agrees with my methods or the madness I wield with my patients. Right now, you're a *colleague* so look the part."

I press my lips together again to keep from laughing for a second time and don the glasses while Jane hits the automatic door button that promises to set us both free. When the doors miraculously open, Jane pushes me out into the full, bright sun.

I have to admit to myself at least that Jane Nelson *is* really something. She makes me want to believe in living again for a few seconds anyway.

A few minutes later, after we've begun our stroll through the hospital grounds, she says gently, "Tally, you're going to get through this, and I'm going to help you."

She squeezes my shoulder with one hand and drives the chair with the other. I refuse to look up at her. I refuse everything—the sun, the light, this day, the outlook.

All at once, I want the darkness again even when she says, "I'm not going to lie. I'm a serious fan of yours already, but I think we can make this work; don't you?"

I'm feeling a little whipsawed by her mood swings.
I'm feeling a little whipsawed by my own.
"Do I have a choice?" I finally look up at her into the light of day.
"I don't think so," she says thoughtfully.
And then? She smiles.
She leans down and touches my hand, and effectively blocks out the sun for me for which I am eternally grateful.

CHAPTER TWENTY-NINE

bleeding out

LINC

Love is my religion - I could die for it.
~ John Keats

What could I possibly say?
I know why you lie, sometimes. I do it, too.
To spare you pain. To spare myself pain.
I understand you now. I do.
~ Lincoln Presley

November 29th

STILL RECOVERING FROM EMERGENCY SURGERY, TALLY still insists on attending Cara's and Theo's funeral. We bury our little girl and our baby son in a pearl white casket together so they will never be alone. We lay them to rest next to Holly and Tessa. Our children will be in good company and watched over by these two angels, if you believe in that kind of thing. I have lost too many loved ones to continue to harbor those beliefs. I share this cynicism equally with my wife. In truth? I find it hard to determine, which is worse, watching our children's casket get lowered into the ground for burial or watching my wife's stoicism that grows exponentially as two more things that she loves in this world have died and left her behind.

With the subtle innocence, like that of a child sneaking forbidden candy, I knowingly watch as she pops a pill I easily recognize as Oxycontin into her mouth. She slips it under her tongue without anyone else noticing but me. The woman can take drugs without the aid of water now. She is a wonder to behold.

I am in search of a placebo as I recognize her continual use of them has become a dangerous crutch. No doubt Tally has pain, but her physical ones are all but gone now, according to her medical team. Dr. Nelson, *Jane*, as she insists upon being called; Jane and I are working on it. We are allies and in this together determined to carry out an intervention with Tally should it become necessary. We have a pact, Jane and I, as it relates to my wife.

Tally is a prime target for addiction. Too much tragedy. Too many losses. Plus, she has ready access to her father's prescription tablets. Adam Landon seems less concerned about Tally and her massive pain medication intake than Jane and me, but he doesn't see what we still see in Tally on a daily basis. Tally's dad watches his daughter from afar in his own kind of haze. Adam Landon has his own set of personal problems and battles his own grief. Tessa has only been gone a few months. And now, we have this—our beautiful Cara and our newborn son, who never had a chance, have been taken from us. Two more senseless deaths that no one has been able to fully explain to any of us. Even Dr. Adam Landon has run out of explanations. *It is God's will* and *this is just the way things are as* expressed by close family and friends doesn't provide enough solace for any of us any longer.

Grief works on all of us and effectively tears us apart in different ways.

I've begun to wonder whether we will ever recover.

I've begun to believe that we won't, in fact, ever recover.

I continue my ill-fated vigilance and keep watch over her. Tally leans heavily on her cane. An apparatus she refused at first, but since the alternative was a wheelchair, and that she would not do that again after that first day she met with Jane Nelson, she acquiesced to the wielding of a cane, so she could get around mostly by herself.

She is too unsteady to actually be upright since she's still recovering from emergency surgery along with having ingested a few too many painkillers that must course through her system and effectively numb her pain because she weighs all of a hundred pounds these days. Yet, she is too sadistic, especially when it comes to herself, to actually stay away from the pervasive grief that invades this funeral and all of us.

Stoic, indeed.

Mercifully, the service comes to an end. No words, no songs, no prayers are going to bring enough solace to anyone in attendance. The large gathering begins to disperse and seemingly heaves a concerted sigh of relief that this part is over. Burying any loved one is difficult, burying a small child and a premature baby is beyond tragic.

Marla and Charlie wave and indicate with subtle nods they are headed home to Palo Alto. Their baby, our niece, is due to come home from the hospital in a few more days. Her heart condition is much improved thanks to the miraculous cardiac skills of Dr. Adam Landon, but no one speaks of baby Alexandra on this day. This day is dedicated to little Cara and baby Theo.

I watch Adam and Tommy trudge toward their SUV after they stop and hug Tally. My own father's absence was remarkable, but then again, it saved me from having to actually talk to him. There's that. His excuse for being absent was that he was tied up in L.A. on ESPN business, so he sent two identical flower arrangements— white lilies adorned with baby's-breath that was downright gaudy and far too pungent—instead of actually showing up for the service for his only granddaughter and grandson.

But he promised to call us next week. *In a card.* That came with the flowers. He promised to give us a ring next week.

His dickhead status with Tally remains in full effect. Tally was the first to say this when the flower arrangements arrived. And I agreed with her. Out loud. And for a second or two, we actually shared a laugh over my father and his dickhead status.

We are making progress. We are finally on the same page when it comes to my father.

On every other page though? We are pages apart.

Volumes apart.
Worlds apart.
An entire universe actually separates us.
And, if it doesn't, yet?
It will soon enough.

Graveside, we have stood alone and a good two feet apart from each other. And yet, now that the crowd of mourners has left us, I console myself with the singular fact that we are finally alone with one another.

Yes, after days and nights of constant vigilance with the interruptions and interference from the doctors and nurses and well-meaning family and friends, it has come down to just Tally and me. She winces as if this fact has telepathically reached her even though she hides behind these incredibly large Jackie O dark sunglasses. Her lithe body is ensconced in a heavy fur coat (PETA be damned) that I bought for her months ago on a whim. The plush mahogany mink coat effectively hides the black dress she insisted upon wearing beneath it.

She hides it all from me. She hides herself from me. This much I know.

With a deep sigh that seems to reverberate from her very soul, Tally suddenly turns and walks away from our children's grave. Her black stiletto heels sink into the damp earth with every step she takes. I race to catch up with her and then grip her by the elbow in a vain attempt to keep her steady and upright.

A few seconds later, she trips on an upturned stone on the path, and I barely catch her. My heart races with the thought that she could have fallen, and I hold onto her even tighter as we make our way to my car.

With the magical touch of the key fob, I unlock the Porshe—a purchase I made in defiance in early November after the Giants' World Series win and after my life with Tally had blown up. I open the passenger side and help her into the car. I close the car door with a decided thud and race to the driver's side determined to slide in and get us on our way before she can change her mind about coming back home with me at all.

Holding my breath for a few seconds, I turn the key grateful the engine purrs to life as if it is performing some kind of miracle just for me. God, if he were to exist, is on my side for a few precious moments. I've escaped with Tally in my car.

Perhaps, my life will return to the way it was before—a few short months and a whole lifetime ago.

But it's a naive thought if there ever was one.

We roar away from the cemetery and share in nothing but the silence for the next forty miles on the drive back from Atherton to Sea Cliff along the 101. Although, Tally sucks in her breath and seemingly holds it when we pass the mile marker on the 101 where fate had us meeting for the first time almost six years ago. Even so, other than that moment, Tally stares out the passenger window and essentially ignores me. Every so often, she reaches up to adjust her sunglasses that still partially cover her beautiful face—sunglasses that don't need adjusting nor are required at this time of day since the sun went down over an hour ago. I spy dried tear tracks along with trails of black mascara upon her face, but say nothing.

What could I possibly say?

I know why you lie, sometimes. I do it, too.

To spare you pain. To spare myself pain.

I understand you now.

I do.

Yes, I'll admit it. I'm afraid of the protracted silence between us that stretches out like a two-land deserted highway, but more afraid if I say anything to her at all, she will demand that I take her anywhere but home. And that request, I cannot abide. Tonight, I need Tally. She might not need me, but I need her. We just buried our children. Tonight, we have to be together regardless of the sins that rock us in our not too distant past or the ones up ahead in the not too distant future.

An hour after the service ended, we pull up to the house.

My house.

Our house?

She turns to me with her eyes still obscured by the dark sunglasses.

"I have no place to go," she says in a low trembling voice. "Tremblay's is out. I don't even have the key anymore. Sam's still in Afghanistan. Too many memories there anyway. Of Cara. Of us. Old times. Good times. And bad. There's my dad's I guess. But no. Not tonight. So, here we are."

"Yes."

She doesn't say anything else. No, she just swings open the passenger door and attempts to get out of the car by herself, but she is too weak to actually accomplish that particular feat. As her designated knight for the evening as well as to the end of all time, I hurry to her side and carry her into the house half expecting her to protest loudly for doing so, but she is surprisingly silent.

The fight in her is apparently gone. I mourn its absence. Instead, she rests her head against my shoulder until I gently lay her down on the sofa in the living room. I have to hope she doesn't detect my racing heart at just being able to touch her again like this, but I think she knows.

Her lips part in the promise of a smile when I let go of her, but it quickly disappears when she looks directly at me. She still hasn't spoken to me since the car, and I transform to serf status with my next words. "I'll make you some tea."

"I don't want *tea*."

She's said this with such disdain it's as if I've asked her for sex, which is completely out of the question according to her entire medical team with the exception of Jane.

Upon her release, Jane had said to me with a wicked little smile, "Do what comes naturally."

Everyone else said, "No sex." Over and over.

That one edict has been drummed into us for the past several days. She still has a few weeks more, maybe longer, before she is fully recovered. According to her doctors, Tally is to take it easy and just rest. No physical effort beyond daily walks, which are only to be considered if the path is flat. No exertion of any kind. Sex is off the table, for the time being, until she heals, inside and out, literally, so we've been told.

I still haven't told her everything about the accident about Nika's involvement in the accident nor about my involvement with Nika. And yet? I can't bring myself to tell her that on this day. Not this day. Not the day we buried Cara and Theo.

Tomorrow will come soon enough.

Guilt and grief prepare me for my complete annihilation.

I already know there will be no coming back from this for us.

I view this night as our final goodbye.

"If you don't want tea, *what* do you want then?" I ask somewhat put out at attempting to read her latest mood to no avail.

She sighs and looks up toward the ceiling but still hides behind the Jackie O sunglasses. They serve a purpose—to antagonize me by not being able to read her most precious thoughts in any way whatsoever. "I want to forget. I want to drink away this pain and not feel it anymore tonight. *Can* you help me do that? *Will* you help me do that?"

"Yes," I say simply. "I want that, too."

I head to the downstairs master bedroom and rummage through the dresser drawers looking for some of her clothes. When I return with them, I undo the buttons of her fur coat, toss it to one side, and then with renewed purpose slip off her dress.

I remember this dress; it used to fit her like a glove, but now it falls off of her frail shoulders as soon as I undo the single button at the nape of her neck and unwittingly expose her sexy black lace bra and a good part of what is underneath. She basically swims in the dress now.

And I still swim in her.

My body responds. The symptoms of her pregnancy, including her full breasts have begun to fade noticeably, but she still turns me on.

Tally touches one of them now and seemingly acknowledges my unspoken thoughts. "Back to the old Tally soon enough," she whispers in this haunted voice. "Disappointed?"

I detect so much sorrow when she asks this that I rush to reassure her. "They've always worked for me."

This rueful smile plays upon her face for a few seconds at my declaration and then it's gone. "Pervert," she says with a defiant lift of her chin. "Don't lie to me. Not tonight."

"I'm not lying." I try to smile but guilt plays havoc with my emotions.

She brushes her hand against me. "So, you're not."

"What do you want to do?" I feel helpless and vulnerable and found out all at once.

"I already told you."

"How far do you want to take this?"

She just looks at me but then her hand falls away from me. "I don't know yet," she says softly. "I don't know anything anymore."

I put on some classical music. She closes her eyes and virtually ignores me.

Then, about a half-hour later, she slowly gets up and makes her way to the guest master bedroom while I mill around trying to determine what we will do next as if I have any power over that decision. Any influence at all. *She's clearly running this show.*

She reappears wearing a sexy red camisole and a matching thong. The bra is now gone. My mind, body, and soul react, but she doesn't seem to notice.

"So what do you want to do next?" I ask sounding like her first prom date. It gets worse when I add, "do you want to talk about us?"

"I can't talk about *us* tonight. I can't talk about anything with you tonight."

With a single glare in my direction she dismissively waves off my offer of help as she stiffly lowers herself onto the sofa again with the aid of her cane and not my arm. I think she hates the cane and me equally in this singular moment.

She's shut me down. I stand here feeling uncertain.

From a long way off, I feel the warning signs of an impending storm between us. My insides twist. I have so much more I need to tell her, but tonight, I cannot do that to her or me or us. I can't.

We buried Theo and Cara today.

My infidelity can wait.

It will find us. This, I know. If she only knew the rest of it, we might not even be here in this house together.

That's my fear.

Our ending.

I should tell her. But I can't. Not tonight.

I can't take any more of her rejection than she's already doled out on me. Tonight, she could effectively kill me with the wrong glance or the wrong words. I can feel the inner strength I've been counting on to survive all of this ebb away from me.

I am powerless.

Tally will destroy me soon enough.

We are in uncharted waters. I am unsure of her. She is fragile and broken, and I'm not sure what I should be doing for her from one moment to the next.

Still, she manages to sit there and look ethereal. Once settled in, she seemingly surveys the room like a queen would her most loyal subjects.

She is all kinds of sexy wearing nothing more than the lingerie now and yet the sunglasses still obscure much of her face and all of her thoughts. I reach up to take them off, but she holds up her left hand—still ring-less, duly noted by me with a grimace—and says, "No. Not yet."

I nod, not understanding her motives nor her wishes on any level whatsoever. She declines the clothes I offer up with a dismissive sweep of her hand.

"Tally? What are you doing?" I ask in exasperation. "How far are you going to take this?"

"Fix me a drink, and I'll show you."

And then, she actually smiles.

I am a goner.

CHAPTER THIRTY

second chance

LINC

"I was about half in love with her by the time we sat down.
That's the thing about girls.
Every time they do something pretty...
you fall half in love with them, and then
you never know where the hell you are."
  ~ J. D. Salinger

Tomorrow will come soon enough.
Guilt and grief prepare me for my complete annihilation.
I already know there will be no coming back from this for us.
I view this night as our final goodbye.
  ~ Lincoln Presley

November 30th

HOURS LATER, WE ARE DRUNK AND watching *Outlander*. It's just past midnight. We are almost through season one having watched the first seven episodes one after the other on cable. We have drunk the entire fifth of Jack Daniel's whiskey straight from the bottle. She has kept up with me shot for shot.

Now, we've moved onto leftover champagne from our wedding, which is apropos because the next episode in the series holds all kinds of promise; Claire and Jamie are getting finally married.

We watch the next half-hour in raptured silence. It's a pretty good scene build. I sit next to her in my black Calvin Klein's which she insisted I wear to match her own scanty attire since she never got dressed in the clothes I brought her.

The house is completely dark save for a few candles that we lit hours ago and the flickering images of near-naked bodies that openly copulate on screen. She sucks in her breath next to me when the two main characters, Jamie and Claire, finally get it on. It's a few more minutes before she turns to me and says, "I had no idea this kind of show even existed. We really must watch more of these kinds of shows, Prez."

I zero in on the word, *we,* and the intentional use of my nickname, *Prez,* which usually indicates she's pissed at me on some level, but lately I know the many reasons why by heart.

"Where are *we* going exactly?" I ask as tension begins to fill the room. *Guilt swoops in. I shouldn't want this.* I shouldn't take this, but I don't allow guilt and sanity to rule. Instead, I look over at the only ruler in this room tonight. "What do you want from me?"

"I'll show you." She downs the last of the champagne straight from the bottle. "I want you to take me. Do what he's doing to her." She inclines her head toward the screen. "Do it to me just like that sans the endless layers of clothing. Make me forget, *Prez*. Help me remember. Do *something*."

"Are you sure you're up for that?"

"Sex?" I nod ever slowly unable to form a single word for her. "There are a variety of ways to satisfy me," she says with a slight smile. She lifts up her chin in defiance; her eyes become slits. "But yes. Sex. I want it. With you. I want you. Frankly, if you don't make a move on me soon, I'm going to go out tomorrow and find you a Scottish Kilt to wear for next time. I may, in fact, do that anyway."

"It does make for easy access," I deadpan.

Tally laughs. It is still the best sound in the world. I allow myself a private moment to savor it, to remember it.

"Take me." She deftly climbs on top of me and settles in. "Take me away from here, Linc."

"Are you sure you're up for this?" I ask again feeling all kinds of concern for her and her weak body and this somewhat exhibitionist state she's got going. Additionally, the guilt over what I did with Nika and the sudden urge to confess tries to makes its way out of my chest through my mouth.

Tell her.

"I don't know, Tally. There are some things you should know."

"I don't *want* to know them. Not tonight. Tonight, I need you, Elvis. We've made a mess of things. Tonight we need to try and fix it." Her words are slurred.

Tomorrow will come soon enough.

Guilt and grief prepare me for my complete annihilation.

I already know there will be no coming back from this for us.

I view this night as our final goodbye.

"Come on. I need this. Help me." She holds my face between her hands and starts grinding away on me. Her lips claim mine and within seconds there is no going back.

Sex with Tally has always been good, but I've rarely seen this side of her, and I'm not sure what to make of it. I remind myself that we have no promises here. She's filed the divorces papers which I still refuse to sign. We are, technically, still married, but I think we both feel like strangers at this point.

There is nothing left of us.

I pull back from her and scrutinize her face. "You've just been released from the hospital after major surgery. Maybe, we should take it easy."

She leans in while her amazing green eyes narrow in on mine. "You say that to me again, and I'll slap you."

"I think I'd like that." She raises her hand, and I catch it before it reaches its intended target and bite it softly. "Are you sure, Tally?"

"Come back to me." She reaches up and strokes my jawline.

"Are you sure that's what you want?"

"Very sure. Now, don't talk anymore," she pleads.

"Okay, no more talking."

She tilts her head to one side and studies the scene on the t.v. screen for a few seconds. Then, she turns to me with this lascivious grin and holds me in her very capable hands and kisses me.

And I am a goner.

There will be no talking tonight.

There will be no confessions tonight.
Tomorrow will come soon enough for those.

It's a few hours later that I am drunkenly looking for Tally. We have been playing a game of hide-and-seek, anointing every room with our mutual need for sex. This has been a night of seduction not romance.

Forbidden.

Unleashed.

I've never seen her act quite this way before. Tally told me what she wanted, and I gave it to her whichever way she wanted because I am afraid of losing her all over again no matter how tenuous this bond might be.

I'm still not sure where we are going after this because now I've strayed into the lies just as much as she has. We are both sinners in this new universe. I broke my vows. According to Nika, Tally broke hers with Sam, although I've begun to wonder. Tally doesn't mention Sam. I'm not sure now.

I don't ask. I don't understand anything anymore.

What's true? What isn't?

Does it matter?

Can we find our way back to each other after what we did tonight?

Maybe.

Naiveté reigns over me.

I want to believe we can.

I want to believe it's true that love conquers all.

Our night together has been a strange mix of pleasure and pain, both physically and mentally, for us.

We needed it.

We were driven to it.

"Tally," I call out. "Where are you?"

It's been more than ten minutes since she went to *hide*. Suddenly, the game isn't seem fun anymore. The hairs on the back of my neck rise as I head down the other end of the long, dark hallway on the second floor near our master bedroom. That's where I find Tally lying on the floor about ten feet in front of me.

"What are you doing?" I kneel and take her into my arms.

"I'm fine," she slurs although she can barely lift her head. "I am *fine*."

She's not fine. It takes a few precious seconds to realize her left side is soaked in blood.

"You're bleeding," I say stupidly. "Why didn't you tell me?"

"I didn't know. It hurt quite a bit, but I didn't want to stop." She frowns. "I like this game of having sex with you in every room in the house. This house. This house that I hate and love at the same time." She looks up at me intently. I'm pretty sure she's not talking about the house. "I didn't want to stop with you tonight. Not tonight."

"Tally, stay with me. I've got you." I hoist her over my shoulder and head for the master bath.

Once there, I strip off her red camisole and prop her up against the edge of the bathtub and start the water. We're both naked at this point. I set her down gently onto the bathroom counter and proceed to examine the extent of her injuries. She is shy all at once and defiantly crosses her legs so I cannot see where the blood is coming from.

"Did I hurt you?" A lame question asked far too late in the game.

"No."

Both of her surgical wounds bleed profusely. We are slammed back into reality and the playful intimacy we shared between us for the past several hours disappears.

Her eyes gleam with fresh tears. I watch, helplessly, as a few of them spill over; it takes all the willpower I have left not to reach out and wipe them away. Yet, I fear her outright rejection of me is imminent more than anything else right now so I don't acknowledge her pain in any way.

Instead, I hastily grab a wet towel and press it to both incisions one located just below her hip bone and the other one farther up near her last rib. She slumps against my shoulder with exhaustion and what I surmise to be pain. "You're exhausted."

"No. I'm fine. I'm hungry." She lifts her head up and stares up at me in admitting this mild complaint. In the harsh bathroom light, I can plainly see the dark circles beneath the bottom row of her eyelashes that the candlelight hid from me so well. I lift her up and place her in the warm bath water. She leans back against the edge of the tub after I tuck a folded towel behind her neck. I take out a fresh washcloth from one of the drawers and proceed to gently bathe her. She sighs with a mix of strange contentment but whimpers with fresh pain.

After fifteen minutes in the warm bath, I play doctor for a few more minutes by drying her off and then redo the bandage of her surgical wound with fresh gauze and tape.

She allows me to wrap her up in a bath towel and carry her into our bedroom. "Time for bed," I say gently.

"New sheets," she says sinking into the black silk sheets I ordered on-line after the thing with Nika. She opens her eyes and stares at me with a little smirk. "Trying to forget me? Or, getting ready for new conquests?"

"I could never forget you. I burned the old ones."

"You *burned* them."

"I did."

She runs her tongue over her lips and looks wounded. "You hate me that much that you burned our best bedroom sheets? Those were a wedding gift you know."

"Not you. It was me. After the divorce papers came," I lie.

The lie come easily enough. I should tell her the truth.

I don't even deserve her. I don't and yet here I am trying to get back in her good graces in any way I can.

"I filed. That's right. I did." She sinks further down into the pillow with her hair fanning out all around her. I take her left hand and press it to my lips. "Still hungry," she says as she closes her eyes and breathes in with a little sigh essentially ignoring my little gesture.

"I'll go downstairs and find you something to eat."

She opens her eyes and stares at me intently for a second time. It throws me off. *Guilt surrounds me. Remorse, too.*

"Thank you," she says this so sweetly I think I'm going to cry.

I hand her a fresh glass of water and a few Advil. She drinks the water and swallows the pills and then she lays back down and closes her eyes again. "Stay here. Wait for me."

It's a desperate plea from a desperate man.

Ten minutes later, I carry a plate of sliced cheese and crackers and green grapes up to her. She's asleep, but when I climb in next to her, she awakens.

"What are you doing?" she asks while taking the plate from me.

With reverence, I just watch her hungrily eat, which is truly satisfying and rare. I take my sweet time in answering her.

"What are you doing?" She points at the bed and then at me.

"Sleeping with you. After tonight's festivities, it's all I want to do." I start to smile but then the guilt couple with true remorse returns and both lance me. I take in air while she's looking at me because I'm unsure of what I'm doing and of what we've just done to each other or what I'm about to do to us. My confession swirls all around us and attempts to suffocate me. "Tally, I…"

"I *told* you. I can't talk about us, tonight. We'll see." She sighs big. "Festivities, my ass," she adds tartly.

"Aye, that too, mistress," I say doing my best imitation of the famous Scot, Jamie Frasier, while managing to push the guilt down far enough once again to answer her and even smile.

Winning.

Tonight, I'm winning.

Tomorrow? I won't be.

Tomorrow? I'll be losing.

My smile disappears because the truth looms demanding to be told.

I'll lose her forever once it's revealed.

CHAPTER THIRTY-ONE

blue jeans

TALLY

I can't take the truth.
I'd rather hear the lies.
~ Talia Landon Presley

November 30th

THE SUN IS TOO BRIGHT AGAIN today. I squeeze my eyes shut to keep the world out. Linc quietly moves about the bedroom while I feign sleep.

I'm pretty sure I smell of the odd combination of whiskey and champagne, all kinds of sin, and sex. The images of last night rush back to me. I more than slept with my almost ex-husband last night, and I liked it far too much.

Desire for him works its way to the surface while I make a vain attempt to solely focus on breathing. Linc leans right over me and gently tucks a strand of my hair behind an ear. His breath is minty and fresh. I breathe in his cologne and the faint musky scent of his brand of soap. A drop of water falls onto my skin from him, and it takes all my willpower not to open my eyes, gaze up at his amazing face, and take up where we left off last night but my body unconsciously protests with fresh bouts of pain. Then, uncertainty sets in because I'm not sure where we go from here.

I force myself to remain still. I do not answer him when he whispers, "Tally, are you awake? I *need* to talk to you."

I don't respond. The desperation I detect in his tone tells me that the battles between us are far from over. I can't take any more revelations. Not today.

I can't take the truth. I'd rather hear the lies.

"Tally, I love you. I want you to know that. I never stopped loving you, and I will always love you."

There's an atonement in Linc's voice I haven't heard before. It's so acute I cannot respond.

There's more.

The obvious remorse in his voice confirms it. I stay motionless because I'm acutely aware of how close I am to crying because suddenly I know that whatever it is he needs to tell me is far worse than what I already know to be true.

My mother is dead. Cara is dead. Our baby boy is dead. What else could possibly be taken from us?

It's another five minutes before I hear Linc shut the bedroom door and leave.

And it's another long five minutes before I open my eyes and survey the room ascertaining that Linc has indeed left.

He's picked up the room. My castoff clothing and lingerie are nowhere to be found. He's laid out a pair of yoga pants and matching sports bra and one of his sweatshirts and a fresh pair of underwear on the chair by the night stand. My cane leans up against the side of the bed nearest me.

He's thought of everything.
He is so thoughtful.
I'm being paranoid.
I'm imagining things.
Lincoln Presley is perfect.
I am far from it.

My cell goes off. Linc brought me my phone.
See? See how thoughtful he is?

Jane: "Just checking in. How are things going? The service was so beautiful and moving. Sorry couldn't stay. Marston had the night off. We had make the most of it. That sounds bad."

Me: "I think I'm fine. Yesterday was hard. Linc brought me home. We made the most of it. Last night."

Jane: "You had SEX? I will NOT tell Marston about that. He's right here. He will not be pleased."

Me: "Well, we are."

Jane: "Well, I'm glad he told you everything. That's good.

Me: "Told me everything? There wasn't a lot of talking going on…"

Jane: "OH. Look, I'm in Sea Cliff later today. Coincidence? I'll stop by SOON. We can talk and you can show me that opulent house of yours that you say you hate so much."

Me: "Fine. I tell you too much."

Jane: "Never! See you soon…"

Me: "So you said."

I'm glad he told you everything.
Everything?
Did he tell me everything?
No.
That's what he's been trying to say.

I drag myself across the bed and slide my feet somewhat gingerly to the floor. Fresh pain assails me with this simple movement. I suck in air as if that will somehow alleviate it and then look down and note I'm wearing a pair of Linc's boxers. How did I get these on? I have no memory of that particular feat. Strange.

I reach for the cane and pitch my body forward and up to a cringe-worthy stand and then proceed to gasp as the incredible pain assails me all over again. Damn! It amazes me how much I hurt. I suck in more air hoping to alleviate this latest round of mind-numbing agony and slowly make my way to the bathroom.

All I can do is stare at Linc's latest thoughtful gesture. He has run a bath. For me. The steam comes off the water, and I breathe in the intoxicating scents of cloves and vanilla. He remembered my signature scent.

He *remembered*. Not all is forgotten.

I revel in this thought for a few moments and then spy a fresh packet of Lavender Epsom salts he's set on the side of the tub, rip it open, and pour it into the warm water. I swirl my hands around mixing it in before descending into the luxurious bath.

It's perfect. He's perfect. I am still imperfect.

Cara is dead. Theo didn't live.

The world is still dark although Linc seems to promise me that there will be light some day again.

I feel hope swirling close enough when I'm near him.

He grounds me. He anchors me still.

With Linc, I may survive this staggering loss. The staggering losses.

Jane's text comes back to me.

Well, I'm glad he told you everything. That's good.

But he didn't tell me everything.

That's what he's been trying to say.

The thought sinks in on me. My hand stills on to of the water. "It's not over." My words echo off of the walls like a bell tolls. *Knowing it tolls for thee.*

Dressed in the outfit Linc laid out for me, I take the stairs at an interminably slow pace. I am without pain medication. A thorough search of the bedroom and subsequently all the upstairs brought about nothing.

No Oxycontin for Tally today.

I already know who's withholding the pills. And who does he think he is to be deciding that for me? The anger builds and I already know it will serve as a protective shield for whatever it is he needs to tell me.

Three distinct voices can be heard from downstairs: Marla's, Linc's, and another I fail to recognize. An older woman's voice. She speaks in gentle soothing tones, and I admit to myself that I like her already sight unseen.

"She's sleeping. I think she'll be awake in less than a half-hour," Linc says.

"What did you two do last night?" Marla asks. "The place was a mess when I got here. Don't worry, Mrs. Lightner, I put it back into order before you arrived."

"I'm not worried, dear. Call me Eddie, sweetie. I've seen quite enough in my day. What Mr. Presley does with his off time is none of my concern. I'm just thrilled that Mrs. Presley is finally home, and that I finally get to meet her. I hope she's feeling better. What can I make her for breakfast? What does she like to eat?"

"Tally, doesn't eat," Linc says with a hint of frustration.

I roll my eyes at his tattle-tale declaration and almost miss a step. I'm only halfway down the stairs, and the landing is looking mighty far away from me at this point. I stop and rest and take in a few deep breaths cajoling my body to finish the task at hand. My head feels like it's going to explode. The pounding sensation started about fifteen minutes ago when I climbed out of the bathtub.

My body betrays me in moving this slow. The landing now feels impossible to reach. I sit down on the stairs in a broken humph, determining that all I need to do is rest for a few minutes and wait until the pain subsides. Meanwhile, the conversation about me continues below.

"Tally won't eat. She hardly eats at all," Linc says emphatically.

"Nonsense. Every girl eats," Eddie says.

"Not Tally." His resentment is obvious.

Granted, we have had several fights about my eating habits. My *lack of eating* habit. *Irreconcilable differences?* My food intake is on that list.

"I'll make her waffles and eggs with bacon," the woman says in triumph. "Everyone like those. And no one can resist mine."

"She won't eat it," Linc and Marla say at the exact same time.

"Nonsense." Someone stomps off toward the basement stairs. I lean back further against the stairs so I won't be detected.

So far, the eavesdropping has proven enlightening indeed.

"What *did* you two do last night?" Marla asks just above a whisper but her tone is packed with all kinds of judgment and protectiveness for me.

We've hardly spoken in the past week or so. She's busy going back and forth to the hospital visiting baby Alexandra while Linc and I attempted to forge a temporary alliance in planning Cara and Theo's funeral. The truth was in order to get released from the hospital and attend the funeral, I needed Linc to reassure Jane and all of my other doctors that he would take care of me at home. I needed help. All of my doctors insisted I needed help, and Linc said he'd be there for me.

We do what we have to do.

And now, here we are.

I'm glad he told you everything.

Everything?

Did he tell me everything?

No.

That's what he's been trying to say.

"We'll get there," Jane had said when I brought up my relationship with Linc at one of our many meetings.

"I'm not sure where we're going," I said.

"We'll get there, Tally. Right now, you just need to take one day at a time. I'm going to be checking in with you daily for a while. That's how I work. We'll just keep talking through things, one issue at a time. Okay? We'll get there. All we have is time. Sometimes," Jane said on a sigh, "time is all we have."

"Thank you for that, Yoda."

Jane talks in strange metaphors and says, "we'll get there" a lot. I find solace in her simple words. A touch of hope? Jane helps me believe that there is a tomorrow. Maybe.

She promised we'd talk about my marriage at some point and get at the reasons why I have such profound trust issues with relationships in general. "We'll work on it, Tally. We will. We'll get there." Jane makes me feel almost normal whenever I talk to her. I feel slightly less broken when I open up to her and tell her more parts of my life story.

Whereas, Marla expects me to be broken and tends to help me fix it. Jane assures me 'we'll get there'. *There's a difference.*

"So what did you do last night?" Marla asks again. "This place was littered with your clothes. There's a half bottle of syrup in the laundry room and Tally's mink coat was on the floor in the guest room. What *were* you two doing all night?"

"We were up late watching *Outlander*," Linc says sounding vague enough.

"*Outlander*? Geez, that show is practically porn by the end of season one."

"Right."

I can practically hear the wheels turning in Marla's head. Her next words confirm it. "Well. Okay. Then. You guys are good?"

"You know it's never quite that simple with Tally."

Linc's reaction both disappoints and guts me.

He regrets last night. He regrets it.

I take a shallow breath as a new kind of torment swarms me.

"Soon enough, she'll hate me for everything we did together last night. We…it was…we are not…we can't be explained."

There is so much remorse in his voice; I swear my heart skips a beat. Jane's text comes back to me. *Well, I'm glad he told you everything.*

What does Linc need to tell me?

I force myself to a stand and decide I need to face this as much as he does.

To me, last night was its own kind of miracle for both of us. I saw a future for us, and Linc was in it. But now? Now, I do wonder.

I start the downward climb again.

"Have you told her, yet?" I've never heard Marla talk to Linc with so much contempt. "Charlie told me," she adds quietly.

"No." Linc's one-word answer is distinctive—a heavy admission.

I'm not imagining contrition. It's there.

Whatever it is he needs to tell me sounds like the worst thing possible in the entire world; I can't even imagine what it could be. I move faster and barely catch myself from falling.

No more hiding out.

I have to face this.

Whatever this is.

What can possibly be worse than what's already happened to us?

The two of them are still stonily staring at each other when I appear in the doorway of the massive gourmet kitchen that I have never felt was mine. Ten seconds later, Mrs. Lightner comes in from the side door ladened down with pantry items from the basement. They put the pantry in the basement. It's another thing I hate about this house.

"Tell me what?" I ask.

Marla and Linc exchange a weird look as if they've just been caught stealing. They are essentially stunned into silence by my unexpected appearance.

Linc hangs his head and won't even look at me. And, Marla does the same.

"Later," Linc says harshly when he finally looks up. "I have to swing by the stadium."

"Whatever for? The season is finally over. What could the Giants possibly want with you in late November?" Linc gives Marla a predatory kind of look—the I-will-kill-you-if-you-say-anything look.

Marla flips him off, while I stand here in shock. She has always seen Linc as a winner. She has always taken his side, stood up for him, and pointed out his goodness to me even when I failed to see it. This is unprecedented.

I feel the small bit of happiness about last night with Linc and the intimacy we shared disappear completely.

"Waffles and eggs and bacon it is. Sit down, Mrs. Presley, I'll make those straight away." Mrs. Lightner rewards us all with an easy smile.

I surprise at least two of them when I say, "sounds good. I'm starving. And *please* call me Tally." I shake the older woman's hand. The warmth in hers steals over me for a few moments and I attempt to smile at this woman that Linc has hired and surprisingly bestowed upon us.

"Please call me, Eddie," she says with an sweet smile.

"Eddie it is. Welcome to our home. Thank you for making us breakfast. I'm sorry the house is in such disarray."

"Nonsense."

Eddie's favorite word.

I smile at her and like her instantly as I knew I would in just hearing her speak minutes earlier.

"I told you you'd like her." Linc helps me scoot in my chair to the table. He avoids touching me at any contact point and doesn't look at me at all. *Something is up.*

Eddie delivers a fresh cup of coffee with a dollop of heavy cream to me which I know better than to protest on this day.

"Thank you." I'm muted for all kinds of reasons that I'm not at all certain about.

Before long, wafts of cooking bacon permeate the air. Eddie has already set a large plate of waffles in front of me.

Marla volunteers to retrieve the syrup from the laundry room. Upon her swift return, she sets it down in front of me with a wicked grin that only I can see and then proceeds to slide onto the chair next to mine.

"How are you feeling?" I grab Marla's left hand. "God knows the past few weeks have been all about me and my problems and my life blowing up again." I sigh and take a breath. "Granted, I was in a coma for a few of those days, but still. Marla, how are you? How's Alexandra?"

"I'm better. She's out of intensive care. Your dad's going to sign for her release from the hospital in a few days, probably Thursday. Charlie's been staying home with us as much as he can. He's been great. We're fine. Don't worry about us."

"So you decided to just swing by and hang out at the house of… rampant sex horrors with me?" I say in a low voice so we won't be overheard.

She rewards me with a fake smile and won't directly meet my gaze now. "*Outlander*, huh? I told you you'd like that series. I just wanted to make sure you were okay. We barely talked yesterday after the—" Her green eyes swim with tears.

"Don't. I'm okay." I touch her hand again where it rests on the table. She grabs mine and squeezes it. "You have to be okay, too."

"I know."

"So don't fucking cry on me now." Eddie looks up and over at us in surprise with her eyebrows raised. "We swear around here, Eddie. *A lot.* I'm afraid you're just going to have to get used to it."

I subtly nod at my best friend and then quickly glance over at Linc, who is busying himself with getting ready to leave. He's put on his leather jacket and makes a point of check his cell phone more than once. He looks preoccupied. *On purpose.* He avoids my intense stare for a number of seconds before he finally looks up and over at me, but his face is a mask of indifference as if last night and the two of us together never even happened.

Marla follows my gaze. "He should tell you. He should be brave enough to tell you." Her eyes tear up all over again.

"Tell me what?" I whisper urgently.

Marla makes this sad face and just shakes her head side-to-side apparently refusing to let me in on this secret burden that Linc must carry that she knows all about.

"You should just tell her, Linc. Man up. Maybe, the truth will set you free." Marla's voice is so cold and judgmental. It's unmistakable how she's said this to him. Her allegiance to me was just made clear to everyone in this room.

This agonized look crosses Linc's handsome face. He looks like he hopes the floor will open up and swallow him whole even as his eyes meet mine from across the room.

Marla pushes herself up from the chair and adroitly starts to lead Eddie, who still has a spatula raised in mid-air, out of the kitchen.

"Let's give them some privacy." Marla glances back at me and with one telepathic look she tells me that *she is here for me* and that *she will stay.*

Oh God, it's bad.

CHAPTER THIRTY-TWO

without you

TALLY

The thing about
chaos, is that while
it disturbs us,
it too, forces
our hearts to roar
in a way we
secretly find
magnificent.
~ Christopher Poindexter

Ruined.
So like us.
We are ruined and most assuredly destroyed.
~ Talia Landon Presley

November 30th

I CONCENTRATE ON CUTTING UP THE WAFFLES on my plate and manage to take a few bites and swallow them down while Linc takes his sweet ass time in coming over to me. He eventually sits down with a heavy resigned sigh in the chair Marla's just vacated.

"I should have told you before. Before last night."

The looming confession must cost him a great deal because his face goes white under his tan if that is at all possible as soon as the words are out of his mouth. He looks like he is about to throw up. "I didn't want to ruin it, but I should have told you before…I was trying to tell you before last night. *Several times.* But I couldn't do it because I thought maybe if we had one more night together that I could change things, but it doesn't change anything."

He is silent for so long I've forgotten how to breathe.

"Tell me," I finally say.

My choice of words seems to lance him. He throws his head back and stares at the ceiling for a few minutes before he gathers himself enough to even look at me.

"That day. The day of the accident. Nika was driving. The car that day. The car that hit you was Nika's. She was driving." He pauses for so long that I gasp for air before I even realize I've been holding it.

"*What?*" All the air leaves the room and the two of us at the same time. Linc struggles to breathe just as much as I do. "Nika was driving the car that hit us?"

"Yes. She was driving. She'd just left here. This house. Me." His grey-blue eyes fill with tears. He looks away for a few seconds, then squares his shoulders, takes a deep breath, and glances over at me.

Our gazes meet up.

The betrayal I see in his is as palpable as if he took a baseball bat and swung it at me.

I struggle even more for air.

"I watched her speed down the street, and then I went inside and four blocks from here you had the accident. It was Nika's car that hit yours. She'd just left. This house. *Me.* I…We were together." He pauses for so long I realize he's stopped breathing. He shakes his head and says in a tone full of remorse, "in all the ways you can possibly imagine. While you were picking up Cara from preschool and inadvertently coming back here instead of your dad's, I was with Nika, and then she left. She was late. And she ran that stop sign and hit your car."

His words burn through me slowly—like acid someone's been careless with—that then proceeds to drip onto the floor and destroys everything it touches.

We are just like that.

The room starts to spin. I push the chair back so hard that it crashes into the wall. I stumble to the middle of the kitchen trying to make sense of all of this.

This.
The words he's just said to me.
His confession.
He was with Nika.
With her.

Time has run out for both of us in the same way sand runs out of an hourglass.

It's just gone.

It just runs out.

We have run out of time.

Anger swoops in and saves me. "Her car. She ran the stop sign. She was late for wherever she was going. Because you *fucked her. Here.* In this house. *Our house.*"

He rises up from his chair and comes to stand in front of me. I face him in the middle of the room with fisted hands as if I'm taking up my mark in the middle of a stage performance.

I don't know where to put this pain.
This pain reverberates up from my very soul like an evil spirit that has been released from Pandora's Box.
I struggle with the weight of it.
It's crushing all of me because it is so intent on its escape and my inevitable annihilation.

"*Where?*" The word is torn from my lungs. I practically shout it at him. "*Where?*" I don't know why it is so important I know this, but it is.

"In our bedroom. The shower. She was here for a few hours. I'd been drinking. I'd taken some painkillers for a headache, and she showed up to tell me I was being traded. Was about to be."

"You fucked her in our *house*, in our *bed*?" My mind stalls out. "*That's* why you burned the sheets."

"Yes."

"You fornicated with her. You fucked Nika so much and for so long that she was late for wherever she was headed and she hit my car and killed our daughter and our unborn son. You son of a bitch.

"And then, you didn't tell me, not to protect me or *save* me, but to save your own sorry ass self because the *omission* saved you from revealing your intricate, most intimate part in all of this for a little while longer."

"I lied. I didn't say anything for all the reasons you just said. I knew it would be over between us, and I didn't want it to be over. It just got all messed up. The truth is I fucked up; I lied to you. And I needed you last night even if it is our last night together for all of time."

"You *needed* me? Last night? *You. Needed. Me.* Well, that just makes everything all right then, doesn't it?" My chest heaves with this unknowable rage. It rushes at me from all sides.

"We went to a funeral for our dead daughter and son just yesterday. We buried Theo with Cara so he'd never be alone," I say slowly. "You led me to believe that you cared for me. That you loved me but you *lied* to me about Nika and what you did with her and what she did to me and Cara and our son and the two of us. She destroyed *everything* just like she threatened she would at my mother's funeral."

A memory flashes.

"Wait a minute. Is she *dead*?"

"Yes."

"That day at the hospital when I first met with Jane. You were in your best Armani suit. Why?"

He looks down at me with renewed agony. "I went to her funeral. I felt like it was the right thing to do."

"The *right* thing to do. You went to her funeral."

I fall to my knees because suddenly standing is impossible. I look up at him in disbelief.

"Well, I hope you two will be really happy together now. Tell me, Prez, is she still as attractive now that rigor mortis has set in? Do you still want to fuck her even though she's dead?"

"Don't do this. Don' talk about her like that. She's fucking *dead*, Tally. Have a little compassion." He towers above me.

I rise up from the floor in one swift motion and slap him. He staggers back from me, holding onto his left cheek, which already bears a red streak across his face.

"Don't you *dare* defend that woman in front of me. Cara *died* because of her. Have a little *compassion*? She *killed* our unborn son. The son you always wanted is gone, and yet you're standing there defending her—*mourning* her—in front of me?"

"I'm sorry," he says slowly looking dazed. "I love you. I wanted us to be together. I just didn't know how to fix this."

"Stop it. Stop it. Stop it. *You. Can't. Fix. This.* You can't. You can't fix this." My words sound alarmingly permanent. Shock reverberates through me like sounds echo off walls that appear to be closing in on me. It seems to reach Linc at the exact same time.

"I know." His throat convulses upon admitting this.

I actually shudder as I watch him literally fall apart. The anger recedes for a few seconds, and empathy takes its place, but it's fleeting leaving almost as fast as it came.

"Usually, I'm the liar," I say with a hysterical laugh. "But somehow you've managed in one prolonged week or two of insanity to upstage me."

"I still love you, Tally. I wanted to be with you last night." He tries reaching out to me but I shake him off and step back. "I wanted us to have some kind closure because of losing the baby and Cara and because we've been losing us. I foolishly hoped we could move on. I thought we had lost enough—Cara, Theo—I saw their loss as some kind of sign for us—that we could share the grief together and reconnect somehow. I know I should have told you about Nika and my part in all of this sooner, I just couldn't. I was…wrong. So wrong. I'm sorry. I thought us being together last night…that we might overcome this. That you would forgive me."

For some unknowable reason, his omissions—his lies—all but harden my heart. The truth from him is far too late to save us.

Suddenly, I am unable to see past this visceral hate I feel for him now. It engulfs me.

I turn inward to that old familiar crutch of mine used for coping. *Cruelty.* "You just told Marla in so many words you hated what we did to each other last night."

He looks up at me in surprise shaking his head back and forth in denial. "No. No, I didn't. I didn't mean it to sound like that if it did." He looks completely undone now. Yet, I watch him, bizarrely detached, as he begins pacing the floor. "I was ashamed of myself… for the things I did with you." He stops and looks at me intently. "For what I did. To you. For lying to you. I hated myself for wanting you that much when I knew you were hurting. I took advantage of you, and I didn't tell you everything."

"It didn't hurt me." I return his gaze full on, ensuring he understands what I'm saying and hears me say it. "I *liked* it. That's the difference between us. I'm a sadist, and you're a fucking saint."

"I'm obviously not a saint for Christ's sake!" He runs his hands through his hair.

The nervous gesture attempts to tug at my heart and reignite my love for him, but it's too far away from me now. All I feel is anguish and this incredible agony—a tsunami wave of grief and loss and hate—that has surely come for me and is intent on destroying every joyful feeling I've ever felt for this man.

It's coming.

What am I saying?

It's already here.

I loved him.

I stagger back gasping for air with this fresh revelation that I'm already thinking of my love for him in the past tense.

Past tense.

I loved him.

Unable to stand I fall upon my knees for a second time realizing the wave of loss is far too great this time. I look up at him.

"I hate you so much right now."

"I know." He hangs his head. "I wanted you so badly, but now I've hurt you more than I ever thought I could. I don't deserve you. You're right. And I'm so sorry. I shouldn't have done that. You were in so much pain. And I've lied to you about Nika and my part in all of this for too long." He winces. "I'm no saint, Tally, far from it." His grey-blue eyes darken with remorse.

I push up from the floor and stagger back gripping the back of the bar chair in a desperate effort to remain standing this time as I turn to face him. "We can't go back. You can't build a relationship out of lies. We are not good for each other, Prez. Maybe, we never were. Maybe, that is what the gods or fate have been trying to tell us all along." I swallow hard overcome by the grief and profound sadness of this latest loss. "I loved you so much, but I…"

With morbid fascination, I watch the pain from my words travel across his features as if I've sliced him open with a Samurai sword.

Maybe, I have.

By the look of despair on his face, it appears to be a mortal wound; I've made sure of it.

And I feel *nothing*.

"You need to leave." I pause for a few seconds suddenly fearful of the finality of what I'm saying and then plunge ahead as if I've just stepped off the highest cliff. And, maybe I have. "We're done. Completely done. Sign the fucking divorce papers. *Please,* let me go."

With cold detachment, I watch him leave the room without a backward glance. I stagger back to the kitchen table and slide into the chair.

Then, with sudden violence, clearly provoked by what just transpired, I push away the plate of food having only taken a few bites as my world craters in. Somehow, the coffee spills. Riveted, I watch the dark stain spread wide across the table and solemnly drip down onto the kitchen floor.

Who is going to clean that mess up?

Who is going to clean up our mess?

Who is left to do that?

❧ ∾ ❧

Five minutes pass.
An eternity.

I'm still sitting in the debris when Linc returns with the divorce papers in his hands. He drops them onto the kitchen table narrowly missing the spilled coffee and leaves the house and me without another word.

Eventually, I glance over at them. *He's signed them.*

My marriage to Lincoln Presley appears to be officially over.

The spilled coffee gets drawn into the stack of papers he's just signed ruining them within seconds as if suddenly magnetized.

Ruined.

So like us.

We are ruined and most assuredly destroyed.

PART III - ABSOLUTION

The truth is life is full of joy

and full of great sorrow,

but you can't have one without the other.

~ Andre Dubus III

"Two souls are sometimes created together

and in love before they're born."

~ F. Scott Fitzgerald, *The Beautiful and Damned*

CHAPTER THIRTY-THREE

body electric

TALLY

Sometimes the most
beautiful people
are beautifully broken.

~ r. m. drake

December 6th

His call comes in as I leave the studio. The fifteenth call from him in two days. I press the ignore button and start across the parking lot intending to head toward the metro station just two blocks away for the forty-five minute bus ride home.

My body protests the constant movement. Almost two weeks in the hospital took its toll. I'm still a little slow in returning to normal—whatever that is—these days. My muscles still ache after hours of rehearsal and the heavy dose of Advil I took just before has clearly worn off. I long for Oxy and vow to take some as soon I get home. I made it through rehearsals, yet my body hurts in places I didn't think were possible.

My heart is officially broken and irreparable, but my body seems to be too as I've managed to subject it to brand new, endless bouts of pain. I've resumed my dancer's life in an attempt to fulfill this ever present, fervent need to keep my mind, body, and soul occupied throughout the day with this impossibly demanding schedule. This zealous quest for constant movement along with perfection burns through me. It appears to be without end.

Seven days ago, I returned to the San Francisco Ballet reprising the role of the Sugar Plum Fairy for the upcoming performances of *The Nutcracker* which will open in less than a week. It seems the tabloids' endless coverage of my most recent tragedy ginned up a ton of sympathy for me. I remain a hot property with the fans as well as the press. So many people called up the SFB's artistic director demanding to know when I would be able to return that Mikhail was compelled to hire me back at the board's insistent urging, of course.

I didn't re-sign. I'm merely helping Mikhail out which I remind him of in as many ways as I possibly can. I agreed to dance with SFB on a temporary basis through Christmastime *on my terms*, which are simple—as long as I feel up to it. Mikhail doesn't like the terms, and he doesn't like me dictating them. However, I no longer care what Mikhail Rostov likes, dislikes, thinks, or feels. Dancing for myself appears to have made all the difference. If I think, I need ten hours of practice, I do it. If I think, I'm too tired after five, I leave.

I have choices as Jane continually reminds me.

They are all mine to make. She tells me this, too.

It's somehow freeing.

Sasha keeps calling. She wants to know when I am going to take her up on her offer with the Bolshoi Ballet, but I can't answer that anymore. I have told her it depends upon when I feel brave enough to get on a plane and actually leave.

For some reason?

The thought of actually leaving terrifies me.

On a subconscious level, of course, just out of reach of my psyche, I tell myself I can't answer as to why I'm so terrified to leave.

Consciously, I tell myself I can *feel it*—the reason as to why—but I still refuse to answer.

I'm suddenly too afraid what the truth about me and the reason as to why I can't leave yet reveals about me.

And him.

I still hate him.

I tell myself that every day, every waking moment of every day.

I tell myself I hate him, but I don't believe me either.

My cell rings again. *Rob. Again.*

This time, I answer.

"*What* do you want?"

"I thought I should call first so I wouldn't take you by surprise."

"*Why* are you calling me. That's the bigger question." I sigh big ensuring he hears it. "Look, Rob, I can't talk to you right now. I'm in the middle of rehearsals."

"You are? Because I can *see* you, Tally, and you're in the middle of SFB's parking lot."

I look up then and there is Rob Thorn leaning against his very expensive and rare Bugatti Veyron. He texted me a photo of the car along with all of its stats months before. It's probably one of the last times I'd heard from him before he came to my mother's funeral three months ago. I remember him being stoked about the car, while, at the time, I was embroiled in all the turmoil with Linc's head injury and the aftermath of all of that. We were worlds apart then, and we—Rob and I—still are, for a whole new set of reasons now.

"What do you want?" I say into the phone even though Rob's thirty feet away from me in the flesh.

"I want to talk to you. I thought I should call you first, and now I have." He ends the call.

There is a hint of the smirky smile on his face, but it is so faint I can't be sure. His surfer's hair is askew as if he has run his hands through it one too many times. His white dress shirt is only half-tucked into his dress pants, and his suit, which I know to be tailor-made for him by the Italian designer, Brioni, is wrinkled as if he has worn it a few too many days in a row and has forgotten to consider his dry cleaners.

Rob Thorn is undone.

And, I know the reasons for all of that, too.

"I can't help you." I hold my hands up when I reach him. "I'm not *that* altruistic."

"I know you can't help me. You *are* too altruistic." I roll my eyes at that impossible declaration while he hangs his head for a few seconds and then looks at me intently. "That's not why I'm here."

"Well, tell me my *why* you're here then. I've got a bus to catch." I take my phone out and search the app for the bus schedule.

"I can't believe you still use the Metro. This late at night? It's *dangerous*, Tally."

"Really? *Really?* You think taking the bus is dangerous? You should try riding in a car and see what happens."

He flinches. "I'm sorry. I'm sorry I said it like that. It was thoughtless. I'm so sorry about…Cara and the baby…I'm so sorry for your loss…*losses.*"

He trips over the plurality of the word.

They all do.

I feel his pain. I think his pain transfers directly to me. Empathy hangs in the air for a few minutes asking me if it can stay. Or, should it go?

He helped me bring Cara into this world. We share that.

Now, we stare warily at one another.

"Can we *please not* do this?" I finally say. "Believe me, I think about my little girl every moment I'm awake, but when I actually hear her name being said aloud, like you just did, it twists me all up inside. I know you are dealing with your own loss, but I certainly cannot sympathize with you about *her*. Please don't ask me to."

I continue toward my metro train destination and essentially ignore him even as he falls into step right beside me. We are five miles from our prospective homes in Sea Cliff, a year and half away from our shared past in Manhattan, and although I seem to intent on continuing down the path of imminent destruction I didn't invite Rob along for the ride down the dark abyss this time and my dagger look telepathically tells him all of that now.

In growing frustration, I stop walking and glare at him. "Why are calling me? Why are you here?"

I wave my arm around SFB's fine parking lot. There are still a number of cars here. For a brief second, I scrutinize the Porshe 911 parked near the back entrance that looks so much like Linc's, but I abruptly turn away because *that* is an impossibility and it proves painful to dwell upon.

"I wanted to see you. I *needed* to see you," Rob says simply.

His beautiful blue eyes are awash with such profound sadness I feel his invisible reach for my help.

He's drowning but so am I.

"You look like shit despite the look of Brioni." I point at his suit attire. "I'm sorry. I don't know what to say to you. I'm sorry about… for your…loss. *Too.*"

"It hasn't been the best three weeks of my life."

"Understatement," I say with derision. "I see you still have the car." I wave back towards his prized Bugatti, which is about twenty feet away from us now. "It's very nice."

He frowns. "It turns out it's just a car. It doesn't buy happiness, at least not for very long, but now I can't bring myself to…she fucking loved that car." His voice is filled with all kinds of pain.

I step back from him and hold up my hands to ward him off even as he attempts to step closer to me. "Don't. Let's be grownups here. We're not in high school anymore. I think we're both aware that the love for the car, even when it costs over a million dollars, isn't going to bring her back."

This isn't going well. He looks like I just punched in the gut.

"Look, I'm not in the best place right now, and I cannot do this with you. I'm sorry about your loss, but I'm not…" I leave the rest unfinished and then my cell goes off with a new text notification. "Sorry. Shit. I have to check in with Jane before she does something crazy like calls the police or rings up the National Guard demanding a search ensue for my body parts STAT."

"Who's Jane?" Rob asks looking confused.

"She's my therapist," I say with an airy wave. "I was supposed to check in with her after rehearsals, but they went long." I look up at him. "As I said, she gets a little intense and slightly beyond paranoid when I don't check in with her."

I concentrate on my phone for a few minutes and read her text.

Jane: "How's it going? Are you done with rehearsal? Just checking in with my favorite sugar plum fairy."

I smile and shake my head. Rob looks at me with renewed interest as I read the text aloud to him. Then, he smiles, too.

Jane was the only one who advocated my return to SFB. She thought it was a good start and she clearly supported any endeavor that would aid in my resuming a normal life.

Jane is all about fine living, good heartfelt decisions, and anything remotely Zen-related or magical. I have decided she is a goddess, a mermaid, and a fairy godmother (or the woman's sidekick) all rolled into one. Jane Nelson is all of that.

"Going back to SFB is a great idea as long as it's something you want to do," Jane said.

"My dad thinks it's too soon. And I *know* Linc will side with him. Not that *his* opinion *matters* to me anymore."

"Sure, who cares what Linc thinks, besides you?" Jane smirked. "But, Tally, it isn't about the two of them; in this particular case, it's about what you think and what you want. Okay, I'll admit it; I *live* for your performances each year at Christmastime. And yes, I already bought tickets for this season's *Nutcracker* performance for me, Marston, and my mom long before we met. Although, why would we even go if not for you? Our season-ticket seats are two rows back from the stage. We'll be able to see you up close, although strictly in a fangirl sense capacity, but we'll pretend we don't know one another until it's over." She smiled big. Then, she got this hopeful look. "I do need to confess, I was kind of hoping for backstage passes. Can you swing them for us? My mom would just about die. And Marston, well, okay, this is really about me and Stella."

I didn't know if she was serious or not. "It's not a rock concert, Jane. There are no backstage passes to give out."

"Well, you can get us back there; can't you? We'll come visit your dressing room and ply you with long-stemmed red roses and stuff."

"You're *serious*?" She nodded. "Okay. Sure." I grinned. "Mikhail is doing whatever I tell him to these days. Come on back."

"See? Total win here," she said.

"Is this a two-way relationship? Because sometimes it feels like it's only going one-way. *Yours.*"

"Don't be snarky, Tally. You're the star here, but yes, let's be honest like we promised, I want the access. That's the give and take we get out of all of this."

I laughed because I knew she didn't mean it. Jane seemed to get me when no one else did.

"I suppose you'll want suite tickets to all the Giants' home games next year, too," I said. "It's probably why you've been encouraging me to give the baseball player another chance."

"It would go a long way in impressing Marston for sure. There's that," she said tartly. "But I don't want you to do anything you don't want to do, Tally. If getting back in bed with the baseball player, both literally and figuratively, is not in your best interest, I will full-on support it. Like I've said many many many times before, you just have to give me a valid reason, so I can see my way to your side of things. You know how this works."

"So you keep telling me."

"I'm just waiting to hear it."

"Hear what?"

"The valid reason." Jane had gotten this cheeky smile.

Jane had a smile for every hour of the day. I swear I've seen them all.

So, I reminded her once again of the one and only valid reason that I had by rehashing my nuclear fallout with Linc some eight hours earlier. Yes, Linc left and so did Marla, eventually, after my many assurances that I was okay and after Jane arrived to take over the hand holding. Eddie, oblivious to what had gone down with Linc, had left for the store after Jane arrived and Marla left.

But for Jane's part? She did not react the way I thought she would.

Nevertheless, I can't think about that right now. Because, in the here and now, Rob Thorn is staring at me and probably wondering where I've gone to.

Join the fucking club.

I get back to the task at hand, checking in with Jane.

Me: "Heading home. Ran into Rob."
Jane: "Addicted to Love Rob? Say it isn't so."
Me: "We're talking.
Jane: "OK. Talking is good. Well, call me l8tr. Must hear more about THIS."

"She lives vicariously through me or I through her," I mutter as I read and respond to her quirky texts which I now consciously hide from Rob. I'm not sure he would appreciate being referred to as Addicted to Love Rob. He would also probably be taken aback as to how many times in my most recent conversations with Jane that his name has come up.

My life story has become quite a revelation for Dr. Jane Nelson. The long and convoluted life of Tally Landon with so many *liaisons*, as Jane put it, has her wanting to put together a chart just to use for quick reference.

"You have a therapist you check in with daily?" Rob asks me now, portraying all kinds of protective concern. "Tally, are you really doing okay? I guess, that's partly why I wanted to see you to make sure you were doing okay. Your dad said you were mostly fine, but I wanted to see for myself how you were really doing."

"Why does it matter whether I'm okay or not?"

"Because I care about you. I always have."

"I'm sure that went over well with your fiancée." I wince at my immediate need for cruelty. "I'm sorry," I say for what must be the fourth time during this unexpected encounter with him. "In answer to your question, I'm not exactly great, and I'm angry, obviously, and surprisingly unfiltered in saying what I think or feel at the moment to anyone who dares to ask me how I am doing or feeling or what I'm thinking. This is probably not the best time for either one of us to meet up. Maybe we should wait, table this whole encounter, and just see where things are light-years from now when I don't hate your fiancée quite as much as I do now for killing my kid, taking my unborn child away from me for all of eternity, and ruining my..."

He gets this dazed look because I've dealt him yet another serious blow.

"Maybe in a different universe altogether you and I could be friends again, but in this one? I can't do it. People keep saying time heals all wounds so maybe light-years from now I won't feel this rage and this overpowering desire to lash out at you or anyone who else who dares to ask how I'm doing. Yeah, I'm all kinds of crazy and cruel, and I have to check in with my therapist every fucking day to hold onto some semblance of sanity as if there is any *left*. Maybe, I won't be so crazy then and things will work out for all of us. We'll all get what we want. We'll all drive cars that cost a million dollars, and we'll all live happily ever after, and nobody will die on us anymore and—"

He puts one hand over my mouth and the other behind my head. "Stop, Tally. Just stop," he says gently.

My chest heaves as I fight for air and equal doses of sanity. The tears start to roll down my face, but he just keeps applying gentle, reassuring pressure with both of his hands to my mouth and the back of my head.

Leverage.

He has it.

And I don't.

I convulse with tears—tears I haven't allowed myself to shed in days. The heartbreak over Cara's and Theo's deaths has been staggering. But the loss of Linc? I haven't even been able to cry about it. Until now.

We stand like this for a long while—two ex-lovers caught in a vortex of time where we inextricably share both the connection as well as the pain.

Then, ascertaining for himself that I've run out of tears as well as words and possibly the desire for cruelty at least, temporarily, he slowly moves his hands to each side of my face and simply gazes at me.

Rob is a sucker for punishment. I must fix this.

"Still so beautiful, Tally." His thumbs gently smooth away my mascara runs and the tears.

I look up at him then caught off guard by his sincerity. Then, his lips brush mine. Our history together rises up to greet us. Kissing Rob back is not a choice. It appears to be some kind of twisted destiny clearly decided by fate and served up with equal doses of irony and doom, and, perhaps, attempts to appease this unfulfilled quest for some kind of closure for us.

He lifts his head and looks at me with this hooded, sultry look I know all too well. "Want to go somewhere?"

I surprise him when I say, "Yes. Yes, I do." Then, I grin at him—a Jane Nelson come-hither-I'm-running-this-show grin. "In-N-Out Burger. I'm starving. Do you think they're still open?"

"Let's find out." He lets go of me then and looks only slightly taken off of his game by my strange, unexpected request for food.

In the next, he mysteriously grins and hands me the keys to his precious car.

"What is this?" I shake the keys at him and try to give them back.

He hides his hands behind his back. I start to stuff the keys in his pants pocket and then think better of it based on what we just spent the last five minutes doing to each other in a still surprising make-out session and whatever solace we derived from that weird encounter. Jane will experience all kinds of excitement over that particular indiscretion, *when* and *if* I tell her.

Of course, I'll tell her.

Sometimes, she calls me Tally Entertainment Tonight.

Sometimes, I don't have to wonder why.

"I brought you a car." Rob nods as if he's just closed the biggest deal of his life. His face is one of supreme satisfaction. "I know you need one." He inclines his head toward his car.

"I don't have a million dollars to *buy* your pretty car, Rob."

"I'm not asking that much for it."

Okay, I'll play this game. I find myself intrigued and after the way I've behaved the past few minutes ago subjecting him to the special brand of a Tally tirade and then crying and ultimately kissing him, I decide to play along.

"How much then?" I point at the car.

He grins and puts his hands in his suit pants pockets and looks at me shyly. "I don't want anything from you, Tally."

"*Nothing?* Well, I can't take the car for *free*."

"Okay." He nods playing along with me now. "How much do you have on you?"

It takes three minutes to go through my purse and count out $143.59. He holds out his hands. I count it out for him laying the bills one by one in his cupped hands and then top it off with the coins.

"That's all you've got?" Rob asks. I nod and watch as he stuffs the money and change into his pants pocket. "And now, that cleans you out?" I nod charmed on some level by what he's doing. "Okay then. The car is yours." I'm rewarded with the infamous smirk, and I return it. "I guess I'll have to spring for In-N-Out Burger then, but you'll have to give me a lift home after that. Does that work?"

"That's works."

I play with the car keys and then stare at the Bugatti. It is shiny and black, and it sparkles with hints of chrome coalescing into this rich, almost artistic, Italian design. It sits there all supreme and beautiful begging to be driven. It is exquisite and now *mine* according to Rob Thorn.

"Why are you doing this again?"

"You need a car and I have this inexplicable need to do something for you. Come on. Just drive it, Tal, and if you hate it, I'll buy it back from you for a $144 dollars."

"Always looking for a good return, aren't we?" I grin at him across the top of the car.

"Something like that," he says as we climb into the car. There's a hint of his smirky smile and for a few minutes it seems the circumstances of the world may have us in the right place for once.

CHAPTER THIRTY-FOUR

the game of love

TALLY

But love?
Love eludes me.
It breaks me.
I don't have love anymore.
~ Talia Landon Presley

December 6th

I THINK ROB IS ACTUALLY IMPRESSED WITH how carefully I drive the car. We make our way to In-N-Out Burger by Ghiradelli Square. We look for the perfect parking spot which takes another half-hour to locate and then we walk out another fifteen minutes from where we safely parked the Bugatti to In-N-Out Burger. I keep turning back to the check on the car while Rob gets the biggest smirk on his face of all time.

"You like the car," he says at one point. I nod. "Good. That's good." I find us a table while he orders food for us. It's another twenty minutes before we're eating the burgers and carrying on a somewhat surreal, casual conversation.

"Do you think the car's okay?" I ask after I've eaten about half of my burger.

"The car's fine, Tally."

He grins. "Actually, I tipped the parking attendant sixty bucks to watch it for us and *not* steal it." Now, he stares at my plate of food and then at me.

This happens a few more times. "What?" I finally ask.

"You're *eating*."

I slowly acquiesce to a wan smile and dip my head. "I'm trying. I'm trying to get better. It's all part of the healthy Tally regiment Jane has me doing." He nods with new understanding. His blue eyes gleam at me.

"Tally?" I look at him with an arched eyebrow. "I don't think I have ever taken the time to say it, so I'm saying it now. I hope it's not too late. I just want to say I'm proud of you. "

I shake my head at him. "We're just conducting a business deal. I just took a car you've grown to hate off of your hands. Don't make it into something it's not." I slyly grin at him.

He laughs and then gets all serious on me. "Do you ever wonder what it would have been like if we'd gotten married?"

I stop chewing because suddenly I find it hard to swallow. I wave my hand around until I gain enough control again to swallow the food down without choking.

Then, I take a sip of water and finally say, "I think we would have been happy enough, but I also think we would always be wondering and searching. If you hadn't loved Holly and I hadn't loved…the baseball player, things would have been different for us.

"The truth is, and don't think less of me for saying it, you always belonged to Holly. You say you fell in love with me first, but I know better. You and Holly were perfect for each other. You always will be. And someday, I think you're going to find someone who reminds you enough of her in all the good ways, all the right ones, and you'll know what to do. I truly believe this, Rob. You'll find her."

"Talia Landon Presley, right now, your sister is so proud of you, your mother, too, and so am I." He takes my hand and presses it to his lips. "So," he says thoughtfully, "You're going to be okay; aren't you?"

"I think so. I am mostly okay. I'm taking one day at a time, getting good counseling, and some days when the grief tries to take over, I just concentrate on breathing in and out. It's going to take some time. And you're going to be okay, too, Rob, and then you'll be ready to find the one you really belong to."

"Hey," he says as we head back toward the car. "I almost forgot another reason I wanted to see you in person."

"Besides roping me into buying the Bugatti for $143 and change?" I grin. "What?"

"Yes," he says thoughtfully, "I wanted to give you this." He stops on the sidewalk and reaches into the pocket of his suit jacket and proceeds to hand me a check. I recognize Linc's handwriting. It's a check made out to him for six million dollars.

"What is this? Where did you find this?" I ask warily. "Damn, now I owe you *more* for the car."

He laughs and then gets this serious expression. "We found it in her car in her purse at the wrecking yard. I've been looking for some kind of closure trying to understand why she was in our neighborhood at that time of day going in the wrong direction away from our house. I know she had a fitting for her wedding dress that day. She must have been running late. Anyway, her cell phone records indicate she called Linc and I was wondering if she saw him that day. Did he tell you? Do you know?"

"What do you want me to say?" My voice shakes and I have trouble looking at him directly. The need for lying versus telling the truth automatically resurfaces. I hesitate. I'm conflicted. I know it would be easier to lie, but I don't do that anymore. Do I?

"I want the truth. I want some kind of closure. I want her to not be dead. Geez, to think I was going to marry her less than a month ago and now she's gone from me forever. It's just like losing Holly all over again." He tears up. "Sorry. I'm not being fair. You don't have to tell me."

I put my arms around him and hold him close. The contact stirs up the old feelings for him again. Rob feels it, too. He starts kissing me again, and I'm kissing him back again.

Linc left me over a week ago.

Correction.

I asked him to leave.

I haven't heard from him and yet being without him has become almost unbearable—it's a special kind of torture like no other.

All these warning bells go off in my head—the things Jane and I have talked about during our daily sessions for the past several weeks—about how I use sex as a way of coping and for validation when all I really want is love to come back to me.

But love?

Love eludes me.

It breaks me.

I don't have love anymore.

A connection from the past with Rob seems like the closest I'm going to get to feeling love for a very long time.

The thing is Jane took the news of Linc's *indiscretion* with Nika—*her words, not mine*—in stride.

"He fucked his old girlfriend Nika," is how I put it. "In my house, in our bed."

The only thing Jane said in reprimand was, "Tally, you *left* him. You'd been gone almost a month. You were separated. You'd just filed for a divorce from him a few days before. I'm not saying he's not wrong, but please own your role in the breakup and in all the aftermath that followed. He's a *guy*. Guys like sex. Sometimes, they need sex. You like sex. So you've told me and based on your history, I'd say that's definitely true. You are, or have been, promiscuous to a fault and to your own detriment at times. Do I need to remind you that for a long while you thought you were pregnant with another man's child? Boom! Own your mistakes, Tally. Own your role in all of this. Try to learn from it. If you want him back, say so. If you don't want him back, then you have to let him go. Nevertheless, don't decide right now. Give it some time. We have enough issues to work through. Let's table the one with Linc for the time being. We'll get there. Just know the difference," Jane said. "Don't confuse love with sex or vice versa. Be careful with yourself. That's all I'm saying."

"That's all you're saying? Because it seems like you are saying *a whole lot* more than that."

Of our own volition, Rob and I quickly move into the alcove of some closed art gallery for some necessary privacy, intent on exploring the here and now with our lips and hands. Rob pushes my skirt up a little higher. His fingers travel up my inner thighs causing this tingling sensation to take me over. Yet, he seems to hesitate before exploring me any further obviously waiting for my consent. I moan in his ear somewhat conflicted about wanting to give into the pleasure his touch brings, and yet I'm still undecided about this quest for closure with him although it seems to demand my serious consideration.

It feels good.
And it's Rob.
I know him.
I used to love him.
It will be okay.

And then?
Damn!
Jane is here.
In. My. Head.

Are you sure, Tally?
We talked about this.
Sex is not love.
It's not.

It's not.
Shit.
It's not.

Her words are messing with my ability to focus and let things go any further with Rob.

Although Rob's tongue continues to explore my mouth and all these memories flood back as to how good it could be between us again. Those thoughts begin to rule my head. The buzz of sexual tension connects with desire; both seek inevitable release. Those sensations take over. They take precedence over everything else.

Logic. Reason. Thought. Morals. The high ground.
Sexual tension and mutual desire hook-up.

Hook-up?

Jane is here.

Jane's fucking wisdom arrives.

Fuck!

Yes!

I *want* to do this. I *need* to do this.
Want.
Need.

I want this with Rob.

Don't I?

"I need you, Tally. I need this," Rob says against my lips as his roving hand travels further between my legs.

Guilt rises up.
Or Jane.
One or both of those.

Oh God, even Linc is here.
Tally, what are you doing to us?

"I. Can't. Do. This. I'm sorry." I push Rob's hand away and in the next pull down my skirt in search of a conscience and something else or someone else. One of those. "I can't. Please, I just can't."

He gazes at me with this tortured look, but I conclude rather quickly that it doesn't have anything to do with me turning him down.

Instinctively, I know it has everything to do with his own demons. *Loneliness and heartbreak.*

These two feelings are palpable between us.

"Let's go," he finally says taking a jagged breath and releasing me.

"Let's go then." I put my arm through his.

We walk back to the car without saying anything more. I think we both dwell in the thought of being lost—suffering within our own heartbreak—and secretly acknowledge and share this desperate search for solace and closure. The overriding need to grieve our loss separates us and yet sustains us at the same time. We hold hands in a valiant attempt to keep the last of our connection as we're not quite ready to sever the ties that bind us.

According to Rob, I drive the Bugatti like a pro. I do experience this weird thrill at the way the car handles with me driving. My fears over driving a car have been annihilated. I think it's because I secretly hope that death will just come and take me.

Now, that I'm no longer afraid of death? Boom. I conquer another fear.

The car purrs along and seduces me with each passing minute I consider it to be mine.

It's a car.

It's just a car, but it's magnificent.

Rob stares out the tinted windows as we cruise the streets of San Francisco back toward our neighborhood. I can't decide if he's getting despondent about giving me the car or something else.

He breaks the silence first. "Was she with him that day? Is that why you and Linc are separated?"

"How do you know about that?" I ask suddenly wary. *Am I ready to do this? Say this?*

"It's in the papers, Tally. You filed weeks ago. It's still all anyone is talking about. Speculating about. What happened to you and Linc? You just lost Cara and your unborn child, and yet you're *not* together. What drove you two apart?"

I park the car on one of the side streets intent on having this conversation without wrecking the Bugatti in the process.

"Truth or dare," I finally say on a heavy sigh.

"Well, a dare could be fun, but I think I've had enough of those for a while. Truth."

I turn to him. "You already know the answer."

"Tell me anyway. I need to hear you say it."

I take a deep, sorry breath. "Yes. She was with him that day."

A chill comes over the car and the two of us at warp speed when I utter this truth.

Still, now that I've opened Pandora's box for both of us I cannot stop. "Yes. She was with him that day. It's the exact reason why we're not together. He didn't tell me. Big omission that. Then, a little over a week ago, when he couldn't really look at me anymore because the guilt was twisting him all up on the inside, he finally confessed that it was Nika's car that had hit my car and he admitted that he'd been with Nika that day—that they slept together in our house, in our bed—and then he apparently watched her speed off in her car afterward. She was late for her fitting. She ran the stop sign at the intersection and hit my car, injuring me, killing Cara and our unborn son, and herself. She got all of us in some way. She actually seems to have killed the best part of me and Linc, too. It seems to be the end of us. It's all gone. There's nothing left."

Rob is speechless at this point. His face contorts with fresh grief and pain and he covers his faces with his hands and shakes his head in disbelief.

"I'm sorry. Maybe, I shouldn't have told you, but then again, I'm done with telling lies. I'm sorry if the truth hurts you, but there it is. Do with it what you can bear or need to believe. Take solace. Find solace. Find *something*."

Rob lifts his head and looks over at me in anguish. "No. No, I needed to know. I needed to hear it." He frowns and looks away for a few moments and then he turns back to me. "Thank you for telling me the truth."

I nod.

Telling the truth doesn't feel so good.

I'm going to have to have an extra session with Jane about this one. The truth hurts. Why is that?

We drive around for another hour just talking about the past and bringing closure to a number of things we've left unsaid to each other for the past few years. I finally pull the car to a stop in front of his enormous house. An estate really.

It's all gated and dark surrounded by nicely trimmed ten-foot hedges. He tells me he has two full-time gardeners on staff who have two full-time workers that work for them. *It's nonsense really.*

He doesn't seem to want to go inside his big empty house. I don't have to ask or wonder why.

"I thought she loved me," he finally says on a huge sigh. There's regret in his tone. Remorse.

I touch his hand briefly where it rests near the stick shift. "I think she did. It was a one-time thing with the baseball player." All at once, uttering Linc's name becomes too much for me. "He told Charlie that, and Marla told me, and now I'm telling you. He told Charlie he asked her about getting together again before the wedding, and she turned him down." I falter at this revelation and swallow hard. "This is a little hard to talk about." He grabs my right hand and holds it in his. "I think she loved you in her own selfish way, Rob. I think she loved sex, too. I think she loved men. She seemed so driven to always try and prove herself—prove that she was smarter and sexier than anybody else, including me—and she probably was."

"No, Tally, she wasn't sexier than you." He presses his lips to my wrist.

"Can you *not* do that or say that?"

"Well, it's true," he says simply and squeezes my hand and then lets go of it. "She admired you. She did. She told me that many times. She admired you in so many ways, and yet she was threatened by you in so many others. Nika wanted to win and possess everything and everyone around her. I think it was something left over from her childhood that surfaced in her as an adult that made her extremely insecure. I don't know. We'll never know. Will we?"

"Truth?" He nods. "I saw you two together in New York that time. Right before we broke up. I remember thinking what a good match you two were—so smart, so successful, and so into each other—you and Nika." I stumble over saying the woman's name but recover and attempt to smile. "I think she loved you more than anyone else. I really do. She might have been driven by demons to possess others but I think she always loved you the most. I don't think that ever stopped. From what I've learned she was truly looking forward to starting a life with you. She was rushing to her gown fitting because that was important to her. She loved you. She wanted a life with you. And the car accident?"

I shake my head slightly as this new feeling—*forgiveness*—washes over me. Just like Jane predicted it would happen one day. "One day, you'll just stop and forgive her, Tally. Forgive *him*. Forgive God, maybe," Jane said.

I turn to Rob. "The accident just happened. We were both in the wrong place at the wrong time, and it just happened. There is *nothing* that is going to change that. All we can do is move on and remember the ones we have loved and lost and try to do better with the ones who are still here with us. That's what I'm trying to do. Not very well most of the time. Obviously." I brush at my face. "I'm nowhere near perfect, and I've come to accept that I will never be perfect, but I am trying to live my life and embrace it more fully. That's all I can do. I'm learning to accept that."

"I miss her so much."

"I know you do. Eventually, you'll start over, just like you did before when you lost Holly."

"I started over with you. I fell in love with you."

"I'm a mess, Rob. You don't want me. You want the *idea* of me, and I can't be there for anyone else right now but myself. I've lost everyone. I can't give you anything right now. I'm just attempting to find me." I smile over at him. "We could be together tonight, but what does that change for you and me? We can't hold onto the past. We're different now." He looks unhappy with what I've just said.

"I know you want me to walk hand-in-hand with you in that house tonight because you're lonely and you're convinced you need me, but tomorrow I'll leave you just like before because I'm still searching for that rare thing that I had with Linc, although I'm not sure I'm even on a quest to look for it again right now. I'm trying to find myself. Get over the losses of my mom and Cara and this baby and Linc and all theses losses that I carry with me as I try to figure out my life and myself.

"In talking to Jane daily, she keeps telling me not to take too much on right now beyond my career and that quest is plenty, right now, believe me. I'm broken. I'm just trying to put myself back together so I can move on. The thing is…" I stop and take a breath and half-smile. "I'm trying to protect myself and do the right thing and not use sex as a way to cope, and it's very hard because there is a part of me—the old Tally—who would very much like to go with you into your big gigantic house and let you have your way with me. Nevertheless, I'm trying to forge a new path here, and I need you to let me do it. And yes, I'm whining and complaining. Two things I never used to do all that much." I try to smile.

"I think that the most honest you've ever been." Rob looks at me in wonder.

I nod. "Maybe."

"Tell me something true," he says. "Something you think I need to hear."

"She wasn't Holly. She was never going to be Holly," I say in consolation. "But someone else is out there, someone like my sister who is not me, who deserves your love. The hardest part might be finding her, but you'll know her and recognize her when you do."

"Don't take this wrong way, Tally, but I don't want to be with you tonight. Well, I really *do*, but I'm not going to be. It wouldn't be right. I'd just be looking for Holly in you like I did before."

Kids, we have a breakthrough.

It's something Jane would say if she were here. *As if she isn't here in some way.*

Rob kisses the inside of my wrist once more. "Thank you." There are tears in his eyes.

Breakthrough, indeed.

"Thank you," I say back to him.

It's simple and honest.

And, I can breathe again, and I believe so can he.

We sit together in front of his enormous estate in Sea Cliff for at least another hour. He shows me how all the gadgets work on the car and connects my iPhone with the Bluetooth connection so my music is playing through the car speakers now instead of his. We open the sunroof and Rob points out all the star constellations he recognizes.

He holds my hand as a friend. It's new and different and nice.

I listen to Rob as he talks about traveling more and the things he wants to do with his life. Life after Nika. He talks about his businesses—his father's legacy as well as the start-up venture he moved from New York to San Francisco for and the upcoming IPO launch.

"I'm sure that's what the six million check was for," he says softly. "Nika probably told him about it. She was so excited about it and made most of the rounds with me when we pitched investors. We're being selective. It's going to be huge. I can't say anything more than that, but if you want in; it could set you up quite nicely, Tally."

I reach into my purse and hand him the check back. He looks momentarily surprised.

"I believe in you. We want in. I'm still married to him *technically*." I half-smile and point to the account number on the check bearing both our names. "That's a joint checking account Linc's written it from. Take the money. Invest the money for us. Maybe, it will bring us all some kind of closure."

"Maybe."

"Are you sure you don't want more money for the car? Obviously, I'm good for it."

"No." He gets this wan smile. "I don't want your money. Right now, I just want to be friends. We're practically neighbors."

"Ten minutes away. Call me if you need me. I'll do the same."

"What are you going to do with that big house of yours and living all alone in it?" He sighs. "I'm thinking of selling mine."

"Yes, I was thinking of selling mine, too, but I've learned a few things recently. You have to fill it. Your life. Your house. With people. I have Eddie. She's my house manager. Just think of Alice from the Brady Bunch, and you'll get the idea of her. And I think she's dating my house painter, Luther. So between the two of them, they keep things interesting enough for me and they both take good care of me. They're like family. They're enough."

Rob shakes his head and laughs a little. "I'm sorry, Tally, but that sounds kind of sad."

"Oh, but it's not though. I have Jane, and you should meet her, too, some time. You'd love her. As you can see." I hold up the latest text from Jane asking where I am. "She makes sure I'm not too sad. And I'm not some of the time."

My smile is genuine. He traces my lips and then leans over and kisses my forehead.

We laugh together, and the demons of grief we share leave us both alone for a little while.

"Thanks for the talk, Tally." He climbs out of the car where even the sound of his door closing is all kinds of magnificent.

I roll down the window and call out to him, "Rob, thanks for the car and the talk."

Closure.

We have it.

CHAPTER THIRTY-FIVE

lies

TALLY

*The resignation on his face looks permanent
and no matter what I say he doesn't believe me.
It's clear; we have reached a point of no return.*
~ Talia Landon Presley

December 6th

THE HOUSE IS BIG, TOO BIG, and so empty. I look around in the dark noting Luther's return and steady progress. He's painted the once plain beige kitchen a stark white adding noticeable contrast to the red trim and stainless steel appliances. It looks stunning. Even *I* like it.

The color scheme was Linc's idea, not mine. For some inexplicable reason, I thought it best to follow through with his design ideas.

Luther is also repainting the baby's room from Baby's Breath Yellow to an innocuous Seafoam Green. Almost sage.

It will ultimately be soothing. Calming?

Let's not get carried away.

The baby furniture has been dismantled and put into storage, but I still feel my baby's loss everywhere including my body, heart and soul.

Yes. We desperately seek closure now.

We're all intent on covering up any reminders of Theo, although I wonder if the change in paint color will do anything to take this pain away from any of us.

He's gone.

Cara's gone.

We don't even venture into Cara's room yet. Not even Luther.

Everyone's gone.

My mind still doesn't have those messages wrapped up tight enough to begin to understand them clearly let alone dwell on them.

In an attempt to outrun the grief, I keep busy every waking hour of every day. That's what I do.

It finds me anyway.

Every single day.

"Are you sure about the Seafoam Green?" Luther asked me a few days ago.

"I'm not sure about anything."

As usual, the quiet man didn't even question my strange response. He just shook his head and told me how sorry he was for my loss.

"Which one?" I asked.

"All of them."

Yes, the house is dark and huge and empty, and I hate it. I move through the downstairs rooms touching the shiny flat surfaces of the countertops and furniture as I go. Eddie has the weekend off. I called earlier and told her I had a late rehearsal and she should get a head start on her weekend with Luther. They had plans.

Sexy plans as Jane would say. Jane *would* say that. I think Jane likes sex more than I do and that is saying something.

I thought I would be working late, but then Mikhail cut the rehearsal short recognizing we were all too tired and there wasn't much he could do if his dancers weren't ready for our opening performance next week.

His lead dancer was weary. I was weary. I wasn't even supposed to be performing yet, but that didn't stop me.

Yet, an early night off was welcome. And then, Rob called. And then I saw Rob. And I bought his car.

Our strange encounter brings a weird smile to my face.

Closure.

It's fantastic.

I stand in the living room staring into its deep, dark recesses attempting to get my eyes used to the blackness when one of the living room lamps is switched on. I flinch from the blinding light as well as the stony expression on Lincoln Presley's face.

"You're home."

"I am. Surprised?" He doesn't sound sarcastic as much as angry.

"I didn't expect you. You've been gone a while." I nervously play with my hair and avoid direct eye contact. Seeing Linc again has me spinning. "I haven't heard from you. What are you doing here?"

"I talked to Marla. She told me you were working late tonight, so I headed there. To the studio." His chin lifts and his grey-blue eyes narrow in on me. He's obviously pissed on a number of levels, and it takes a few seconds to discern why for myself before he tells me. "I *saw* you as you were leaving. I saw you get into his fancy car. I saw you with *Thorn*. I saw the two of you *together*."

"It wasn't like that. It—"

"Don't tell me what it was like!"

I close my eyes while his accusations seem to fly like arrows straight for me.

I did this.

I lied one too many times and now he doesn't believe a word I say.

"Did you fuck him?"

My eyes fly open. Still, I don't speak. I shake my head vehemently.

Finally, I find my voice. "Nooooooo. No! We didn't. It was… he came to find out the truth about Nika. We went to dinner. We talked. Yes, I kissed him and we did go to In-N-Out together for dinner, but nothing happened. We talked about closure. He knows I'm still married to you and—"

"Well, that never stopped you. Being married to me never even enters your mind, does it, Tally?"

"He needed closure as it related to Nika. He could just have easily gotten the answers from *you*. We said our goodbyes. We talked about stars. We talked about…starting over," I say in a rush. "Wait. No. That didn't come out right, I meant—"

"You shared all these intimate things with him that you won't even talk to me about. You're married to *me*, but you were talking to *him*. You weren't even thinking about us, about still being married to me, were you?"

"It wasn't like that. He needed some closure. He wanted to know about Nika and you."

"Was this while he was *kissing* you next to his car?"

My face gets flushed. I can't keep up with the accusations. I'm guilty with some of them, and Linc won't believe me in denying the rest.

"I'm gone a week, Tally. *A week.* And I see him kissing you in the parking lot at SFB and you're kissing him back. *I saw you.* You'll take anybody who can make you feel good; won't you? Anybody can stand in for me. And he's kissing you. Was it his idea to go one last round with you or yours? He made good on his promise? He wanted to say good-bye in his own special billionaire way; didn't he? " Linc says softly, "And, I bet you were more than willing and ready to get things on with him again, weren't you?"

Honesty trips me up. "It wasn't like that. Yes, he kissed me and I kissed him back, but then that's not what happened. He wanted to make amends. He gave me his car. He knew I needed one."

"His million dollar car—*the Bugatti*? And what? *This* is supposed to make me feel *better*? Geez, Tally, can you even keep the lies you tell straight anymore?"

"The car's in the garage. Go check it out. Don't worry I paid for it, and he already signed over the title. We went to *dinner*, Linc. We talked about Nika. His IPO. *Things*. We talked. That was it. I dropped him off, and I came home. *Nothing happened*."

Linc won't meet my gaze any longer and I know he doesn't believe me anyway. The chill in the room seems to go down about twenty degrees.

Then, he turns and goes out to garage. "What the hell? He gave you his *car*?" he yells out.

I trudge out to the garage. Linc is just standing there staring at the car and looking defeated in a thousand different ways like that of a soldier returning home from a lost war.

"He wanted me to have it," I say in a low voice. "Like I said, he knew I needed a car. I didn't take it for free I paid him every cent I had in my purse."

"I bet you did."

"We're finished," I say referring to the situation with Rob.

"Yes. We are," Linc says darkly as he turns back to me. "You and I are *finished*. I can't take it anymore. The things you do. The way you behave. The way you treat me. Our relationship. This marriage. Even the way you treat yourself." His voice breaks. We both seem to be reeling from his words. "You're addicted to sex, Tally," he says tiredly. "It validates you. You confuse the act of sex with love. And yet, the truth is you don't even know what love is. You don't know how to be faithful or love somebody back. You're cruel and calculating and heartless. You don't know how to love anyone because you don't even love yourself. You all but abandoned our daughter when you abandoned me, and then she died because of…"

"Of me," I say unevenly finishing his sentence.

He doesn't answer. He doesn't have to.

His vision of me—his version of the truth of me—shreds me.

It's not that Jane hasn't been observing some of the same things about me. It's that Linc recognizes them in me, too, and the temporary act of trying to be better—to get better—and do the right thing disintegrates inside of me with his obvious loathing.

I'm a lost cause and even Linc seems to accept this now. *It's devastating.* I shatter like a crystal vase that's been dropped to the floor.

"I was not good enough, not good enough for her, not good enough for you." My voice is far away. I can barely hear myself speak let alone think of what I'm saying or doing.

"Yes, you are! But it doesn't matter what I say, does it? What anyone tells you. It's what you believe. It's what you allow yourself to believe to be true." He turns away and retreats back into the house.

I turn off the garage light and follow him back inside. "I'm seeing Jane. Every day, I talk to Jane and I'm trying to work through my issues. She's trying to help me. There's a lot to go through because I'm seriously fucked up."

"Well at least, Jane's got that much right."

"She's trying to help me. I'm *trying*."

"Not hard enough. Not soon enough." Linc stands to his full height and towers over me. We face off in the kitchen but I cringe at the look of indifference on his face. "Seeing you with Rob tonight did something to me, Tally. The thing is I can't do this anymore with you. And it doesn't matter anyway. Not anymore."

He hesitates for a few seconds. "I've been traded to the Seattle Mariners and—"

"*What?* Why? How could they do this to you right now with everything we have going on?"

"A trade has been a long time coming. It's *business*, Tally. It's part of the game. I'm lucky it didn't happen mid-season. It doesn't matter. I didn't think it would be Seattle though, but it really doesn't matter anymore. I can play ball anywhere."

"At least you'll still be on the West Coast. There's that."

I go into self-preservation mode still reeling from all the things he said and now faced with this new reality.

Linc's leaving.

He's leaving me anyway.

"It comes with a lot of expectations, Tally. They're paying a substantial amount of money. They want a title. I'll be part of the select ones expected to deliver. Big fish. Smaller pond. Where it rains six months out of the year."

"I thought Seattle's weather was a lot like ours here?"

"Kind of," he says shaking his head. "I don't know. They have lakes. It's very beautiful, but it's not my home town."

"It's a ninety-minute plane ride away from here. It's practically in your backyard. Their clubhouse is beautiful. Their fans must just want a winning season."

"All true but it's not here. It's not home. But I guess it doesn't matter anymore. I have nothing left to come back to."

"That's not true," I manage to say even though it feels like he just sucker-punched me. "We have…" The words die on my lips.

He's right; we have nothing. There's nothing left of us.

"Look, my dad mostly lives out of suitcase and spends more time in L.A. than he does here. Like I said, it doesn't matter. The thing is it's a big deal all around with this trade. That's what I wanted to tell you. It's why I came to the studio to give you a ride home only you already had one."

The resignation on his face looks permanent and no matter what I say he doesn't believe me.

It's clear; we have reached a point of no return.

"There will be an official announcement within hours. I fly to Seattle for a press conference tomorrow." He hesitates. "Kimberley wants you there with me. She and my agent would like a united front. It's a big contract. About ninety-six of those cars you just got bestowed upon you that's sitting in the garage. Five years. It's a big trade, including Hillman and Delgado and me. Scott wants everything to go off without a hitch and so does Kimberley. She and Brad are flying out for the presser event. Scott is flying in, too, for the contract signing." He runs his hands through his hair and gets this pleading look. "It's hard to believe I'm asking you this, but can you manage a united front with me for a few days? A week at the most?"

"A united front?"

"Yes. They want to see us together. The Seattle Mariners' brass, Kimberley, Scott, the press. Everyone." He sighs deep and won't even look at me.

I think he's holding his breath awaiting my answer.

"Yes." It comes out shaky but I try to make light of it with a weak smile. "A united front. Of course."

I'm trying to wrap my mind around what a trade to the Seattle Mariners really means to him and inevitably to the two of us.

There is no way out.

It gets harder to breathe, but I do my best to hide it from him while Linc goes on to tell me about the presser event and the contract signing and some of the specifics.

"It won't be for long," he says, "It will be just a few weeks more; and then, we'll tell them."

"Tell them what?" My worst fears coalesce inside and start to spew forth like evil spirits as soon as he opens his mouth to deliver the final blow.

"That we're officially filing for divorce. *Irreconcilable differences.* I finally understand what that means as well as you do, Tally." He pulls out the sheaf of divorce papers—the coffee-stained ones. I flash to the scene from days before when he signed them. "It turns out *you* still need to sign them, Tally. You forgot your part."

He won't even meet my gaze now. His jaw clenches and I can't tell if he's still angry or as upset as I am at what's transpired between us in about the same amount of time it takes to deliver a gourmet pizza to the house.

I take the papers from his outstretched hand. In a daze, I walk into his old office in search of a pen. *I haven't been in here in weeks.*

I'm still frantically searching some five minutes later for a pen to sign the papers with when Linc comes up behind me and impatiently hands me one. My hands shake, and my eyes won't stop tearing up. I can't even see the typewritten words on the page at this point. I set the papers down on the desk and eventually look up at Linc feeling conflicted over all of this, over so many things.

"I can't see the words to even sign these. I've got dust in my eye or something."

"Right. Okay then. You can sign them tomorrow. Your lawyer probably needs to update them anyway. He needs to take out all the clauses dealing with custody."

We hold our collective breaths together.

"Right," I eventually manage to say. "I'll text Everett and have him do the updates. We can get the documents redone and we can sign them when we get back, I guess."

"Right." He takes a deep breath and finally looks over at me. "I'm heading out. I've got a hotel room downtown."

"You can stay here if you want," I say without thinking it through. "There are plenty of bedrooms here, far too many to count. The house is huge." I sweep my arm around like Vanna White does with the letters.

"And you hate it," he says softly.

I ignore the bait.

I don't want to fight about this house anymore.

I don't want to fight with him anymore.

"You can stay here…if you want."

He looks a little uneasy, which is so surprising for the newest star baseball pitcher of the Seattle Mariners with a multi-million dollar contract. He eventually nods. "Okay. We can take this up in the morning." He points at the divorce papers. "If I stay over, we can leave directly for the airport together. I have a car service coming. I guess we could begin the united front thing sooner and at least make Kimberley and Scott happy. She wants to get ahead of this thing before the latest news about us breaks in the next couple of weeks. It helps me out with the Mariners—not allowing for any more drama or side rumors—until the contract is signed, and the press goes away. Thank you for that. Does that work?"

"That's fine."

"But what about you with Mikhail?" he asks looking at me with fresh suspicion. "I heard you're back rehearsing again at SFB for *The Nutcracker* despite what your doctors have told you. Eddie told me. Jane, too." He looks a little guilty. I try not to glare why he is checking up on me since he obviously hates me so much now. "Can you be gone for a few days as many as four or five? Doesn't that make things difficult with Mikhail? It's right in the middle of rehearsals for your next *big* performance."

I don't miss his sarcasm. Obviously, Linc's unhappy I'm dancing again against doctors' orders. I half-smile anyway because telling Mikhail I'm missing a few rehearsals and even possibly next week's opening performance will put him in a very bad mood indeed, and he'll probably make a note of it and add even more documentation to his ever growing file about reprimands and misconduct involving me. I shrug. "I'll tell Mikhail I'm going to be gone for the next five days. He'll just have to deal with it. That's the deal we made.

My terms. I do what I want. Besides, let's be honest; I can do *The Nutcracker* in my sleep. Lila will be thrilled to stand-in for me if it comes to that. After all, that's what an understudy is for."

Linc looks distrustful as if believing anything I say, especially this, is all but impossible for him. He knows very well that I've never been an advocate for my understudies. I've always been threatened by them, and I've never missed a rehearsal or a performance in my career, unless I was on my deathbed, literally, and that only happened once. In Moscow.

We share a look remembering that turbulent time together.

"Moscow," he says quietly putting living color to a place we've delegated to a dark, distant memory.

He remembers. I nod. "And to think how much worse things could be, like where we are now," I say with true remorse.

"I can't do this tonight, Tally. Please don't go there." He looks less sure of himself and of me. We stare at each other a few more minutes swamped with painful memories of a distant past and well as the here and now. "Okay then." He slowly nods as if finally accepting the idea. "I'll take the guest master down here. I've got a suitcase in my car. I was on my way to the hotel."

"So you said."

I watch him leave and stare long and hard at the papers bearing his signature while he's gone retrieving his things. I slide the papers into the top drawer because I can't stand the sight of them any longer. I need to text my lawyer with the changes but the thought of typing those words about leaving out the custody clause language in a text or saying them on a phone call is impossible to fathom.

Cara. I miss you.

The guilt and grief over everything that's happened to us suddenly weighs me down again.

I did this. We did this.

The lies. The omissions. The truth always eluding me. Us.

Linc did this too, when it came to Nika, but I taught him well.

I was the best teacher.

I have to own my part. I did this.

CHAPTER THIRTY-SIX

valley of the dolls

TALLY

so perhaps we do want
happiness but we also
desire to keep the pain
close. close enough to
destroy us, close enough
to make us feel
a little less cold.
~ r.m. drake

"Glass cuts. Grief cuts. Death cuts. Love cuts. All true."
~ Talia Landon Presley

December 6th

MY PHONE GOES OFF PULLING ME out of my twisted trance that had me traveling down a bad memory lane.

Jane.

Jane: "How's it going? Are you home, my little sugar plum fairy?"

Me: "Yes."

Jane: "Linc just sent me a text. He's there??? You're going to SEA w/him?? United front?? You okay with that?"

Me: "Yeeeesssss. You okay with that?"

Jane: "It's your LIFE, Tally. Not MINE. You're the one who is married to him. REMINDER."

Me: "Says YOU."

Jane: "Girl, you know it's true."

Me: "Ha! Milli Vanilli."

Jane: "See? You know it. You got this. Talk to you in AM."

Me: "Don't do anything I wouldn't do."

Jane: "Damn, Tally. You should have texted me sooner."

Me: "I'm going to bed ALONE."

Jane: "Such a good girl. At least one of us IS… Marston is calling my name. Must go."

I asked her once why she called Marston by his last name all the time. Her sunny smile slid off her face. It was pretty obvious she had to prepare herself to share her own little story. I had begun to suspect that she had one. She was deep. Too deep. She understood personal pain too well to not have her own tragic story.

"I call him Marston because it keeps things in perspective for me. I lost someone. Five years ago? I went a little crazy. Thus, the change in college major from pre-law to psychology. Anyway, I had this the whole epic love story going on for over four years with the hottest solider-boy in the universe bar none, who wanted to marry me as soon as he finished serving his last eighteen-month tour in Afghanistan. We had big plans, Tally." Her voice broke down.

She looked away in an attempt to compose herself. Then looked back at me with this twisted up face. "But it turns out?" she finally said with a trace of bitterness. "You can't marry a purple heart. He got blown up by an IED two months before he was to be honorably discharged. My life blew up along with his and my plans suddenly changed. For-fucking-ever."

"I'm sorry, Jane."

"I know. Everybody is."

Déjà vu set in on me.

Her face contorted with memories I would bet she didn't normally allow anyone else to see. "So. I thought my life was over. My life with Steven was most certainly over." Her beautiful face clouded up, and she swallowed hard.

Then, she held out her wrists. She solemnly showed me the jagged white scars on each one.

Thus, the long sleeves she was so fond of were explained.

"It took a long while to come back from it. Obviously, I almost didn't." She winced and took a deep breath. "So, I lost my mind for a little while, was lucky enough to get a second chance, and find a new perspective to start over, and finished up my degree in psychology. So to answer your question—very astute, by the way—I call him Marston because I like to remind us both of who we are and who we are not and who I am with and who I am now."

"That's a lot of reminders."

"I know, right?" She flashed me a bright smile and shrugged. "He's this big-shot ER doc, and an exemplary surgeon with Chris Hemsworth looks that manages to keep me hot and bothered, and I'm just the best psychologist he's ever had the pleasure of fucking. It's all good. He saves people's lives every day. It's what he does. And I try to do the same. And, it works for us." She smiled wide.

I waved my finger at her. "Don't lie, Jane. It's bad for you. Bad for business. Bad for you. Don't teach your patients to lie either. It's bad and you know it."

"Oh, you're doing so good, Tally. Just parroting the lessons right back to me. God, I'm so proud right now."

"Stop it. You're going to make me cry."

"That was my evil plan all along." She stopped and looked over at me then and got all serious which is very un-Jane-like. "The thing is I learned firsthand that bad shit happens, when I lost Steven in that war zone, so I try to keep a perspective around me now." She sighed and shook her head. "I'm not fucking perfect. See? I'm not the only one."

When she quoted a song lyric like that I was supposed to give her the artist. It's a game we'd begun playing the week before. It's supposed to trip up the mind whenever we've had a conversation that has gotten far too serious and deep. "Sam Smith. I'm not the only one," I said gently. "Something harder *please*."

It took the edge off of her like it was supposed to do. She laughed. I squeezed her forearm and leaned in to give her hug in this strange camaraderie of we had uniquely choreographed together.

"I'm sorry you lost Steven."

"I know you are."

"You didn't have to tell me. I could have continued to wallow around thinking I fucking *owned* the title as the girl with the most heartbreaking losses and setbacks that has *ever* lived."

"Yeah, I know. But you're not. You're close. I'm close. But there are others out there besides us, Tally, who have suffered greater losses. We must always remember that and never wallow, as you say, too long with our own."

"Thank you for that assessment, Mother Teresa."

"You're welcome."

"So. Tell me. Does Marston have a first name?" I asked her surprising myself that I didn't already know his first name already. He was my surgeon after all. I smiled at her. She didn't return it.

"Yeah." She gave me this weird little look as if she was about to blow my mind. "Steven," she'd said his name all breathy like Marilyn Monroe.

"Noooooooo."

"Yeah, tell me about it." She frowned and then laughed. "I asked him to change it, but he won't. And he doesn't allow me call him *Stevie* either, so Marston it is."

"I like it. I like him very much."

"Yeah. Me, too." She flipped her mermaid hair over one shoulder.

It was a sign that this part of the sharing was clearly over, and we continued our hike up into the hills north of San Francisco.

Hike.

Did you catch that?

Me.
Hiking.
With Jane.

Yes. I've taken up hiking with Jane. As she constantly reminds me every time we go, "if the exercise doesn't kill you, Tally, a cougar surely will and that will be big news around here. You'll be fucking famous."

"Yes, but I'll be dead from the large fangs of a cougar, and I don't think I'd like that very much despite the lure of being famous."

"Well yeah, but it would be beyond epic! Anyway, the rule is never hike alone and try not to be in the front or the back of a group."

"But there's only two of us," I protested.

"Maybe we should just head back to town and get a drink."

We both laughed the first time she said this.

In fact, we always laugh when she says this.

And yet?

She still makes me go every single time.

I step into the hallway just as Linc reenters the house. He wheels his carry-on luggage right past me but then turns back. "This will be easier I guess, staying here," he says looking more uncertain than before. He tries to smile but he looks weary and worn out. "So, I'll see you in the morning. We can sleep in, but just keep in mind the flight is at noon. We'll need to be at the airport by ten thirty. We'll get in around two in the afternoon, maybe sooner. I already called Kimberley. She's working with the Mariners' staff and getting us booked in a private suite with two masters at the Four Seasons downtown. We have dinner reservations with the Mariners' head coaching staff—the general manager, the pitching coach, and a few others at The Metropolitan Grill downtown—and then we're supposed to have drinks with Kimberley and Brad around eight to go over the schedule and what all is involved. If you pack for a five-day trip for the City, keeping a couple of dressy social events in mind as well as your regular black jean ensemble, you should be fine."

"Ooooohhhh."

He must sense my growing apprehension at presenting a united front and what all that might involve. "Tally, it's going to be okay. Thanks for doing this, for helping me out."

"Sure," I say trying to sound certain when all I feel is more unsure by the minute about this entire trip.

"So. I'll see you in the morning." He inclines his head toward the guest master and turns away from me.

"Congratulations, by the way," I say to his retreating back. He turns back, looking surprised. "On the trade. I'm just surprised that it's with Seattle; that's all."

He pauses for a few seconds and then grins. "I needed the money. Highest bidder. I've got this pain-in-the-ass-soon-to-be-ex-wife. We didn't sign a prenup. She gets half of everything."

His words sting.

He must think it's funny on some weird, twisted level, but I have a problem with the label he's bestowed on me. I frown and quickly come to terms in understanding his entire agenda. "Pain-in-the-ass-soon-to-be-ex-wife and half of everything. So, this is what the whole united front thing is about? I get half of everything. Well, I told you I didn't care about that." I glare at him feeling like I've just been played.

"Hardly," he says with a hint of sarcasm. "You know me better than that to even ask such a thing or think I would do that to you. I don't care about the money either. I shouldn't have said that. I'm sorry. The truth is I just want you to be happy again, Tally. I know it's a stretch for both of us, at this point, but I've decided that's all I want for you."

I finally meet his intense grey-blue gaze, and am unable to look away.

He smiles ever so slightly. "The thing is…I just want to do what's right from now on. *Move on.* After all, that's all we can do, right? That's all that remains between us—doing what's right for the other."

His sincerity trips me up and brings brings tears to my eyes as well as his. "You've always done the right thing. *Usually.* You're good at it. *Usually.* Probably to a fault. *Always.*" I reach up and wipe my eyes with the back of my hand while he watches.

His features soften. The anger in him from earlier seems disappear completely. It's been replaced by this deep sorrow reflected so clearly in his eyes. "Something like that. But not always. I really screwed up with you."

I can't take his remorse right now. I'm still reeling from the wounds he inflicted with his harsh words for me less than an hour ago. "Let's not talk about this anymore tonight, okay? I'm really tired. Let's not do this. Let's just concentrate on doing the united front thing and take it from there." I smile wide. The star smile—the no-more-tears-from-Tally-tonight-winner-takes-all smile.

He looks defeated, shakes his head, and then waves a famous finger at me as he saunters off again with a small laugh. "Save the star smile for the press, Tally. You're going to need it. You know how this goes."

That reminder about the press wipes the smile right off my face. After he's gone, I say in the empty hallway. "The press. And to think they're the least of our problems."

Surprisingly, I hear him call out, "To think."

The irony of it all isn't lost on either one of us. I retreat upstairs away from him.

I swear it feels like the longest climb of my life.

CHAPTER THIRTY-SEVEN

the state of dreaming

TALLY

December 7th

IT'S TWO IN THE MORNING. I lie awake in the middle of our king-sized bed surrounded by the proverbial emptiness.

Not quite accustomed to the dark, even after laying here for a few hours, I stare at the ceiling and wonder how our life together got to this irrevocable point of destruction. It's as if I am at the edge of a cliff looking over once again. I feel the imbalance of it all take over and sense the absolute nothingness in staring out at my future. In this melancholic metaphor I can't go back, but if I even take one step forward all will be lost including me. Sheer panic sets in like a stone pulling me down into the abyss. I feel as if I'm drowning or free falling, one of those.

I can't breathe.

I fight off the panic attack by taking deep breaths and center my mind on the visual Jane gave me. In desperation, I try to imagine a pool of water where all I can see are the rings of water being formed by each drop being released from above into the pool. Each droplet causes the water rings to spread outward into perfect circles. And, here I am, at its center attempting to feel the ensuing calm of its perfection.

I cause the calm.

I am the calm.

I am water.

My breathing gets easier. I've calmed myself in a matter of minutes.

I should text Jane.

I'm supposed to text her whenever I have an attack. But I don't because she's with Marston.

It's half past two in the morning.

I'm okay.

For the next few minutes, I search around in the dark for the prescription of Xanax that I swore to Jane I did not need that she insisted I get filled.

"Just a ninety-day starter pack, Tally," she said. "It will take the edge off of your anxiety and help you out giving you some control. It's not forever. Just enough to get you through it. Grief ebbs and flows. Xanax can help you with that. Let's just see how it goes. You have to start somewhere."

Do I? Do I get to start somewhere?

Am I starting somewhere or stopping somewhere because right now my life feels completely over, especially with Linc. The grief is there for my mother and Cara and the baby we lost, but it's more than that now. Something new and incredibly large is taking up all the remaining space in my heart and seems to reach all the way to my soul. It weighs me down with its incredible force in an entirely new way.

This thing is even stronger as if this profound feeling of loss or grief—or whatever this is—seems to have found a permanent place. It's as if I've been carved out with a dull knife. This massive loss—this great chasm—seems to be with me constantly now. *I can feel it.* I have merely become the vessel that barely exists within its realm. Yet, it's not a matter of it just taking over with a flimsy promise of eventually going away. No. From a long way off? I already understand its significance. Its permanence and the desolation it most assuredly brings.

I'm losing Linc—Linc and his love. And this thing that has come for me? That's carved me out? It's showing me that losing Linc may be the greatest loss of them all.

I'm alone.

I've never felt this alone in my life.

I finally text Jane.

> Me: "Sorry to bother you. Had a panic attack. Took the Xanax. Letting you know."

I don't expect a text back. She'll see it in the morning.

She and Marston are probably fast asleep after a wild night of sex. *Passion. Love.*

"It works for us," she'd said once.

What works?

Teach me.

I'm okay.

I'm fine.

It's just a setback.

A thing as Jane likes to call it.

This strange euphoria envelops me. *Warm. Soaring. High?*

From the Xanax? No way.

I make my way toward the master bedroom closet, fling the doors open, switch on the closet light and stare in newfound wonder at all dresses I have hanging in here. "So many colors. There's a red one, a black one, a white one and of course, the ultimate one—Catherine Deane's silk satin gown with French tulle. All those buttons missing now."

I pull the wedding dress from its hanger and get a little lost in its heavenly scent—a mix of my favorite perfume hinting at cloves and vanilla, spilled champagne, and wedding cake frosting.

"God, this dress is awesome. I fucking love this dress. I still do. Even though my life has turned to shit." I start to laugh." I feel good. Man, do I feel *fine*."

"Cupcakes. It's a great idea. They'll be perfect. We can order them right away, jazz them up anyway we like," Mom had said the day before the big day. "No one will care, Tally. It's the best we can do on such short notice. The kids will love them. You can have a wedding cake on your first anniversary. I'll make it or buy it, one of those." I remember how my mother laughed. She was happy. So was I.

So happy.

The wedding was almost five months ago. A whole lifetime ago. We had eight weeks of happiness, though I was far from perfect, and then all these months that have followed have been filled with this unbelievable turmoil and unbearable loss.

And now?

Here we are.

I know, right?

Here we are putting on a united front—putting on a show, so he can get his contract signed and everyone can think we're together—getting through the grief of losing our daughter and newborn son—together, at least, for a few more weeks.

A united front.

See how cool we are?

See how the fabulous couple unites together for the world and shows them how it's done.

We are stars.

We can handle this.

I smile at the girl in the mirror and continue to admire her wedding dress that I hold in my hands.

It's a crossroads.

We are definitely at a crossroads.

Did we pass the crossroads?

Are we at the point of no return?

Point of no return.

Does it matter?

I don't really care anymore, do I?

The girl in the mirror looks excited. She looks ready to take on the world.

This high is weird.

This cannot be Xanax because that stuff is tame compared to this!

"This! This is Oxy. Whoa. This is *good*. I love this stuff. I feel *fine. Mighty fine.*"

I should get this dress cleaned and boxed.

I should have the buttons sewn back on.

That's what brides do, but not me.

"I didn't have time. I was pregnant. My mother died. I got fired. I lied to Linc about my relationship with Sam and in the process fucked up my marriage. Cara died. We lost the baby, too."

"We lost us. We lost everything."

"I got my job back. There's that. I don't have Linc, but I have my job back. And I have myself. *Not nearly enough.*"

I strip off all of my clothes and pull the wedding dress on over my head. I look in the mirror again.

It is quite the sight looking back at me.
I have myself.
And you are enough.
You are?
The girl in the mirror seems to think so.
She has this wide smile.
She plays with her hair.
She is suddenly beautiful.
The world is lighter
She is going to be okay.
Someday.
I am enough!
Me!
I have me!

I smear the face in the mirror suddenly disgusted with her smile. I wipe it away.

"What did Linc say?" I nod slowly preparing my little speech to the girl in the mirror. *She needs to hear it.*

"You're addicted to sex. It validates you." I bow. "All true."

"You confuse sex with love." I incline my head and stare at the girl in the mirror. "All the time."

"You don't even know what love is." The girl's face gets sad. "Maybe not."

"You're not faithful. You can't love somebody back." She slowly nods. "Maybe not."

"I am cruel. Calculating. Heartless. I don't know how to love anyone. Not even *you*."

I point to the girl in the mirror and she points back and we share a smirky smile. "True. All true."

"So what? Who cares? I can do what I want," the girl in the mirror says. "You are enough. You are a star. Stars rise up and they unite." She raises her fist at me and in the next smashes it into the mirror.

The cracks in the mirror distort the girl. She is broken now.

She looks at her right hand and dully notes the trickle of blood running down her arm onto the beautiful white dress.

"That blood will be impossible to get out. It's ruined. You're ruined."

"Glass cuts. Grief cuts. Death cuts. Love cuts. All true."

"Who is she? Why is she so less than perfect? Why does she care so much about being perfect? Why, girl?"

"Stop it."

"Don't look at me anymore. Let's go."

I stumble out of the bedroom, holding onto the walls smearing more blood along the walls as I go.

Who's going to clean that up?

I float down the hallway in bare feet. The dress swishes with each step I take and I attempt to twirl around in it because I love the sound it makes.

I hesitate in front of Cara's door.

Grief is coming. Fucking grief is coming for me.

It takes two seconds to turn the knob. I choke back a sob.

My hand throbs with this faraway pain. It takes just another two seconds for the sadness and the grief, which can never really be denied for too long, to find me and essentially bring me to my knees.

I crawl across the floor and over to her bed and climb in.

"I miss you. Cara. I miss you so much. I'm sorry I couldn't hold onto you. Mommy is so very sorry I couldn't hold on."

The scent of my sweet girl still lingers. Sugar cookies and frosting and Play-Doh and hints of dried-up fingerpaints assail me from all sides.

The room is a little sad. It is a little sad like me.

I pull her favorite stuffed animal into my chest and hug it hard. It's the gigantic pink unicorn, Linc gave to Cara on her last birthday.

"Elsa? You miss her, too; don't you?"

"These pills are *definitely*...working."

"I...am...amazingly...*high*."

"How many...did...I take?"

"Was it three or four? More?"

I lay on Cara's bed and try to lose myself in it finally pulling the duvet up over me in my beautifully exquisite wedding dress and close my eyes. "The drugs are working. I feel mighty fine," I say to the room and Elsa. "Just say no to panic attacks and yes to drugs." I start to laugh and I cannot stop for a long while.

My head is swamped by the thoughts of the man sleeping in the guest master downstairs and directly below this one.

Is he sleeping now? Does he sleep at night?

Or, is he like me? Does he just wallow around too engulfed in the grief and swamped with regret to even function?

Is he drowning like me? Or, does he stand on the shore and just watch me drown because he doesn't care about me at all anymore?

His words for me earlier were harsh. He has never talked to me quite like that before.

Is this how it's going to be? A war of words between us?

Will we ever get past this? Could we ever be friends?

What happens when he finds someone else? What happens then? How will I feel?

What am I thinking? He found Nika. He lost me.

Why do I ruin absolutely everything and everyone who is important to me? Why is that?

Does it matter? No. Not right now. Not this very second.

Right now, I have Elsa and this dress and the smell of sugar cookies and frosting.

And all of this just stretches out into the…nothingness of it all, and it doesn't matter anymore.

And Jane will know what I must do.
I must talk to Jane.
Tomorrow.

"Tomorrow, I will ask Jane why it is again that I ruin absolutely everything and everyone that is important to me. Jane will know and she will finally tell me why."

"And, I'll ask her how I stop. Yes, because stopping is…so important."

I have no answers, tonight. The thing inside—the true terror at losing Linc's love—begins to fill me up and overflow.

I can barely breathe.

And I think?

I need to stop trying.

CHAPTER THIRTY-EIGHT

collide

LINC

*i admit she had a little
madness. but i didn't care;
she was magic and i was on
the edge. she wanted to fall
and i wanted to fly. and
somewhere in-between we lost
direction in our heads. we
collided, and i lost my
heart on impact.*
~ r.m. drake

*Do I expect Tally to be perfect?
Is that where this all started?*
~ Lincoln Presley

December 7th

I FIND HER IN HER WEDDING DRESS in Cara's room wrapped up in our little girl's bedding. Her left hand is cut in two places—the edges of her cuts jagged obviously made by the broken shards of the glass mirror I first saw when I went looking for her. I quickly wrap a wet towel around her hand and hoist her up from the bed and onto the carpeted floor in the next.

I went to check on her with a fervent need to apologize for all the horrible things I said to her earlier and then I'd heard the sound of breaking glass. My apology couldn't wait until morning.

She isn't breathing. Instinct kicks in. I open her mouth and breathe into her. I start palpitating her heart and try to think of all the steps involved with CPR. I drag her small body out of Cara's room, down the stairs, and into the middle of the foyer and restart compressions.

How much time did I waste doing that?

Fifteen seconds.

One. Two. Three. Four. Five.

I reach up and grab the phone and dial 911 and put it on speaker and call out our house address when the dispatcher answers.

One. Two. Three. Four. Five. Six. Seven. Eight. Nine. Ten. Eleven. Twelve. Thirteen. Fourteen. Fifteen. Sixteen. Seventeen. Eighteen. Nineteen. Twenty. Twenty-one. Twenty-two. Twenty-three. Twenty-four. Twenty-five. Twenty-six. Twenty-seven. Twenty-eight. Twenty-nine. Thirty. Blow. Blow. Repeat.

Again.

Thirty count. Blow. Blow. Again. Repeat.

Thirty count. Blow. Blow. Again. Repeat.

Thirty count. Blow. Blow. Again. Repeat.

"Taaaaalllllllyyyyyy, don't you dare fucking die on me!"

It's only a few minutes, but a lifetime away before the paramedics arrive. I throw open the front door all in a matter of five seconds and restart compressions on Tally while they assess the situation and set up.

But time is precious, and it cannot run out for Tally.

I won't accept that outcome.

The paramedics pull out the portable defibrillator and take over the scene. It takes two tries to get her heart started. She is fitted with an oxygen mask over her face and begins to respond when they ultimately decide to give her Narcan. An overdose, they grimly conclude. Soon, she's strapped to a gurney with her wedding dress flowing out from her as they rush her to ambulance. They tell me she's breathing steady and somewhat impatiently instruct me to follow in my car.

With a unique grip on crazy now, I call Jane Nelson and tell her I'm on the way to the hospital with Tally, and that we need to keep this locked down. "You're the only one I'm calling beside her dad. I thought you should know. She took something," I say in a clipped broken voice. "They don't know what. They found Xanax and Oxycontin upstairs. I think it was an accident, but we had a fight. I said some things that I shouldn't have said."

Jane consoles me with soothing words and promises to get there as soon as she can. I call Tally's dad and relate the same story.

I'm beyond exhausted, by the time I arrive and meet up with the chaos that is the ER, just as they're wheeling Tally through the emergency-room doors. "I'm her husband," I say to anyone who will listen. I flash my insurance card and my driver's license. I sign papers. I am vigilant and undeterred by the uncanny red and white horror scene that greets me as soon as I arrive. All I want to do is get to my wife.

Forty-five minutes later, Tally's come around. She's somewhat disoriented but awake and most importantly alive. She's confused by the mayhem talking place all around but her vitals are good according to the ER doc on scene. The cuts to her hand are deep but won't require stitches. I watch them as they wrap the cuts in butterfly band-aids and gauze.

It seems based on their interviews with her that she mistook a bottle of Oxycontin for Xanax. A simple mistake made in the dark that they've seen enough times before that they do not seem to question it. They believe her. They believe me when I somewhat automatically confirm her story. It's a simple mistake we tell them already assuming our roles as part of a united front.

Her father finally arrives and takes charge. He consults Tally's chart with enough swagger and authority that the ER resident steps back and allows this transgression to occur. The chief cardiologist has a word with Jane, who arrives on scene after Tally has been

     Katherine Owen

pronounced in the clear. Dr. Landon and Dr. Nelson edicts seem to rule. *It was an accident.*

Even so, my bravado about all of this begins to disintegrate. I'm not so sure anymore. I'm not so convinced of Tally's innocence in all of this. I'm secretly terrified at the thought of what could have happened. I cannot get past this singular thought. *I almost lost her.*

The rage builds. Rage at myself for saying the things I said to her. Things I should have apologized for long before now which I still haven't done.

Rage because bad things seem to keep happening to us.
Why is that?
And when will it stop?

Jane and Tally are talking. They put their heads together as if they're working a crossword puzzle instead of meting out the story of what happened. Tally's dark hair contrasts with Jane's siren red, and I wonder what these two incredible beings are talking about and coming up with.

"I know you didn't. I got the text. Fuck! You scared me good, Tal."

"Me too. I'm fine. I just…" Tally looks up and over at me and then looks away. She whispers something to Jane; I'm unable to hear.

Jane looks up and over at me now with this intense scrutiny, but then she looks away and hugs Tally tight. "I don't think so. Let me talk to him."

It appears a conspiracy theory has been decided upon because suddenly it becomes all about me. The nursing staff takes over the patient, and I helplessly watch them lead Tally down the hall to the restroom. The ER doctor on call wants to keep her for observation and makes his views known, but Jane and Tally's dad have already overruled him and said she can go home.

"You all right?" Jane leads me out into the hallway with a firm hand. She's wearing sweats and a black t-shirt with white script lettering that reads, *"Ask me how I know?"*

She is a dichotomy—*Jane*—but I like her, and I know Tally does, too.

"She just scared the shit out of me. Sure. I'm fine. Fine. Fucking fabulous."

"She's okay, Linc." She touches my forearm. "You got there in time. She made a mistake." Jane pulls her phone out of the pocket of her grey sweats. "She had a panic attack. See? She texted me like I told her to and well, look what she said."

Tally aka Sugar Plum Fairy: "Sorry to bother. Had an attack. Took the Xanax. Letting you know."

"That's not a suicide note," Jane says easily.

Too easily.

It sets me off.

Jane's charm isn't working on me tonight.

"Tally almost *died*, Jane, and then it wouldn't really matter if she overdosed on purpose or not; now would it? It wouldn't matter whether she left a note or just a cheery little text that vaguely tells you what she's done. Just so long as you felt *good* about it. It's all good; right? Well, let me tell you something, lady, you weren't *there*. *I was.*

"She wasn't breathing. They had to restart her heart with a portable defibrillator in our *foyer*, Jane. *Twice.* Before they brought her back and felt she was stable enough to transport. Thank God for Narcan. But let me ask you something, what if I hadn't found her? What then? I couldn't…I couldn't live with myself if something happened to her." I attempt to get my anger under control and fail miserably.

"But it didn't! You were there. You found her in time. Look, she's scared herself pretty bad. She knows she's still in recovery. She *knows* that. She's already dealing with a lot—far more than the rest of us put together—so, let's not give her anymore to deal with than what she already has. Okay, Prez? Now, man up, and take her home, and let her get some rest because she obviously needs it, and then you can get her on the plane later today, if at all possible, and carry on with your plans and try to show her a good time in the Emerald City."

"You're really twisted," I say meaning it. "I don't think we should even go now."

"She made a mistake. The crisis is *over*, but you're not going to let it go, are you?"

"You don't know Tally the way I do."

"Don't I? I've pretty much gotten her life story over the past several weeks. I know her *plenty*. Look, she's not a plant you forgot to water. She's not a baseball you can learn to grip a certain way and make a spectacular throw with. She's not a *doll* either. She's a human being. She made a mistake. She was careless. Aren't we all? Jesus Christ, man, let it go. You can't fix this one.

"And, while we're on the subject, stop trying to make her perfect. Frankly, that's the last thing she needs from you right now. You need to move on from this. It happened, but now it's over. Take her to Seattle. Take her on a date. Maybe she'll let you fuck her brains out, but that's up to her right now, not *you*. Live a little, Linc. Love her lots. You know you do." She knocks her shoulder against mine like we're friends and are just having a simple disagreement about our choice of beer at a bar.

"I kind of hate you right now," I finally say, feeling bulldozed by this woman and I continue to seethe inside.

She is Tally's psychiatrist. And yet, even Jane fails to recognize the signs.

The signs.

The signs that are fucking everywhere.

"Yeah, well I kind of hate you right now, too, Prez. I was having this fabulous dream, and Marston was in it, and yet now here I am talking to you in a hallway with a hole in my sweats while so many of my colleagues are getting a free show of my flashy rather spectacular ass because we're standing here talking about something that is already over and done with.

"It's not over and done with. *That* is what you *fail* to recognize. It's just another in a long line of crises that we've had to deal with. Wait a minute, you're sleeping with Dr. Marston? Tally's surgeon?"

"*That's* all you've got out of what I've just said? Are you seeing someone professionally, I mean like *psych*-wise? Because maybe you should. You are entirely too focused on the wrong thing here."

"I'm focused on the wrong thing? *I'm* focused on the *wrong* thing here? I just saved her fucking life! I'm focused on my *wife* while you're busy trying to minimize the implications of what we're dealing with here. She's been on full oxygen for the past two hours and given a big enough dose of Narcan to counter the overdose effects from the pills she took. I'm sorry does it matter whether it was an accident or not, if I didn't get there in time, and she ended up dead either way? And now? Here I am again dealing with the fallout. This is your first time dealing with something like this with Tally; it isn't mine. What's next? I'm sorry was that the wrong thing to do here? What did you want me to do let her die so I could *really* teach her a lesson? I'm sorry I'm just not buying your easy shtick of hey everyone; it's all good; Tally just took a pack of pills she mistook for Xanax and the paramedics just had to swing by and start her up again."

Half the ER has turned around to stare at us.

So much for keeping things quiet.

"It was a mistake!" She jabs her red manicured nail into my chest. "A mistake! I'm sorry I must have misunderstood. Is she not allowed to make them? Is that it? You're fucking perfect, so she has to be perfect, too? Her career is all about perfection. That's what they demand of her and what the people want from her. But now, I think I get it; you're looking for the same thing from her at home, too, aren't you? Well, let me tell you something, *big guy*, she is not one of her trophies that you place up on a mantel and admire from time to time. She is a human being just like the rest of us who makes mistakes and tries to learn from them. God knows you've made your share of *yours*."

Her emerald gaze lasers in on me. "She *told* me," Jane says in hushed tone. "And I fucking defended you because everyone makes mistakes, but, apparently, only *you* are allowed to make mistakes, *not* your wife. Because somehow Tally's mistakes are judged by you as much worse than your own. *Now*, I get it. She's *not allowed* to be less than perfect. Well, that would be a hard act for anyone to keep up. *God!* No wonder she left you!"

"Janie girl, is there a problem?" It's Dr. Marston. He rubs his neck and has this somewhat bemused look on his face. He's wearing grey sweats that practically match his girlfriend's. He leans into our little huddle and hangs his arm across Jane's shoulders in a united stance as soon he comes up to us. *Well, at least I know where I stand.*

Jane sighs deep and rolls her eyes and then flashes him a sexy smile. "I may have gotten carried away just now."

Dr. Marston arches an eyebrow her way and says softly, "You *think*?"

Jane sighs big and looks over at me with the hint of an apology. "Sorry about…before."

I shrug and then shove my hands in my pockets without saying a word. I'm beyond pissed at this woman, and I'm not ready to just let things go. My mind is still trying to get wrapped around all the things she said.

Do I expect Tally to be perfect?

Is that where this all started?

"Mr. Presley, it's nice to see you again, even under these circumstances," Dr. Marston says easily.

We shake hands.

"My friends call me *Prez*," I say quietly.

"All right, *Prez* it is, but only if you'll call me Marston. All my friends do." His blond head bobs and he looks over at Jane and smiles wide. "Her bark is far worse than her bite. Right, Janie?" He looks from Jane to me and then back at her again. "Everybody okay here?" Jane shrugs like I did a few minutes before. "You two have given the entire ER quite a show, and now they want something from you to remember it by, Prez." He inclines his head.

I look around and vaguely note that quite a few people have gathered around and hold onto scraps of paper, or their jackets, or their baseball caps and probably hoping for an autograph while most of them still pretend to look anywhere else but the three of us.

Jane mumbles something about getting Tally's some surgical scrubs to wear home in lieu of the fabulous wedding dress she arrived in and moves off from us. Marston and I watch her saunter down the long corridor going in the same direction a few of the nurses took Tally minutes before.

He proffers me a Sharpie. "Go get 'em, Prez. Time for autographs. Your fans await. This will take the notice off of Tally, which is a very good thing."

"Right. Thank you."

CHAPTER THIRTY-NINE

chances

LINC

love lingers when the
heart remembers to touch
the light leaking from
the soul.
  ~r.m. drake

and she always had a way
with her brokenness.
she would take her pieces
and make them beautiful.
  ~r.m.drake

December 7th

IT TAKES TWENTY MINUTES TO SIGN autographs for all the fans. Then, I quietly talk to Tally's dad, who tells me he is headed out because he has an open-heart-surgery to perform at noon, and he really believes that this was just an accident and that Tally is going to be fine. "She's fine, Linc. Believe me, I'd know if it were something more. It was quite a scare, but she's going to be fine. She'll be more careful from now on. She promised." He has this wistful look as if he wants to believe his daughter as much as I do.

"Are you sure, sir?" I can't help but ask. I need some kind of reassurance here, too. I'm not feeling any reassurance whatsoever from Jane Nelson right now. I'm still pissed off and there's nowhere to go with this much anger roiling inside of me.

My father-in-law clasps my shoulder, leans in, and tells me everything is going to be fine one more time. Then, I helplessly watch another believer in Tally's story walk out the door.

I debate on calling out him back and having him tell me one more time that he really thinks Tally is going to be fine, but decide against it. I've already made enough of a scene in this place.

After Adam's exit, I look up to find Marston watching me closely. He stands with his back against the hall wall his right foot holding him in place and casually crosses his arms while he patiently waits for Jane and Tally. I take up the same stance right next to him.

"Is she always like that?" I incline my head towards Jane, who stands at the far end of the hall conversing with the ER doctor on call one last time.

"Intense? Passionate? Fucking perfect and right every time? *Yes.*" He gets this keen look as he seeks out Jane. She and Tally are now headed back towards us and walk down the hallway arm-in-arm. Tally is dressed in blue surgical scrubs that are about two sizes too big for her.

"Jane has her reasons for being the way she is. We all do." Marston glances at me and then back over at the two women making their way towards us. The two remain in a deep conversation and seem oblivious to the chaos all around them. "Hey, where did you park?" He pushes away from the wall. "I'll bring your car around that will help speed up your getaway from here."

"Emergency parking lot. It's a grey Porshe 911." I toss him the keys.

"Nice. I have one, too." He holds up my keys. "I may have parked next to yours."

"Marston, thanks, man," I say putting out my hand. He shakes it for a second time.

"No problem. You guys have had it rough. Sometimes, you have to go all the way to the bottom of a dark well before you can figure out just how you're going to climb back up out of it. Somehow, I think—and I know Janie thinks this too based on her passionate speech for you thirty minutes ago—that this just might be the breakthrough you were hoping for. For both of you.

"Just remember, Prez, we're all fucked up in some way. We just have to find somebody we want to spend the rest of our lives with who accepts the worst parts of us and can handle being with fucked up right along with us."

"That makes sense despite being one of the most fucked-up philosophies of marriage or a relationship I've ever heard." I find myself smiling despite the somewhat dire circumstances we find ourselves in. "Nevertheless, *thanks, really.*"

He shakes his head and we both laugh, which is surreal given where we are standing. It appears that Jane and Marston believe there is life and second chances given, even in the ER.

Maybe I just have to believe in them.

And Tally.

We drive back from the hospital in wary silence after a strong—or was that a *stern*—sendoff from Jane and Marston who tell us both to get some rest, take it easy, and enjoy Seattle. I'm pretty sure those marching orders were solely directed at me.

Everybody believes Tally.

Except me.

Driving toward home, Tally dozes off after a few minutes, and I allow the raging thoughts to battle me from all sides. The truth is I don't know who or what to believe anymore. I want to believe what Jane and Marston and Tally's father think, but I don't know anymore.

I almost lost her last night. Tally almost died. If I hadn't been there she would have. They didn't see her lifeless body while I performed CPR. They didn't see what I saw and experience firsthand what could have happened.

I can't reconcile all of this in my head yet. I'm worried about Tally and what almost just happened to her. My forearms start to spasm because I'm gripping the steering wheel so tight. The stress and shock begins to reverberate through me.

I almost lost her.

I glance over at her sleeping form. I've been watching her like a hawk tracks it prey from the sky above since she was finally released while the one unanswered question in mind continues to trouble me.

What if it wasn't an accident?

I glance at my watch. We are still scheduled to fly out of here at noon today. Less than five hours from now. How is that even possible? How can I even think about going? Not that I would leave her. That's not an alternative for either of us at this point.

I pull into the garage next to the Bughatti. With extreme effort, I attempt to table any and all thoughts of Rob Thorn and his possible ulterior motives in giving Tally his car.

I sigh big because I actually ordered Tally a new car—a BMW sedan this time—with so many airbags that an accident would feel like falling into a feather bed or so the car salesman told me last week. I guess my chivalrous act is a week too late and a million dollars short of what Rob Thorn gave her.

My cell phone buzzes.
Kimberley.

> Kimberley World Dominatrix: "Hey, just boarding. We get in SEA at 1 PT. U good?"
>
> Me: "Everything is FINE. Fly out at noon. We'll be in SEA at two. Meet you at hotel."
>
> Kimberley World Dominatrix: "Gr8t. 4Seasons. PrezSuite. 2 Masters. Dinner with SEA brass at 5. Drinks w/us at 8."
>
> Me: "Everything is fine then."
>
> Kimberley World Dominatrix. "You've said fine 2X. Are things NOT fine???"
>
> Me: "We're FINE."

Getting Kimberley all riled up right before she boards a flight to come to the West Coast is not a good idea. I can't deal with Kimberley right now. I can barely deal with myself. Tally still rests next to me in the car. I stare at her in the dim light of the garage for a few minutes to ascertain she's actually breathing and that it's nothing more sinister like she's stopped breathing because she's overdosed on one too many pills she's carelessly taken in the dark.

I allow myself to collapse inward just a little as the rush of adrenalin with everything that's taken place in the last fours hours swarms me yet again.

It was an accident.

Because she said so?

Because today I choose to believe her?

Which is it?

Tally must notice the dead silence because she slowly opens her eyes and looks at me. "I'm sorry," she says softly.

I think she means it.

"I'm sorry too for what I said earlier. I shouldn't have said those things. I didn't mean them. I shouldn't have ever said anything like that to you. I hurt you, and I'm sorry. I won't do it again."

She pauses a few seconds and then slowly nods. "It hurt me—the things you said—but you were right about all of it. Jane has been saying the very same things to me for quite a while now. What you said was true. I've used sex for some kind of twisted validation since I was in high school and, up to recently, I confused sex with love all the time. I have for years. You're right; I don't know how to love other people. I don't love myself very much." Her eyes fill with tears. "I'm sorry for so many things, Linc. I'm just so sorry."

I push a tendril of her hair behind one ear. "Tally," I say but then I hesitate and close my eyes for a few seconds before reluctantly meeting her gaze. "*Please. Please* tell me you didn't do this on purpose. Please tell me this was simply an accident. I need to hear you say it, but please don't lie to me if it isn't the truth. Don't lie to me anymore. *Tell me.* Tell me something true."

She studies my face and reaches up and traces my jawline and then my lips. "I didn't do this on purpose. I *swear.* I started to have a panic attack. I was thinking about the things you said, realizing they were true and that you believed them most of all, and I couldn't breathe and I reached for what I thought was a bottle of Xanax. It was dark. Jane prescribed them for me a few weeks ago. She said they would help me find some balance. Only they weren't Xanax. They were leftover Oxycontin pills. I didn't do this on purpose. Please believe me."

It's a long time before I answer. "I do."

Her lips part ever so slightly and the world is put right on its axis with the promise of her smile.

I will never be free of her.

I will never *want* to be free of her.

There is solace in knowing that much is true.

She fidgets with a thread on the surgical scrubs and looks uncertain. "Are we still good for Seattle? I don't want to mess things up for you with your new team."

"I'll only go if you go. If you're not up for it, I'll re-schedule. And, they'll just have to deal with it."

"Kimberley won't like that."

"I don't really care what Kimberley likes or dislikes. Right now, all I care about is you. You being okay. You being well. That's it. Nothing else matters. The Mariners can wait. You being well is all that matters to me, right now."

She touches my hair and attempts to tuck it behind my ear like I've done to her so many times before. She slowly nods. "No, I'll go. If this gets out—please pray it doesn't—it could cause problems for you. For both of us. Please, I'm fine, Linc. I can do this. We'll go to Seattle. It's important to you, and I want to do this for you."

It's a long time before I can speak.

"Thank you," I finally say because saying anything else would seem inadequate. Then, I decide to be honest because somewhere along the way I think I must have determined we both need to start there from here on out. "Tally, if anything were to ever happen to you, I couldn't live with myself."

"Nothing is going to happen to me, Elvis." She gets this sweet smile, then kisses her index finger and touches it to my lips. "Thanks for saving my life again."

"The paramedics did that. I just found you in time."

"No, you saved me in time because you always find me. That's what I can always count on, you finding me and saving me, so thank you."

Impulse and desperation work hand in hand and essentially take me over. "Tally, can we just pretend to start over while we're in Seattle? Can you do that for me? For us?" I hold my breath while she contemplates an answer.

"Elvis, are you asking me out?" she finally asks. Her eyes get glittery. The girl that rarely cries looks like she's about to.

She doesn't like the mushy stuff. It's right up there with being called baby. I know this about her, so I make my tone lighthearted when I say, "I guess I am. Will you go out with me while we're in Seattle? Can we just pretend to start over at least for a little while?"

"Yes."

I'm not sure which question she is responding to, but I fill them both of them in with her answer.

Yes.

CHAPTER FORTY

TALLY

We are the epitome of the perfect couple,
and we've avoided the loaded questions
about our relationship. We look perfect.
We act perfect. Everyone wants to believe
that we are, in fact, perfect.
~ Talia Landon Presley

December 9th

SEATTLE. LINC AND I PORTRAY TO the world that we're the perfect couple. We are photographed together as he holds up his new jersey emblazoned with the Seattle Mariners logo. The cameras flash, and we smile for the gathering press.

Kimberley is happy. Scott is happy. We are not exactly, but no one knows but the two of us as to the reasons why. I accidentally overdosed. We're trying to keep a lid on that. Linc hasn't even told Kimberley yet, but the woman is clairvoyant and has an uncanny ability to find out things like that all on her own.

We pass the test with the Mariners' coaching staff, our publicist, Linc's agent, and the press, for the first few days in Seattle with a tight schedule of press events often followed by expensive dinners and champagne and the inevitable Seattle vice of coffee that seemingly overflows just as much as the wine. I've smiled so much and often that my mouth aches from the concentrated effort. Even so, the Mariners are happy and so is Kimberley for now.

We are the epitome of the perfect couple, and we've avoided the loaded questions about our relationship. We look perfect. We act perfect. Everyone wants to believe that we are, in fact, perfect. At least in public. At least when the spotlight is upon us like it has been since we arrived.

Yes, everyone believes that the perfect couple has ninety-six million different reasons to be happy despite their most recent, unspeakable tragedy. And nobody wants to dwell upon that. I secretly think that Kimberley has instructed them not to ask either one of us about Cara or the baby we lost. I can easily imagine her threatening them with permanent black ball status and no access to either one of us whatsoever if they were to bring it up.

On our third night in Seattle, Brad and I meet up to have a drink together while we wait for Kimberley and Linc, who is finishing up his exclusive interview with *Sports Illustrated*. They'll be joining us within the hour.

After the waiter takes our drink orders, the man steeples his hands together—conveying his signature signal for deep thought. "Everything okay?" Brad finally asks.

"Everything is fine."

"A truce of sorts in the works?" Brad cocks an eyebrow rewarding me that intense quizzical stare he's so famous for. "Linc told me that you two were putting on a united front."

"Something like that."

My cryptic answers aren't going over very well with Dr. Stephenson. He's frowning. "I'm here as a *friend*, Tally. Do you want to talk about it?"

"There's nothing to talk about."

Dismay crosses his features. He shoots me are-really-going-to-stick-with-that-mantra? look.

"He *told* you."

"He told me." Brad slowly nods.

"But we're not supposed to be telling anyone. He…we promised each other that we wouldn't because if the press were to find out. Or, if Kimberley finds out…"

"It's only a matter of time before Kimberley *finds* out," Brad says dryly and inclines his head in the familiar clairvoyant way of his.

"Oh." I cringe because I know he's right. "I don't know why he told you…"

He touches my left hand where it lays across the table vying for my undivided attention. The diamond and wedding band glitter as part of the united front and seemingly mocks us both right now.

"He loves you, Tally. He freaked out because he almost lost you. He needed to tell somebody. He was beside himself imagining if he hadn't found you in time, so he confided in me last night about what happened this past weekend. I've assured him, as your friend and his and also as a psychiatrist, just as yours has, that you can handle this. I don't take that position lightly. I know you well enough now. You don't want to end it all. You don't," he says emphatically when I look up at him in surprise.

"If you did, you would have done that a long time ago. You've experienced loss many times and yet; you're still here. You have so many things to live for. Yourself. Ballet. And perhaps, starting over with Linc if you two agree to try and work things out." I start to shake my head. "*Perhaps.* That's what I told Linc. You're still here. You made a mistake. Everyone does, at some point. Just know, I believe in you. Linc believes in you. Now, you just need to believe in yourself, and I actually think that you do."

His words disarm me. He seems to know the truth about me— the essence of me, at least. "Well, it sounds like you have me all figured out."

"It's not a matter of me knowing you and having you all figured out, as you say. It's a matter of you knowing you and accepting yourself."

"That's it? That's all I have to do?" I tease.

"You've already done the work, Tally. Now, you just need to look around and appreciate what all you've accomplished and embrace your life for what it is and what it isn't."

"Is this like the Dorothy in the Wizard of Oz with the ruby red shoes? I've been able to go home this entire time? All I had to do was figure that out and click them together and say I want to go home?" I reward him with the star smile.

"Something like that," Brad says, and then he laughs. "He loves you very much."

My star smile fades. "He does?" I try to take in Brad's reassuring stance on the subject of love and Lincoln Presley. "You he does love me?" I ask in wonder.

"He loves you Tally. It's obvious to anyone who watches the two of you interact for any length of time. Five minutes at the most."

"He does, doesn't he? But why did I not believe this before now? Why have I wasted so much time and not believed in us or put all my faith in Linc?"

"You already know those answers."

There's a long pause between us. I slightly tip the water glass in my right hand and watch it swirl. Then, I eventually look over at Brad. "I was afraid of losing him. I was so afraid of losing him and knowing I wouldn't be able to bear the loss of him that I pushed him away."

"And yet, he still loves you."

I nod. Words seems inadequate.

"Yes," I finally say.

"You two have been tested in ways most couples never experience, and yet you're still standing together." He raises an eyebrow; I nod. "Mostly together. A united front as you say for the world to see. The thing is you're still here. And you love him, Tally. That's pretty obvious to everyone. You think you're putting on a show? But really you're just living it. With him. United with him. Because you are.

He toys with his wine glass and takes a sip. "So, really, I think you're at the point where you just need to decide if you are better off being with him and loving him here in Seattle or being some eight hundred miles away in San Francisco and not being a part of his life, but still loving him. It's your choice to make. But, let me just say, in all my years of practicing psychiatry, I've found that you can't rule love. Nobody can. People try, of course, but love always wins out."

He nods as if he's just dispensed a magical spell. He probably has.

"That's where you're at. It's your choice to make—to be with him or to be without him, but just know that love is the constant in that equation either way."

"Love is the constant. In the equation."

"Yes."

"So, it really doesn't matter if I live in San Francisco, and he lives here in Seattle." I sweep my arm around the bar for emphasis. "Love is the constant in that scenario either way it goes. I can be miserable without him and let the fear of losing him constantly rule my life, or I can just let love rule and see where it takes us."

"Exactly. You love him, Tally. You can't really change that. You can fight it. You can rail against it. You can make yourself miserable trying to change things or how you feel about them, but love is the one constant for you two, and it transcends everything else. Love wins. It always does."

"You really believe that?"

"I do. I see it every day."

"So. I love him, and I can't change that no matter what I do. Is that what you're trying to tell me?"

"Whether you're here or there, you'll still love him. Time and distance won't change that. Love is your constant. It's your guide. Love. It's powerful stuff. You love him, Tally. You can't change that."

"I love him." My throats closes up and I swallow hard while my eyes tear up. The fear of losing starts to rise within me and I ask the question that constantly haunts me before I can think it through. "But is love going to be enough?"

"What do you think? What do you *really* think?"

I lean back in my chair suddenly overwhelmed by the answer formulating in my head. "I think, sometimes; love is all we have," I say shyly looking across at Brad.

"There you go." The great Dr. Bradley Stephenson smiles wide.

CHAPTER FORTY-ONE

good for you

TALLY

Welcome aboard to the let's-be-honest-Tally-Landon-Presley-ship.
You liking it so far?
~ Talia Landon Presley

December 10th

SOMEHOW, WE MANAGE TO DODGE KIMBERLEY in a direct confrontation about the incident, but I'm fairly certain that it is Brad, who talks her down from the ledge when she finds out about the accidental overdose that took place with me just days before. A text from Brad early this morning confirms this.

It's day four of our stay in Seattle as a united front. This morning Lincoln Presley seems as preoccupied as am I.

I continue to mull over what Brad and I talked about last night. *Love is the constant.* The mantra runs through my mind over and over.

Linc hands me a cup of coffee after putting in a generous dollop of cream and gives me this curious look when I sip at it without protest. I don't even do the caloric calculations like I normally do. He hands me a bagel generously spread with cream cheese.

"Thanks," I say. "I'm starving."

"Everything okay?" He looks somewhat taken aback now.

"Yes. Why?"

He points at the plate with the bagel. I look down. I've already polished off half the bagel.

"Everything is fine. I'm hungry. What can I say?" I attempt an easy carefree smile, but I'm nervous around him today because Brad's conversation continues to run through my mind. *Love is the constant.*

"What did you and Brad talk about last night? You seem…I don't know…*fine?*"

"Brad is always a good guy to talk to. I like him." I swirl my coffee and take a sip then nervously look up at him. "I know you told him about the thing." Linc looks guilty. "It's fine that you told him. He was helpful. He was understanding. He believed me." I lift my chin in defiance and look at him intently.

Linc looks a little unsure of himself even when he says, "I believe you, too, Tally. It was an accident. I know that now."

"Kimberley knows," I say in a low voice after a few seconds.

Linc gets this fearful look. He doesn't like to be the brunt of Kimberley's wrath. No one does. "Damn."

"I think Brad took care of it. He explained it all to her. That's what his early morning text to me said anyway."

"Oh good. That's a relief. Brad's a good friend. He helped me through a lot with the memory thing. He's helped me talk through things about you so many times."

"I know."

He nods and takes a butter knife and spreads cream cheese across his own toasted bagel. "So, today, I have some things to do with a real estate agent. I need to find a place to live that's near the ballpark." He hesitates and looks over at me with this hopeful expression on his handsome face. "Did you want to come?"

"Actually, I can't. I have some things of my own to do. Kimberley set some things up for me, remember? Her branding campaign with Lancome for one and Capezio; they have a new dancewear line they want me to consider endorsing. Print advertisements. That kind of thing."

"Seems like she's taking the united front thing a bit too far. Do you really want to do all of that?"

He sounds disappointed with all of my reasons for not going with him.

"It might be fun." I shrug. "It hasn't exactly paid off trying to avoid the spotlight now has it? Maybe, Kimberley is right. I need to get a handle on my image as it relates to my career. Maybe, I do need to start paying better attention to things like that. And I'm here and Kimberley's here so we thought we'd take advantage of the situation. She set up a few things for me to consider as it relates to branding and merchandising. You know I want to dance just as much as you want to throw a baseball. The branding image stuff kind of comes with the territory as they say and now that things are somewhat on track with Mikhail; well, I'm evaluating my options. Kimberley's been fielding calls from ABT in New York. There's Sasha's offer. Things. I need to pay attention to." I can tell he's getting agitated with the mere mention of Moscow and New York so I stop talking and just wait for his response.

"Lots of options," he says with a heavy sigh. "I just thought… never mind what I thought." He frowns ever so slightly and runs his free hand through his hair. "It sounds like you have a busy day ahead of you."

"I've never been to Seattle. I just want to explore the city on my own," I say gently and hide a smile but not nearly as well as I should. It cheers me a little to see Linc this frustrated that I won't be spending the day with him today, but in a good way. "I thought I'd look around and maybe get fitted for some new pointe shoes, several pairs, if I can find some."

"You can never have enough of those." He half-smiles, knowing I annually go through dozens of pairs of pointe shoes.

"Maybe, we can meet up later this afternoon if that works out for you," I add trying to placate him now.

"Sure. Sure. I just thought you might want to check out a few of these places before you have to fly out tomorrow."

"I don't really have much interest in traipsing through a bunch of gigantic mansions with some real estate agent that is intent on showing you what all your money can buy."

He looks a little dejected by my honesty.

Welcome aboard the let's-be-honest-Tally-Landon-Presley-ship.

You liking it so far?

I smile to take the sting out of what I've just said. "Look, I'll tell you what, if you run across something you think I would actually *like*, and you want to show it me; I'll come see it with you. Okay?"

"Sure. Okay. Fair enough. So, we'll meet up this afternoon then?"

"Yes, Elvis, we'll meet up this afternoon; okay? Find something good for me to come and see."

He seems to accept my reasoning and all the excuses I've thrown his way in the past few minutes. I don't want him to know where I am actually going for a number of reasons. The triple threat of fears still rules me and today I may manage to confront all three—failure, losing and falling. Nothing else has changed about me except that the mantra—love is the constant—now rules every waking thought I have since Brad and I discussed it last night.

"This afternoon then," Linc says.

"This afternoon then."

I head into the master bathroom we share and strip off my workout clothes as I go. I know he's watching me. A smile steals across my lips he cannot see. I hold my breath under the hot stream of the water until I hear the suite door click shut behind him. Then, I finally breathe freely and begin to put my plan for the day into action.

I look the part of a rising star ballerina on her way to being named a principal, by the time she's twenty-five. A year or two from now. I twirl my hair up into a chignon and pin it up into place. Years of practice with hair styles and cosmetics have made me into an expert. I do up my make-up so it's slightly dramatic but not over the top. Demure. I line my lips with red and ensure my complexion is a shade darker than true porcelain. I don't want to look like a doll, but I want the sophistication that comes with being a star. I want the allure of star status to shine through. I've paid my dues, on some levels, much more than other dancers, and today I'm hoping to make good on that.

I'm to have lunch with the artistic director of the Pacific Northwest Ballet Company. At first, this was part of the staging of the perfect-couple-comes-to-Seattle shtick that Kimberley has been endorsing. In fact, she set up the meeting between the director and me. I went along with Kimberley's plans, although I knew I could never be in the same town as Linc if we were not married to each other.

My conversation with Brad last night and all the conversations with Jane have finally resonated with me.

They've changed me.

Now, I'm going to meet the PNB director for an entirely difference reason, a far more important one. I need a job. In Seattle. And I just might be capable of landing one.

CHAPTER FORTY-TWO

gold

TALLY

"Now, I just want to find a home with my career
that supports the rest of my life,
if that makes any sense at all."
~ Talia Landon Presley

December 10th

Pacific Northwest Ballet's Artistic Director is charming. A former dancer with a long career spanning more than twenty years with the New York City Ballet, Daniel Hollis has performed everything from George Balanchine's *A Midsummer Night's Dream* to *Prodigal Son.* He is extremely talented and quite famous as a dancer in his own right as well as a very gifted artistic director. Facts that somehow only resonate with me now when I am sitting across from him at this lunch meeting Kimberley has arranged in downtown Seattle.

Daniel has been the artistic director of the Pacific Northwest Ballet for almost a decade, and I find myself extremely nervous in his presence. He's listed off all of my accomplishments in a matter of ten minutes, and I've peppered him with questions for the last twenty in talking about all of his. It didn't matter before when I first acquiesced to Kimberley's request to just meet with him as part of the ongoing united front shtick we have going, but now this meeting has become something else entirely.

For her part, Kimberley stayed for the first half-hour of our lunch meeting, and then she surprisingly begged off for another event she insisted she was already late for. *She left me. With Daniel.* And now, I'm all but terrified. All the unconquerable fears that continuously dwell inside of me rush to the forefront. Despite perfecting the art of sophistication and looking the part, I'm pretty sure I'm not acting sophisticated at all at this point with PNB's famous artistic director.

After Kimberley's abrupt departure, the director does look a little perplexed by me.

Aren't they all?

"I saw your performances in *Swan Lake* and *Giselle* a few years ago. Both, actually, with NYC Ballet and San Francisco Ballet last year."

"You did? I didn't know that."

"You're extremely talented, Tally, but you know that." He pauses and takes a sip of his wine. "How's SFB treating you?"

"Mikhail can be difficult, but then again, so can I, sometimes." I shake my head and reward him with a little smile but then it fades. "He fired me at one point not long ago. I'm sure you heard." He nods but I detect nothing but sympathy for me in his gaze. "Not for insubordination. I was pregnant and I didn't tell Mikhail right away, and he fired me before I could tell him, but I think he knew. I'm pretty sure he knew. My being pregnant messed with his fall schedule, and he wasn't happy. Then, the fan base started asking about my return after my car accident where we lost our daughter as well as the baby I was carrying. And so, he's hired me back on a temporary basis for *The Nutcracker*, but it's different." I shrug. "My options are open, although unclear."

"I'm sorry to hear about your loss...losses," he quickly corrects himself.

"You are? I'm sorry. That's not what I meant. I'm cynical, you see. I know why Mikhail fired me and I'm just a little..."

"Cynical," he adds the word for me and looks sympathetic again. It's both disarming and distracting.

"Yes, I'm a little cynical, these days. I love to dance. I've sacrificed everything for it. I just…" I half-smile and shake my head slightly. "Now, I just want to find a home with my career that supports the rest of my life, if that makes any sense at all. My former director with SFB, Sasha Bennett, is in Moscow with the Bolshoi. She wants me to come there."

"Sasha is very talented. The Bolshoi Ballet. Wow. That's quite an opportunity."

"Yes, but it's in…"

"Moscow," he finishes for me with a slight smile.

"Right. Yes, the job is in Moscow." I smile back feeling a little more at ease with him.

"A little far from the baseball player pitching baseball in Seattle at Safeco Field."

"Yes. Exactly."

"Tally. Can I be frank?" Daniel leans in so we won't be overhead, and I do the same.

"Yes, I'd hoped you would be."

"We want to offer you a three-year contract."

I raise an eyebrow. *Three years is unusual.*

"I wasn't aware this was more than a introductory meeting. I'm not really sure of the next steps I'll be taking with my career. Right now, I'm just here in Seattle to support my husband's newest career endeavor."

Kimberley's words.

I know them by heart.

I smile at my perfect delivery.

"I know, but this is a rare opportunity to meet with someone of your talent and caliber. Kimberley told me and the board as well that I should make the most of it in meeting with you. I know the American Ballet Theatre is interested as well."

"Kimberley told you that? About ABT, too? I wasn't aware of that."

"Yes, well, I wanted to be prepared and make the most of the opportunity to talk to you about your career and what you would gain by landing here with us with the Pacific Northwest Ballet. I spent twenty-two years with the New York City Ballet, believe me, Tally, I know how it works."

"I'm sure you do. Mikhail threatened to blacklist me. Has he made good on that?" I ask with a little laugh. It's very freeing to not be afraid anymore of what Mikhail might do.

"I'm not sure. I didn't think to check *the list* before meeting with you for lunch today." His smile is genuine. His honesty is refreshing. "We *do* really want to offer you a three-year contract. Three performances a year, possibly four," he says softly so we still won't be overheard. "Summers off, if you wish, so you can spend the majority of the baseball season with your husband. You two face quite the challenge with dueling schedules, some would call downright *grueling*, and seasons that can overlap. We understand that. We want to support you in any way that we can."

He smiles again and I return it. I allow myself to feel hopeful that things might work out for me here in Seattle. For just a few minutes anyway.

"The dueling schedules have made it challenging for us. Difficult, actually," I say quietly. "And it's true; we're not perfect. We've had our challenges both in our careers and our personal life. We've come to accept that the constant hounding of the press seems to come with the territory. I'm just telling you that right now, upfront, to be fair. There's a lot of press that comes with being married to somebody famous, especially baseball players; it seems."

"Well, what would Kimberley Powers say? Any press coverage is good for all of us?" Daniel laughs.

"Kimberley would most definitely say something to that effect. Kimberley's been good to us, I must say. Good for Linc. Good for me as it turns out. Her defense of us when it comes to dealing with the press, negative or positive, is exemplary; she cannot be matched. We are very grateful for her support and due diligence. She's our publicist as well as a good friend. To both of us."

"Kimberley speaks very highly of you. All your coworkers and mentors alike do. Your resume and body of work speaks for itself. You are gifted. Any dance company would be lucky to have you. But I also want to emphasize that we would ensure and accommodate and support you in any way that we can in making it all work for you and your family. The salary is generous, I'm guessing more than what you have with SFB and dare I say more than Sasha Bennett can offer with the Bolshoi Ballet." He slides over the contract for my review. I'm pretty sure my mouth drops open at the dollar amount.

I take a sip of water and then switch to the untouched wine glass in front of me because I am at a loss of words at the dollar figure I'm staring at. Daniel seems to realize I need a minute or two to compose myself. He breaks into a gentle speech about the heritage of the Pacific Northwest Ballet and its long tradition of working and training exceptional dancers and producing prestigious performances.

"That's a lot of pointe shoes," I finally manage to say with a wan smile as I point to the dollar amount clearly displayed on the contract he's given me. "And three years is a long time. It's very generous."

"We cover the shoes by the way, up to one hundred and twenty pairs, more than that though, and you're on your own." He laughs.

I laugh, too. "Yes. Okay. A hundred and twenty pairs then. No more."

"It's generous. The contract. Our terms." He steeples his fingers together. I'm instantly reminded of Brad Stephenson. I smile.

"It *is*."

"With product endorsements and branding assignments and featured advertising, you'd be well above seven figures. Granted, it is not your husband's contract, but it is huge in our world as you well know."

Linc's five-year, $96 million-dollar contract is the talk of the sports world right now. Constant banter in discussing the merits of his contract as to whether it's too high or too low floods the airwaves wherever we go.

"So I wanted to tell you a little bit more of the why. *Why* are we willing to go this far with an offer for you."

"Yes, please. Tell me why. Why me?" I'm charmed by his generosity and his kind nature. The man is a god in the dance world. He certainly doesn't need me to shore up his roster as it were.

"Your stage presence is exceptional. We've heard the rumors about you. Frankly, Allaire Tremblay told me about you some eight years ago. "She's one to watch," she'd said. I remember her saying it like it was yesterday. The comparisons to Polina Semionova captured my interest. It is quite an accomplishment to even to be compared to her but you have been and you are that kind of rare talent just like Polina is. When you left the New York City Ballet for San Francisco I wondered why for some time, but then I saw the links being made to Lincoln Presley and I knew you'd sacrificed your career advancement for love. Don't get me wrong the San Francisco Ballet is up and coming as is the Pacific Northwest Ballet, but they are not New York, London, or even Moscow. We're aware of that.

"The fine arts are ruled by prestige and patronage. Don't underestimate my eagerness in having you come on board, building upon your brand in the hopes of drawing in the crowds during high season. I want that. We need that to survive. We count on it. In a world where everything goes much faster and farther, ballet as an art form can just as easily be left behind for far cheaper entertainment. We constantly battle that kind of competition. People have choices. Many. The fine arts doesn't always make the top of that list except at Christmastime. Tradition is eschewed like last week's newspaper these days. We are aware of that.

"So we are in constant search of the finest talent—the huge draw where fans will take notice and bring patrons of the arts in droves back to our theater. You have that talent—that rare gift—that people will pay top dollar to see. You will draw in the fans from the youngest to the oldest. I want that. I covet that. I'm willing to pay homage to it wherever I can find it.

"You've fought adversity in your professional life as well as your personal life. I don't take that lightly. You've suffered the loss of a young child, a baby, as well as your mother in just the past four months. And yet, here you are. You persevere. You're already back on stage and always the consummate professional in doing your best and performing at the highest level. You're a survivor, Tally. I admire that. I think your empathy lifts you up even higher when you're on the stage. You have that rare gift where ballet makes up part of your DNA. It's not a choice with you. It's part of who you are. It's rare.

"It's hard to make it in the dance world as you well know. We battle injuries. The dedication it demands. The burnout it engenders. We fight all these things to make it look so beatifically elegant and effortless on stage. You have all of these qualities and more. I envision you dancing with us and anticipate seeing you named a principal dancer before too long. That would be my goal with you in our dance company. You're a star, Tally, a rare talent and the Pacific Northwest Ballet wants to play a part in your rising career. We want you to find a home with us."

He points to the contract documents at my fingertips. "I didn't give you those to be presumptuous. I just wanted you to know that we are serious with our offer and give you some time with your attorney to look over the contract. We can only hope you'll accept our offer. Just know that we're prepared to buy out your full contract with SFB as well as the temporary one you've just signed if necessary. Mikhail cannot hold you hostage. I've seen him do this before to other dancers, so we've already prepared the contract language to protect you and us both. We'd like you to start with us in early January, unless you're willing to make a surprise appearance for *The Nutcracker,* which we would eagerly accommodate. In the first two weeks of February, we do a two-week run of performances of *Roméo et Juliette,* and we'd like you to be our Juliette. We think you'd be perfect in the role."

He is saying all the right things. My head spins. I'm desperately trying to remember what all Jane said about making choices and doing things for the right reasons and what Brad said last night, for that matter, but their wisdom is all starting to run together. Love is the constant is the only thing coming to mind.

"I'm overwhelmed by what all you've said." I look through the documents while Daniel casually sips his wine. He's all calm and cool and collected, but I know he's a little nervous because he thinks he might lose out to Sasha and the Bolshoi Ballet or the American Ballet Theatre in New York.

I skim the pages but stop and read the fine print about the contract buyout. They really are buying out my contract with SFB.

The salary is beyond generous; it's an amazing offer, even for Seattle. I could get a place of my own, if things somehow still fall apart with Linc.

What do I mean if things somehow still fall apart with Linc?
Things may very well continue to fall apart with Linc.
They have fallen apart.
There are no guarantees that they will come back together.

Love is the constant?
Says who?
We'll see.
I still have to cross that bridge and need to actually take those steps toward my future.
My uncertain future still awaits me.
"Tally? Are you okay?" Daniel touches my hand vying for my attention. The artistic director looks a little concerned.

I brush at my face with the back of my hand feeling the wetness from tears. *I'm crying in front of the PNB's most famous artistic director.*

"It's just a little overwhelming. It's a generous offer. Thank you so much."

He smiles. "We want you to dance with us, Tally. You're a star, and we want you to be part of our family." He removes his hand from mine and looks slightly embarrassed. "I'm sorry. I just wanted to make sure you were okay. I'm a little enthusiastic about this opportunity with you in possibly coming on board with us."

"I'm okay. I'm amazed by the offer." I smile reassuring him. "It's fantastic. *Really.*" I sigh big feeling somewhat torn. It is really tempting to just sign the documents and be done with it but I know I need to perform due diligence. I bite at my lower lip and finally look over at him. "I'll have my lawyer look these over. Would it be possible to meet again tomorrow and check out the studio and meet the other dancers? I don't see why I wouldn't sign; I just want to ensure I've had my attorney read these over first."

"So, if the terms are agreeable…are you saying yes?" Daniel looks all hopeful.

"Yes, I'm saying yes if my lawyer doesn't see a problem with the terms." I extend my hand, and he shakes it.

"This is so exciting. Yes, let's plan for you to swing by the studio at ten tomorrow morning if that works for you, and I'll introduce you around."

"Ten sounds perfect. Thank you."

I will not allow my mind to even contemplate what I've just done, what I've just committed myself to. Instead, Daniel sends the documents to my email and I quickly forward them to Everett Madsen requesting he look them over so I can sign with PNB as soon as possible and request he get back to me by tomorrow morning at the latest. The whole communiqué with my lawyer takes less than the time it takes to order our afternoon coffee from the waiter.

We finish our lunch and share the last of the white wine between us. Daniel seems willing to carry the conversation and tells me all the nuances about Seattle and the Pacific Northwest Ballet.

Meanwhile, I revel in the moment of being wanted and of being valued. This surprising feeling as if I'm coming home resonates with me deep inside. The idea of working for a dance company that is intent on creating a balance between a home life and a professional one would be hard for any dancer to turn down. Saying yes to the Pacific Northwest Ballet feels like I've finally arrived. I'm coming home. That's how it feels. I'm coming home to Seattle, which is weird because I never would have thought as Seattle as home, but then I realize it has nothing to do with Seattle or even the Pacific Northwest Ballet.

It's Linc.
Home is where Linc is.
Home is where the heart is.
Damn.
Jane was right.
And Linc is coming to Seattle.
And now so am I.
Love is a constant.
Home is where the heart is and Linc is my home.
eE
My phone buzzes with an incoming text.

Everett Madsen: "Tally, this contract looks good. You're covered with SFB by PNB's buyout. Sign away."

Tally Landon Presley: "Signing."

I smile at Daniel. "Do you have a pen? My lawyer says I can sign them."

He proffers a pen, and I sign the papers without another thought. It takes a few seconds to register what I've just done as I slide the documents back to him.

He quickly produces another identical set of documents, and I sign those as well.

"Two originals. Signed. One for each of us to hold onto," he says with an engaging smile.

I smile back a little dazed in suddenly realizing I'm coming to Seattle to dance with the Pacific Northwest Ballet. I'm coming home to Seattle.

I'm coming home.

To Seattle.

Love is a constant.

Well.

It better be.

CHAPTER FORTY-THREE

money power glory

TALLY

It's all wrong. It's all wrong but why does it feel right?
Why does it feel like destiny?
Love is the constant.
Love is the destination?
Love is destiny?
  ~ Talia Landon Presley

December 10th

It's ten blocks back to the hotel where Linc and I are staying. I weave my way past the traffic and pedestrians using both time and distance to clear my head. My copy of the signed contract is tucked away in my purse. I can feel it there like an extra set of hands holding on to me, guiding me. I confirmed the plans to meet up with Daniel tomorrow morning to meet the other dancers and get a tour of the studio. Surprisingly, I didn't demand to do any of those things before I signed a three-year deal. Funny that.

I stand in front of the Four Seasons for a few minutes and steel myself for the next scene. Linc texted me about a half-hour ago wondering where I was and how things were going.

I texted him back. "I'm on my way home." Let's not even examine why I said that.

I glide across the lobby and take the first elevator to the penthouse floor. We have the entire floor and a suite with two masters. It must have cost the Mariners a small fortune to put us up here. It's so unlike Linc to be so demanding, but he hasn't been himself in some time. This version of Linc is clearly pissed off and all about getting what he wants. This version is like me. Selfish. Self-indulgent. Understanding him as well as myself is big news all around. Yes, I've finally figured it out. I smile at my newfound wisdom.

I'm still smiling as I step off the elevator and make my way toward our private entrance.

I took the job. Why did I do that?

Because love is the constant.

Love is all I can count on.

Now, I just have to show him.

Be ready to show him.

Linc is already in the suite. He's dressed in a black Polo shirt and his favorite pair of jeans. I know he had a photo shoot with Calvin Klein at one point today and another one with the Mariners as well as meeting which included a uniform fitting. We've been apart all day, busy with our own stuff.

"I have a place I want to show you," he says by way of greeting as soon as I walk through the hotel door. "I have a car waiting. You look amazing by the way."

"Thanks. Can I change? Do I need to dress up like this?"

"No. You can change, but you look stunning, incredible really." He stops and stares.

"Thank you," I say looking away from him because the longing I see in his eyes would prevent us from leaving this hotel room at all, and I can't deal with that right now.

Or, I could very well be imagining things.

I am off my game.

I have sworn off of sex as part of my new repertoire for a while; and yet, he is already causing me to rethink the whole vow of celibacy thing. And, it's only been five days since I made this pact with myself. He seems to be thinking the same thing. He runs his hands through his hair and grins as if he's been caught looking at dirty pictures.

"Tally, can you hurry? I…I really want you to see this, and like I said I have a car waiting."

"Okay, I'll hurry."

I change into a new red silk blouse Jane talked me into buying and a pair of black jeans and slide into with the black ankle boots I brought with me. My feet are already killing me from the long walk in heels back from my lunch meeting with Daniel. I pull the pins from my hair and pull at the strands with my fingers while Linc stands in the doorway watching me.

"I like your hair down like that."

"Thank you." Our eyes meet in the bathroom mirror.

"How did your day go?" he asks.

"It was…truly amazing." I smile wide and shake my head in wonder. "How about you?"

"Jury's still out. It could be considered truly amazing too, if things go the way I want them to." He stops talking and seems to hesitate. "Tally? Are you ready? The car's waiting for us."

"Sure. Let's go." I turn from the mirror and face him. He holds out his hand, and I take it. "Is this like a date or something?"

He laughs then. Apparently, my sense of humor has miraculously put him at ease finally. "Something like that. You'll see."

I let go of his hand to move past him and grab my leather jacket and put it on. He watches me the entire time. He has this bemused look upon his handsome face as if he holds the world's biggest secret, and he can't wait to share it.

Or, I'm just imagining things once again.

We make small talk in the car. A limousine. The man is full of surprises all of a sudden. He hands me a glass of champagne from the limo's bar. I give him a quizzical look.

"I know you like champagne. So what? It's okay to know what you like."

"Okay."

I don't know what to make of him or myself.

I signed the contract with the Pacific Northwest Ballet so I'm moving to Seattle. I think that particular shock of the day has finally caught up to me. I lean back in my seat, sip the champagne and gaze at the beauty of Seattle as we make our way through downtown and then take the bridge that spans across the water. Linc goes on to explain how a bridge can float on the water while I try not to look too closely at how that all works as the limousine whisks across this two-lane floating miracle of a freeway.

Lake Washington is immense. Linc tells me it's more than two hundred feet deep in places. It is this beautiful cobalt blue and goes for miles in every direction as we cross the bridge. He points out Mount Rainier as we head to what is commonly known as *the Eastside.* We take the first exit off of the bridge and circle our way back to a neighborhood which Linc tells me is referred to as Evergreen Point which is part of the small city of Medina where Bill Gates and Jeff Bezos reside.

"Really? Bill and Jeff as neighbors? Say it isn't so. The homes are huge. It definitely reminds me of Sea Cliff," I say airily.

Linc just secretly smiles. "No *judging* yet. Just wait, Tally. I think you'll like this place."

Does it matter whether I like this place?

Linc and I are separated. Separating? One of those.

It's all wrong. It's all wrong but why does it feel so right?

Why does it feel like destiny?

Love is the constant.

Love is the destination?

Love is destiny?

"What are you thinking about?" He looks a little excited as well as nervous; \it's as if he can barely contain himself.

I smile at him and down the last of my champagne. "Destiny."

"Destiny." He raises an eyebrow. "*Destiny?* Isn't that a little too optimistic even for you?"

"Maybe?" I shake my head slightly. I lick my lips while he watches. "Maybe not anymore. I don't know. I'm just being honest and telling you what I was thinking about."

He starts to say something. He leans into me even more and I do as well, *waiting*—waiting for him to say something, do something.

The connection between us is so strong it's as if we're suddenly magnetized and drawn into one another. But then, the driver is driving up this long drive lined with all these immensely tall trees on both sides and I'm momentarily distracted. I turn away from Linc and gaze out the darkened windows at this wondrous scene that seems to be straight out of a movie.

"Wow."

He leans into me. "I know. It's something to see; isn't it. It's an old estate. It's been in the same family for years. It's a shared driveway. If you go to the left you'll be at the neighbor's property. Or this one. These are fir trees and there are some Cedar trees as well that are more than fifty years old. They're indigenous to the Pacific Northwest."

"They're so beautiful. This is amazing. I love this driveway and... whoa." I turn to Linc in surprise.

He smiles wide. "I had the exact same reaction the first time I saw the house."

The limousine has stopped at the top of a circular drive directly in front of long, white brick house. The ranch-style home is all one story with large windows on either side of these red-painted double doors.

"Love those red doors," I say turning back to Linc and grinning wide.

"I know. I knew you would."

He opens the passenger door before the driver can even get out and pulls me up from out of the limousine in the next. I make a full circle taking in the drive and the trees and the circular fountain lined with mosaic tiles in various shades of blue. You can hear the water as it splashes from the urn of a cherub little angel into the blue mosaic-tiled pool below.

"I love this," I say pointing to the fountain. "It's so charming."

"Come on, Tal. There's a lot more to see." Linc holds up a key and unlocks one the red door on the right and then steps aside allowing me to enter first. "The house was built in the 1970s. It has a Frank Lloyd Wright kind of feel. Everything is either made of wood or materials native to the Northwest." I make another full circle standing in the middle of the great room trying to take it all in while

Linc lists off all the features of the house like a dedicated tour guide. "There are three bedrooms plus a master. Two full baths. A kitchen. Dining room. This great room."

The house has been designed as an open floor plan, and my eyes are automatically drawn to the large windows that line the back of the house. I stare at the massive green lawn lined down each side with six-foot hedges making it completely private from the neighbors. The lawn stretches out to a sandy beach, a boat dock, and the cobalt blue water's edge. The view is spectacular.

"That's Lake Washington," Linc says pointing to the gigantic blue lake where the waves gently lap at the shore. We have laughed several times already about how many different bodies of water surround this city so I'm glad he knows. "It's not that far from downtown or the ballpark. Both are just across the bridge."

"That's good, right? An easy drive to Seattle." I give him a weak smile and avoid looking at him directly.

I am captivated by the house. It's pulling at me.

But, just as suddenly, things feel uncertain between Linc and me. There is too much *not* being said right now.

There's a long hallway with a black and white marble floor in a checkered pattern. "I love this, too." I point to the patterned floor.

"It's great, right?" Linc continues to play tour guide and grabs my hand as he prepares to lead me around the entire house. "This is the living room—the great room—I guess. It dominates the house. This is where everyone must have hung out. The kitchen is a good size. It probably needs to be redone."

"I don't know about that. I like it. The marble countertops are pretty. It's not like I'm a great cook or anything. Well, you *are*, of course, but if everything works…"

I feel foolish for inserting myself into the scenario about the kitchen. Nervous now by the way captivating way he's looking at me, I turn on a burner; a blue flame comes on proving my point. "See? It works." I turn it off quickly. "I don't know," I add hastily, "*you're* the one thinking of buying it. Gut the kitchen if you want. It would be fine for me is all I'm saying."

"Is that all you're saying?"

His sudden flirting throws me off. "What are we doing here?"

He shrugs with indifference. "You told me I could show you a property that I thought you might like. This is the one. I saw five others. This is the only one I knew you'd approve of. Anyway, the real estate agent said it comes with a few caveats per the seller's request, but she also subtly suggested that the property could be sold with the idea of tearing it down and building a new house here."

"Noooooooooo. You *cannot* allow that to happen. The house is perfect just the way it is. You'll have to buy it on the principle alone of saving it just to preserve the charm.

He takes in air and slowly lets it out as he looks down at the floor and then back up at me. "I know, right?" He hides a smile now. I get the distinct feeling I'm playing right into his hands. "I thought the same thing. And I knew you'd love it because it's not too big and… why are you looking at me like that?"

"What? I'm not looking at you like anything. Finish the tour, Elvis. Show me what you've got…I mean, what you've found." I try to smile at him but the bantering back and forth is weighing on me because there is so much more not being said between us.

"There's a master on the south side," he says. "Come on. This way. I'll show you."

I follow Linc down the white and black marble hallway still marveling at the cool geometric style. The design of this house has all these little touches that make it charming, but not overdone.

I think I'm falling in love with it a little bit more with every moment I spend in it. And for some reason, I think Lincoln Presley knows this.

We step into the master bedroom together which proves rather awkward. It seems we're acting like this is our first date—we're both nervous around each other now, which is truly ridiculous.

I busy myself in stepping away from him and start to scope out the view. One entire wall is dedicated to an unobstructed view of the lake.

"It's beautiful," I say quietly. "The serenity of this place…it just seeps right into your soul."

"I know." He points out the open white brick fireplace along the far wall a space that must be designated for a sitting area. "There's still enough room for a king-size bed and a long dresser."

"That's good." I walk into the master closet. "It's not huge, but it will fit the majority of our clothes," I call out to Linc.

Wait. What? I'm not living here.

"*Your clothes*, I mean." I quickly exit the closet and catch up to Linc, who now stands in the middle of the master bathroom. I casually look around noting double sinks and a large mirror lining one wall.

There's a walk-in shower matching the blue mosaic tiles once again, but it's the old-fashioned claw-foot bathtub sitting beneath a large window with a view of the lake that captivates me. "Awesome! I can take a bath and enjoy the view at the same time. Well, *you could*." I climb into the tub to demonstrate.

Linc gets this glazed look for a few seconds. He sighs and then shoves his hands into his jeans pockets and seemingly studies the view of the lake out the window instead of me. "You think that's the biggest selling point?"

I don't think we're talking about the bathtub anymore.

I lean back in the tub, close my eyes for a few seconds, and then turn my head and glance out the window. "Perfect. I can still see the water even when I put my head back like this. Somebody thought through their design all the way to perfection." I attempt to laugh while Linc glances down at me looking tortured in a number of ways.

"What's wrong, Elvis?" I extend my hand and he grabs it and pulls me up. I am about six inches taller when standing in the tub. "Finally, I'm tall enough for you," I say airily, demonstrating with my arms loosely wrapped around his shoulders.

He gets this anguished look. "You've always been tall enough for me." The crevice between the bridge of his nose deepens. "I never meant to make you feel bad about your height or your weight or your size or just being you, but I've done all of that to you; haven't I?"

There's a little silence as I try to figure out how to answer him.

"No more than I've done to myself," I finally say.

"Jane said I demanded you to be perfect. Did I do that?"

"*I* demanded that I be perfect—in your eyes, in everyone's eyes—for a really long time. It has been *me* more than you demanding that

I be perfect, but I'm better now. I'm getting better. I'm trying to not be perfect, and instead I'm just trying to be myself. It's very hard, but that's what Jane and I have been working on."

I run my fingers through his hair at the nape of his neck. We stare at each other for a mesmerized moment.

We are entirely too close.

"Tally," he says in anguish, "I can't do this with you anymore. I can't kiss you right now, even though I want to so badly, because I can't go to the edge with you anymore. I can't risk losing you all over again. I just can't do this with you right now."

"Sure. I know." I force a smile to make light of it as I drop my arms and go to step back, he reaches out and catches me just before I would have fallen backwards.

"Careful." He quickly lifts me out of the tub but then just as fast he's dropping his hands to his sides and moving farther away from me.

He's afraid of me.

His fears of losing and falling and failing have finally taken him over. I recognize the defense mechanism because I've been there and allowed those same fears to rule me and my emotions for far too long.

"Right," I say with sudden understanding. "Okay then." I reward him with a bright smile. "I think I've seen enough. Do what you want. Buy it if you want. It's your decision. Thanks for showing me the place."

"Tally. I…I'm sorry. I just don't want to…I can't go through the pain of losing you anymore."

"I know. I know. It's okay." I force myself to smile. The star smile. He looks pained at seeing it. "I'm just going to go now. I'll wait for you out…"

I've run out of words.

I can't take the look of defeat in his eyes and I can't help him out anymore than I can help myself out. With extreme effort, I make my way down the hallway gripping the walls for support as I go because putting one foot in front of the other has suddenly become the biggest challenge.

Linc does not follow.

Love is a constant?
Well, great, but you have to have love.
And right now?
All I feel is Linc's transference of pain.
His outright rejection starts to burn through me.
Love doesn't appear to be anywhere nearby shoring up either one of us right now.

CHAPTER FORTY-FOUR

gods & monsters

TALLY

We are never on the same page,
on the same plane,
within same vortex,
on the same planet
or in same universe.
Like ever.
Like never.
   ~ Talia Landon Presley

December 10th

LINC STILL HASN'T EMERGED FROM THE master bedroom. I assume he's caught up in the vortex of loss, regret, and remorse and armoring himself up as well along with his heart for our next encounter or parting. One of those.

Great.

Fucking fabulous.

Damn.

We are never on the same page, on the same plane, within same vortex, on the same planet or in same universe.

Like ever.

Like never.

I wander through the great room's old-fashioned sliding glass door, irritably push it open, and head outside to the back yard. There's a patio with four perfectly painted shiny red Adirondack chairs centered around a lovely stone fire pit on one side of the stone patio made of the same type of stone. Everything about this place screams I am loved and cared for.

I slowly make my way down to the boat dock and watch the waves as they lap at the sandy beach. Barely avoiding getting my boots wet by one of them but I jump out of the way just in time. Reaching the end of the dock, I look out across the late admiring the noble, tall buildings of downtown Seattle and the bridge that stretches out across the water that we must have crossed earlier.

You can see for miles. It's truly an amazing place.

It's a piece of paradise right in the heart of the city. Well, close by. Close enough to the city.

There's still no sign of Linc. I make my way back up the luscious green lawn and aimlessly wander around to the south side of the yard and casually glance up at the master bedroom window. Linc is talking rather animatedly on his cell phone. I guess it to be to Charlie or Brad or Kimberley, or the real estate agent. It doesn't look like the conversation is going all that well because he's running his free hand through his hair, and I watch him sigh several times. He looks out at me. I give him a parade wave. He waves back ever so slightly then turns away from me altogether.

I do the same, but can barely swallow down the bitter irony of being so thoroughly rejected by him in this way. The powerful feeling of loss assails me once again. His obvious indifference has quickly become a special way to torture me.

I did this.

Well, okay I started it, but he performed the grand finale of our demise rather spectacularly now, didn't he?

And now?

I'm thinking of Nika Vostrikova.

Damn it.

Stop it, Tally.

Moving on.

There's a bench hidden in a little archway that catches my attention. and I go and sit down and breathe in deep.

It's true. I'm feeling sorry for myself. Maybe it's finally happened; Linc doesn't love me anymore. Or, he's afraid to.

Either way?

Not good.

This stressful situation calls for Jane's input. I send her a text.

> Me: "Tally Landon Presley aka Sugar Plum Fairy. Hi. Checking in. How are things?"

It takes Jane all of thirty seconds to respond.

> Jane: "Hey. TOY. How's it going? "
>
> Me: "Am I like you're ONLY patient? That was fast."
>
> Jane: "Answer the ???"
>
> Me: "Crazy. Crazy for feeling so lonely."
>
> Jane: "Patsy Cline already? Crazy for you."
>
> Me: "Already. He's showing me some house. He freaked out. Said it was too hard. He couldn't do it anymore."
>
> Jane: "Whatev. He's just being a guy. No touchy feelings. I'm SCARED."
>
> Me: "I know."
>
> Jane: "So? What are you going to do?"
>
> Me: "IDK."
>
> Jane: Strip naked. Then, try to talk to him."
>
> Me: "You TOLD me that sex is not the answer."
>
> Jane: "It's not always the answer but some Xs it's the ONLY answer."
>
> Me: "ha ha. C.E.L.I.B.A.C.Y. vow in play. Oh, and AND I signed with PNW Ballet. So. Now, I'm moving to Seattle sans husband as the baseball player's ex-wife, I guess. La-di-fucking-da."

She doesn't answer that text.

Jane calls.

"What the hell? You're moving to Seattle?"

"Hi to you, too."

"Tally, are you sure about this?"

"The director is fantastic. Three to four performances a year. Three-year contract. Major bucks for a girl like me. I couldn't turn it down."

"Wow. That does sound like you couldn't turn it down. Congratulations. I assume you told Linc? But then again, based on what you sent via text, I'm assuming you haven't told him yet. *Maybe* you *should*."

"I don't know. I don't want to look like I'm *begging* him to reconsider our relationship. Love shouldn't be that hard." I play with my hair and try to figure out what my next move should be even as Jane keeps on talking.

"True. True. Okay, well shit. Now, I need to do some thinking about this, and I actually *do* have another patient, so can we like talk later about this? Damn! I'm so proud of you right now. *Seattle. You.* This is *fantastic* news."

"What you're stepping out on me with a new patient?"

"*Never.*"

"So, Seattle…" I sigh big and feel a major panic coming on. "I'll miss you. Maybe it wasn't such a good idea to sign the contract so soon."

"You won't have to miss me. I'll be up there. It's a 90-minute plane ride. It's a lot better than commuting to Moscow to see your fine, bony ass. No worries. Okay, shit, I've got to go. The patient is in the waiting room. I can see her unhappy little face from the office window. Gah! Some days are harder than others, and I'm late besides. I'll call you in a few hours, okay? You good?"

"Good enough. Talk soon. Go save somebody else."

Jane laughs and hangs up.

I put my phone away and finally pay enough attention to discover the amazing secret about sitting on this bench: you can see the water, the entire yard as well as the back of the house from here. *It's a secret hideout.*

I close my eyes and allow my mind to drift. Soon enough, I conclude that this place is intended to soothe the body, mind, as well as the soul. It's like a special form of yoga. When I finally open my eyes I notice a little picket fence gate right past the bench and the ten-foot hedge that spans the length of the yard with what I assume to be the neighbor's property line.

I unlatch the gate, follow the inviting path made by the stepping stones, and suddenly find myself standing in the neighbor's garden. These people are serious gardeners. The once immaculate plants are now dried out and yellow and brown in color with winter's subtle wrath, but they are draped just about everywhere. I can only imagine how beautiful this garden looks in the spring. Beyond the garden, the neighbor's lawn is a matching green like ours—Linc's—I mean the-house-that-is-for-sale's lawn. The design of the house seems eerily similar.

I'm about to retrace my steps back to the other side when I notice an older woman with dark auburn hair kneeling in the far side of the garden curiously watching me.

She partially raises her hand and casually waves. Then, she's getting up and walking over to me. Her long dark-red hair is tied back with a red, pink and orange-colored scarf, and her head is topped off with a wide-brimmed straw hat decorated with a sash matching the scarf. She's bundled up in this big white winter coat that hugs her body and yet I can already tell the lady has a flair for style.

It's undeniable. It's there. Her style.

I am instantly reminded of Jane.

"Hi, I'm Stella. I'd shake your hand, but I've been *mulching*. Like *that* sounds attractive." She rolls her eyes and laughs. "I know it's the dead of winter, but I read somewhere that coffee grounds are good for the soil, so I thought I'd give it a try. I'm trying to grow this new variety of roses, *Bouquet d'Or*, for next spring." She takes a little breath and smiles wider.

I bet she has a thousand different ones.

I'm reminded of Jane again.

"I'm Talia. Well, everyone calls me Tally."

"Is that what you like? Tally? Or Talia? Which one? I like them both." She leans forward, and nudges my forearm with hers. "You are *stunning* in person."

"Tally is fine," I say, slightly disconcerted that she seems to know who I am.

"Well, I'm Stella Nelson. Jane said you two would be coming by to look at the house."

"Jane? Jane said *what*? I'm sorry. I'm not following. Do you know Dr. Jane Nelson? I was just talking to her on my cell phone. This is weird."

"Well, yes, I brought her into this world almost twenty-five years ago." Stella laughs.

"Wait. What? You're Jane's *mother*?"

"I am. The house belonged to George and Lila Winters." She points back to the house behind me. "It's their house that's for sale. When I heard your husband was coming to Seattle I told Janie to let him know about the house. The estate has been for sale for a long time. The family isn't interested in selling it to just *anyone*; they want to ensure it goes to the right couple. That's why I told Janie to let Lincoln know about it. Welcome to Seattle, by the way, Tally."

I smile feeling instantly at ease with Jane's mother. "Thank you. I'm sorry I didn't make the connection. Jane never mentioned you lived in Seattle. I guess I assumed you were in San Francisco since you go the San Francisco Ballet's production of *The Nutcracker* each year because I'm in it." I pause realizing what I just said and how it must sound. "I'm sorry that didn't come out right."

"I *do* go to *The Nutcracker* each year because you're starring in it. I fly down every year to see your performance and well, because it's Christmas, and I love the ballet, and it's one way to spend some extra time with Jane. We're season-ticket holders here too with the Pacific Northwest Ballet. She flies up when she can."

"You are? What do you think of them? The dance company, I mean."

She purses her lips together as if she's given it a great deal of thought and then she smiles again. "I think they are truly talented ballet company. Their artistry and choreography is amazing. I would classify them as up and coming. Did you meet with Daniel Hollis, yet?"

"I *did*. Kimberley, my publicist, set it up? How do you know about that?"

"Well, I'm on the board. I may have mentioned you were accompanying Lincoln on a visit to Seattle when Jane called to tell me. How did it go?"

"It went well. *Amazingly well.* I signed with them, actually. Three years. It's a huge contract. Not like the baseball player's, of course, but it's…"

"It's a big deal. Oh my goodness, you've made my year! I can't wait to see your performances. You'll be the perfect Juliette." She winks.

"You're too kind."

"Don't sell your talent short, my dear. They're lucky to have you. Daniel already knew that, of course. Your reputation precedes you with the work you've done with the New York City Ballet and internationally with the Bolshoi in the past few years. Daniel just needed a little push and some additional funding to make it all happen. We called in a few favors to ensure it would. I'm just so glad it all worked out." Stella pulls off her right-hand glove and extends her hand.

I clasp hers, and she squeezes mine back in the same way Jane always does. "Thank you. You're amazing just like your daughter."

"She says the same about you. Good thing I live right next door so when she visits, if you two are living next door, Jane will invariably be doing that more often. Win win. All around. Just think we can run back and forth between our houses and do all kinds of fun things together with Janey and Marston. What am I saying? I really hope that she and Marston are ready to take the next step in their relationship by getting married and finally declare their undying love for each other. *That* is what life is all about, but Janie is stubborn that way, and she's had a rough go of it at times," she says with a little frown.

"She told me about Steven." For some reason, I think it's important Stella know this.

"She told you about Steven? *Whoa.* Then you *are* in the special circle."

I nod. "I asked her once why she calls Marston by his last name."

"Aw, I see. Well, Janie doesn't talk about Steven with just *anyone.* She barely talks about Steven with me, and I'm her *mother.*"

She cocks her head to one side. "She must really trust you. That's good to know. And it's nice to see her confide in someone like you."

"She's helped me tremendously over the past several weeks; and if I'm helping her in some way that's the least I can do. I've always been more of a taker than a giver. It's something I'm working on."

"Well, I think you are doing just fine and giving the world quite a bit of yourself already with your talent and your beauty. We all give in different ways, Tally. Maybe you've been looking at it the wrong way. You share your breathtaking talent and all of yourself with the world. You make it all look so easy and beautiful up there on stage, but I know the sacrifices you make. Just know that I think you are amazing." She squeezes my hand and feel the sympathy emanate from her without her mentioning either Cara or the baby. "Hang in there, Tally, you're doing great," she says softly. "And congratulations on the—"

"Tally?" Linc asks from directly behind me.

Stella's eyes go wide, so I know it's him. It might be true that Stella Nelson is all up and involved in the ballet world but clearly baseball is her sport of choice or, at least, the Mariners' newest acquisition, Lincoln Presley, has not escaped her notice.

I glance back at the baseball star. "Hi."

"I've been looking for you," Linc says.

He looks completely stressed out. "Everything okay?" I ask cautiously. He subtly shakes his head. I step aside so the two of them can meet one another properly and proceed to make introductions. "Lincoln Presley, this is Stella Nelson—Jane's mom."

Linc extends his hand out to Stella while I extend mine toward the woman. "Oh right. Jane sent me a text with the address and the agent's name who set everything up and she mentioned you lived next door," Linc says. "Thanks for the recommendation about looking at the house. We love it."

"Stella Nelson, this is Lincoln Presley, the Seattle Mariners' newest star," I say.

For her welcoming part, Stella tosses both gloves aside and makes her way over to Linc. She doesn't even bother shaking his outstretched hand. I think she actually bats it away as she just moves right in and hugs him to her. "Come here, *you*. You are…Oh my

God. I'm so proud of you for shunning those Yankees and signing with the Mariners. Your fastball is amazing, and I think your slider is coming along, and you are exactly what our baseball team needs here."

"Thank you."

Stella steps back from him. Then, she lightly touches the right side of his head where the tiniest of scars is still visible through his dark hairline. "How's the head? You better? Still getting the headaches, I've read. That's related to stress you know. But moving here to this house? That can change all of that for you. I swear it will."

She is—what I imagine Linc's mother or my mother would be doing if they were alive and standing here—fawning over him in the only way a mother can. Linc seems to rather easily give into Stella's motherly ministrations, which are the unique combination of mother, avid fan as well as her own special brand of magic. Stella Nelson is Jane's mother after all, so she must be magical in the exact same way.

"The slider is coming along. The headaches are still there, but I'm hoping there will be less of them here in Seattle." He frowns ever so slightly and looks over at me. "But I just talked to the real estate agent, and she said she was pretty sure the owner wouldn't sell the house to me. They want it to go to a *couple*, not a guy who's separating from his wife. So, it's a no go on the house." He turns to Stella. "Tally's here to help me out with the press, but we're officially filing for divorce in the next couple of weeks." He glances my way looking completely disillusioned. "Gosh, I've got a car waiting for us, so we really need to get going. Are you ready to go, Tally?"

"Sure. I guess so."

Linc turns back to Stella. "It was nice meeting you, Mrs. Nelson. The real estate agent suggested leaving the key with you? It was great seeing the house. I'm glad Tally got to see it at least. And Jane was right; it's quite a find."

"No problem." Stella gets this bemused look as Linc hands her the key. "Maybe, you should talk to the owner, and change her mind."

Linc and I look at each other in confusion.

"Come on, you two," Stella says easily. "We'll make some phone calls together. I'll make you some tea. Tally, you must be freezing.

You're wearing a short-sleeve blouse, and it's the dead of winter, and I've been jabbering on. Come on, loves. Tea makes everything better, and I have cookies baking in the oven to go with it."

CHAPTER FORTY-FIVE

kryptonite

LINC

*I drown in her words but somehow grasp at the ray of hope
she's given me with a ghost of her smile.*
~ Lincoln Presley

December 10th

Stella Nelson's house is almost an exact replica of ours.
Ours?
Not ours.
The Winter's house.

I make a point of cutting the limo driver loose for a few hours since Stella Nelson insists we come over to her house for tea. She might have some insight into this mysterious owner who is making my life difficult since they won't sell the house to a guy about to get divorced. Not that I want that. I obviously don't, but it seems Tally and I are worlds apart at this juncture.

I can't even look at her right now. I'm too pissed off about losing out on the house. Plus, the heartbreak of losing her over everything that's happened between us because of the Nika thing has decided to mess with me again today.

I can barely keep up with the conversation taking place around me. Stella fires questions at me, and I defer to Tally to answer most of them for me. She keeps shooting me this questioning, what-is-wrong-with-you? look but I'm unable to even answer that for myself let alone my wife, my *soon-to-be-ex-wife*.

Stella is the consummate host. She's already served me three sugar cookies straight out of the oven, and she made me this heavenly sandwich with ham and cheese and freshly baked bread. Tally is eating one now, and she must love it because she is actually eating it. I still get a perverse pleasure in watching this girl eat.

I am so screwed here. Designated to live in Seattle while she'll be in San Francisco or Moscow or New York. I've seen the emails from Sasha. I talked to Kimberley, who Tally has begun to confide in again, and I know the American Ballet Theatre wants her to audition with them soon. Although I know she's mostly serious about returning to Moscow to dance for Sasha with The Bolshoi Ballet. *Why wouldn't she?* It's a huge boost to her career, and that is all she can count on now because I let her down. *That's a fact.*

I let her down.

As for the house for sale next door? I thought maybe seeing the house might change things between us, but now they're worse than ever. I've ended up behaving badly with her all day in defending myself against any kind of intimacy with her because, in our heated exchange at the hospital this past weekend, one of the things Jane said me was to give Tally some space and let her make her own way. Unfortunately, that fact that I am giving her some space is now confusing the hell out of us both because I still want her so damn bad, but I need to get a grip and just let her go—let her make own way and have her own life.

Still? One truth remains. I love Tally more than ever, but a part of me doesn't know if I should risk reaching out to her only to be rejected by her and in the process lose her all over again. I tried to explain this to Jane in a phone call earlier today when she texted me about the house and told me there was a property right next to her mom's on the water that I might want to check out since I was in the housing market and bound for Seattle. Jane did say the owner was being picky about who they'd sell it to. I just didn't know how strict the terms were until after I brought Tally here and called the real estate agent a second-time with the intention of making an offer.

Now, everything is messed up, and I don't know how to fix it.

Stella still bustles around in her kitchen as if she's in her element. She reminds me of my mom from long ago. I tell her that now. She stops what she's doing and gives me this sympathetic look. "I loved your mom's films. God, she was amazing on-screen and just a beautiful person. How's your dad doing?"

"He's still a little lost without her even after all this time. I guess you could say he's not himself."

"I'm sorry to hear that." Stella goes quiet and then she looks over at Tally. "I was sorry to hear about your mom."

She moves past the counter that separates us and hugs Tally and then me.

Stella is a hugger.

Then, she turns back to Tally. "You need some meat on those bones, sweetie. I know you've been ill and are already back dancing for that rat Mikhail Rostov. Don't worry," she says with a little laugh, "Jane just texts me the headlines." Her smile slips and she looks uneasy between glances at me and then Tally. "But it's enough to know what's been going on with you. Are you doing okay, sweetie?"

"I'm fine. Much better. Thank you." Tally tries to pull back from the woman's embrace but Stella isn't having it. She just hugs Tally harder.

Eventually, the woman steps back and just looks at Tally. "So beautiful. So talented. God, this is like the best day ever having you both here." She looks over at me and winks. "I wish Wes was here for this. He died two years ago. He probably wouldn't believe it, even if he were here. Getting to meet the Seattle Mariners' newest acquisition for pitcher who is just casually sitting in our kitchen would be hard to believe. It would be very high on his bucket list." She grins at me and then turns back to Tally and brushes tendrils of her hair from her face like I do. "And this lovely ballerina star."

"I'm sorry so sorry, Stella. I take it Wes was your husband? Jane's dad?" Tally asks grabbing the woman's hand.

"Yes," she says getting this unexpected big smile. "He went fast. What a blessing, right? No suffering with that man. He gave me a hard time for some thirty-one years, and then he went just like that." She looks lost in a memory.

"He told me he didn't feel well and went to lie down, and that was it." Stella quickly wipes at her face with the back of her hand and surprisingly laughs. "He was a God. Built like one, too. This big Norseman of a fellow. We met in college, and that was it. *Big love.* He was big in every way with a big laugh and a big heart. He's left a huge space in my life now that he's gone, but I wouldn't change it. We had a fabulous life together and in the end, he didn't suffer. It just ended one day."

"Oh, Stella, I'm so sorry," Tally says gently taking the woman's hand. "I guess it was kind of like that for my dad with my mom. It just ended for them, too. She'd just left for the store, and then she was hit by a drunk driver just blocks from her home, and she was just gone. But she loved him. She loved him big. She was a generous lady, who struggled with her demons, but she had a big heart like that, too. God she loved my dad so much."

"Tally's dad is a cardiologist," I say for no particular reason. Tally and Stella both turn and stare at me quizzically. "Sorry. I just thought I should supply that tidbit of information about Dr. Adam Landon. Tally's dad."

"I get it," Stella says gently. "So. He fixes broken hearts." She laughs and shakes her head at her own little joke. "Invite him up."

"Oh, he'll be up here," Tally says airily. "He will be a little miffed that he's has to travel to Seattle even for Linc's home games, but he won't miss them if he can help it."

"You think he'll still come to see me play?" I allow for this small ray of hope that at least Tally's dad will still be in my life even if his daughter isn't. Obviously, I'm desperate for consolation on any level I can find it.

Tally turns to me. "He wouldn't miss seeing you pitch regardless of what's going on with us."

I drown in her words but somehow grasp at the ray of hope she's given me with a ghost of her smile.

Meanwhile, Stella watches our weird exchange with studious fascination and then shakes her head and laughs. "Aw…young love. So much to learn, yes?"

To which neither Tally or I have an answer. Now, we avoid looking at each other altogether.

Finally, Tally fills in the uncomfortable silence that follows. "Something like that."

Stella grabs Tally's hand and leads her toward the kitchen intent on sharing her recipe for the sugar cookies just in case Tally wants to make them one day. It's laughable because Tally making cookies let alone eating them is an impossibility. She looks back giving me this helpless look and then surprisingly continues to follow the woman to her pantry.

Admiring what Stella has done with her kitchen, Tally brings up the idea of updating the kitchen at the house next door.

"What's the point, Tally? We lost out on the house already, remember?" I say impatiently.

"You don't know that for sure. Maybe, if the owner meets with you, you can change her mind." She actually smiles; I'm at loss for words at seeing it.

She turns her attention back to Stella. "I don't really cook like at all. That's Linc's thing. I think the kitchen next door is fine. I checked. The burner works, and I can boil water with that."

Suddenly frustrated with losing out on the house as well as Tally, I link the two intrinsically when I say, "Tally doesn't eat, hardly at all. It's one of those irreconcilable differences of ours."

"Lots of those," Tally says softly without looking at me.

"There's a balance," Stella says. "Maybe, he was just trying to help you with that."

"Maybe," Tally says faintly.

"Like love, food is important for the soul. There's a nutritionist on staff with…." Tally shoots Stella a warning look and vehemently shakes her head. "Well, I'm sure there's one at San Francisco Ballet, too," Stella adds.

"Am I missing something?" I briefly study the two women's faces.

"No," Tally answers quickly.

"I can teach you how to cook, Tally," Stella says quickly. "People overcomplicate things when it comes to cooking…well, pretty much *everything*. Things don't need to be so complicated."

She looks quizzically at me.

"If you get her a decent grill, both of you can make steak and fish and chicken all year-round here."

"You think a decent grill is all we need?" I like Stella but her simple way of looking at life exasperates me all at once.

Stella ignores my testiness. "People say it rains here all the time, but it really it doesn't. Actually, the weather is fairly mild and not at all that harsh like the East Coast. *Thank God.* The summers are warm enough and the winter storms…" Stella closes her eyes for few seconds. "They are just beautiful to watch as the rain and wind roll in across the lake. Some people might complain about facing due west, but I could never live anywhere else. I'd miss seeing the now without being able to see the immaculate sunset practically every night. I already know how the sun rises. I don't necessarily need to see that. I always want to see the sunset capping off another spectacular day with the promise of tomorrow. You know what I mean."

"I think I do." Tally looks thoughtful while I can only continue to gaze at her. She is like a flower opening up toward the sun in Stella Nelson's presence. I haven't seen her this receptive and almost happy in a long while.

Stella laughs too and then cocks her head to one side in contemplation. Then, she nods to herself as if she's made an important decision. "So, Tally, did you tell Linc about the Pacific Northwest—"

"No. No. I didn't." Tally looks reluctant to say more.

"Tell me what?" I ask getting this strange vibe from Tally as if this is a secret she'd rather keep to herself. Her reluctance is pretty obvious.

"Well, I was going to tell you, at some point, but I guess I'll do that now." She sighs big and is notably nervous. "Stella here is apparently on the board of the Pacific Northwest Ballet." She inclines her head toward Stella. "And…between her and Kimberley, I was able to meet with the artistic director today. We met for lunch. He knows my whole history—the resume—my body of work." She catches her lower lip. "He's been at the School of American Ballet as well as the New York City Ballet, and he knows of me. We had quite a lot to discussion about all of that, and he offered me a job. It's a three-year contract. Nothing like yours, of course." She smiles sweetly at me.

"Doesn't have to be." I feel like I'm spending my very last wish, but remain unsure it will ever come true, so I hold my breath and impatient wait in suspended wonder for Tally to finish her story.

"They want me to play the part of *Juliette* next spring. It's quite an offer. Somebody on the board called in some favors and made it happen." She again inclines her head toward Stella and finally shyly looks over at me. Meanwhile, I can feel Stella beaming from a long way off like an unexpected rainbow after a storm.

"You took the job?" I'm still holding my breath and unable or unwilling to believe that Tally would actually do this.

She turns in her bar chair to face me more fully. "I did."

"Why?" I ask needing to hear her honest answer.

"Because you're going to be here and in talking to Daniel Hollis it just seemed like the right thing to do. He is amazing and he seems to appreciate my hard work and everything I've done and what I've sacrificed to get here. He seems to think I have talent. He said something about me making a principal in the next couple of years, too. You know I want that."

All I can do is nod. I know that's important to Tally, but it's almost too much to hope for that she will be okay with living in Seattle instead of New York.

"It seems they want to do great things at Pacific Northwest Ballet, and he thinks I can be a part of their vision, contribute to it and, more importantly; I want to be a part of that kind of dance company. He knows we have dueling schedules—he said *grueling schedules*, actually—and said they were willing to accommodate me in having most of the summer off for your games." She gets this shy smile as she looks over at me. "He made it all sound very attractive. I emailed the contract documents along to Everett and within a half hour, he got back to me and told me they looked fine, especially since they're willing to buy out my contract with San Francisco Ballet, so I took the job."

"It's not New York." Realistically, for the betterment of her career, that's where Tally needs to return to, and we both know it.

"No, but it doesn't have to be." She gets this benevolent smile. "Daniel understands that I want to have balance in my life in the personal as well as the professional. His offer was generous. I'm supposed to visit the studio with him tomorrow morning at ten and meet the other dancers. He'd love to have me do a guest performance of *The Nutcracker* if it works out before Christmas. He's already said he wants me to perform as Juliette in *Romeo et Juliette* in early February, so I start in early January, which works out fairly well. I don't know. It felt good to say yes to his offer, so I did."

"You're moving to Seattle?" Apparently, this is still surprising news to me and must be reaffirmed.

"I am."

"With me."

"Yes. I am. I'm moving to Seattle to be with you."

"Can I ask why?" Apparently I need to be reassured in a thousand different ways right now.

"Because love is the constant, Elvis. Love is all we need. And Jane once said to me, 'Home is where the heart is.' And now, I truly understand what she means by that corny little phrase." Tally smiles, and then her beautiful face becomes serious and painfully sincere. "My heart is and has always been with you. I love you. I never stopped. I love you, Lincoln Presley. Love. Our love is the constant. It's all we need."

I finally smile and take Tally's hand and bring it to my lips. "You just made my life again."

"Well, you've made mine for a very long time, and I'm just glad I was able to finally recognize that."

Tally rewards me with the most benevolent smile, and I return it as all my long-held fears coalesce and die at the same time once and for all.

"Can I jump in here?" Stella asks sweetly.

We both turn seemingly realizing at the same time there's someone else in the room besides the two of us.

"I would just like to clarify a few things about the house." Stella clasps her hands behind her back and steps toward us.

I still hold onto Tally's hand, intent on never letting her go again.

"First of all, my maiden name is Winter. I am Stella Winter Nelson. The house belonged to my parents, George and Lila Winter. They lived there for fifty-three years. Together. In love. I married Wes, and we bought this house next door to that one some twenty-five years ago. We raised a family here. Jane and her brother Drake.

Anyway, I'm sorry to put you through the wringer this way. I can see I may have been overcautious, but my parents' final wishes were for the house be sold to a young couple who had plans for the next forty or fifty years to live there. *Together.*"

She sighs and then smiles big. "I can see that you two do. Of course, I was hoping Janie and Marston would buy it, but they seem hell-bent on staying in San Francisco so you two living together in the house will be all kinds of spectacular. From what Janie has told me in this very convoluted twisted way of hers, so she doesn't break any HIPAA laws, I understand you two are still married. I assume by the looks you two are giving each other right now that you intend to stay that way. If so, the house is yours."

"We want the house," Tally and I say at the exact same time, although I'm not sure we're talking about the house anymore.

CHAPTER FORTY-SIX

if

LINC

Together all of us watch them go off
into a perfectly clear, starry dark sky
over the water
and become stars.
~ Lincoln Presley

December 24th

YOU START TO BELIEVE IN MIRACLES again. It starts with a promise. It stays because of the only constant. Love.

Inside of a week, we've moved to Seattle. Eddie. Luther. They're busy unpacking and painting and whatever it is that they do for us. There is always a long list, and they work through it. There's a little guest house at the back of Stella's property, and she rented it out to them as soon as she learned they needed a place to stay to get my life with Tally in order here in Seattle.

Charlie and Marla and the kids arrived yesterday along with Adam and Tommy. Jane and Marston got here five days ago. I'm not exactly sure when or if they'll be leaving. Marston told me he was seriously looking at a job at Harborview in their trauma department and wanted to know what I thought. I told him he had to go where his heart told him to go.

Obviously, I learned a few lessons about love and relationships in the past few weeks.

"That would be wherever Jane is," he said with a laugh.

"Well," I said with a laugh, "since Jane and Tally seem to be connected at the hip, welcome to Seattle."

Tally is due home from her afternoon performance of the *Sugar Plum Fairy*. Everyone went to the matinee performance including me, but I left the show a little early because I wanted to get some things done in order to surprise Tally.

It is amazing how you can be so broken apart with grief and admittedly we've both been dreading the holidays since we lost Tessa and then Cara and the baby, but something has changed. The future feels bright and sadness over our many losses seems to have retreated for the past several days from all of us. Tally and I have discovered that we are stronger together. We are able to face the bad days when missing Cara or thinking about how old Theo would have been becomes unbearable by holding each other's hands and assuring the other that we can get through it together.

With Jane's encouragement, Tally talked of doing some volunteer work with Children's Hospital. Of course, Kimberley thought that was an exceptional idea and I told Tally I'd go along with her, too. Tally thoughtfully reminded us both that there were people with worse heartaches than ours and we've already met some of them in the past few days when we made an impromptu visit to the hospital and brought an abundance of holiday gifts for all the sick children and their families.

It was never a question that we would celebrate Christmas here. But then, family and friends rallied once Tally decided she would do a couple of guest performances of *The Nutcracker* with Pacific Northwest Ballet once she got things straightened out with Mikhail Rostov. That's when everyone decided to spend Christmas with us in Seattle. Most everyone is staying downtown at the Four Seasons, but tonight we are hosting Christmas Eve.

Tomorrow, Tally and I will wake up in this house on Christmas morning. It will be just the two of us, although I anticipate Jane and

Marston will join in with some Christmas cheer at some point since they're staying right next door at Stella's.

I've tried to come up with a way that we can celebrate Christmas and remember our lost loved ones without getting too sad about it. I think I've finally come up with something. I got the idea of paper lanterns when we were watching a few half-dozen of Cara's favorite movies one night. With Stella's help, I was able to track them down and an artist who works with specialty paper, after hearing our story, agreed to handcraft the lanterns and finish them before Christmas. Stella doesn't know I ordered one for her husband Wes as well Holly, Tessa, Cara, and baby Theo. It's a simple plan: light the candles tonight for each lantern and watch them drift off into the night all together as tribute.

Sentimental? Maybe.

But we miss them all, especially Cara, and this seemed like one way of remembering everyone that would be touching and not so final. Maybe, it's a tradition we can continue for years to come.

"What are you doing in here all by your lonesome? You left early. I missed you. Of course, you probably just wanted to spend some time driving the Bugatti by yourself." Tally stands in the doorway looking like the best Christmas angel in the universe. She looks amazingly beautiful in a white sweater dress with a large red belt around her waist.

"It's all about the Bugatti." She laughs. "Looking festive; aren't we?" I kiss her and cherish the thought that I get to be alone with her later on after this party of sorts is over. Number nine is already on the Christmas list and Tally has promised to deliver.

"Just wanting to play the part of hostess. Did you put the pastries in the oven already?"

"Yes. Everything's done. Don't worry. It's going to go fine. You've got this."

"First party. First time cooking. *Things.* You know," she says with a slight frown.

"I know but you've got this."

"Can I just say that I am really really happy today? I thought it would be hard but between how great the show went and then just being surrounded by everyone and with you here and us being all right and *together*, I don't know…I feel okay with everything. More than okay. Is that bad?"

"No. That's good. " I lean into her and kiss her on the forehead. "I hear your dad. "

"So? Come here, Elvis." She reaches up and touches my face. "Kiss me properly. I imagine he'll come up with a thousand different reasons to go over and help Stella carry her dishes over here." She gets this secret smile.

"You saw that, too?"

"I did."

"And how do you feel about that?" I ask softly.

The attraction between Stella and Adam seemed to start within the first few minutes of introducing those two to each other.

"I feel good about it. My dad deserves to be happy. It's probably too soon, but I think Stella gets that. She's promised to make waffles for Tommy tomorrow morning so the sixteen-year-old is already on board with the romance. I think she invited them over at seven." She laughs.

"Tal, can I just say, thank you?"

"Sure, but Elvis, what could you possibly be thanking me for?"

"For forgiving me. For being in my life. For being everything."

"Ditto on that. Now, tell me again how much you love me because I promise to never grow tired of hearing the reasons as to why."

She puts her arms around me and kisses me hard. It's the best feeling in the world with this woman in my arms. Everything feels possible.

"Hey, lovebirds, save the make-out session for later. We've got to get this party started. Where's the boathouse, Linc? Marston wants to show me something in there; don't you, baby?"

I keep on kissing Tally while Jane laughs to herself as she walks by us pulling Marston along with her.

Then, it's Adam and Stella's turn as they walk through the sliding glass doors ladened down with stacks of food.

We finally give up on making out and join the party.

The lanterns prove to be a hit. Okay, everyone's crying but they are mostly happy tears. Jane and Marston help Stella light Wes's lantern and then Tommy and Adam light Tessa's and Holly's. Tally lights Cara's lantern and I light Theo's and together all of us watch them go off into a perfectly clear, starry dark sky over the water and become stars.

"Love lives on. I think that's all we can ask for," Tally says to the crowd, and then she grabs my hand and brings it to her lips. I wrap her in my arms and hold her tight. "Thank you for being everything to me, Elvis. Your love is my constant."

"Your love is mine."

CHAPTER FORTY-SEVEN

lucky ones

TALLY

I've learned that sadness shifts
and changes with the light from above
and the air all around
and the love that is everywhere covers and stills
the surface of sadness and eventually makes you whole again.
~Talia Landon Presley

A year later ~ November

I FOUND LOVE IN LINCOLN PRESLEY AND he found it in me.

And love is our one and only constant.

It's our truth.

It's been a year since that fateful accident took our children and almost destroyed the two of us.

The sadness doesn't go away.

I just think it leaves the surface of your life so the pain isn't as raw and visceral anymore.

It's like that pool of water Jane used to have me envision where I imagined the rings of water flowing outward when a single drop of water falls from above.

It's like that.

I've learned that sadness shifts and changes with the light from above and the air all around and the love that is everywhere covers and stills the surface of sadness and eventually makes you whole again.

It takes time just like Jane said once.

Time is sometimes all we have.

Time. Love.

Those two things stay with you and help you survive.

There are days where you are still sad, but then again, there are more days when you feel free enough to believe in tomorrow and perhaps feel alright about putting yesterday away.

My baseball player had a very good season and the Mariners are very happy with his play. He pitched a perfect game in mid-July. Wow, what a moment. The entire stadium was deathly quiet until his last pitch struck the batter out and then the roar from the crowd erupted and it was deafening. It was quite something. Charlie and Marla as well as Marston and Jane just happened to be in the stands with me for the game that day. It was surreal and beautiful. Everybody said so.

But for me? The best moment was when Linc climbed all the way up from the field into the stands and came straight for me. I ran into his arms, and we somewhat spontaneously performed a rendition of the *Dirty Dancing* signature move much to the baseball crowd's delight. Then, we kissed with all the cameras flashing. Of course, it was just about the two of us in that moment, but TMZ ran with it. Kimberley and Daniel were grateful for the coverage.

We were just happy to be together. We still are, because after all we've been through, being together is all that matters.

Stella Nelson is right. Seattle sunsets from our little piece of paradise promising tomorrow are the best. We made a point of spending a lot of time on our dock this past summer where we watched the sun set and began to fully believe and embrace that it would rise behind us again tomorrow.

Even my dad has found that to be true. He has taken a position with Swedish Hospital as their new chief cardiologist starting in January. Apparently, fixing patients' broken hearts are not the only one he's mended. When I asked him where he planned on living, once he and Tommy moved to Seattle, he got this very sheepish look and told me that Stella had them all fixed up.

"How do you feel about that?" he asked looking anxious.

"How do I feel about that? Well, it makes Jane and I related, and since we're practically sisters already, I'm fine with that. More importantly, how does Tommy feel about that?"

Dad said, "I think he fell in love with Stella when she made waffles for him that first Christmas morning."

I smiled. "And you, Dad? When did you fall in love with her?"

"Well, she had me at hello; I swear, but I gave it fifteen minutes before I knew for sure."

"Good job, Dad. Way to hang in there and make sure it's real."

We both laughed.

Linc steals up behind me and holds me close. "Tell me something true."

"I love you more today than yesterday." I turn in his arms and stand on my toes to kiss him. "Clearly, the odds are in our favor."

"Clearly."

"Like I said, more than yesterday," I say sweetly.

"How is that possible?"

"I don't know, but it's true, Elvis. You're my everything. Surely, you know that by now."

"I know it, but I always like it better when you show me, Tally."

And so? I do.

See? Love is a constant. And? Sometimes? Love is all you need.

That much is true.

~the end~

DEDICATION

THIS BOOK IS DEDICATED TO MY daughter Lauren, who has been a great sounding board for me with this novel for the past *year*. There is one particular plot twist she didn't agree with which proved invaluable because, *yes*, I had to fight my way through it and she helped me in that unfiltered, tell-it-like-it-is daughterly way of hers and the story is better for it.

Additionally, her incredible artistry when it comes to visuals as well as music soulfully resonates, and she helped me achieve just the right look for the book cover of *Tell Me Something True* as well as the novel's play list largely comprised of Marina and The Diamonds songs (her favorite singer and now mine, too).

Thanks for shining so incredibly bright in my world, Lauren. What a star you are!

XOXOXO

Mom

ACKNOWLEDGMENTS

Books are not always written in a vacuum, especially this one. *Tell Me Something True* came about because of my core group of fans and their encouragement (or, was that *demand?*) to write more of Linc and Tally's love story. You know who you are. You're the ones that leaves me notes on Facebook or send emails telling me how much one of my stories affected you.

This book is also for those of you who leave reviews for my books on your blogs or on Amazon or other fine on-line book retailers, especially you, because reviews make an author's worlds go 'round. We need to hear the feedback, feel the love, field the hate (*sometimes*) because there is something to be learned even from the harshest critic as well as the most avid fan. *Thank you for that.*

It was encouragement like yours that brought forth the idea of a third book about Linc and Tally.

So.

Here it is, *finally*, a whole year and then some later, for all of you…

Thank you so much for believing in my work and in me as a writer. I appreciate the support you all provide, but, mostly, I treasure all of you for being a part of my *writerly* world.

Katherine Owen

Dearest Readers of the Truth In Lies Series,

IF YOU'VE MADE IT TO THE end of this book, I know some of you hate me at this very moment. I am truly sorry for upsetting you all in this unexpected, devastating way. By now, you must have figured out how terribly difficult this story was to write, which is why it took just over a year to do so. Just know, I had a completely different story line in June of this year that would have had more of thriller intonation to it, but it just wasn't working for me.

I kept getting drawn into really focusing in on the relationship between Linc and Tally and imagining the worst things that could happen, and then I wrote about them. Just know as I dove deeper into Tally and Linc's characterizations, I saw that the explosiveness of their relationship would become a serious factor because they weren't completely healed of the emotional wounds they carried. I began to realize it was an explosiveness that would either ultimately destroy them or rebuild them. I realized their past would catch up to them and their human flaws and the serious emotional issues surrounding them because of their triple threat fears would cause them to react badly. And did it ever.

Most of the plot twists taken were a complete surprise to me, even as the writer. I have numerous outlines that would attest to that fact because the story that unfolded this summer was not part of the plan. The dark moment was much worse than I thought it would be, but once I went there; I found it difficult to retreat from this particular part of the story line (And, it wasn't for a lack of trying!)

The secondary characters of Jane and even Marston started to play a bigger role and then Stella came out of nowhere and the ties between all the characters started to make sense. Even after I finished the novel, I tried to go back and change the story line (soften it up and take out the most devastating plot twist of all), but I just couldn't get it to work.

And so?

Here we are.

Given all of that, I finally told myself that *you just have to feel this one.* When *I cried* the other day at a particular passage on a final read through, I knew I was there. *I* felt it, and I knew I would just have to stop fucking around with it and just put it out there.

And, so I have.

The simplest view I came up with in my self-talk, you-can-do-this sessions about this particular book was that I don't write simple boy-meets-girl romances. I never have. If I did, you'd be getting six books a year from me instead of one.

Okay then?

Okay then.

I believe I own the space right now for writing about the pain and heartbreak that comes along in life and love. And so, I stayed the course with where the story kept taking me, and even though I didn't like where the story and these characters led me; I felt I had to go there. It was heartbreaking. It was real. Bad things like this happen and after a long time thinking about it; I decided that I needed to be the one to write about it. There are other writers who write the sad love stories as well, but I know my particular foray into this hell filled with angst and heartbreak is pretty awful and emotionally raw in comparison to just about anyone else writing it. *I'll own that.*

You want happy? Read somebody else. *Truly.* I don't mind.

I just can't write the happy, I guess. Instead, I write the real.

And this is life, and this is love and sometimes bad things happen and love is all you have left.

There you go.

In any case, I am mostly ready (somewhat emotionally prepared) to hear your thoughts about this story, so please don't hesitate to reach out to me and let me know how you feel about *Tell Me Something True*. I promise to read them all—good and bad.

As it is, I will be starting on *Saving Valentines* straight away. I feel the need to give Linc and Tally a rest. I think we all need it. Looking forward to working on Johnnie McDaniel and Eve Goodlight's love story with *Saving Valentines*.

But didn't you just *love* Jane and Marston?

All the best to you,

Katherine Owen

Play List for *Tell Me Something True*

Prologue - "Young And Beautiful" - Lana Del Rey
1. "The State of Dreaming" - Marina and The Diamonds
2. "Valley Of The Dolls" - Marina and The Diamonds
3. "Your Body Is a Wonderland" - John Mayer
4. "Somewhere Only We Know" - Keane
5. "Wake Me Up When September Ends" - Green Day
6. "Landslide" - Fleetwood Mac
7. "Chasing Cars" - Snow Patrol
8. "Catalyst" - Anna Nalick
9. "Fear and Loathing" - Marina and The Diamonds
10. "Habits" (Stay High) - Tove Lo
11. "Lies" - Marina and The Diamonds
12. "Wicked Game" - Chris Isaak
13. "Starring Role" - Marina and The Diamonds
14. "How To Be A Heartbreaker" - Marina and The Diamonds
15. "You Don't Really Know Me" - Jessie J
16. "I'm A Ruin" - Marina and The Diamonds
17. "Hurricane" - MS MR
18. "Time To Pretend" - MGMT
19. "I'm Not The Only One" - Sam Smith
20. "Better Than That" - Marina and The Diamonds
21. "Your Eyes Open" - Keane
22. "Of Moons, Birds & Monsters" - MGMT
23. "Immortal" - Marina and The Diamonds
24. "Hold Back The River" - James Bay (a fan recommendation)
25. "Solitaire" - Marina and The Diamonds
26. "Teen Idle" - Marina and The Diamonds
27. "Weeds" - Marina and The Diamonds
28. "Hypocrates" - Marina and The Diamonds
29. "Bleeding Out" - Imagine Dragons
30. "Second Chance" - Shinedown
31. "Blue Jeans" - Lana Del Rey
32. "Without You" - Lana Del Rey
33. "Body Electric" - Lana Del Rey
34. "The Game of Love" - Santana, Michelle Branch
35. "Lies" - Marina and The Diamonds (Yes it is a repeat but the lyrics are
    so spot on to Tally's pain)
36. "Valley Of The Dolls" - Marina and The Diamonds (See note above)
37. "The State Of Dreaming" - Marina and The Diamonds
38. "Collide" - Howie Day
39. "Chances" - Five For Fighting
40. "The Heart Wants What It Wants" - Selena Gomez
41. "Good For You" - Selena Gomez
42. "Gold" - Marina and The Diamonds
43. "Money Power Glory" - Lana Del Rey
44. "Gods & Monsters" - Lana Del Rey
45. "Kryptonite" - 3 Doors Down
46. "If" - Bread
47. "Lucky Ones" - Lana Del Rey
Extra Tracks I really love! "Your Loss I'm Found" - Jessie J; "Love, Save The
    Empty"-Erin McCarley; "Old Money"-Lana Del Rey
Visit www.katherineowen.net for links.

ABOUT THE AUTHOR

"I believe that all I can do is inspire (or, is that "grind"?) both my readers and myself in what I construe as reality. Someone has to capture the sad, emotional, angsty love stuff that often collides with fate. It might as well be me. Apparently, I am THAT writer." ~Katherine Owen

Katherine Owen writes emotional, romantic literary fare that can be classified as contemporary romance and/or new adult fiction romance, including the bestselling Truth In Lies Series consisting of *This Much Is True*, *The Truth About Air & Water*, and *Tell Me Something True* as well as these standalone novels: *Seeing Julia*, *Not To Us*, and *When I See You*.

Owen's release of her fourth novel, *This Much Is True*, hit the Amazon bestseller lists in September of 2013 and put Owen into a whole new stratosphere as an author. Readers wanted to read more about the baseball player and the ballerina so Owen wrote a sequel to *This Much Is True* titled *The Truth About Air & Water*. Again, at the request of her fans, Owen's newest release and the third book in the Truth In Lies Series is *Tell Me Something True*.

To keep up with Owen's work about novel updates, please visit: www.katherineowen.net or www.katherineowenauthor.com

Want to stay up-to-date? Sign up for Owen's newsletter where she does periodic updates about the novels, the work-in-progress, and novel release updates/dates at: http://eepurl.com/benyOD

www.ingramcontent.com/pod-product-compliance
Lightning Source LLC
Chambersburg PA
CBHW050957210726
48287CB00004B/1265